Bohemian

KATHRYN NOLAN

Dedication

Washington College's Rose O'Neill Literary House: where I
made life-long friends and rediscovered my love for writing.

Lucia, California: the small town right next to Big Sur where
my husband and I came up with the idea to live in a van for a
year, traveling across the country.

The cute guy working at The Henry Miller Library in Big Sur,
California: You don't know this, but our five-minute interaction
is the reason I wrote this book.

And finally, the poet Mary Oliver: there's not much I can say
except thank you.

CHAPTER 1

Calvin

"The poet Diane di Prima once tried to levitate my grandfather," I told the mourners, clearing my throat through the nervousness.

"She didn't succeed—obviously," I said, and I saw a few smiles. "—but the evidence is captured in this grainy, black-and-white photograph that's framed on a wall in the bookstore. In it, Diane is laughing. Probably stoned."

My parents frowned, but I went on. "Next to her, my grandfather was a veritable lion: tall and broad-shouldered, his smile bright like the stars against a Big Sur sky."

I tugged on my tie, itchy in my suit. My grandfather hated suits.

"My grandfather lived his life for joy. From the second grade until I was in high school, I spent my summers in Big Sur, at the bookstore with him. And those memories are filled with these... with these *shocks* of happiness," I said, wondering how I was possibly going to get through this eulogy without crying.

My grandfather cried often—encouraged it, even—but I was already nervous as hell. Hated speaking in front of people,

1

hated being the center of attention—I was content as a wallflower.

But this was for him.

"Once we spent an entire night on his deck reading Shel Silverstein. Later, as I grew older, we delved into Pablo Neruda, Emily Dickinson, e.e. cummings, Adrienne Rich— and always, always, Jack Kerouac, whose words my grandfather held close to his heart. But, when I was a nine-year-old, he hid the Neruda and pulled out something more age-appropriate." I grinned, and a few of the mourners chuckled softly.

"'Close your eyes,' he'd said. 'Let the words paint you a picture in your mind.' He always said that, encouraging me to drink in the images an author was trying to convey. I remembered this one part from *Where the Sidewalk Ends*, about a 'moon bird' and 'peppermint wind.'"

I let the words linger for a second—recalling, as a kid, how much I'd loved the idea of a peppermint wind.

"He'd ask me questions. '*What do you think a moon-bird looks like?*' '*What makes the wind peppermint?*' We'd spend hours like that until I was exhausted and falling asleep against his shoulder, the poem or book forgotten. We'd pull cots out onto the deck, mugs of hot chocolate at our feet, books everywhere. And in the morning, I'd wake up under the canopy of the redwood trees."

I paused to collect myself. "Filled with that... that feeling you have as a kid in the summertime. Unfettered freedom," I said, knowing my grandfather would have appreciated the alliteration.

"Like all of us," I continued. "My life is no longer filled with too many books. Instead, it's full of too many meetings." I watched as the audience nodded their heads in agreement.

"Sitting in traffic, answering emails—all the aspects of the daily grind. But even when I'm busy, or distracted, stuck in the rat race, the sound of my grandfather's laughter will tumble into my memory," I said, hearing the tightness in my throat, the rise of grief in my chest. "Or the taste of hot chocolate, our endless discussion of poetry—the way he always encouraged me to live my life authentically, to embrace joy."

I was crying now and found I actually didn't care because I was heartbroken, desperately heartbroken, and there was no way I could bottle it up. "And I hope all of you take that with you today as you honor his memory."

* * *

The last day of my grandfather's life, according to him, had been completely banal. He'd been writing in his journal and drinking whiskey, probably by the fireplace in his beloved bookstore.

Took Chance for a walk down by the beach. Windy, but we were lucky to see the sun for a bit. Had a hysterical moment when Chance chased the seagull for an inordinate amount of time. Seagull won. More customers than usual today in the store, including a sweet couple from Sacramento who were thinking of holding their wedding in Big Sur. Was pleasant to talk with them. Finished that little book of poetry I picked up in Petaluma last week—it was delightful. I'm wondering if

That was it. *I'm wondering if.* And then, just like that, an aneurysm burst in his brain, and he died. He was eighty-one years old.

I was standing on the patio of my grandfather's bookstore, holding the journal. Chance, my grandfather's dog, was curled up at my feet.

Susan, his lawyer, approached me with a kind smile. She was about my parent's age, white with short red hair. Mourners were milling inside, but I knew my parents and I needed to discuss the will.

"Calvin?" Susan said, touching my arm. "Let's talk in another room."

I nodded, following her into the small room that held the children's books—such a whimsical place for such a stressful conversation. I sat next to my mother, holding her hand. Grief had made her smaller, but she'd smiled through my eulogy.

My parents and my grandfather had a complicated relationship—one of deep love but also total misunderstanding. Like me, my parents were rational, numbers-driven, orderly people. Both of my parents were engineers, and I'd been a software engineer for almost nine years, ever since I left college. Long hours, tons of dedication, lines of code moving across my computer screen.

My grandfather, however, had been something else entirely.

"I'd like to talk with the three of you about the will," Susan said. "Specifically you, Calvin. As you know, your grandfather purchased this property in 1958 and turned it into a bookstore shortly after. He had stipulations in his will that upon his death, the ownership of this bookstore be passed along to you, Calvin."

"Um... *what*?" I asked, mouth dropping open in surprise. I thought she was going to tell me my grandfather had left me his extensive collection of science fiction. Not *the entire bookstore*.

"You are now the official owner of The Mad Ones," she said simply, and I could hear my parents grumble next to me. My parents and I were *planners* by nature... and this was not in the plan.

"Um... *what?*" I repeated like a broken robot.

Susan smiled kindly. "It does not mean that you must run the store or anything like that. The ownership of the business and deed to the property has been transferred to you. What you do with it, of course, is up to you."

"And what you should do is sell," my mother said firmly, shifting next to me on the couch. I turned to look at her.

"Sell the store? But it's... I mean, this bookstore is famous. An icon."

Was I missing something?

"That was a long time ago, Calvin," Susan said, and my parents nodded in agreement. "Besides, you probably aren't aware of this, but your grandfather's business had been operating off credit for a long time. The finances are in terrible shape. The bookstore is in massive debt."

"You should sell it, Cal. This is Big Sur. Property in this area, especially with this view, will go for millions," my mother added.

On cue, I could hear the waves crashing against the shore. Big Sur was a bohemian paradise once. My grandfather was one of the residents that kept that spirit alive, tending it like a flame about to go out. But like every other part of Northern California, the wealthy had come in droves, seeking the quiet of the redwoods and the dramatic ocean views.

"Bookstores, especially independent ones, are a dying breed. Everyone buys online now," Susan said.

My heart broke at that, even though part of me knew it to be true. I hadn't bought a book in a while—my grandfather would have been so ashamed—and when I had, it certainly wasn't through small, independent bookstores.

"So, you'll probably sell, right?" Susan asked, to which my parents both replied *yes*, and I said, "Um, well...I guess? I don't know..." but they were already talking over me. Of course I would sell. I had absolutely no idea how to run a business, let alone a dying one.

"There is one thing on the event calendar I do think you should stay open for. It's only five months from now."

She showed me the contract: a three-day-long photoshoot for a high-end fashion magazine, scheduled for the middle of

October. My grandfather must have been desperate, since things like "fashion" and "magazines" went against his bohemian values.

The contract he'd signed—the sight of his shaky signature sending a pang through me—promised the bookstore as the main location for three days of filming plus lodging at the tiny cabins he owned in the woods.

"Generate some additional revenue during the final months. Do the photoshoot. Pay off as much debt as you can, then sell it to the highest bidder. Don't worry, some investor will probably turn it into luxury condos. You won't have to worry about it one bit," Susan said.

"Luxury condos," I said sarcastically. "Exactly the vision my grandfather had."

Susan looked at me with a pained expression. "Why don't I leave you with your parents for a few moments?" She left without waiting for an answer, clearly knowing when it was time to make a graceful exit.

"Cal," my mom started, touching my knee gently. "I know how much you loved this place. And your grandfather. And the memories you have here won't disappear just because this place won't exist anymore."

"You lived here too," I pointed out. "Aren't you... aren't you upset?"

"You know my feelings about this place. I loved it, very deeply, but it's not my home anymore and hasn't been in a long time. It's time to say goodbye, to let someone else enjoy the property," she said, turning to my father who nodded in agreement.

"Your grandfather was always very private about his finances, so we weren't aware it was that bad. But... based on the things he told us, and the way the world has changed, it's not surprising. I guess your mother and I always figured that when he passed away, the store would close."

I nodded, comforted by their usual rational wisdom. A wisdom I automatically gravitated towards, even though just being back in this store had me yearning for the wild, whimsical days of my summers here. No numbers, just words on a page.

"Yeah," I finally said. "Yeah, you're right."

"And I'm sorry this burden is falling on you," my mom continued. "You think you can take some leave from work? If not, we can work something out, maybe we can all share responsibility. Hire someone up here to keep an eye on it."

I shook my head, thinking of my grandfather on the patio that night, the all-encompassing love he had for this place, the legacy he'd intended to leave me.

I owed him this. I owed this place to stay open until the bitter end, to close with some dignity and respect—not to bulldoze it tomorrow.

"I'll stay," I said, feeling the weight settle onto my shoulders and not knowing what in the *fuck* I was going to do. But I was going to stay. "Can you get Susan?"

My father grabbed her, and we continued the discussion. Susan was outrageously surprised that I wasn't willing to sell tomorrow and walk off into the sunset, millions of dollars richer.

I was surprised too.

By the end of the meeting, my head was spinning, and I had an entire life in Silicon Valley to figure out, to shift up to Big Sur. A job to put on pause, friends to call.

"Oh, and one more thing," Susan said, pulling out a worn, creased letter from her bag. "This was with your grandfather's will. Instructions for me to give to you on the event of his death."

A folded letter with just my name on the front, *Calvin*, in my grandfather's handwriting.

"What is it?" I asked.

"I don't know," she replied. "I wasn't supposed to read it."

* * *

Now, as I stood on the deck of my grandfather's bookstore—*my* bookstore—I shoved the letter in my back pocket. I had a feeling what it might say, and I wasn't prepared to deal with it right now. My grandfather was a dreamer. I'd looked up to him. Loved him.

But I wasn't him.

My grandfather stared down life's challenges head on with a twinkle in his eye and a glass of whiskey in his hand. He was fearless, always had been. If I was like my grandfather, I would have laughed at financial reports and credit scores and back taxes and said, "To hell with it. Let's go skydiving."

In some ways, that was essentially what my grandfather had done, dying before having to face the realities of the irresponsible life he had lived.

And he'd left me to inherit it all.

Reckless bastard, I thought with a smile. I was loopy with grief and still stunned from the news.

Tomorrow, it would hit me. Tomorrow, I'd wake up in my grandfather's bedroom and begin living his life. Trying my hardest not think about how he'd feel about some smarmy investor buying up the place he loved the most and turning it into condos.

The wind rustled through the redwoods. I inhaled the woodsy scent I associated with my childhood summers: bark and pine needles, saltwater and earth. Tears pricked at the back of my eyes, but I swallowed against them, turning towards the lights of my grandfather's store.

"Come on, Chance," I said, heading back in.

CHAPTER 2

Lucia

I 'd just lost twenty-two followers on Instagram.

It wasn't much. I knew that, deep down, especially since I had close to six million followers (5,989,854 to be exact). But I had been obsessing over it the entire drive up from Los Angeles to the tiny coastal town of Big Sur.

I clicked through my last week of photos. Nothing out of the ordinary: selfies on the beach, Parisian streets and cute cafés, a shot of the expensive sushi I'd dined on last night, a random picture of Josie and me before my last runway walk. The kind of glamorous life (with glimpses of "authenticity") that fans *loved*.

So why? Why did twenty-two people decide I wasn't worth their time anymore?

"It's *gorgeous* up here," Josie said, poking me. I'd driven the first half of the journey, and she'd taken the second half, recognizing that antsy look I got when I'd been off social media for more than an hour.

"Lu?" she poked again. "You're missing this."

"Mhmm," I hummed, scrolling through. I was like the

Nancy fucking Drew of Instagram. *The Mystery of the Twenty-Two Lost Followers.* "I'm busy. And jet-lagged."

"And grumpy," she said, and I stuck my tongue out at her.

"All part of my glitzy new contract," I said, wiggling my shoulders and making her laugh. "Jet-Lagged and Beautiful: The Lucia Bell Story."

"You realize between this photo shoot and your Dazzle contract, you're one step closer to total world domination?" she teased.

"Not if I keep losing followers," I said, then wished I could take it back. *It doesn't matter. It shouldn't matter.*

"That doesn't mean anything, and you know it," she said, dutiful in Best Friend Mode. She watched me obsess over these things every day. She knew the powerful sway social media held over me.

And she was right because it didn't really matter. I was grumpy and jet-lagged because I'd just gotten back from spending two weeks in Paris, finalizing the remaining details to become the face of Dazzle cosmetics.

I'd signed a two-year contract that included billboards, magazine ads, television commercials, merchandising—essentially a supermodel's dream. Not that I didn't love runway shows in Milan, but it'd be nice to model foundation and mascara and not eleven-inch heels.

The announcement had skyrocketed my career in a matter of days. I was used to being on the cover of magazines, but this was different. Dazzle was the largest cosmetics company in the entire world, and out of every single model they could have chosen, they chose me.

I added a million Instagram followers in two days.

And I was already losing them.

I'd need to win them back during this photo shoot we were about to embark on in Big Sur. My mind flashed to the countless Instagram photos I could capture: wildflowers by the ocean, restless waves, goofy smiles with Josie with the sun lilting behind us.

Lilting.

My fingers itched to write the word down but I shook it off. My journal was packed into one of a dozen bags shoved into the trunk. *Lil-ting*. Sideways. Lean. Dandelions in a field, light as clouds.

"Did you say something?" Josie asked, glancing over with a strange look.

Oh good, now I was talking to myself.

"Nope," I said, eyes fixed on the tiny screen of my phone, that word seared onto my brain. That hadn't happened in a while.

"Tell me about this shoot again," I said. "Between the time in Paris and the red-eye flight home, I've completely forgotten what we're doing here."

Josie grinned. "Well, you're about to spend three days in beautiful Big Sur with your best friend in the entire world."

"Interestingly, also the World's Best Makeup Artist," I said, tapping my finger against my chin. "Go on."

"Shay Miller. *Rag* Magazine. Boho-style," she said simply, jogging my memory.

"Yeah, yeah," I said, nodding with recognition. "That's right."

I'd met with Ray, the creative director, and Taylor Brooks, the other male model on the shoot, more than six months ago. I'd known both of them for a couple of years. And Shay Miller was a newer designer, currently all the rage in Los Angeles.

Experimental, a little unconventional, definitely erotic—he wanted his clothes displayed in environments that held a similar feel. His latest line of clothing, *Boho*, was bohemian-trendy, wild-child-with-a-vengeance.

And he wanted the first photoshoot for it to take place in the capital of Bohemia: Big Sur.

As usual, about 98% of my body would be visible. One time, I modeled an honest-to-God parka with cut-outs to ensure my boobs and ass were on full fucking display. For a *winter* coat. And the mock-ups that Ray had walked us through had affirmed Shay Miller's flair for softcore porn.

"So would you say Taylor's dick would be entirely inside me for this shot? Or is it a just-the-tip situation?" I'd asked Ray, pointing an expensively manicured nail at his notes.

He'd grimaced, and Taylor had spit out his latte. Taylor was the newest It-Guy. Younger than me, only twenty-two, and still very much enamored with the shiny world of high-fashion modeling.

"Lucia," Ray had said, a warning in his voice. Directors liked the models to be seen. Not heard.

"Just asking," I'd said. "I mean, I've done *Sports Illustrated, Maxim*. I know the drill. I can do the 'pretend you're being fucked by the camera' look in my sleep. I just didn't realize we'd be actually fucking for this shoot."

"You're not," he said, looking at me like I was a child. "It's just Shay. He likes things to be hot and gritty and *real*, and I need the two of you to really, you know... really let your walls down."

"And the tip *in*."

Ray and Taylor exchanged a look over my head, and I swallowed a scowl. I needed to quit or I'd start getting a "reputation," as my agent said. I'd just turned twenty-six—which was ancient for a supermodel—and luckily, I'd snagged the Dazzle contract.

Because my days were officially numbered.

"Are you excited?" Josie asked, guiding us through the winding turns of Highway 1.

I looked up from my phone for a second at her. Josie was Mexican American, with tattooed arms, a gold nose ring, and lavender-tipped hair. She was the bad-ass I'd always wanted to be. Authentic and *always* herself.

"I'm excited you'll be on this shoot. I missed you the past few times. And I definitely missed you in Paris," I said.

"*Will* miss me. You know I'm not coming, *chica*."

I nodded, something twisting in my gut. "Yeah, I know. It's only two years. You'll come visit, and we'll video chat every second of the day."

"Sounds sustainable," she said wryly. "But aren't you excited for the next few days? Shay Miller is everything right now. The outfits are stellar. Taylor is hot. And I have amazing ideas in mind for your makeup. It should be fun." A quick glance over at me. "Right?"

I shrugged. "I guess. It's also going to be long hours. Tedious posing. Having to listen to Taylor talk about the new Brad Pitt movie he's in—for barely forty-five seconds—all day."

I'd worked with Taylor a couple times in the past year. He was nice but not that bright. And incredibly boring.

Josie bit her lip, eyes in the rearview mirror. "Can I ask you a random, kind of intense question?"

"Go for it."

"Do you ever think about why you're not into your job anymore?"

I snorted. "What are you talking about?"

"I don't know." A long pause, in which she seemed to be gathering her thoughts. "Lately I feel like you used to *love* things like this. I remember because I was there with you. I know it sucks, and it's exhausting, but even with all the bullshit that comes with being a makeup artist, I'm still *mostly* happy going to work every day."

And she was. Josie loved her job, and it was obvious. She was also fucking *great* at it. And so was I—even with my growing "snarky" reputation, I was the hardest worker, the

13

most expressive, the most flexible. I was a supermodel for a reason—because I was the best.

"I love my job," I said, pulling up Instagram again. I needed some social media affirmation to help the slight feeling of dread moving through my body. "And I'm thrilled about the Dazzle contract." It sounded hollow, even to my ears.

"I'm not *People* magazine, Lu. You don't need to give me soundbites," she chided. "Just... I don't know. I also think that Dazzle is a great opportunity for you, and you did seem happy when you got it."

"I am happy."

She looked at me again, continuing to chew on her lip — Josie's main tell when she was worried about something. Apparently, me.

"Forget I said it," she said, shaking her head. "I'm probably just horny."

"You're always horny," I said, laughing. Josie was the queen of hot one-night-stands, but it'd been a while. I looked back at my Instagram feed, desperate to see if I had lured any of my lost followers back. It paused, frozen. I refreshed it again.

"Were you having trouble with your internet earlier?" I asked, hating the note of panic that crept into my voice.

"I think internet is pretty spotty up here. And we'll barely have it while on location. Didn't you read Ray's email?"

"I don't understand the words that are coming out of your mouth." I was *always* online.

Josie laughed. "It's no big deal, Lu. We'll be living the way our ancestors used to live. Or, you know, people in the nineties."

"I hated the nineties," I whined.

"You weren't even ten in the nineties," she reminded me, not biting at my sulky tone. I wasn't usually this irritable when jet-lagged, but Josie's observation was making me feel a little off. Jagged.

"We'll have to do things like talk to each other," she said with a smirk.

"*What*?" I cried, throwing my hands in the air dramatically to the sound of Josie's laughter. I was (mostly) joking now, and as I leaned forward, turning up the radio, I fully looked at my surroundings, tossing my phone in my bag.

It *was* beautiful. We were curving through the woods under a canopy of fir trees. Every so often, there'd be a break, and the ocean would peek out, roaring against a rocky shore.

"Also..." Josie said, slowly turning into a long driveway. "I think we're here."

Redwoods lined the entrance; moss and overgrown bushes and orange poppies along the side. White fairy lights were strung between the tree trunks.

"Where are we?" I asked, rolling down my window to get a whiff of damp forest and ocean breeze.

A building came into view—it was more like a log cabin with a huge deck filled with mismatched chairs. A rickety old sign in front read "The Mad Ones" in bright-yellow paint.

"This bookstore is the main location for the next three days. The true home of Bohemia in Northern California," Josie said.

My eyes were still on the sign. "That's the name?"

"Yep," she said, slowly driving forward and parking. "It's still pretty famous but not like it used to be. My parents used to party up here in the early seventies—during their hippie days. Did yours?"

I rolled my eyes. "My parents only party if the paparazzi will be there. I get the impression this is not that kind of place."

I stepped out of the car, and the scent of the place hit me again. Damp forest. Ocean breeze. Something else... like bonfires on a cool autumn night. I was aware, too aware, of the air on my skin.

"Welcome to Big Sur," Josie whispered, coming up behind me. "It's something else, isn't it?"

Sunlight lilted through the trees. *There goes that word again.* The itch in my fingers was beginning to literally hurt. And the sunlight was like... it was like... "Magic," I breathed.

The front door of the bookstore opened, and a man stepped out. Tall. Wrinkled shirt. Giant glasses and a book in his hand. He waved at us, tentatively. I waved back, and he blushed. He walked down the steps towards our car—behind us, I heard the telltale sign of the entire photo shoot pulling up; car after car of clothes and cameras. High-fashion Hollywood descending on this tiny town.

As he got closer, I could see how nervous he was.

"I'm Lucia. How's it going?" I asked, holding my hand out to shake. He avoided eye contact with me, looking down. Avoided my hand too.

"Good. Um..." he said, hands in his back pocket. "Hello? I guess. Hi."

His blush deepened, and I held back a smirk. Men tended to blush around me.

"I'm Calvin," he finally said with an anxious smile. "Welcome to my bookstore."

CHAPTER 3

Calvin

F ive seconds into meeting Lucia Bell and Taylor Brooks, and I was a nervous fucking wreck. They were the most beautiful people I'd ever met, and now they were standing in the lobby of my grandfather's bookstore (*my* bookstore), and I could barely think straight.

"How about I show you around a bit?" I asked, putting my hands in my pockets to keep from fidgeting.

Lucia looked bored. Taylor looked like he'd never seen a book before in his life. Only Ray and Josie seemed interested.

"I'd love that," Josie said, tugging Lucia by the arm. I thought she was Lucia's makeup artist. The thought of someone having their *own* makeup artist was an astounding fact to me.

"Um... great," I said, clearing my throat. "So... this is the lobby."

I accidentally caught Lucia's eye, causing a blushing attack of epic proportions. She arched an eyebrow in response.

You can do this.

"My grandfather bought this property in 1958 after graduating from UC Berkeley with a Lit degree. He loved reading and books his entire life and was really into the Beat culture that had been centered in the North Beach area of San Francisco. At that time, Big Sur was just beginning to gain a reputation as a mecca of bohemian life. Artists and writers and singers and dancers were flocking to the town in droves. This bookstore became an epicenter of arts and culture, especially for writing."

I indicated the lobby. "This original building was a one-story log cabin. My grandfather added onto it but never wanted it to lose its intimate feel." The lobby was one of my favorite rooms, a veritable paradise for book-lovers. Stacks and stacks and stacks of books shoved against the wall in no discernible order.

"In the other rooms, the bookshelves are a little more organized, but generally, my grandfather believed in a kind of gentle chaos. Most of the books were priced the same so they'd end up in these large, dusty stacks anyone could look through. If a book didn't have a price on it, my grandfather let the buyer choose their own price."

That got a lot of bemused expressions.

That's also one of the reasons my grandfather was massively in debt.

"On the walls, you'll see the first of many, many framed photos, poems, posters for readings and book signings. Until recently, at least one reading a week was held here—and in the sixties and seventies, you can imagine they turned into quite the bohemian parties."

"Drugs and poetry, a great mix," Lucia said softly, eyes scanning the wall. I laughed, a little surprised.

"Um... you got it. My grandfather would tell stories of poetry readings that lasted 'til sunrise, discussions and arguments and dancing."

I pointed up towards the ceiling. "One of the most famous elements of this bookstore are the note cards. My grandfather would hand them out and ask guests to write down some feeling they had. Something they learned. Something beautiful or painful or eye-opening."

"It'd take you years to read them all," Ray chimed in.

I nodded. "I've tried, and I'm barely through this front room. My grandfather pinned them all to the ceiling, in no particular order."

Interspersed among them were scraps of poetry; pencil sketches; scrawled, drunken messages. Someone had drawn a highly accurate portrait of Gabriel Garcia-Marquez years ago, and it was still pinned up by the front lightswitch.

I walked them into the main room. "This is where I'd imagine you'd be doing most of the shoots, right?"

Ray nodded, looking around, sketching in his notebook. He was white, about ten years older than me, with salt-and-pepper hair and an intensity to his movements. "Absolutely fucking perfect, Calvin."

I nodded, oddly happy with the praise. The main room of the bookstore—the Big Room, as my grandfather called it—was one of a kind. Huge fireplace in the corner. Shelves and shelves and shelves of books, my grandfather's handwriting indicating "California, Botany" or "Fiction, Mystery." Coffee tables and plush armchairs, old rugs worn over the years. The walls in here were similarly covered in posters, poems, and black-and-white photos of authors. Two other rooms branched off the Big Room.

"This room is just poetry?" Ray asked, poking his head in the smaller one. It held three shelves of books, a few old chairs, and another fireplace.

"Oh, that was my grandfather's favorite room. He used to ask visiting poets to write a poem on the spot—they're all pinned up on that corkboard."

Lucia was walking through the shelves, fingertips trailing along the book spines. She had a peculiar look on her face, mysterious and almost worshipful. She wandered closer to me, and I fought the urge to back up.

Don't be a nerd, don't be a nerd.

"You, uh, you like books?" I asked.

Great opening line.

She tossed her long, wavy hair. I caught the scent of coconut. Her eyes flashed up at me, almost in alarm.

"I *like* lattes, actually," she said quickly. "Be a dear and make me one?"

I half-coughed, half-laughed. "Um... we don't have lattes in this bookstore."

"Every bookstore in LA does."

"So *that's* why we keep getting one-star reviews on Yelp," I shot back before I could stop myself.

Lucia tilted her head, looking almost as surprised as I was that I'd made a joke. A twitch of her lips—not a smile but almost.

"I mean," I started to say. "I just made a pot of coffee. You want some?"

I watched her eyes track down and then up my body, assessing. She took a step closer to me. I took a step back.

"Calvin, was it?"

"Cal," I said, almost apologetically.

"Cal," she repeated. "A cup of coffee would be great. Thank you."

I turned on my heel and headed towards the tiny kitchen off the bedroom. My cheeks burned with embarrassment. I had a spotty track record with women and *definitely* had never had a supermodel ask me to make her a latte.

I was strangely offended. But also bewildered.

I opened the cabinet of mugs and tried to guess what Lucia Bell would like. I turned back to glance at her. She had that look on her face again, like she wanted to devour every page in sight.

I knew who Lucia Bell was before this photo shoot—
everyone did. Victoria's Secret, *Maxim*, runway shows, magazine covers... sometimes it felt like her face was everywhere.

Meeting her in real life was beyond surreal.

And she looked gorgeous against a backdrop of novels. I'd spent the morning training my jaw not to drop so I could get through meeting her without being *too* obvious. I was hoping to at least appear a *little* aloof. So I barely looked at her when we met, tried my hardest to ignore her presence as we toured through the dusty shelves of books.

But she was gorgeous.

Gorgeous in way that knocked the breath from your lungs. Gorgeous in a way that made you question whether you'd ever truly understood the meaning of the word. Her hair was wild and blonde, curling down her back. She was white, and almost as tall as I was, dressed in ripped, faded jeans and a slouchy sweater that hung off one smooth, tan shoulder. Eyes the color of the sky before rain. And lips...

Those fucking *lips*. I felt the strongest urge to *bite* that bottom lip. Tug it between my teeth and see what it tasted like.

This was concerning.

She was still standing in the "Fiction, Women" section, so I pulled out a mug with Virginia Woolf stenciled on it. The warmth of the hot coffee was comforting against my palm as I walked back towards her, steeling my limited confidence.

She took it from me, our fingertips just grazing each other.

"*A Room of One's Own* is one of my favorites," she said, eyes on mine with her honey voice.

Surprised, I said, "You're a fan of Virginia?" Forgetting, for a moment, I was talking to a woman who had once walked down a runway with nothing but peacock feathers glued to her body.

Because Lucia Bell was potentially *flirting* with me by referencing a literary masterpiece.

A small, secretive smile. "One could call me *avid*," she finally said, voice lowered.

"So you *do* like books," I repeated, and her smile grew.

"You could say that," she replied, taking a long sip of her drink. Tilted her head. "It's no latte, but I guess it'll have to do."

I laughed, still surprised, and I wanted to ask her more, but Ray called her over, breaking the moment.

"Thanks for the coffee, Cal," she said, tossing a wink at me.

I gawked after her before I could stop myself.

CHAPTER 4

Lucia

This bookstore—*Calvin's* bookstore—was like
something out of my wildest dreams. When I was
little, before modeling became my life, all I wanted
was for my parents to drop me off at a bookstore like this one,
where I could lose myself in words for hours.

If they'd taken me here, I would have never left.

It wasn't huge. Calvin was right when he said it was intimate. Except every room had giant windows that made you
distinctly aware of the wilderness outside, pressing in. A fire
crackled in the fireplace. None of the chairs matched. My mug
was chipped and faded, and I pressed it to my chest.

I *loved* Virginia Woolf. How did Cal guess? And why did I
feel the need to impress him with my knowledge of her works?
I usually kept the bookworm side of myself locked away.

Not that I'd read much these past years.

I avoided the poetry room, but I wandered towards the far
wall. Half of it was taken up with framed posters advertising
readings: *Maya Angelou, Allen Ginsberg, Henry Miller, Amiri
Baraka*. It went on and on, writers I recognized and writers I

didn't, but their presence on the wall telegraphed something special: A night of words. A night of communion.

Scattered throughout were tiny torn pages of poems and selections from literature, slid haphazardly into frames or taped onto old photos. From the look of them, Calvin's grandfather must have typed them on an old typewriter.

I closed my eyes, imagining him sitting here, reading. Falling in love with something he'd read and needing to share it with the world.

I tapped my finger against a Pablo Neruda poem, feeling an electric buzz. It was thrilling and scary, and I hadn't felt it in a long time.

At the far end of the room was an old cash register and a long desk similarly covered with stacks of books.

I was sensing a theme.

Behind the table sat Cal, engrossed in a slim novel. I walked closer, still semi-interested in the walls but sizing Cal up at the same time. People didn't usually do things like *read* around me. I expected his ardent adoration: some cartoonish, jaw-drop-to-the-floor, eyes-bulge situation. I would play it cool, of course, treat him like just another fan.

You need the attention.

I shook that thought away and slid a little closer. He turned the page, head in hand, totally absorbed in whatever was on that page. *Not* on me, the 5-foot-10 blonde bombshell standing in front of him.

I sighed loudly, but he didn't look up. I was half-tempted to take my top off but decided against it.

Reputation, Lu.

Cal was white, with thick, dark brown hair and a five o'clock shadow that was almost a beard. Those big glasses which he could have pulled off as "hipster" if he had more confidence. Instead, he just looked like a nerd, one step away from using a finger to push his glasses up his nose.

"This place is perfect, Lu," Ray said, walking up behind me.

I turned, nodding, because he was absolutely right. "Where are we shooting?" I asked.

"This is our first and main location, so I want you and Taylor here a lot. There's tons to work with—the details, the fireplace, the color of the books, the feel of the walls. The camera's going to love it, and you're going to look gorgeous together."

"And when does the rest of the crew get here?" I asked.

"Should be tomorrow morning. You can start meeting with wardrobe, see what looks good. We'll work our way through the other locations during the three days that we're here. Tomorrow morning, we can start talking hair and makeup."

I nodded along, distracted. I'd been doing these shoots since I was fifteen years old. And they were all the same. Hair. Big makeup. Some ridiculous piece of clothing literally taped to my body. Glitter. Five-inch heels. At this point, I'd perfected all kinds of looks: pouty yet serious, irritated yet turned on, carefree yet grounded.

Modeling was a study in contrasts. The viewer wanted you to be everything and nothing. A body to project their own feelings onto, a face to worship or hate and sometimes both at the same time.

I pulled out my phone automatically to scroll through my social media accounts.

No Service.

I sighed in frustration. I wouldn't be able to win back lost followers if I couldn't post sexy photos from Big Sur.

So I sighed again, extra loudly, and strode right up to Calvin's cash register. He was still reading, completely absorbed. I remembered the feeling—except that I was annoyed at his lack of attention.

I looked up at the framed photographs over his head. More authors, some of his grandparents. And then I saw it—I sucked in an actual gasp, fingertips to my lips.

"Are you okay?" Calvin asked, *finally* looking up. Except my surprise was real, not feigned.

"Oh... yeah," I said. I debated if I should share, but before I could stop myself, I blurted, "Is that your grandfather with Mary Oliver?"

Calvin looked up to where I was pointing, smiled and nodded. "It is. He adored her. She did readings here several times."

I want to stay in her cabin.

"Can I stay in her cabin?" I asked out loud, trying to keep the desperation out of my voice.

Cal looked astonished. "Um...yeah, I can look back in the records and see if I can find out where she stayed. Not a problem, Ms. Bell."

"Lucia," I said automatically. "Or Lu... or, really, you can call me whatever."

He broke eye contact, looking away. "Oh, okay. Sorry... just, how do you...?"

"She's my favorite poet. Ever. Like ever, ever," I said, and for a moment, I was thirteen years old again and having a very grown-up conversation about poetry with fellow readers I'd bump into at bookstores.

Calvin's smile was tentative, head tilted. He put his book down, allowing me to finally see the cover. *Tropic of Cancer* by Henry Miller. I knew that book. A sexy romp through Paris.

"I spent my summers up here with my grandfather for years, and Mary Oliver was one of the poets we'd read together. Her words blend perfectly with Big Sur. There's so much nature here, it's almost..." He thought for a second. "*Forceful*. She captured that so well."

I nodded eagerly, in love with this feeling again. *I had*

missed it. "That's so true. I always read her in the concrete jungle that is Los Angeles. Doesn't have the same effect. Reading her here, though?" I said, twirling my finger towards the big open windows. "Would be fucking *fantastic.*"

He laughed, softly, almost nervously, and managed to hold my gaze for five whole seconds this time before blushing and breaking it. His eyes were a dark, dark green, like the forest outside.

On an index card taped to the cash register, someone had written "Word of the Day: *Lilting.*" I stilled, looking at it.

That word again.

"What's this?" I asked.

Cal looked where I was pointing. "My grandfather would choose a word completely at random every day and write it on an index card. I have a cardboard box in storage with all of them, dating back to the late fifties when he first opened the store. Sometimes when poets would come by and he'd ask them to write something on the spot, he'd give them the Word of the Day for inspiration."

"Did you choose this one?" I asked.

"No. He chose it on the day that he died. It was his last one. I just keep it up there for..." he trailed off, clearing his throat. I looked up at him. "Well, I just think he'd like it. It's one of my favorite words, actually."

"Me too," I said, and Calvin's smile was a lot less timid.

CHAPTER 5

Lucia

D ark storm clouds gathered in the distance as Cal walked us from the bookstore to our cabins. It was about a quarter mile through the forest on a tiny, worn path.

"My grandfather built these about thirty years ago. When The Mad Ones was at the height of its popularity, he wanted to extend it somehow, offer something more for the writers who were visiting. So he developed these cabins as writers' retreats. And the writers would spend a lot of time in the store —holding spontaneous readings. Drinking with my grandfather. Being active in the Big Sur bohemian scene at the time."

My heart gave a little squeeze, but I ignored it.

"Hey, Cal," Taylor said, stopping in the middle of the trail. Cal turned around, expertly avoiding eye contact with me. And mostly with Taylor too.

"Yeah?"

"Can I ask kind of a silly question?"

"Oh... of course."

We were standing under a canopy of awe-inspiring redwoods. I so wanted to ask Josie to catch me in some kind of accidentally-on-purpose shot for Instagram—laughing into the sunlight against the trunk of a redwood tree. Perfecting my "I know I'm a model, but I'm also a real *person*" brand.

But of course we couldn't do any of those things because we *didn't have the fucking internet.*

"Why is your bookstore called that? The Mad Ones? Kind of a weird name," Taylor said.

For the briefest of seconds Cal glanced at me. Someone who read Virginia Woolf *probably* knew that reference. But I shrugged, tossing my blonde hair. Playing it cool. Too many people around to impress.

"It's Jack Kerouac," Cal said.

"Who?" Taylor asked.

"He's a famous author, a Beat poet actually. He was a big part of the literary scene in San Francisco and spent a lot of time in Big Sur. He wrote a book called *On the Road*, which was my grandfather's favorite. It came out the year before my grandfather opened this bookstore. And the name, weird as it sounds, is from that book."

We turned one more corner, and then I saw the cabins, six of them. Tiny and built almost like row-homes, squeezed together. Each had a postage stamp-sized front porch, a railing, and a chair. A small table perfectly sized for a cup of coffee.

And then...

"Holy shit," Josie said next to me, and I turned, seeing the view fully for the first time.

Up ahead, Calvin shrugged, but there was pride in his voice. "So... this is why writers wanted to stay here."

Because the cabins were perched on a cliff that overlooked the coast of California. A rocky, untamed beach. Wildflowers and small, bright green bushes. On a clear day, you could probably see down the coast for a mile, totally uninhabited.

All yours. Behind the cabins stretched the woods, dark and mysterious.

"I wish I could take a selfie here," Taylor said, and I had to fight the urge to reply, "Same."

I walked over to the cabins, which couldn't be more than a bedroom and a bathroom.

"They're basically studios. You can use the kitchen in the bookstore while you're here, or there are some restaurants close by," Cal said.

"Internet?" I said, hopeful.

Cal shook his head. "Not even a little."

I nodded along, trying to be nonchalant. I strode up to the closest cabin, walking onto the porch, and plopped myself down in the chair. As I looked up and into the ocean, my fingers started itching again. Stronger this time. It felt like the ocean would swallow me whole, the roar of the waves drowning out any thought I had beyond this present moment.

It was exquisite. It was aching. It was scary and real. There was danger in that ocean—buried ships and the skeletons of pirates, red tide and great white sharks.

And there was beauty in that ocean—an entire delicate ecosystem we might never lay eyes on. A world, free from the push and pull of societal pressures.

I closed my eyes and let the thunder of the waves wash over me. When was the last time I sat and just listened... to anything?

The others walked further down the cliff, but I stayed. I desperately wanted to post a picture of this. Snapchat it to millions of people. Obsessively read their comments, their jealousy, their desire to be living my exact life. Calvin had stayed behind but still at least six feet from me. Every time I'd move closer to him, he'd take a step back.

It was like a fun little game we had.

"Calvin," I purred, tossing my hair. His eyes followed my golden tresses before re-focusing on my face.

Gotcha.

"What's a girl gotta do to get some internet around here?" I crossed my legs, leaned forward. Gave him my best "I've been on the cover of *Maxim* magazine" pout. Calvin looked away.

Okay, maybe not.

"I don't know what to tell you," he said, shuffling his feet. I was starting to wonder if subtle flirting was lost on Calvin. Except I wasn't being subtle. In the absence of social media, I needed attention, dammit, and Calvin wouldn't bite.

"There's an internet café in town. And service pops up sometimes in the oddest of places. It's just spotty," he said.

I gritted my teeth. *You're only here for three days.*

"What do you do for fun around here?" I asked. "*You* specifically."

"Oh," he said. "Well, when I inherited this place, I didn't exactly know how to run a business, especially an independent bookstore. I've spent a lot of time in the internet café googling things like 'what are property taxes?'"

I laughed, which seemed to spur him on.

"Also, um... reading. A lot. I used to love to read when I was younger, but my job before this was really time consuming. Now I basically spend every night with a book in front of the fireplace or on that back patio."

I thought of my nights recently, being photographed at clubs. Bars. Restaurants. Strobe lights and dance music and re-applying my lipstick twelve times in a darkened bathroom. I pictured Cal's nights.

I wasn't sure which one I'd prefer.

"Sounds quiet," I finally said.

"It is. But I'm starting to like it. There's tons of hiking around here, so I'll take Chance with me. Go to the beach.

Take long drives. It's really..." He stared off for a second. "Peaceful. Like going back through time."

"No internet. Cable TV. Like the Ye Olde Nineties," I said, and Cal laughed. He had a great laugh.

"See? Models can make jokes." I smirked. He made eye contact, for real this time, and held it.

"Sorry, it's just... it's a little surreal making jokes with Lucia Bell."

"I get it," I said. "First time I ever went to a real Hollywood party, with celebrities and movie stars, I kept thinking I was dreaming. But... and I know this sounds cliché, they really are just people. Like, food stuck in their teeth, awkwardly standing around, guzzling glasses of wine *people*."

"Hard to imagine," he said. "So different from here. From this place." He indicated the giant view behind him.

"Yes," I said softly, thinking. "It is."

The others were coming back. He threw me a conspiratorial look. "I checked my grandfather's records. That's the cabin Mary Oliver stayed in." He pointed to the one all the way at the end, balancing almost precariously on the edge of the cliff. It looked the same as all the others but somehow different. *Mine*.

"Can I...?"

"Yes, absolutely. Should I put Taylor in there, um, I guess, also?"

"Oh, *Taylor*?" I asked, confused. "Oh, he's not my boyfriend. He's just the other model on the shoot."

Cal laughed nervously. "Right, sorry I assumed. You're both just..." He trailed off, and I shook my head, dismissing the idea.

"Plus, we'd never fit all of our outfit changes in these tiny cabins if we shared," I said, shooting him a kind smile. He looked like he needed rescuing.

"For only three days?" Cal asked.

"Don't tease," I said, but loving it. Calvin's attention was like real life Instagram.

I traced my fingers up the curve of my neck, down to my collarbone. His eyes followed but only for a second. *Maybe he has a girlfriend*, I thought.

"We have a lot of clothes, you know. It's a fashion shoot. I'll wear, easily, between ten and twelve different outfits a day. Most of them completely see-through. Get used to seeing me basically naked," I deadpanned.

He didn't laugh this time but held my gaze. And for the briefest of moments—the *briefest*—I caught a flicker.

Lust.

My cheeks burned—even though *I never blushed*—but I re-crossed my legs, regaining the power.

"Well, I've officially died and gone to heaven," Josie called out, laughing with Taylor and Ray. I liked seeing her laugh— she needed that after the year she'd had.

"You love it?" I asked.

"I adore it," she said, glancing back as Ray reached us. He glanced out at the horizon where the storm clouds were growing darker by the second.

Ray pointed, looking at Calvin. "Bad weather supposed to come through later?" he asked.

"I think so," Cal said. "Big Sur can have some pretty dramatic weather, but you should be fine. Just a thunderstorm, I think. And if you get rained out, any number of Big Sur businesses would probably let you do a photo shoot there."

He nodded, making a note on his phone. "It would make for a pretty epic shot though, right? Lucia and Taylor in the rain, overlooking some cliff?"

I rolled my eyes. Easy to say when you weren't the person holding some twisty pose and a gorgeous face as hail beat down on your head.

"Sounds rad," Taylor said, and Josie made a face at me.

"So which cabin can I have?" Josie asked.

"Lucia's already called the last one," Calvin spoke up. I mouthed a *thank you* his way.

He shrugged it away, then nodded back towards the bookstore. "We should probably get back," he said. "Get you all unpacked and set up before the sun sets. Which is beautiful from here."

"Which I can't even post a photo of online, so it's like... what's the point?" Taylor mused without a touch of irony.

I grimaced, biting my tongue, since I'd *almost* said the same thing.

CHAPTER 6

Calvin

The first month I lived in Big Sur I'd missed sitting in traffic. I'd missed a lot of things. My apartment, even though it was dark and small and dingy—all white walls, tiny dishwasher, windows that looked out into the back of a parking lot. I missed my gym, where I went at least four nights a week. I missed my job as a software developer. There was nothing I loved more than sitting down in front of a computer, earbuds in, and coding for ten hours a day.

There were some days when I didn't talk to a single human being—just woke up to my alarm (always set to the dulcet tones of the local NPR reporters), sat in traffic for forty-five minutes, zoned out in front of a screen at work, sat in traffic on the way home, ran on a treadmill until I was exhausted, and went home.

I had inherited my mother's innate sense of order—and strong dislike of chaos. I liked routine. Numbers made sense to me. Traffic patterns were soothing.

I had done everything right. Went to Stanford for computer science. Made friends with the other nerds in my program, spending weekends watching *Star Wars* and bickering about comic book characters. Barely had sex... and I mean *barely*. Which was exciting, since I spent high school *never* having sex—no surprise, really, since I was essentially a walking stereotype.

After graduating with honors, my friends and I all landed jobs immediately. And I wound up in a three-year relationship with Claire, whose initial sense of order and routine complemented my own.

My family and I always thought of my grandfather as a lovable weirdo. Even me, and I'd spent most of my summers with him, growing closer and closer, ultimately seeing past the one-dimensional view my extended family had: the old hippie living in the woods and off the grid.

He was so much more than that, obviously. But deep down, I still thought it *was* weird. A life I wasn't cut out for.

A year before my grandfather died, I'd driven up to Big Sur with Claire for a long overdue visit.

My grandfather had teased me about the tie I was wearing, about looking stern in my button-up. We were sitting on the back patio, glasses of whiskey in our hands.

"I have something for you," he'd said, pulling out a stack of books. Asimov. A slew of Vonnegut. An old collection of pulpy sci-fi he'd found at a pawn shop. He pressed them into my hands.

I remember inhaling that smell—that smell of used books, a combination of sun and dust and whatever happens to paper pages as they age. The kid in me wanted to squeeze them to my chest. The adult in me sighed.

"I wish I had time to read these," I'd said, cracking a smile. "Work is so busy, you know? I never have the time anymore."

My grandfather laughed. "You sound like a robot. And not the good kind."

"You mean the kind that will one day take over our planet?"

"Of course," he said. "You're not the kind of robot over-lord I'd want in charge. Too boring."

I laughed. I'd missed his odd sense of humor.

"Well," I continued, "I'm too tired at the end of the night to read. And on the weekends..."

"On the weekends, what?" he asked. But when I opened my mouth to answer, I found I didn't really have an excuse. I just didn't read anymore.

"Too busy laying the groundwork for the robot revolution, you know? You can't overthrow the human race in a day," I finally said, and his laughter rang out on the patio. I laughed too, glancing down at the books in my hand.

My grandfather read every genre voraciously, but knew I had a passion for science fiction. As a kid, when I'd show up prattling on about the old episodes of *The X-Files* my parents showed me, he'd smile, nod, and then come back with a stack of science fiction classics almost never suited for my age.

"Here. Start from the beginning," he'd say gently, and I'd usually devour them in a single sitting.

"What about a vacation? Go anywhere beautiful lately? It's a great time to read books," he'd asked, sipping from his drink.

I caught Claire's eye. We had just been having this conversation, about the last time either one of us had taken a legitimate break from work—more than just a long weekend here or there. It had been years for both of us.

"You know how it is, Grandpa," I said. "I've got so much work to do, I basically have to kill myself to get ready for the vacation."

"And then when you get back," Claire cut in. "—it's even worse. It's like, why even go? Just makes work harder."

My grandfather just smiled, giving me a look I remembered well from childhood. I shifted in my chair, changed the subject. But I could feel his disappointment.

Later, after Claire had gone to bed, he convinced me to go on a walk with him. His walks were famous in Big Sur, and he was known to show up at people's houses for unexpected conversation, sometimes bringing Chance. Sometimes bringing food. Sometimes just bringing a couple glasses and a good bottle of wine. My grandfather believed in spontaneous socializing, building community instantly with just about anyone he made eye contact with.

This walk, though, was through the woods, lit brightly by a full moon. We were heading out towards the cabins. I'd been feeling something all day, some feeling I couldn't put my finger on, a discomfort. Itchy. I'd torn off my tie, undid the first few buttons on my shirt, but the feeling didn't fade.

"I'm sorry if I seemed a little judgmental back there," he finally said after we'd walked in silence for a while.

"I doubt Claire noticed," I said. "Only a few people recognize your 'I'm secretly judging you' smile. Most people just think you're really nice."

"I *am* nice," he said, elbowing me. "But I don't want you to think I'm sitting up here in Big Sur, the King of Bohemia, and looking down on you in judgment."

I laughed. "You think I'm wasting my life, don't you?" I wasn't offended, not really. We had a close relationship, and I'd heard him argue with my parents enough about this topic to know he only said it out of love.

"Not at all, Calvin. Not at all," he said. "Life is beautiful. We live our lives differently, which is one of the best things about living. I've lived long enough on this earth to know that to be true. I just... I want to know if you're happy."

"Of course," I said. "I got my dream job. I go to as many science fiction conventions as I want. I've got Claire. We've got an apartment in the city. I have a car." I shrugged. "I'm not sure what else I need."

But even as I said it, something was stirring. I didn't know what it was.

"I'm not sure either, Cal. And I'm not saying you need any more than what you have. What you have is amazing and a real privilege. But..." He trailed off.

"I'm not like you," I said hastily, sensing where he might be going. "I don't want to go against the grain all the time. I don't want to always have to explain my different life choices to people. I like my routine. I like that Mondays we always do pizza. And Wednesdays I play Dungeons and Dragons. And Fridays we go to the movies. I *like* all of that."

He sighed deeply, stopping for a second to identify a constellation for me. The stars up here were brighter than in the city. I couldn't star gaze there, the universe looking milky and pale against an onslaught of lights. In Big Sur, the stars demanded your attention.

We stood in silence for a moment, and I suddenly felt tiny and insignificant.

"Staring at the stars up here can get you in trouble," my grandfather finally said. He knew me too well.

"I feel..." I struggled to finish the sentence, awash in the Milky Way, shivering slightly under a canopy of trees, the pounding of ocean waves steps away. All of nature, crashing down around me.

"I feel like living in Big Sur is like living on another planet," I finally said. "It's isolating."

"I felt that way too, when your grandmother and I were first up here. We were really going against the grain, although back then we could barely go a day without having young kids —younger, even, than you—showing up at our doorstep, looking for a place to crash."

"Running away?" I asked.

He shrugged. "Sure. Or just exploring. Going on a grand adventure. Didn't always turn out well, but the spirit was there. I'd felt the same way then, staring society in the face and saying *why*? Scoffing at the career ladder, at a culture that seemed obsessed with buying things. At that time, we had so many writers coming through—some famous, some not—and they'd sit in the Big Room and have these long, drawn-out conversations for hours on end just... questioning."

We neared the cabins. They looked spooky in the moonlight. I shivered.

"But then I'd have to go into the city to buy books, or meet with my accountant, and I'd be startled. Just... shaken up. By the busyness. How quickly people seemed to move through their lives, never seeming to be fully present in the moment. In comparison, yeah... I bet my accountant thought of me as an alien," he continued.

"And not the good kind," I said, grinning. "Not the kind I'd want to be my future overlord."

My grandfather laughed. "Exactly. I had long hair and only wore sandals, and he probably thought I was stoned out of my mind. I wasn't. I was just used to a slower pace of life."

We were silent for a second before he said, "I can be a bit dogmatic in my beliefs, Calvin." We perched on one of the cabin porches, our feet swinging in the darkness. "I know that. I know that I've pushed family members away, burned some bridges."

I nodded. My grandfather had never done any real damage (he was too kind), but I'd spent plenty of holiday dinners attempting to mediate an argument between my grandfather and some uncle. Or my parents.

"And the last thing I ever want is to appear judgmental. People need to live the lives they want—I guess, at the end of the day, *that's* what I'm dogmatic about. It's not how you're living it, Cal. You could be an investment banker and own six houses, and if you were happy—*truly* joyful—I'd congratulate you. Since finding comfort and peace in how we live our lives is not easy to do. Believe me." He turned to me, and now I wondered if he knew he'd be dead in a year.

He couldn't have—it wasn't like he had an illness, or even an inkling, that an aneurysm lay dormant in his brain. But he seemed desperate to get through to me.

"I know you," he said. I felt that shift again, something awakening. "I think we're more alike than you realize. When you used to come up here, I'd see such joy on your face. An excitement for the world around you." He paused, and I knew what was coming next. "Do you feel like you still have that?"

I don't remember exactly what I said, probably some assurance. And I'm not even sure I was lying to him at the time. I might have been a little confused, but it wasn't hard for me to tell him something like, "Of course I do."

We switched subjects after that, moving on to his recent favorite books. A poem he'd found the other day he couldn't wait to show me.

I didn't tell him I hadn't fully read a book in over a year—I read Facebook articles and scrolled through Reddit. Talking to him that night, I felt that feverish desire I'd had as a child, to consume as many words and worlds as possible.

The next morning, I woke early and sat in front of the old fireplace, reading the Isaac Asimov novel my grandfather had given me cover to cover. Because it was good, and because I needed to—needed to remember the simple pursuits of my childhood, a world outside the magnetic pull of the internet and its myriad of distractions.

My grandfather joined me after a while, and we spent the morning like that, quietly reading. Chance at our feet, the fire burning down to embers.

* * *

I ran hard this morning with a smile on my face, remembering my longing for traffic that first month in Big Sur. My new routine was different, and as I ran up Highway 1, the ocean to my left, I relished in the burn of my calf muscles, the fog clinging to my skin.

Big Sur fog was my new favorite weather condition to run in—thick as a shroud and pressed so close I could only hear my breath, my footsteps, the waves. So different from the manufactured brightness of the gym.

I stopped at the Big Sur Bakery for coffee and flipped idly through our local paper, liking the combined hum of locals and tourists. Laughing at the small-town crimes written about in the back. Guzzling a glass of water and then running home, fog just beginning to burn away. The storm clouds stayed, though, low and threatening in the distance.

I felt closest to my grandfather when I opened the store every morning—a new routine I didn't expect to love so much when I first moved here. I expected to feel emotionally divorced from the daily acts of bookstore business—because it didn't matter, not really. I'd be closing up at the end of October. And yet, every day the enjoyment I got from the multitude of small tasks grew until I actively looked forward to it.

Again, so different from my life before. And something I was beginning to feel comfortable enough to admit I was going to miss: the gentle act of dusting the piles of books, straightening spines and pages, tucking wayward poems back into their place—pinned on the ceiling or framed on the wall. Lighting three fireplaces.

I read voraciously now, keeping a long list by the register of what I'd read and what was next, my recommendations, even though some days not a single customer came in. But my grandfather had done it, and he would have wanted it to continue.

Flipping the sign to "open," I propped open the door, pulled out my stool, and waited for customers.

During my first month, I'd had no idea what to do with the types of people who wandered into the store: tourists, locals, free spirits making the pilgrimage to a Bohemian touchstone. I didn't know how to have small talk with people, my old high-school insecurities rearing back up.

My grandfather was warm and chatty and loved meeting strangers. In comparison, I was the wallflower at the school dance, stuck in my head and easily embarrassed.

On one of my first days running the store on my own, a group of women came in, pulling up in an old VW van— daffodil yellow with printed curtains inside.

They were young, about my age, and awash in self-confidence. Airy dresses and long hair, limbs jangling with bracelets. They wanted to know all the stories about my grandfather: Beat poets, anti-war demonstrations and famous authors scrawling masterpieces on index cards.

They grew quickly tired of my nervous rambling, their disinterest evident. I felt gawky and too tall, and wished at least one of them was wearing glasses, even ironically.

Except for Claire, and a handful of awkward hook-ups, my experience with women was severely limited. I'd been single for more than a year at that point and was constantly wondering if I'd ever meet a woman like Claire again—not that I was pining for her. She'd been too serious, too moody, too quick to judge. But some part of her had been okay with the fact that I was just an awkward nerd, stumbling through human interactions like a bull in a china shop.

But nothing—absolutely nothing—in my life thus far could prepare me for the next-level-awkwardness of having a supermodel suddenly strut into my store with an entourage of people and cameras following in her wake.

I knew the general shooting schedule—knew that I'd have an open store with a photo shoot happening at the same time —but they still caught me completely off-guard. I had been thumbing through *Letters to a Young Poet* by Rilke, sipping my fifth cup of coffee and idly looking out the window.

"Calvin." Lucia grinned, breezing past me. I choked on my coffee. Her hair was piled on top of her head in a messy bun, and she was wearing a short dress she must have slept in. She was barefoot, drinking lemon-water and holding her phone in her hand.

"Uh... good morning, I guess?" I finally managed, aware of the coffee spilling down my shirt.

She didn't respond, lowering herself gracefully into a makeup chair. Josie buzzed around her, setting up bags and brushes and a rainbow palette of makeup.

She chatted easily with the myriad of folks swarming around her: Ray, camera guys, a few people with sketchpads and pencils. I watched, mouth slightly open, as an army of superbly trendy people began to drag in rack after rack of clothing, shoes, scarves, hats.

Taylor strolled in next with an easy confidence, flashing me a winning smile. "Calvin, what's up, man?" he said, shaking my hand and then draping his body over a black makeup chair. He was tall, charismatic and broad-shouldered, with a supermodel's smile and the kind of floppy, hipster haircut I could never pull off.

I was taking it all in, my quiet Big Sur paradise suddenly filled with the busy hum of a Hollywood film set.

I ached, slightly, to imagine my grandfather here. He would have made everyone laugh, regaling them with stories of Elizabeth Taylor and Richard Burton stumbling through the bookstore at midnight on a Tuesday in the late sixties, drunkenly mistaking The Mad Ones for their cabin. They had stayed the night, chatting with my grandparents until the sun rose. A card was pinned up near the cash register—a thank you note signed by them both.

But in so many ways this photo shoot represented what my grandfather hated the most, the reasons he lived in Big Sur with its rugged individualism: Capitalism. Commercialism. Magazines that told you how to eat and what to look like and how thin you should be. Beauty ideals that made women hate the way they looked. The obsession to need things, buy things, own things, and the endless, incessant compulsion to compete with one another.

I swallowed, took another sip of coffee, and caught Lucia staring at me: one long assessment—my messy hair, my three-day stubble. The plaid shirt I had probably buttoned incorrectly.

"You're not hiding a latte behind that Rilke, are you?" she finally asked.

I tilted my head, surprised again. Was she flirting with me? Just being friendly? Also, and maybe this was stereotyping, but I didn't peg her for a reader of early-twentieth-century German poets.

So I begrudgingly left the comfort of the desk and wandered over to where the action was slowly developing. Ray was moving everything everywhere, cocking his head, examining light. I stepped around him, slid past tangled computer cords, and ended up in front of Lucia. She was perched in the makeup chair, one long leg crossed over the other.

"Um... what?" I asked, affecting a disinterested air.

Lucia Bell didn't need one more man to slobber all over her, which is what I would have done if I hadn't steeled myself for having to look at her every day for the next three days.

Without makeup, she looked younger, her eyes wider. Her dress hitched up her thighs, just stopping before the curve of her ass. She had, literally, just woken up, and my mind scrambled to fight off an image of rolling over in bed to find her next to me, my hand sliding beneath that dress, the other hand threading through that thick golden hair.

"Good morning," she said, hand clutching her phone again.

"You know we still don't have internet," I said, pointing at the screen.

She scrunched her nose, sighing. "Force of habit," she said. "It's no big deal."

I narrowed my eyes at her.

Lucia's smile tugged at those full lips. "What? You think I have an addiction to the internet or something?"

I smiled. "Nope. I mean, no worse than me when I first moved here. Want me to make up some news stories? Act out some Instagram drama for your viewing pleasure? Maybe a cat video?"

She was smiling broadly now. I was killing it with the jokes.

"What I want is a latte," she said simply, snapping her phone down. I opened my mouth, closed it.

"Oh, right, we're back to that again." I sighed, looking around. "Don't you have a craft services person to do that for you?"

"They haven't arrived yet," Josie said, glancing at me apologetically. "They're stuck in some massive traffic on Highway 1. And Miss Lucia here is even more addicted to caffeine than she is to the internet."

She released Lucia's hair from the bun on top of her head, and as her hair tumbled to her shoulders, I caught the scent of her shampoo again—something beachy, like coconut.

"Ahhhh," I said, hand rubbing my jaw. Lucia was still looking at me, and I remembered our bizarre conversation last night—her love of Mary Oliver. The look on her face when she was surrounded by books—so different from what I expected. So interesting.

But now she looked disaffected and bored, a gorgeous model used to being waited on hand and foot.

"Ray, what's the first look again?" Josie called back, rummaging through her makeup. A hair stylist walked up, arms filled with bundles of fresh flowers.

"We're going to weave these through your braids," she told Lucia, who nodded. The hair stylist began pulling at Lucia's tresses, winding them around her finger.

"Beautiful," Josie said. "And it looks like first look is that white dress thing."

Another woman was now at Lucia's feet, measuring the size against about fifty different types of shoes—all with stacked wedge heels. Another woman was pulling at Lucia's fingernails, examining the cuticles and rattling off color ideas to her harried assistant, taking notes in a giant notebook.

Lucia arched an eyebrow. "It's the Lucia Buffet. Everyone gets a piece."

I laughed, which seemed to make her happy. "Let me call a few folks in town, see what we can't do. What do you eat for breakfast?"

"Ten small watermelon seeds. Five almonds on the side."

I paused, glancing back. Her face was as serious as a heart attack.

"Are you fucking with me?"

She unleashed a smile that would have killed a lesser man.

"Totally. I eat like a normal person, so, like, eggs and bacon? Bagels?"

"Got it," I said, grinning. "I'll see what I can do."

A quick phone call, and I activated what was affectionately known as the Big Sur Channel, the network of Big Sur locals who would step up and help any person in need, even a bunch of high-maintenance LA models. Twenty minutes later, and the bakery was delivering lattes and bagels and bacon galore.

I sat back behind the register and watched Lucia munch happily on a piece of bacon, laughing with Josie. Our interaction had used up every element of "cool" that I had, which meant I'd need to go back to ignoring her for the rest of the day and praying she didn't talk to me—just like every interaction with a woman I'd had since the time I hit puberty.

CHAPTER 7

Lucia

I woke to the sunrise—something I hadn't done in years. Not unless it was stumbling home from some club opening, tipsy in high heels, waving away paparazzi waiting for me at my doorstep.

No. This was different. As soon as my eyes opened, I sat up, yanked on a sweatshirt, and pulled open the front door.

"Paradise," I breathed. The fog hung like a blanket over the coast. The air was wet on my bare legs, that scent of rain, the threat of thunder. I wanted tea and a good book. A fireplace and flannel. My fingers drummed against the doorway, and I wondered where my notebook was.

And then, just as quickly, I grabbed my phone and went to open one of seven social media apps I used regularly.

No Service.

I contemplated chucking the phone right into the ocean.

I had probably lost another hundred followers—followers who were used to me posting sometimes hourly, providing a glimpse into Lucia Bell's Glamorous Life. And this—*this*—was the kind of sunrise I needed to post a picture of.

Now, not an hour later, I was perched on a stool with ten different women touching ten different parts of my body, intent on making me beautiful.

"Bacon me," I said to Josie, who cheekily fed me a piece. I was getting a simultaneous pedicure and manicure, and the hair stylist, Joanna, was scrunching a thick gel into my hair.

"Latte me," I said, and Josie held the steaming cup up to my lips.

Josie had been my makeup artist (and best friend) for a decade, and we'd done this song-and-dance a million times. As a model, the only way you could ensure you got to eat on set was to have your makeup artist feed you. That, and I also usually stuffed my face when they allowed me a rare five minutes to use the restroom.

"Calvin really came through, eh?" Josie said, tilting my head just slightly, her fingertips cool against my cheekbones.

"That he did," I said, my gaze sliding towards the big desk he was currently hiding behind.

He was reading that Rilke like it held the secrets of the universe, barely glancing my way since our little interaction half an hour ago. I'd caught his eyes snag ever-so-briefly on my bare thighs before composing himself.

His self-control was intriguing—I'd been fawned over by rock stars and celebrities and European diplomats and even other models, younger women who want to worship at my feet.

But Calvin was content to ignore me.

Although it *was* nice to have someone on set who would finally laugh at my jokes (besides Josie).

"What are you thinking about?" she asked me as I let my eyes flutter closed.

This was my favorite part of modeling—letting a group of people take total control of your body, their fingertips like tiny hummingbirds landing on your skin, over and over. Hands in my hair, on my cheekbones, on my ankles and wrists.

"Oh, nothing," I said. "I was actually thinking about Cal. He's... interesting."

She made a sound of assent. "And this bookstore," Josie said, "I swear I got chills when we came in here. I wonder why all of those writers don't come anymore, you know?"

"Mmmm," I said, thinking about my own reaction. Even now, with Ray manhandling every piece of furniture in this gorgeous room, I felt the energy of all the books waiting to be read. I think Cal had picked up on it, that and my ridiculous overreaction to his Mary Oliver story.

"Lucia," I heard in my ear. Ray.

"Yeah?" I said.

"I'm estimating nine hours, minimum, today in this location. We'll work through the first thirty-five outfits with you and Taylor."

"Perfect," I said, waiting for him to walk away and then heaving a giant sigh. Suddenly I was exhausted, and the thought of holding poses for nine hours through thirty-five outfit changes was the last thing I wanted to do.

Josie laughed a little. "See? This is kind of what I was talking about yesterday," she said lightly. She knew I was unlikely to take it seriously, at least not while on set.

"I know," I said. "I don't think I'm unhappy, though," I said, hoping Joanna and her assistant were ignoring me. "It's just not as... I don't know, *thrilling* as it used to be. And I'm not sure..." I trailed off, surprised at how quickly I was about to spill a dark thought that had invaded my mind a year ago and wouldn't let go, spreading like a nasty weed.

"What?" she prompted.

What the hell else am I supposed to do? I was twenty-six, which was incredibly young in Normal Years but practically *ancient* in Model Years. I was like a Great Aunt to the new, younger faces, my time in the spotlight nearing the end. Those Instagram followers would find the next It Girl and want a piece of *her* glamorous life, not mine.

Which is why I needed the Dazzle contract.

"*Estoy feliz,*" I finally said, wincing as Joanna yanked my scalp. "*Lo prometo.*"

"I believe you," she replied. "*Estoy preocupada porque te amo.*"

"*Yo también te amo.*"

I opened my eyes to find Josie grinning kindly at me, holding a mascara wand in her hand. "Look up, *chica.*"

I had been fifteen years old when I landed my first modeling gig and spent the majority of that first day longing to be with other ninth graders at my high school. It was weird to be both the center of attention but also surrounded by adults so much older than you.

Josie was twenty-one then and newly hired, an assistant makeup artist, and could see right away how brave I was trying to be. How cool I wanted to seem in front of the adults, even as I stood, almost naked and shivering, in the cold studio lights.

"*Hablas español?*" she'd whispered, holding a tube of scarlet lipstick like a weapon. Josie was fucking *cool*—nose pierced, lip pierced, a few tattoos already decorating her arms. Josie was born in Mexico but raised in East LA, the youngest of five (and the only girl).

"No," I'd said, miserable.

"Ah, *no te preocupes, cariño.* Don't worry, darling. I'll teach you. It'll take your mind off things." And she had. My memories of my first year of modeling were colored with memories of conjugating Spanish verbs with Josie by my side. It got me out of my head until, at sixteen, I could walk onto a modeling set and feel like I owned the world.

"I'm really fucking happy about Paris," I said, ignoring the tendril of doubt as Josie coated my lashes with thick mascara. "And I'll be even happier when you come visit me."

"Good," Josie said. "That's the Lucia I know. I like seeing you happy."

"I like seeing *you* happy," I said, reminded of holding a prone Josie, picture perfect in a crisp white wedding dress, as she sobbed for hours. The memory made me flinch, even though it'd been two years, and even though she'd sworn up and down that she'd moved on—from Clarke, from the wedding, from the heartbreak.

"You don't have to worry about that," she said, examining her handiwork. Josie was a goddamn cosmetics genius. "I saw you this morning, watching the sunrise. When was the last time you did that?"

I shrugged. "Never? Maybe... high school?" I held my hands together to stop them from trembling. I'd had a writing teacher once who told us to wake up with the sunrise every morning for seven days straight... to see if it affected our poetry.

It had.

"Hmmm," she said with fake nonchalance. "That's an interesting development."

"Probably just jet-lag," I said, but she arched an eyebrow at me, and I capitulated. "Okay, I wanted to watch the sunrise. Take my LA Cool Kids card from me."

She laughed, holding up eyeliner pencils like Edward Scissorhands, one stuffed between each finger. Josie was a trendy night owl like me, a frequenter of nightclubs and bars that only opened at four in the morning. We'd sworn to dance the night away at the darkened, scarlet-toned nightclubs of the LA underground, stopping only to have our picture taken by paparazzi.

Sunrises, we'd always said, were for suckers.

"It'll probably never happen again," I said, holding three fingers up like a Girl Scout. But the look she gave me suggested otherwise.

"You know what would be fucking rad? Snapchat," Taylor said, pulling up a stool and sitting next to me.

"I'd have to agree," I said, my hand feeling naked without a phone in it.

Josie layered magenta gloss onto my lips.

"You ready, Tay?" I asked, eyeing his bored look. Earlier, Ray had been giving him some intense instructions, and he'd looked extra stressed.

"Ready as I'll ever be," he said, stretching his arms overhead, exposing his perfectly sculpted six-pack. Everyone on the set seemed to stop, sneaking a glance at the hard ridges of his stomach. Sighing collectively.

But I wasn't impressed. After a decade of sculpted abs everywhere I looked, I was losing interest. Instead, my eyes landed on Calvin, adjusting his glasses and turning the page in his book. Quietly reading. Totally absorbed.

* * *

Hour six of this shoot, and my neck was killing me. I was wearing my 26th boho outfit of the day—a black crop top with high-waisted, cut-off jean shorts. A wispy, see-through cover-up on my shoulders, my fingers dripping with turquoise rings. Joanne had given me lioness hair, with tons of tiny braids, daisies woven through to the ends.

And from the moment we started, for reasons I still wasn't sure of, Taylor and I were just *off*. He was sitting down on one of Calvin's chairs; the set designer had stylized it with flowers and lace. It should have been a simple first shot—him seated, legs spread, looking directly into the camera. As usual, I was some type of human adornment—draping over his arm, straddling his leg, standing behind him. I re-arranged my face to appear both interested yet disinterested. Aroused yet irritated.

But we couldn't pull it off. In the first minute, Taylor nearly elbowed me in the face.

"Hey... watch it," I hissed, pushing his arm back into place.

"Sorry, I just... gah, I'm sorry," he whispered back, coughing awkwardly. We sounded like two high schoolers fumbling towards losing our virginity.

We changed poses. We changed outfits. Ray pulled Taylor off to the side and had a special "chat" with him—the kind every model has been given a million times: What's going on with you? Why isn't your face working?

These were the times when being an Older Model helped —years of experience and endurance. But two hours in, Taylor was yawning again.

"Chin up, Tay," I murmured, gripping his hair with one hand, my other drifting into his jeans. "We've got at least seven more hours of this."

"Whaaaaaa," he'd said, creatively, and I'd fought the world's biggest eye roll. I might have been currently less than enamored with modeling, but it was still a job that I took seriously. Sometimes It Guys like Taylor strolled onto a set, expecting a bunch of standing around and looking pretty.

Which, it was, a little bit. But it was also physical and boring and oddly intense and tedious, and you had to contort your body into strange shapes for hours on end.

"On his lap, Lu," Ray said, setting up the camera a few inches from our faces. "Let's try some extreme close-ups."

"My favorite," I replied sweetly, then proceeded to make a hideous, monstrous face directly into the lens. The camera guy burst into laughter.

"Taylor, you've gotta wake up for me, buddy. We need your face as animated—"

"Yet passive," I chimed in.

"—as possible. Yes, what Lu said. Also, I need you to barely breathe."

I'd perfected the art of Barely Breathing, but Taylor was struggling. Ray wanted us to do a lot of intense gazing into each other's eyes, and we just couldn't do it. I'd hear Taylor's scarcely concealed wheezing, and I'd crack up.

We had no connection. Which was an issue.

"Let's switch it up for a bit, and then we'll take a break. Get a little coffee, re-orient. Sound good?" Ray said, finally.

We both nodded, a flurry of stylists rushing over to primp and fluff me, pulling things up, yanking things down. I looked up and made direct eye contact with Calvin.

For the past few hours, he'd been either reading intently or answering the questions of bemused customers who weren't used to wandering into an active photo shoot.

He was more comfortable around them than he was around us—still awkward, but warmer. Funnier. A few times his laugh rang out, and I had to work to keep from smiling automatically.

Now his eyes were boring into mine—probably by accident—so I shrugged, arching my eyebrow. He was going to see me primped and fluffed *a lot*. I kind of wanted him to walk over again, but he kept his distance.

"Lu, let's have you face me now," Ray said. "Taylor, you're back in the chair but facing the fireplace. Lu, you straddle him. Let's get a series of shots where you're being kind of intimate with each other. Aware of the camera—"

"—but not aware at the same time. Got it," I said, throwing my legs over Taylor and getting into position. Taylor gave me a wolfish grin, probably trying to work his nerves out.

"Be serious," I chided, tossing my lion-hair and staring directly into the camera.

Which was now directly facing Calvin.

"Taylor, I want your hands kind of... well, kind of everywhere. Let's do a bit of a peep show, sound good?"

I rolled my eyes, and Ray caught it.

Reputation.

"It needs to be fucking sexy, Lu, you know that," he said, dismissing my eye roll with his hand. Calvin was definitely only *pretending* to read now, looking up every other minute as I essentially made love to the back of Taylor's head. Eye-fucked the camera. Exposed my throat, arched my back. Pulled Taylor's hair.

"Ouch." He winced.

"Get used to it," I said back.

"Can you lick him, Lu?" Ray said, and I complied, running my tongue up the side of Taylor's neck.

I looked up at the camera, inadvertently catching Calvin's gaze again. He didn't break contact this time, still staring. Taylor's hands smoothed up the backs of my legs. I nibbled on Taylor's ear. He grazed his hand on my stomach, pushing up the crop top and exposing the lower swell of my breasts.

I bit my lip, made eye contact with Calvin, expecting him to blush or cough or faint.

Instead, he gave me that look again, the one from last night.

Pure fucking lust.

"Take her top off, Taylor," Ray said, and Taylor's fingers glided up my rib cage, the fabric lifting off. I wasn't completely exposed, but if you used your imagination, you could get there.

I was pinned beneath Cal's gaze, trapped against Taylor's body, and growing more aroused by the second. Gone was Cal's nervous demeanor, replaced by something almost *savage*.

And then a family with six children walked in, breaking the moment.

"*Holy—*" the teenaged boy said, whipping out his phone.

The mom gasped, the dad tried to stay composed, and the youngest children were distracted by the lollipops Cal quickly found for them.

"So sorry," he said, moving from behind the desk and escorting them back to the front parlor. Taylor laughed, Ray grinned, and I wasn't entirely sure what the hell had just happened.

"Let's take an actual break this time, eh?" Ray said, standing and stretching. Josie handed me my top, and I put it back on.

"That's a great idea," I said quickly, slipping off the six-inch platform sandals I was wearing. "I'm going to wander for a minute, get some air."

Josie gave me a questioning look, but I shook her off. I walked towards the back of the store, discovering a few hallways I hadn't noticed before. One of the hallways was comprised entirely of built-in bookshelves, and I ran my hands down the spines, seeing some well-loved titles.

I breathed in the scent of dust and words. My heart was still racing, my body keyed up. I suddenly longed for someone to press me against these shelves, skin-to-skin.

Oddly enough, I wanted that someone to be Calvin.

I shook my head, dismissing the thought entirely and wandering further. I looked up toward the ceiling, seeing the postcards Cal's grandfather had pinned. I was tall enough to be able to read some of them—they appeared to be older.

Tonight, a group of us listened to Diane di Prima read some new poems in The Big Room. Amiri Baraka was also there, joining in on occasion. Smoked good weed and had the oddest sense that I could feel Diane's words on my skin. Robert opened the windows, and the night air was so clean and cool I cried.

I swallowed against a sudden wave of emotion, feeling the enormity of this place. Of the moments that happened here, of this person, now probably sitting at some desk, filing paperwork or answering emails, but with the memory of hedonistic nights at this bookstore.

"Lucia?"

I spun at my name and fell directly into Calvin's arms.

"Sorry... ah, fuck, I didn't mean—" he started to say.

"—oh, no, it's not your fault," I mumbled over him, looking up into his face.

At first, he wouldn't look directly at me, shoving his glasses back onto his nose and trying to slide past me. But the hallway was too narrow, so we stood, locked together for a moment, so close we were practically hugging, his hand the only thing I could focus on, clamped like steel around my wrist.

He stepped back first. "I'm so sorry, I... um... really didn't mean to scare you."

I waved it off, willing my heart rate to slow to normal. "You're fine. I'm kind of jumpy today." I smiled at him, and he smiled back, tentative.

"I think, um, well, I think you might have given that dad a heart attack," he said.

"Not the first time," I said, stony-faced, and pointed at my barely covered breasts. "These things are real killers."

His laugh came from deep in his chest. He was cute when he laughed.

He was cute when he wasn't laughing.

"I was reading this card." I pointed up, and Cal moved closer again, tilting his head to see. I thought about his gaze back in The Big Room, his hand on my wrist. "I just had the strangest feeling reading it. I was... I don't know... *enthralled*."

My tongue rolled around that word—*enthralled*. It was a good word.

"That's beautiful," he said softly. "You know, there are days where I would give anything to be here during that time.

59

I can't imagine seeing someone like Diane di Prima reading poems, and at the height of Beat poetry no less."

"Yes," I breathed. "I went through a heavy Beat phase when I was younger. I loved this one of hers called..." I tipped my head, trying to remember. I'd been in eighth grade, fighting with my parents about modeling and escaping through poetry.

"'An Exercise in Love'?" Cal said, eyes finding mine. The air became charged, the hallway growing smaller around us. I wanted to hold onto this moment: two near-strangers talking about poems.

"That was it," I said, a smile practically splitting my face. "I loved that—"

"Lu, you back here?" Josie stumbled into the hallway. When she saw us, she could barely conceal her reaction—a blend of excitement and confusion. We were standing closer together than I realized.

"Hello," I said, waggling my fingers at her. "Ray need me back?"

"He does. And he sent Taylor back to the cabins for a bit. Told him to get his head on straight."

Cal glanced at me. "It's common," I said, shrugging. "Modeling is hard. Sometimes you're just not in the right headspace for it."

"This girl, though—this girl could model balancing on the tip of the Empire State Building," Josie said, leaning against the bookshelves. I laughed. I wanted to snap a photo of her and Instagram it, some cute caption about best friends. She looked so pretty.

"You're thinking about Instagram, aren't you?" she said, and I sighed, my hands aching for a phone that wasn't there.

Cal moved out of the way, letting Josie grab my arm and pull me down the hallway. "I just miss it so much," I whined.

"It's only been a day," she said. "I'm pretty sure you'll survive."

I turned back towards Calvin, his shoulders broad against the narrow shelves. He gave me a small smile, and I winked at him. He blushed and looked away.

I turned back to Josie, feeling confident again.

At least *Calvin* liked me.

CHAPTER 8
Calvin

I slid onto a barstool and motioned over to Gabe, who was chatting with another Big Sur local. Without even looking, he opened a beer and slid it towards me. This bar had been around as long as my grandfather's store, although it had been through several different permutations. I wasn't even sure of its real name, but I'd been coming in a couple times a week since moving here.

A few tourists came in, immediately obvious. They were laughing, pointing at some of the strange artwork on the wall. Like all Big Sur institutions, this place was half bohemian, half leave-me-the-hell-alone.

I wondered when I had stopped thinking of myself as a tourist. I'd only lived here for five months, yet it seemed that taking over my grandfather's store gave me automatic "local" status. That, and many of the folks here actually remembered me from when I was a kid spending my summers here.

I wondered what they'd think of me when I sold his store a month from now and moved back to Silicon Valley.

"Calvin."

I looked up to see Gabe, the bartender and owner—and the first friend I'd made here.

"Gabriel," I said, grinning.

I liked Gabe, a lot. He was funny and chill and didn't seem to care that I was a bumbling mess of nerves most of the time we hung out. He was a true Big Sur bohemian: messy bun. Full beard. He looked like a hippie lumberjack. He was white, with tan skin and dark blond hair.

"I've heard through the Big Sur Channel that you have a bunch of Hollywood starlets at the store right now," he said.

"I do. And I have no idea what to do about it," I said, sipping my beer. "I have a hard enough time talking to normal people, let alone *famous* people."

"Ah, you'll do fine," he said. "They probably barely notice you, right? Maybe I've lived in Big Sur too long, but I get the sense they wouldn't care too much about us lesser folk."

I nodded, thinking. "That's pretty much true. And it hasn't been *too* hard. I've mostly been showing them around, giving them a bit of 'inspiration.'"

Gabe grimaced. "Stories about your grandfather?"

"Yeah," I said. "The usual."

Gabe was an institution in Big Sur, even though he was only a few years older than me. But his family had lived here for generations, and tourists often sought him out for stories about communes and acid trips. Like my grandfather, Gabe actively worked to keep the memories of this place alive.

But sometimes having to share the same stories over and over to drunk San Jose State students got old.

"Right now, the biggest issue is the fact that none of them knew they would have little-to-no internet connection."

Gabe laughed. "Amateurs. Don't they know we send letters up here?"

I laughed too. "I remember the shock of it when I first got here. I used to be so connected, especially in programming.

There was always some new blog post to read or community thread about a new thing Google was doing. I loved to just scroll through Reddit—"

"—down in an internet rabbit-hole—"

"—and then look up and realize two hours of my life had gone by while I watched cat videos."

Gabe nodded, picking up a towel and starting to dry glasses. "You get so used to the luxury that coming up here feels shocking. Which you know I technically prefer," he said with a smile. Gabe lived his life pretty much off the grid.

"Yeah, and I think the two models, Lucia and Taylor, both have a big internet following, so they've been extra twitchy."

"Interesting," Gabe said, stepping away for a second to help two customers, both locals.

Gabe was one of the only locals *not* curious about the 'Hollywood starlets' camped out at the bookstore for the next week. But I'd already shooed away countless others (the Mayor, two waitresses from the diner, a handful of local musicians) who'd been sneaking around, trying to get a glimpse of the action.

Although now I was getting in on that action.

I was closing the shop early and taking the crew into the Ventana Wilderness, the long stretch of forest that ran alongside Highway 1 in Big Sur. I had mentioned to Ray that my grandfather used to camp there in the 60s and 70s with some of the poets and authors that came through town. Ray wanted my help in staging a camping scene for Lucia and Taylor, which I was happy to do even though none of this entirely made sense to me.

On the phone, before arriving, Ray had told me all about high fashion, and how avant-garde this designer was, and how the 'new' thing in Hollywood were photo shoots that had the feel of modern art. And I nodded along, taking notes and wondering when we started caring about clothing so much.

Gabe walked back, grinning at the two customers. "They're both planning on coming back this week to spy on the photo shoot. You are suddenly *very* popular, my friend."

I sighed, shifting on the barstool. "That's good because we need customers," I said wryly. "After the shoot is done, I need to start putting things together to sell."

A look of disappointment flashed across Gabe's face, and I cringed. I knew, deep down, how he felt about it—he was part of a long list of residents who had both subtly and not-so-subtly pleaded with me not to sell.

"Have you, uh... have you reconsidered on that at all?"

"No," I said, honestly. "It was the hardest decision I've ever had to make, but my parents and I looked at the finances, and I just don't think it's possible."

"You don't want to revive it? Bring it back to its original glory?"

I shook my head. "I can't. I can't run a bookstore, especially not *that* one. My grandfather was this big, bold person who didn't give a fuck about society or doing anything the normal way."

"Which is why he was so awesome," Gabe interjected.

"True," I said. "It *is* why he was so awesome. But that's not me. I can barely..." I paused, coughing a little, "I mean, I can barely ask a girl on a date, and I'm almost thirty years old. I don't take risks. I'm not spontaneous or impulsive like he was."

I thought about my routine back home: commute, work, commute, gym, sleep.

The American Dream, although my grandfather would have considered it a nightmare.

"And running that bookstore isn't the same as it used to be. Writers don't want to come through and do readings anymore. We barely make enough revenue a month to pay costs." I finally stopped, feeling myself blush and hating it. My inner introvert seemed to be in constant turmoil up here. Sometimes when I felt comfortable enough to talk or share a lot, I'd feel embarrassed afterward.

"I don't know," Gabe said, thinking. "You left your job for six months to move here. You drink with me most nights. You're currently hosting two world-famous models at the shop. That's pretty impulsive, Cal."

"Hardly," I said, smiling sadly. "And I've got a meeting with these investors I really like in two days. It's all but done."

Gabe nodded, switching subjects. He never pushed, even though I knew part of him wanted to beg me to keep it open. He had a lot of good memories at The Mad Ones and considered it a historical landmark of Big Sur. I knew it was painful for him to think of it being sold and turned it whatever the hell it would be next—a hotel? A spa?

Gabe and I chatted the rest of the night, but I felt unsettled. Every time I thought about my life back home, I felt an odd blend of homesickness and dread. Every time Gabe would tease me about being "wilder than I thought," my stomach would clench.

I couldn't tell if it was anxiety over selling the store or my body trying to tell me something else, something deeper. Like that night in the woods with my grandfather, his deep belief I was living an uninspired life.

I walked home late, a little tipsy but mostly happy, the cold air and storm clouds forcing me into the present moment. It was going to pour rain at any moment, but I didn't care. A gentle reminder that I liked talking with Gabe, I liked sitting in a bar surrounded by my neighbors. I liked walking home beneath a Big Sur sky—I knew why my grandfather loved it up here: beneath the expanse of these stars, every wild idea you'd ever had felt possible.

And I had a wild idea.

When I got home, I walked into the Poetry section of the

bookstore. I slid my fingers down the spines until I found *Di Prima, Diane* and pulled out a collection of her poems.

I couldn't stop thinking about Lucia.

She was so... strange. One second whining about lattes or Snapchat. The next, impressing me with her knowledge of Mary Oliver or 1950s Beat poets. The photo shoot today was the definition of surreal, being in the same room as a famous model slowly stripped her clothing off. I worked hard to keep my eyes off her, picking up Rilke again and trying to lose myself in the poems, attempting to ignore her. And I hadn't wanted to stare, didn't want her to feel like I was the pervy guy in the corner, watching her like she was an object. Already the day had shades of high school—the nerd, quietly reading in the corner while the cool kids made out before fifth period.

But at some point, I made the critical mistake of looking up for a split second to see daisies in her hair and those luminous blue eyes. The soft muscles of her stomach, her perfect breasts. Lucia was flirtatious and a little outrageous, and I was drawn to that like a moth to a flame. She seemed to *like* that I was looking—maybe it was the performer in her. She'd held my gaze as she worked her body over Taylor's, posing for the camera.

Posing for me.

In the closeness of the hallway, I'd had to fight down something primal that roared up at her proximity. My hand on her delicate wrist. Breathing in her scent as she spoke so reverently about a poet she loved. I'd had a brief fantasy—of twisting that wrist behind her back and pinning her against those shelves. I'd liked thinking about dominating a woman who was such a force of nature.

Now, alone in the store and tipsy, I chastised myself, like I always did when my sexual fantasies turned dark and aggressive. I'd never had sex like that before, and I wasn't sure if I even wanted to.

And there wasn't a *single universe* where I'd be having that kind of sex with Lucia fucking Bell.

I flipped the pages, finding the poem that she'd mentioned loving: "An Exercise in Love." It was beautiful—short, but powerful. I grabbed a highlighter from behind the cash register and highlighted my favorite passage. I stuck a small Post-it Note inside: *Thank you for reminding me that this poem exists. It is perfect. - Cal*

I walked toward her darkened cabin, finding my way down the trail through memory alone. Some part of me that existed beneath the layer of alcohol fizzing through my bloodstream knew I'd be embarrassed that next morning, that leaving a poem for Lucia on her doorstep was too romantic, that'd she laugh when she opened it, and I'd remember why shy nerds never get the girl.

But the stars were bold and big, and the ocean was roaring against the shore, and I felt, so clearly, the rightness of the universe.

CHAPTER 9

Lucia

The last time I'd read "An Exercise in Love," I was in eighth grade and had just been approached by a modeling agent while at the mall who asked me if I'd ever considered modeling.

From the tender age of eleven, my parents had already *been* considering it for me.

That year, my mother had had a huge movie premiere—some action blockbuster—and we'd walked the red carpet as a family. The media loved my parents' love story. My mother was a Hollywood director who had fallen in love with—and married—the star of her first movie, my father. She was also ten years his senior.

The red carpet was terrifying—the constant flash, people screaming, a steady stream of celebrities I recognized and wanted to faint over. It was old news for my parents, but I didn't know how to stand. Where to hold my arms, how to tilt my chin.

I just smiled for the camera—beamed, really, like a dorky eleven-year-old does when someone points a lens in their face and says "smile." Later, looking at the photos in *People* magazine, it was obvious my parents had training—they were smiling, but it was attractive. They were happy but not *too* happy.

Underneath the caption, the magazine had written: *Lauren Paley posing with her husband, Mark Bell, and their daughter, Lucia.*

We looked like the perfect Hollywood Family. Afterwards, I'd been featured in a couple of those articles: "Mark Bell's daughter... a stunner already at eleven!" My mother had showed them to me, asking me how I felt about it.

"About what?" I'd asked, sinking lower in the passenger seat. It was Saturday, and on Saturdays, I begged my parents to take me downtown so I could walk to my favorite bookstores. Sometimes I wouldn't call for a ride until nightfall, having spent the entire day reading.

"Well, about that magazine saying you were pretty. More than pretty, a stunner. Did you like that?"

I glanced at my mother. I didn't know if I was pretty, but I thought she was. Even though she was behind-the-scenes, her wealth and status kept her focused on image just like other famous people. BOTOX, yoga, facials, crystal meditation, juice cleanses, kale smoothies... at forty-four, she looked ten years younger, a combination of health, good genes, science, and a ton of fucking chemicals.

"I don't know," I said. "Hey, later, can we get ice cream?" I asked, because I was eleven and too young to realize that my mother saw an opportunity.

I was smart for my age and a voracious reader—at ten, I'd finished *Catcher in the Rye*, and I was in the middle of reading *I Know Why the Caged Bird Sings* by Maya Angelou. I didn't have the emotional maturity to understand those novels fully at the time, but the words had a powerful effect on me.

At the age of twelve, I'd gone rollerblading with my father down Venice, and the paparazzi had snapped a photo of us.

Lucia Bell: all grown up and looking hot! My mom had shown me the caption on the photo, and I grimaced.

"Ew," I said because, even at twelve, I thought that seemed gross.

"Not what I would have said, true," she replied, tapping her finger against the photo. "But it's interesting, don't you think? I mean, you're already a little famous without even trying."

I crinkled my nose, mostly grossed out and just wanting to go back to what I'd been doing before she'd knocked on my door—writing.

The summer before, I'd begged my parents to send me to a creative writing camp since the only time I felt happier than when I was reading was when I had a pen in my hand. Those four weeks were the best of my life. So much uninterrupted time to just write. The camp was set in a beautiful nature refuge, and we were encouraged to walk and hike and sit in gorgeous meadows, taking in sights and textures. The different birdsongs, the way the grass swayed in the wind, the peculiar shape of a dandelion.

Away from the image-obsessed pressure of LA, and my mother's constant pushing, I felt lighter somehow. Free. The camp was filled with writers my age, and they were weird and cool and dorky, and I loved it.

"You have the soul of a poet," our instructor, Gloria, had said, smiling as she read the small collection of poems I'd written by the end of the four weeks. My heart felt close to bursting. When I got home, I told my parents all about the camp, talking a mile a minute, flushed with excitement. I wanted them to read my poems.

"And when I grow up, I'm going to be a *writer*!" I declared with all the sweet naiveté of a twelve-year-old. I spun around the kitchen, laughing.

"Oh, sweetheart," my mother said calmly, in between

barking at someone on the phone. "Writing's not a *real* job. Not poetry, anyway."

Just a year later, at thirteen, my picture was appearing at least semi-regularly in celebrity magazines. My mother was pushing my father to take me *everywhere*. I never suspected a thing, but it had been part of her grand plan.

She'd show me the pictures, and I'd scoff. But I was a new teenager, an intense mixture of huge ego and horrifically low self-esteem. The comments in the magazine were complimentary.

So I found myself becoming a little more curious.

When I was fourteen, my mom and I were back-to-school shopping at a downtown mall. A scout approached us as I was looking at jeans. In my hands was a collection of Beat poetry I'd just bought at the bookstore nearby. As the woman chatted with me, examining my bone structure and complimenting my smile, my mother was sharp-eyed and hawkish. The grand plan was coming to fruition: a director, a movie star, and a model—the trifecta of fame.

I'd glanced at my mother for an answer when the scout asked if I'd like to come down and do some portrait shots. She had nodded coolly, the epitome of aloof.

I did it, and it was easy, and it taken so little time I was still able to meet my friends at the movies that night. I hadn't seen the big deal, but I'd heard the murmurs of people in the studio. After the first shot, the photographer paused, looking at it. Called a few folks over who made similar serious faces. I thought I'd done a bad job. But they'd taken a few more, my head tilted eighteen different ways, and when it was over, the agent asked me if anyone else had seriously approached me for modeling.

"Oh... no," I said, laughing nervously. "Can I go now?" A boy I had a crush on was going to be at the movies with us.

"Yes," she'd said slowly. "You can go. And, um, Lucia, just

so you know, I'm going to give your parents a call." She paused. "Immediately."

That night, she strongly urged my parents to take me out of formal schooling and have me sign with her modeling agency.

"High fashion," my mother had said, perching on the edge of my bed with barely concealed excitement. I had been sitting there, surrounded by the remnants of my Algebra homework, texting my friends on my flip phone. "Runway in Milan and Paris. *Vogue* covers. This could be your life, Lucia."

I remembered laughing since the models I saw on runways were grown-ups and I was definitely *not* a grown-up.

"There's a short timeline for modeling," my mother pressed. "Most of them retire in their mid-twenties, so we're not talking forever here. We don't have a lot of time to make this decision before you get too old."

"Can I still go to school?" I'd asked, thinking about English class, my favorite. It was how I could be a secret book-worm without the popular kids finding out I was a big nerd. "And back to writing camp?"

She'd shaken her head but didn't seem upset by that.

"Aren't parents *supposed* to want their children to stay in school?" I asked, arching an eyebrow. My natural sarcasm had really started to kick in that year.

"You'd still get an *education*, Lucia," she said, rolling her eyes at me. "Just not the typical one. Like the kids who are in my movies. You'd have an on-set tutor. After high school, you'd test for your GED. It's the same as a high school diploma."

"But it's not the same as going to actual *high school*," I'd said, sitting up straighter and disturbing the delicate balance of my Algebra homework. Papers spilled to the floor. "I thought... I don't know, I thought I could do, like, fun model-ing. Like be on the cover of a magazine for the downtown mall. Or a pageant or, I don't know, easy stuff. The girl who lives down the street does it, and she never has to miss school. She just makes extra money and gets her photo taken."

Which sounded like a good deal to me: feed this newly wakened desire for attention while still getting to go to English class and prom and football games. At fourteen, I'd *just* had my first kiss. Who would I kiss on a photo shoot?

"High school is nothing," she said, smoothing her hand down my hair. "I know this doesn't make sense now, but you'll forget about high school as soon as you're in your twenties. It won't matter. What *will* matter is you'll be famous," she said. "Lucia, that agent sees something in you, something she took very seriously. She saw, in you, an amazing amount of raw potential. She told me she hasn't been this excited about a new talent in a very long time. You could be famous."

"Like Kate Moss?" I'd asked, trying to understand. It was a big concept.

Her eyes gleamed. "Yes. That's what I'm telling you. There's no guarantee, but if you work hard and meet the right people and get the right jobs... your life could look very different in a couple years."

I swallowed, wondering how we could be having this conversation surrounded by calculators and homework and my friends texting me winky emoticons. Some part of me recognized this as "not normal," but I'd grown up in Hollywood, and everyone I knew was image-obsessed and desperate for fame. Why couldn't I be a part of that?

After she'd left me to "think about some things," I'd pulled out that collection of Beat poetry, reading Diane's words obsessively, trying to find some meaning. Because even though my dream had been dismissed earlier, I *still* wanted to go to college for creative writing.

Be a writer.

A lost dream now.

* * *

This morning, I'd woken at sunrise again, flinging open my cabin door for a glimpse of the rocky coastline. It had rained hard last night—the beginning of a storm—and the waves seemed angry. There, right on the front step, was a collection of Diane di Prima's poems. When I flipped it open, "An Exercise in Love" was marked with a Post-it and a handwritten note. Cal's handwriting was neat and orderly, and he'd highlighted the last lines.

They were my favorite too. I clutched the book to my chest, perching on one of the rocks overlooking the beach. I read the last lines, over and over. It was the dual w-words, the hard "v" sound in the word "weaving." The contrast against the harder consonants.

I sat like that for a long time, reading it over and over. When I finally stood up, brushing rocks from my legs, I was startled to find my cheeks wet with tears, although I hadn't realized I'd been crying. Which used to happen to me all the time when I read poetry.

"You getting ready, Lu?" I glanced back to see Josie and Ray, packing up their supplies for the day. I wiped my face hurriedly.

It was barely seven in the morning. I needed to sit in makeup and hair for at least three hours, and then we'd be filming until dark. Suddenly, I longed to be back at that creative writing camp, letting my pen move across the paper.

"Born ready," I lied, slipping the book into my back pocket. "What's on the docket today?"

"Calvin's taking us to the woods," Josie said excitedly.

"Calvin's coming?" I asked, perking up. *Someone has a crush.*

And suddenly the day looked a little brighter.

* * *

As soon as we met up with Calvin on the trail, I wanted to thank him for the poem, for how perfect it was this morning, that specific moment. But he was standing there, looking kind of cute in his flannel, his ever-present scruff, and I got a *teeny-tiny* bit nervous.

Just a little. But it was there.

He avoided me though, chatting with Ray about the setup. I wasn't sure why I needed Cal's attention so much. That morning, getting ready in the cabin, I caught my reflection: makeup-less, hair a giant tangle. I was wearing an old sleeping shirt that was stained and fraying at the bottom.

I crinkled my nose, feeling gross and unglamorous—a byproduct of being on these shoots. You spend all day having experts make you look like a perfect human specimen, so when you see yourself without fake lashes and airbrushed makeup, your self-esteem plummets.

Instinctively, I'd picked up my phone, opening Snapchat. It was the kind of thing I would have posted about—taken a #wokeuplikethis selfie and waited for the compliments to roll in.

Even just two days without those interactions had left me feeling weird. Adrift. I hadn't realized how much I craved it. Wondered, briefly, if my parents had known how much this job would turn me into a fame monster.

But then we turned the corner, and the beauty of the natural landscape stunned me into silence.

"Wow," Taylor said beside me. I heard Josie suck in a breath.

I walked up ahead to where Calvin was standing. "What is this place?" I asked.

We were in a forest of mostly redwoods, towering over our heads. And evergreens, ripe with the scent of Christmas.

Colorful wildflowers dotted the forest floor, and the air was alive with birdsong. And in the middle?

"My grandfather's campsite," Calvin said, grinning. I smiled back at him, and for a second we were the only two people in the entire world.

"Fucking cool, man," Taylor said, pushing past us towards the fire ring. Josie was already setting up a makeshift hair-and-makeup set, and Ray was scouting location ideas. Joanna was with wardrobe, unpacking outfits they'd wheeled out in huge suitcases.

I perched on a log, and to my great surprise, Calvin sat next to me. Our thighs brushed, and I turned, about to make a snarky comment. But he noticed, immediately sliding a foot away from me. With one finger, he slid his glasses up his nose.

"Sorry, I didn't mean to—" he mumbled.

"I don't bite. Unless you want me to," I said, trying to save him. He started to cough uncontrollably, and I gave him three hard whacks on the back. "Did you swallow a bug or something?"

He shook his head, coughing a few times more before clearing his throat. "Thanks, uh, and sorry."

"Calvin, you can sit next to me. And I was totally joking about that biting thing," I said, giving him an easy smile. He returned it, and then I said, "Or... *was* I?"

He laughed, which was the point, and seemed to visibly relax. Now would have been a good time to bring up the poem, but we were surrounded by people. I kind of liked that it was a secret. Our secret.

"So this is it, huh?" Ray asked, indicating the space in front of us. Josie joined us, interested. Ray had wanted a background on this campsite to "inform the narrative" of the shoot.

Which I'd rolled my eyes at since Taylor and I could be

semi-naked and groping each other, with expensive clothing on, literally *anywhere*. No narrative needed.

But this was *Shay fucking Miller,* as Ray had reminded me.

"Yeah, so... as I was telling you all before, my grandfather hosted tons of writers, famous and non-famous, at the bookstore regularly. Some did readings or held workshops. Others were 'in-residence' and would spend their days on a permanent retreat, writing in the cabins and drinking whiskey with my grandfather in the evening."

He paused, rubbing his jaw for a moment. "But there was a time, in the late 60s, when Big Sur was really known for naturalism. Living off the land, going back to a more primitive lifestyle."

"But with drugs," I said, and Calvin laughed again, nodding.

"Ye-es, I'd say LSD was pretty popular. And weed, like a *lot* of weed. But my grandfather would lead these artist retreats, and they'd camp for days, sometimes a full week. There was nothing overtly special about it, but I know from reading his journals that these experiences out here were spectacular. Moving and mind-blowing, all of these now-famous writers swinging through Big Sur on their way to—and from—San Francisco. Trying out new pieces, experimenting. Sitting around a campfire, talking about everything and nothing. It's easy, under a canopy of trees like this, to stare up at the stars and wonder about the meaning of your own life."

I had been leaning closer and closer to Cal, drawn into the image he was painting. I wanted to be with those writers. I wanted beautiful words under a wild sky, sweet communion around a campfire.

My fingers itched but not for my phone. I hadn't brought my journal, but there was a poem there: Calvin, perched on this tree, remembering his dead grandfather. The sweep of his dark hair. His strong, aquiline nose. His mouth forming around the word 'canopy.'

"So... um, yeah, I guess that's it," he said, looking suddenly embarrassed. Josie and Ray had been standing right next to us the entire time, but Calvin was talking to me. Only to me.

"That's beautiful, Calvin," I said softly, and he smiled, tentatively. "Also, I think that's the most words you've said at once for the entire time we've been here."

"Ah, well," he said, smiling wider now. "You take an introvert into the wilderness, and they usually open up."

We sat in silence for a moment, taking in the trees. "It's one thing I've always loved about the people who choose to live here," he finally said. "It's like reverse-suburbia, this desire to live in such a rural place. Not only rural but completely chaotic, uncontrollable. The waves aren't calm, and the water is freezing. The trees are gigantic. There are no box stores or chain restaurants or movie theaters. You're just... completely vulnerable."

I opened my mouth to respond, but Josie interrupted. "Lu, *mija*, I'll need you in makeup ASAP. I'm thinking some body paint, Haight-Ashbury-style," Josie said. She looked at Calvin, smiling. "Cal inspired me."

"See? It informs the narrative," Ray said, stalking off to fret over lighting.

"Happy to, uh, help," Cal said, standing and brushing tree bark from his jeans. He reached down, offering his hand, and I grabbed it without thinking. His warm palm closed over mine, and I remembered his steel grip on my wrist yesterday—so much power in those fingers.

"Thanks," I said, disentangling quickly. "And thanks for the story. I kind of wish I'd brought, like, a lot of LSD for this shoot today."

"It would definitely make things more interesting," he laughed before turning away.

"Wait," I said, and he turned back. "You're staying, right?" I didn't want him to go.

Plus, I still needed to thank him.

"For the shoot?" he asked, pointing to the slew of cameras. "To be honest, I hadn't planned on it. Won't I just get in the way?"

"It'll be fun. And we'll never find our way back without you," Josie chimed in. "Just stay. Craft services has coffee and donuts."

"And I'll be walking around with my top off for a lot of it," I said, propping a hand on my hip and winking outrageously.

Cal reddened before saying "Oh, well, okay then." He walked back towards the log we'd been sitting on, removing a slender book from his back pocket.

"Always with the books with that guy," I said, rolling my eyes at Josie.

"You're such a flirt," she teased, opening a rainbow palette of eye makeup.

"It's part of my charm," I said, leaning over to plant a big kiss on her cheek. "And you love me for it."

* * *

"Maravillosa, chica," Josie said, standing back to assess her handiwork. She held a thin makeup brush in her hand, head tilted.

I made a silly face at her. "Gorgeous, hey?" I said. Joanna was putting the final touches on my hair: a giant floral crown of dark pink peonies.

"Ray, what do you think?" she asked.

I stood completely still, Ray to my left and a bevy of cameras to my right. I couldn't speak when Josie was doing the body painting, so I had to listen to Taylor prattle on about his time with Brad Pitt on the movie they'd just done together. If I heard Taylor say the words "He's just a chill dude, man. A chill, chill dude," one more time, I was going to punch something.

Ray's face came into my line of vision. "Perfect," he said, nodding. He leaned closer, dropping his voice. "Listen, you're probably going to carry this shoot again today."

"Yep," I said, stretching my neck, already aching from the weight of the flowers. "It's all good. I'll handle it."

Reputation or not, I was known in the industry as a "one-and-done" type of model. I usually nailed it the first time, every time.

Taylor, though, could throw off the whole day with his nerves... and our serious lack of chemistry. I swallowed, conscious of the cameras a few feet away.

"Let me snap a photo of you," Josie said. "If we had internet, I'd have you all over my Instagram."

I groaned. "Ugh, with the flowers and the trees and the body paint."

"Mhmmm," she said, indicating I should strike a pose. I did, and her smile told me it was a good one. "Looks like we'll have to just make memories the old-fashioned way."

"I hate that," I said, but when she showed me the photo I smiled. "Well... I do look cute." I was in brown suede boots that laced up the backs of my legs, up over my knees to the middle of my thighs. A cream, sleeveless shift dress barely covered my ass. The dress had a deep v-neck, and I was bra-less. I felt kind of wild and Woodstock—flower crown and hippie boots and my boobs out and proud.

And the crown jewel? Josie had hand-painted an intricate pattern of floral designs in gold and silver paint up the entirely of my right arm and across my chest. Delicate leaves fanned out from around my eyes.

"Wood-nymph Woodstock," Ray declared, squeezing my

shoulders and nodding over my head to his camera guys. "Just what Shay Miller wanted. Now let's get this show on the road. We have about four hours of sunlight left and approximately one million outfit changes."

I sighed, tossing my hair, trying to dredge up an iota of the excitement I used to feel. Josie's words of concern rattled around, but I chalked it up to being tired.

"Where do you want me?" I asked.

* * *

"Gorgeous, Lucia. Fucking *gorgeous*," Ray said. "Keep that face, got it?" I gave a subtle nod that I'd heard, then went back to "the face."

Taylor and I had moved through the first couple poses already—not too bad, considering Taylor was nervous. But we hadn't had to face each other, or really interact off each other —we were both just working the camera separately.

I looked over at Calvin, perched maybe twenty feet away on a fallen log. Coffee in one hand, his book in the other. So far he hadn't looked up once, not even when I'd walked right past him. I was surrounded by cameras, but I just really wanted Calvin to look at me.

I didn't know why. Except that he was alternately nervous around me yet seemingly immune to my charms. It was weird.

"Next pose, guys," Ray said. "Taylor, on the log, laying down."

"Um, what?" Taylor asked.

"Laying down. Shay wants—" He flipped through his notes. "He wants the scenes in the woods to be 'erotic.'"

"What's so erotic about the woods?" I asked. I mentally prepared myself to dry-hump Taylor on a log in the middle of the wilderness in front of dozens of near-strangers.

It was actually not the most awkward thing I'd ever done in a photo shoot.

I glanced back at Calvin, who was still immersed.

I'd changed outfits: the boots were still on, but now I wore short cut-offs and a white bikini top. The flower crown had been replaced with a high bun.

"Am I naked? Semi-naked?" I asked Ray, voice a little raised. I thought I saw Cal sway a bit.

"Maybe in a bit," Ray said seriously, although I had been totally joking.

He came over and walked us through what he wanted: me, miming crawling towards, and on top of, Taylor. Some scenes of me licking and/or biting his bare chest. Alternately, Ray also wanted some sweet kisses, adoring looks.

"After this, it's up against the tree," Ray said.

"Excuse me?" I asked.

Ray shrugged. "Shay wants it. Like kind of this animalistic, carnal, fucking-in-the-woods type thing. All the sexy parts of Woodstock but on steroids." When I arched an eyebrow, he said, "You heard it from Cal himself. Things used to get wild back here in the bohemian days. You don't think a few people fucked against this tree?"

Cal looked up at that, hearing his name. "Um... what?" he asked.

"Fucking. Against trees," Ray said, somewhat impatiently. "Don't you think some of these camp parties used to get a little sexual?"

Calvin met my eyes. "Yeah. Um... I mean, I think Ray is probably right. You mix drugs, horny writers, and the outdoors, and I'm sure..." He swallowed, held my gaze. "I'm sure there was a lot of fucking."

My blood heated under Cal's appraisal. I caught his eyes wandering: my bare stomach, the almost see-through bikini, my dark magenta lips.

"I can see it," I said. "Yeah." I tilted my head. "Thanks Cal."

He nodded before settling back down. And immediately going back to his book.

For an hour, I gave it my all. Erotic high fashion wasn't hard. I'd done *Maxim and Vogue*, been on the cover of *Cosmo and* walked the Milan runway. But it was different: attempting to embody a softcore vibe in a high-class way. Taylor had to basically just lay there while I crawled, licked, bit. I made my way up to his face... and immediately hit a roadblock.

"All right, kids. Time to turn on the romance," Ray said.

Except Taylor and I could not pull off the romance. I mean, I thought I was probably doing okay, but Taylor's face was wooden. Tired-looking. Every time I tried to kiss him, we'd almost headbutt each other.

I burst out laughing at one point. I couldn't help it. I was straddling Taylor, his hands on my thighs, and every time I leaned in close, he'd make this 'kiss me' face that was a blend of both constipated *and* confused. I didn't know how he did it.

Ray came over, looking like a disappointed dad. "What's going on with you two?" he asked quietly.

"Nothing," I said immediately, but Taylor cleared his throat.

"I'm just tired," he said. "We've been shooting for hours."

"Um, *one* hour," I said. "And it's not that bad. You've basically just been laying down."

"Taylor, I need you to work off Lucia. Look at her: she's gorgeous. She's like this sweet, fuckable wood nymph you've stumbled upon in the forest. Tell yourself a story in your head. You know, get into it."

Ray and Taylor kept chatting, and I climbed off Taylor's lap for a second. I swigged water, munched on a few almonds, my mind distracted. I looked at Calvin, who was now chatting amiably with Josie and Joanna. They were laughing at something he said.

I wondered what Cal would do if he'd stumbled upon me in the forest, looking like a sweet, but fuckable, wood nymph. Flowers in my hair, wrapped in some gauzy white fabric. Naked underneath. All wide-eyed and innocent. The few times I'd seen Cal's guard fall, I'd glimpsed an inner sexuality that was more intense than his shy demeanor—or maybe that was just my imagination.

But I secretly thought he'd know what to do with me.

How to corrupt my innocence. Maybe against this tree.

"And now the tree part. You good, Lu?"

"Um... oh yeah, Ray. Feeling great."

Taylor looked a little pale, having just had his ass handed to him by Ray.

"Okay, then. Let's get sexy in the woods."

Josie and Joanna scurried over—touching up lipstick, fixing my hair. Josie took my shawl and the top.

"Time to get naked, I guess," I said, my hands covering my breasts. I didn't know why; I was never shy on these sets. But Cal had moved closer, was leaning up against a tree not fifteen feet away.

I stepped backwards until my skin hit the bark. It was rough, abrasive on the soft skin between my shoulder blades. Taylor followed, covering most of my body with his.

"Hands on her thigh, Taylor. We need to focus in on the boot."

I hitched my leg up, Taylor's hand holding up my knee. The jean shorts slid higher. I arched my back, fingers trailing up his spine.

"Okay, don't look at each other for... uh..." *For the rest of the shoot*, I thought. "For the time being. Taylor, you're looking down at her body. Lu, you're looking off to the right. Let's play off that."

I turned my neck, closed my eyes for a second.
And opened them to find Calvin staring right at me.

CHAPTER 10

Calvin

I had finished my book and had nothing else to do.
That's what I told myself, repeatedly, as I shame-
lessly watched Lucia and Taylor's photo shoot. I'd spent
most of the day ignoring her—or attempting to. At one point,
I'd looked up to see her climbing over Taylor's body, her ass in
the air, her hands sliding down his stomach.

I'd been hard all day. She was painted and glowing and
sexy-as-hell. But I kept looking down, forcing myself to read.
It was a worthless endeavor to torture myself. Plus, we'd had
an actual conversation this morning, and she hadn't once
mentioned the poem I'd left her.

Lucia was probably embarrassed for me, laughing with
Josie about my silly crush and, out of sheer kindness, had
chosen not to mention it. I knew when to cut my losses—had
done it with countless women, countless times.

I'll just look for a second, I told myself. *Then I'll take a
long, long... long walk through the woods until they're done.*

I leaned against a tree, hoping my erection wasn't totally
obvious, and fully took in the scene. I couldn't see Lucia's
body, except for a sliver of her toned upper thighs, exposed

between the tops of her boots and the frayed bottoms of her shorts. I wondered what it'd be like to fuck her in just those boots. I pictured the feel of the suede, her legs propped up on my shoulders.

The bottom of her shorts slid higher, and I could just begin to see the curve of her ass. Ray gave her some directions, and she tilted her head away, exposing her beautiful throat. She looked down and away and then up, directly at me.

I held it—*god help me*—I held it. I didn't think about how embarrassed I'd be later or how I'd have to awkwardly apologize. I didn't think about the dozens of women who'd turned me down over the years. I didn't think about any of that because I was operating on pure instinct.

I wanted Lucia Bell. And not in a "hey look at that hot model" kind of way. It wasn't opportunity or an obsession with her fame. I just *wanted* her.

I recognized the purity of that desire in that moment, the way I pictured myself in Taylor's position. He nuzzled his lips along the side of her neck, and I pictured doing the same thing. Wondered what her skin would taste like beneath my tongue. Wanted to feel her shiver.

My fingers, gliding up her thighs and sliding under the frayed threads of those shorts—*almost* grazing the lips of her pussy.

But holding off.

Making her wait.

Lucia continued to hold my gaze as I let the images I'd locked up the past few days finally shake loose in my mind. It must have shown in the way I was looking at her because there was something... *exhibitionist*... about her reaction to me. She bit her lip. Gripped Taylor's hair. Licked his bicep. Raised her arms over her head and arched dramatically, almost exposing her breasts.

I swallowed a growl. There was not even a remote possibility that Lucia was doing this on purpose—she was just a fame-starved model, hungry for the attention of a socially inept loner.

But I didn't care.

I turned on my heel and stalked off towards the woods—a trail I ran about once a week. I wished I had brought running shoes, needing the distraction of intense physical exertion, something to direct my body towards.

Instead, I knew what I was going off to do. As I put the shoot further and further behind me, I recreated the campsite in my mind. No people—no cameras. No Taylor, or makeup artists or hair stylists.

Just Lucia in those fucking suede boots... and nothing else. Her wild hair, the gold and silver body paint dancing up her skin. An outstretched finger, beckoning me closer. Her lips, moaning my name.

Almost a mile away, I found a quiet clearing and a large tree, which I leaned up against. Unzipped and took my cock in my hands, already groaning at the contact. I should have felt shameful, jerking off in the woods like a teenager. Instead, I liked it—liked that Lucia had driven me to such a carnal act in the middle of nowhere.

And Fantasy Lucia was relentless. I stroked my cock and shoved her back up against that tree. Lifted her in an instant, those suede-clad legs wrapping around my waist. No foreplay, not now: we were already too hungry for each other.

My hand moved faster and faster, my panting breath the only sound in the clearing. In my fantasy, I was fucking Lucia against that tree with a mindless fury, one hand slapped over her mouth to quiet her screams, my teeth bruising her neck. It wasn't romantic. It wasn't sweet. It wasn't nice.

It wasn't *me.*

Except that I came harder than I had in months.

* * *

Later, after I'd walked back and given Josie some simple instructions on how to get home, I left, already feeling the shame that would creep up whenever I let a sexual fantasy get the best of me. Especially one about Lucia, who probably spent most of her life batting away the awkward affections of men like me.

The darker desires had started when I was in college—a powerful urge to dominate. To take. To keep a woman on the edge of release for hours, on her knees and pleading.

I thought it was due to years of pent-up sexual frustration, but the fantasies didn't relent while I was with Claire. So I told her about them, as openly and honestly as I could. Made some suggestions on how we could—safely—act out the things I was thinking about constantly.

"Too weird," she'd said, dismissing the idea immediately. Which was fine—sexually what I desired was not was *she* desired. But she wasn't willing to try, even a little, to make me happy.

And her instant dislike seemed to be proof that I was destined to be stuck in a vicious cycle: too shy to get a date. And, on the off-chance I *did* get a date, I'd scare any woman off with my sexual proclivities.

CHAPTER 11

Calvin

Today, *Chance and I watched the sunrise from the back patio. The news is predicting a massive storm, and it's been mistier than normal, the sky a dramatically dark gray. The clouds made the sunrise look like an Impressionist painting. Chance was sprawled at my feet as I downed cup after cup of coffee.*

I haven't slept well the past two nights—I think it's the sudden arrival of an entire Hollywood camera crew plus two models and a makeup artist. I've gotten really used to being alone these past months. Their presence is... distracting.

I stopped, taking a sip of my grandfather's favorite whiskey. It burned. It felt good. When I moved into my grandfather's place, I unearthed one giant box of slim black notebooks—his journals. Since he wrote every day, even it if was only a few sentences—*Woke up. Busy day at the shop. Can't seem to find my glasses anywhere*— he'd easily filled close to a hundred of them over the five decades he'd owned The Mad Ones.

I'd been reading them, slowly, each night—like peeling the layers of an onion. They showed the banality of his life, yet his joy was so real I could almost taste it. I was still reading through the first few years before all the hippie-bohemian wildness started. Currently, it was 1960 (two years after opening the store), and my grandfather was trying to figure out how many copies of books to order and how on earth they would all get to this middle-of-nowhere place.

It was fascinating.

It wasn't that my grandfather's life was without pain or grief. I knew what was coming in his journals—meeting my grandmother on a beach in Monterey. Moving her into this wild little store. To this day, I still found touches of her: the hand-knit napkins I used, photos of the two of them shoved between his favorite books. On the wall behind the register was their wedding photo, something she must have hung in the early sixties. It still rested there, their faces young and happy, the cliffs of Big Sur rising behind them.

And I knew that when I got to the entries from 1985, I would also read of her sudden death.

A car crash, so stupid. The winding, dark roads of Big Sur dangerous for a woman in the early stages of Alzheimer's. I wasn't sure which would have been worse: to have her die so suddenly or to watch her lose all memories of her life. Her loves. My grandfather.

Although it didn't matter, not really. Because what had happened was that she overcorrected, swerving to avoid hitting something in the road (A dog? A deer?), hit a tree, and died on impact.

I was young at the time and barely remembered my grand-mother, but shortly after that was when my parents started sending me down to Big Sur for the summers. I think I was part of the antidote to my grandfather's grief.

And maybe that was why his joy seemed to stand out so strongly to me. Before my grandmother died, he was happy, truly happy. But after she died, he seemed to need to

BOHEMIAN

remember what it was like to be *alive*, that the moments the rest of us take for granted—eating a good meal, hearing a good joke, relaxing into a hot bath on a cold day, watching the flames in the fireplace—she was no longer a part of.

Because really—wasn't that what life was all about? The small moments?

Went to the internet café to check my email, I scribbled. *Justin had emailed, curious about my start date to come back. The final month of my sabbatical is starting, and he seems to need to verify that I'll definitely, absolutely, 100% be back.*

I'd been surprised at his nonchalance when I first told him about the bookstore, the sudden need for a sabbatical. I'd worked there since graduating—more than nine years. Long hours and complete loyalty. But he'd waved it off.

"Six months? Sure. But if it's anything longer than that, we'll just hire an intern to replace you."

At first I'd been a little hurt, but it was true—at the end of the day, I was totally replaceable, my job able to be done by any number of recent, bright-eyed college graduates.

If I wasn't coming back, Justin needed to know so he could hire that intern. And I was coming back, so it didn't matter.

But I didn't answer his email.

I sat back, thinking. To be honest, I hadn't checked, or responded, to my email in months, except to schedule meetings with potential investors and buyers of the property. I'd let friends drop off, especially since they were mostly friends from work, and outside of talking about software, new technology, and mild Silicon Valley gossip, I was learning we had absolutely nothing in common. Especially since *none* of them could understand why I was still up here. Why I hadn't just sold this place for a zillion dollars and bought a nice penthouse in San Francisco with a view of Alcatraz.

I tapped my pen against the page.

I mean, I wasn't entirely sure either.

"Hey."

I looked up to see Lucia leaning against my doorway.

"Hey," I said back, startled. I knocked part of my drink over. *Fuck*. "How, uh... how long have you been standing there?"

She pulled her long braid over her shoulder. "Just a few minutes. You seemed really into..." She gestured towards the journal.

"Oh this? It's nothing. It's..." I struggled for a second. *Journaling* suddenly sounded juvenile and silly.

"Do you write?" she asked, stepping further into the room, her face brightening. She sat down in the chair across from mine. My first instinct, as usual, was to back up, put distance between us so that what happened in the woods would never happen again.

But I was sitting down. Nowhere to go.

Control yourself.

"No, it's... well, it's my journal. I never kept one before, but my grandfather did, every day. I've been reading them, and it made me curious. About why a person would do something like that. Just document everything, every part of their day."

She leaned forward to sneak a peek, a mischievous look on her face. Lucia was wearing a loose, pale-pink tank top, and as she leaned forward, she pushed her breasts together expertly. I didn't look though, keeping my eyes on her face.

"What are you doing?" I asked.

She grinned cheekily. "Have you written about *me*?" she asked, arching an eyebrow.

I still couldn't make sense of her. Because women did not typically flirt with me. At all. I might *try* to flirt with them and fail miserably... that happened a lot in my twenties. Even Claire didn't flirt with me. Too serious. Too goal-oriented. Life, for Claire, was like a game you were actively trying to win every moment of the day. Something as frivolous as *flirting* would never have interested her.

And yet Lucia Bell sat not two feet from me, long, bronze legs in tiny shorts, dark-blue eyes wide and beautiful, and every bit of her body language was saying *Fuck me.*

Except she still hadn't brought up the poem.

Maybe she never got it. Maybe a bear ate it.

"I did, actually," I said tentatively. "I just wrote that you and your entire crew are a huge distraction."

"What's distracting?" she asked.

You. I wanted to say. *You've spent the last two photo shoots actively trying to get me to watch you take every single scrap of clothing off your perfect body. I got drunk at a bar and left you a poem on your doorstep—and you haven't even mentioned it. Oh, and then there was the time I got so turned on looking at you that I jerked off in the woods.*

"Oh... nothing," I said. Because Lucia Bell wasn't really flirting with me. She was attention-seeking. And I'd been on the wrong end of that countless times with other women, misreading their attentions and not realizing that beautiful women thought of shy, quiet nerds as a safe repository for their innocent flirting. A way to get out some sexual energy without having to actually *do* anything about it.

"What can I do for you tonight? Is there something you need?" I asked, sliding the journal back onto the table and standing. She did too, her heels putting us eye-to-eye.

"It's our second-to-last night," she said. "We've just been laying around. Bored out of our fucking minds." She laid a palm on her chest. "I was sent as a goodwill emissary."

I grinned. "And it's barely been two days," I couldn't help but say. "You really miss LA that much?"

"I miss the *internet* that much," she said quickly. "And, you know, Netflix."

I shook my head, fighting a smile. Her life was so different than mine, although six months earlier I was plugged into the internet every second of the day too. I remembered that craving.

"You could read a book? Take a walk? Star-gaze?" I said, rattling off ideas. She crinkled her nose, stuck her tongue out.

"Any other options?" she asked, sighing.

I laughed, twirling my keys. "Um… you could have some beers with me and my friend Gabe on my patio?"

"A party?" she asked.

I shook my head. "No, no… well, I mean, I guess if you invite the whole crew over, that's party-size. I'll have Gabe bring the beer and any locals who are hanging around. He's a bartender at the only bar in Big Sur, and he's got the access."

"Party it is!" she said, throwing her hands in the air. She grinned at me, and I fought the urge to touch her. *This*. This small moment, in the quiet of an empty bookstore. Lucia Bell grinning at me after I'd made her happy.

But I knew the truth. And it couldn't be real.

"Go round everyone up," I said. "I'll call Gabe. Give me thirty minutes?"

Lucia reached forward to squeeze my arm, the brush of her fingers a shock to my system. And then she whirled around and left.

* * *

The patio off the back of the bookstore was magical, and with a few strands of white string lights and two firepits, it did kinda-sorta feel like a party. The patio was surrounded by forest, but you could still hear the ocean. I pulled out some chairs, threw on some music, and called Gabe.

"You're having me over for beer with models?" he'd asked, sounding surprised. "You want me to bring some other folks over?"

"Sure, I think. I mean… I think they kind of want to meet people. Or something," I said. "Bring beer. Bring liquor. We'll see what happens."

And now, an hour in, I leaned back against the railing, beer in hand, and observed. The camera crew had put together a game of beer pong. A few Big Sur locals were sitting around the fire pit. Gabe and Josie were standing close together, having an intense conversation. I sipped my beer, content. I wasn't lonely up here—in fact, I was learning to love the silence.

But I did miss this… this *community*. My grandfather had a community easily; in fact, the week before he died, he'd thrown a party like this. Beer, trees, music, fire. A simple recipe. I was happy he'd had that, happy he'd been able to enjoy the unpretentious pleasure of drinking whiskey with friends.

"How's it going?" Taylor asked as he and Lucia walked towards me.

"Oh… good, you know," I managed to reply. "I guess… well, I guess I'm still a little surprised that models are standing on my patio. I know you probably hate when people say that." But it was true. Taylor had probably spent the day texting celebrities and having his photo taken with his shirt off. Tonight, he looked comfortable being The Sexiest Guy at the party—shirt un-buttoned, hair on-purpose-messy, Lucia Bell hanging off his arm.

"No way, dude, I love it," Taylor said, flashing me a grin.

Lucia looked away, pulling her phone out automatically, then rolling her eyes when she realized we still didn't have internet.

"I wanted to be a model my entire life… I mean, I'm only twenty-three but basically since I was like, I don't know, ten years old, it was what I wanted to be," Taylor said.

"Huh," I said, taking a sip of beer. "I'm pretty sure at ten I wanted to be a dinosaur. Or a stormtrooper."

Lucia laughed, delighted, while Taylor said, "Why? And what?"

"Oh, you know, a stormtrooper? From *Star Wars*? I'm a nerd in the classical sense, I guess. Very sci-fi."

"Natalie Portman was in the one when we were kids," Lucia said softly, tugging at his arm. "You know, the ones with Darth Vader?"

"Aw fuck, I *loved* that movie. You wanted to be Natalie Portman when you were ten?"

I shrugged, laughing into my beer. I liked Taylor. Maybe he wasn't the brightest, but I could tell why people gravitated towards him. A pure soul. "Something like that. When did you start modeling?" I asked.

I was impressing the hell out of myself with my social skills tonight. Must be the beer. I dutifully took another sip.

"When I was twenty, which is kind of old for modeling? Lucia was fifteen."

"Wow," I said, glancing at her. "So young for something so... adult, right?"

Taylor shook his head, but something flashed across Lucia's face before she hid it. "It was pretty fun for me. Just hot women and staring into a camera. Easy." He smiled that golden smile. "What about you, dude? How long have you been running this bookstore?"

"Only five months," I said quickly. "My grandfather died at the end of April, and he left me the bookstore in his will."

"Before that?" Lucia asked.

"I was a software engineer in Silicon Valley," I said. "*Am* a software engineer, I mean," I corrected.

"You're a real computer nerd, aren't you?" he asked but with a smile.

"Through and through," I said, laughing, enjoying an easy social interaction with two famous people.

"Taylor, we need you at beer pong!" one of the camera guys called out, catching Taylor's attention.

"Fuck yeah, dudes," he called to them. "I'll be back in a bit," he said, and Lucia waved her fingers at him.

And then she turned back to me, flashing a smile that could knock the redwoods over. "Calvin and Lucia," she said. "Finally alone."

CHAPTER 12

Lucia

Calvin was having some kind of coughing fit—or maybe a heart attack?

"You okay?" I asked, stepping forward to pat him on the back. He stepped back, shaking his head.

"Totally," he finally managed to say. "Just... swallowed wrong is all."

"You seem to do that a lot around me," I said, biting my lip to keep from smiling. He was cute when he was jumpy.

I leaned my arms against the railing, sipping my red wine and staring out into the woods. I felt the breeze in my hair, the back of my legs warm from the flames of the fire pit crackling softly behind us. The storm was holding off, and the air held that delicious just-about-to-rain smell I forgot I loved.

After a moment, Cal joined me. If I slid six inches to the left, our arms would have touched.

"So you started modeling when you were only fifteen?" he asked, returning to our earlier conversation.

"Yep," I said. "Fifteen. And it was only through the sheer force of my will that we didn't start doing it earlier." I paused. "My parents are in the business."

"Modeling?"

"No..." I said, shaking my head. "It's a Hollywood term. The Business, with a capital B. Film. She's a famous movie director. He used to be an actor but is now a producer. When I was eleven I first started to get noticed and they were *ecstatic*."

"They didn't want you in school?" he asked.

"School is not important to them. They've both worked with child actors who have to take classes while on set, so they know all about minimum-schooling, believe me. But they love being famous."

"They wanted a famous daughter," Cal finished.

I sipped my wine and nodded. I turned to face him, liking it when he did the same. "My parents *really* wanted me to start when I was fourteen, but I just wanted to be a regular high schooler."

I watched him grimace. "It's... I'm sorry, but I guess I always think of modeling as being..." He paused, looking for the word.

"Sexual?" I chimed in.

"Ye—yeah, I guess. Or selling something at least. Something about having a *fourteen-year-old* use her body to sell something feels totally wrong to me."

"Same," I said, laughing. He laughed too but looked surprised. "It's okay," I said. "I didn't do it. I'm pretty fucking stubborn, and I had my teachers write letters to my parents about why it was important for someone going through puberty to have a normal childhood experience."

Cal looked impressed.

"I'm determined when I want something," I said, and he nodded, bringing his beer to his lips but holding my gaze.

"I can see that," he said.

I swallowed, suddenly hot. "Anyway, fifteen isn't much better. But it could have been a lot worse. I did have to kind of drop out of traditional school. I still graduated high school," I said hurriedly, because I was suddenly nervous standing in front of someone who was clearly brilliant.

I leaned a little closer, the wine and the trees and Cal's sudden penchant for eye contact making me a bit woozy. I looked around, confirming we were out of earshot. "I actually was on track to be our school's valedictorian."

Cal visibly brightened. He reached forward, like he wanted to touch me, but then pulled back. "I uh... well, me too actually. I mean, I *was* our school's valedictorian."

"I'm not surprised," I said, throwing my head back and laughing. Hurt crossed his face, but he hid it. "No, I'm sorry," I said, laying my hand on his arm. "I meant that as a compliment. I actually think you might be the smartest person I ever met."

"Don't let the glasses fool you," he said, lips quirking up.

"Not a lot of people can do computer programming *and* run a small business. It's impressive." I sipped my wine. "Very impressive, actually."

We were silent for a moment before Cal said, "Wait... but you weren't valedictorian? In the end?"

"Oh, *god* no," I said. "I ended up having to get my GED instead. I missed graduation, I missed prom, I missed... well, a lot of things."

"I'm sorry to hear that," he said, sympathy lacing his voice. But *actual* sympathy.

I shook it off. "Don't be," I said. "I grew up in a privileged world, and my life has been nothing but. Being a model at a young age was sometimes... *difficult*," I said, blocking a handful of memories before I went too deep. "But I basically get paid a tremendous amount of money to look pretty." I shrugged. "Much worse things happening in this world."

Cal looked thoughtful for a second, almost like he wanted to ask another question, but stopped. "We're so different," he said, finally. "I'm not super into celebrity culture or anything, but like all people, especially growing up in California, I'm *aware* of it and that it exists. I have no concept of what that would be like. You know, before coming up here, my work days were, like, I don't know..." He blushed, thinking. "Something like: hit the snooze alarm, get dressed in my tiny, cramped apartment, sit in traffic, totally zoned out. Um... be at my desk for nine hours staring at numbers on a screen. Meetings, annoying coworkers. A kind of constant, unending sense of bleakness," he deadpanned.

"*Calvin*," I said, squeezing his arm, and for a second I couldn't tell if I was fake flirting or real flirting. "It couldn't have been that bad. This is going to sound like such a stereo-type, but usually on my tenth straight hour of holding some ridiculous pose, half-naked and with, like, a lion cub in my lap or something," I said, delighted when Cal grinned. "I'd wonder: what would it be like to just work in an office? You know, gather around the water cooler and talk about HBO shows. Sit in staff meetings. Say things like 'thank god it's hump day,' to my coworkers."

We were leaning closer and closer together, the night sky and the smell of the forest doing strange things to my sense of balance.

"Question," he started. "Why are you always holding a lion cub?" Cal was relaxing, some of his natural shyness dissipating.

"Oh, who the hell knows," I said. "Creative directors *love* sticking wild, deadly animals with models. Something about ferocity and taming beasts and a little bit of the scare factor. I've modeled with cobras, pythons... once a tarantula."

"Dear god, why?"

"It was for *leg waxing*." I said, and Cal burst into laughter. Deep and joyous.

KATHRYN NOLAN

"Have you laughed much since your grandfather died?" I asked, the wine totally going to my head now.

Cal looked briefly startled and then thoughtful. "I mean, yes, definitely. But I don't have a ton of company up here. Gabe is hilarious, and I spend a couple nights a week at the bar with him, hanging out with some locals. And my grandfather had a real wry sense of humor, and he filled his journals with that. I'll definitely burst out laughing while reading them. Which is nice... for a second, he feels very alive again."

I bit my lip. "I'm sorry he died. I didn't know him... also I don't really know you, but still. I'm sorry."

I couldn't quite make out his expression. "Thank you. I... well, um, I miss him. A whole hell of a lot actually. It's hard living here because he's everywhere. And he died suddenly, so there was so much regular *life* stuff still around when I moved in. Like, on his nightstand was the book he was in the middle of reading."

"Which was?"

"*On the Road*. Again. His annual re-read. Jack Kerouac meant a lot to him. I mean, Kerouac's life mirrored my grandfather's in that Kerouac didn't give a fuck about following the rules or living within society's random pressures. Obviously, they were different too."

"Kerouac lived life way harder than your grandfather. Your grandfather also didn't, you know, help his friend bury a dead body. Or drink himself to death."

A small smile from Calvin. "Yeah. Yeah, you're right. How do you..."

"I've read *On the Road* at least ten times." I shrugged. "One of my favorites too."

Cal's eyes bored into mine, and I thought about the woods. That look on his face.

I held his gaze, my thoughts drifting to his lips. Did he take his glasses off when he kissed someone?

104

"You read a lot, don't you?" he finally asked.

Yes, I wanted to say, desperately. Although the real answer was *I used to.*

I started to say more—what was *in* this wine? —but Cal's friend Gabe showed up, and it was clear it was time for me to go. I waved goodbye to Cal, whose expression was completely unreadable.

* * *

I couldn't stop thinking about the woods.

And I'd drunk too much. Not, like, *too*-too much, but I felt lighter and sillier and more honest than usual. And something about that patio... it had worked some kind of magic on me.

I'd shared *a lot* with Calvin—except for Josie, no one in my current life knew about my desire to stay in school or my failed attempt at becoming our school's valedictorian. LA, in its image-obsessed glory, could give a fuck about a high school diploma. And it could give a fuck if you were the smartest kid in your school, the hardest worker, the most intellectual.

I had a role to play and a reputation to keep. Sure, I sometimes got snarkier and more sarcastic than my handlers would like. But in general, I'd spent the last decade being the goddamn best at my job. Holding poses the longest, wearing the most outrageous outfits, the tallest heels, working the most bizarre shoots with *ease*.

I never purposefully played the role of vapid model. It didn't suit me.

Yet, when I was younger, I found it a lot easier to not actively fight *against* that label. I got the impression that my millions of fans followed me for a glimpse into the glamorous life of a supermodel. Not because I offered some interesting perspective on the world. Or because two-thirds of the time I just wanted to post photos of the books I wanted to read.

Or the poems I felt desperate to write.

But tonight, with Calvin, I was *compelled* to show him a different side of myself. I didn't know him well, but he seemed so incredibly smart. Worldly and knowledgeable—writing code while simultaneously reading Margaret Atwood.

And I couldn't stop thinking about the *fucking woods*.

Calvin had been *watching* me... leaning up against that tree like a nerdier James Dean. The look on his face was so intensely sexual I wondered if he was even aware of it. It lit me up inside. I performed for it. Was greedy for it. Wanted to spend the entire day being photographed while Calvin watched.

It was unsettling.

And unexpected. I'd been chalking it up to boredom, hormones, and the fact that I was probably just a little horny.

But... he had left me a poem.

A *poem*.

Blame it on the alcohol, but between the moment in the woods and this party and our run-in in the hallway, Calvin was becoming more and more intriguing.

Maybe I *was* developing a crush.

I was Lucia fucking Bell. I could literally have *any* man on the planet, and I was (*lightly*) crushing on someone who spent most of his time ignoring me. And was definitely smarter than me.

But the alcohol had made me brave. So after the party died down and I'd tried, and failed, to fall asleep, I snuck into the bookstore. Cal had told me he left it unlocked a lot of the time, and tonight was no exception.

I'd had a poem in mind as I walked through the path in the forest, spellbound by the trees at night, that intoxicating sound of wilderness in the dark. I felt *everything*—the brush of branches against my skin. The slight squish of mud beneath my shoes. The full moon lighting my way, pale and enchanting. The entire walk was one long, glorious poem, and my notebook was still packed away, unopened and not here for me to capture it.

When I snuck inside, I found the poetry room, my heart expanding at the presence of so many of my favorite poems. And this one, the one I would leave for Calvin, was one of the best.

I pulled the Mary Oliver collection out, finding it quickly. I grabbed a Post-it Note from behind the desk and a pen.

Your grandfather's campsite had a profound effect on me. The entire time I kept thinking about this poem. Do you know it? -Lu

P.S. Diane di Prima is a goddess. Thank you for the gift of her words.

I grabbed a pencil and circled my favorite lines from her poem, "In Blackwater Woods." I crept down the hallway towards his bedroom, alive with the knowledge he was sleeping behind that door. I loved men in bed, sleep making them sexy and vulnerable. I wondered what he wore, if anything. I wondered what he'd do if I crept in, crawled into bed, the covers warm from his body heat, the sheets smelling like him: woodsy and masculine.

I was turned on. A little drunk. And holding a poem for a computer programmer who, after tomorrow, I would never see again.

I felt more alive than I had in months. I left it, propped up against his bedroom door.

And as I walked home, grinning uncontrollably, my phone buzzed with an international text: an odd time for me to get a smattering of cell service. I stopped, holding my cell up, attempting to keep the signal.

It was Sabine: *just checking in.*

She'd seen the first photos of the shoot and was thrilled about it. *There is so much good buzz around you right now, it's ridiculous*, she'd written. *I didn't think Lucia Bell could become even more famous, but between Shay Miller and this new contract, you're going to be unstoppable,* ma cheri. *Do you have time for a phone call in a couple days? I have mock-ups for you.*

I stopped, sighing. Yanked back down to Earth.

I read the message again and re-read it, until the attention-seeking beast that lived inside me roared back to life.

I didn't think Lucia Bell could become even more famous.

Which is what I wanted, desperately. Because 26-year old models had a short shelf life. I'd be lucky to book shoots like this much longer, and Paris offered a new world of fame.

My Wi-Fi icon winked open—I had about a half a bar, suddenly, and I used it to open Instagram. My notifications flared up instantly, but I only cared about one thing.

894 new followers. Not bad for a few days where I'd posted basically nothing. Those twenty-two Instagram followers could suck it!

I did a little semi-drunk dance in the woods, grateful that no one could see me. I lost my internet and cell connection as soon as I'd gained it, but it had given me a glimmer of hope.

Fuck Big Sur. Fuck the wilderness.

I was back on top.

CHAPTER 13

Calvin

L ucia left me a poem outside my bedroom door last
night. It was Mary Oliver's "In Blackwater Woods," a
favorite of my grandfather's. She'd circled her favorite
lines, which, curiously, are also my favorites.

I looked back at the page Lucia had left for me, her curling
handwriting on the Post-it Note. I lived for the lines she'd
circled.

I'd almost tripped over the book when I woke this morning, figuring it was something I'd left out and forgotten about.
When I discovered Lu's note, I almost fell over again. Who *was*
this woman? And was this *actually* happening? Was I
currently sweetly flirting with a supermodel via our favorite
poems?

I've never met someone like her before, I wrote. *And I don't
quite know what to do about it.*

I was more ashamed about what happened next. I had
been delightfully surprised by the discovery, awash in that
feeling you have when you *think* the girl you have a crush on
might have a crush on you. Which was still incredibly unlikely
—given my track record and the fact that I wasn't a model,

wasn't famous, and didn't have a six-pack—but Lucia seemed *intrigued* by me.

Hell, I'd take it.

But the happiness dimmed when I realized what she must have done: Coming into the bookstore at night while I was asleep. Standing outside my door. Did she press her ear up against it, listening for my breathing? Did she contemplate slipping inside?

Because I sure as shit did. Before I could stop myself, I was back in bed, masturbating, an image of Lucia waking me up floating in my mind. Crawling over my body the way she did with Taylor at the shoot in the woods, her blonde hair brushing my chest. In my thoughts, I threaded my fingers through those waves and pulled as hard as I could, sitting up to press my chest against hers as she straddled me.

I came quickly, again. And hard, again. So hard I had to close my eyes for a minute, slightly dizzy.

I don't know what to do about it... and I don't know what is happening to me, I finally wrote. *I might be a little obsessed.*

I stared at it, my handwriting on a mostly blank page. It was almost too honest, and if I'd written it in pencil, I would have erased it. Embarrassed that I wasn't strong enough to withstand Lucia's charm. That I was joining legions of men *across the world* who jerked off to her. I didn't want to be the computer nerd lusting after the model—it was too John Hughes.

But... she'd left me a *poem*.

I glanced at my watch, sighing when I noticed the time. Ray was doing another shoot in the bookstore today, and they were due in an hour. Plus, I was meeting with investors this evening—I had hours of tedious work ahead of me to prepare for it.

I think these investors will be the ones I sell to, I wrote. *They're offering a good price, and they plan to build a spa on the property—use the cabins for private massage suites. I'm not sure if they're going to tear down the actual building or not. But they seemed the least nefarious of all the other investors I've been meeting with.*

Sitting on this patio, staring at this view, every bone in my body screamed *don't sell*. I'd felt it a bit the day of my grandfather's funeral, receiving the news I was now the owner. I'd been so surprised, astounded really, when the lawyer suggested I sell off the property immediately. With the reputation it had, how could The Mad Ones not be thriving?

With the memories I'd made here as a child, with the memories my *grandparents* had made here, how could I just tear it down? There was so much history here—the landscape of literature and poetry was irrevocably changed by the existence of this store. Authors and poets traveled from miles away —flew from other countries—to read here. To speak here. To just *be* here.

And yet... there was also *so much* debt. I'd never owned a business before, and certainly didn't know what the hell I was doing. The few advisers I'd met with took one look at the numbers and all said the same thing: *sell it.*

A mercy kill—demolishing this beautiful piece of history while it was still on top, at least from the public's perspective. Maybe they'd put a plaque here or something, honoring my grandfather's legacy.

I quieted the voice that popped up—a voice that sounded surprisingly like my grandfather's. A voice laced with disappointment.

The first month I'd lived here I couldn't wait to leave. Same with the second month. But now, during my final weeks here, that voice was growing louder and louder. Pushing back against every rational thought that I had. I *needed* to go home. I needed my orderly, quiet, respectable life back. And one day, I'd look back on these wild times in my life with fondness. *For six months, I lived the bohemian life in Big Sur. Not for me, but it was nice for a little while.*

Let it go, I wrote in my journal. *Love it and let it go.*

* * *

This morning Taylor and Lucia breezed past me like I wasn't even there. Which, to be honest, was the kind of treatment I'd *originally* expected. Instead, they'd surprised me from day one with how friendly they seemed to be; different lives, for sure, but they hadn't been outrageously snooty.

Today Lucia didn't glance my way once. No flirty winks or sarcastic remarks.

She certainly didn't say anything to me about leaving an emotionally charged poem outside my bedroom door. After spending an evening charming me with her honesty, her sense of humor. Her beautiful mind.

So I swallowed the familiar taste of disappointment and instead yanked out boxes and boxes of my grandfather's financial files, beginning the arduous process of making sense of everything for investor meeting. Eventually, the sounds of the shoot became an almost comforting blur, my only breaks to help the occasional customer who stopped in.

Everything was a goddamn mess. I stared at numbers until my eyes blurred. I should have been used to this since I'd spent my entire adult life staring at numbers on a computer screen. But this—this was my grandfather's *livelihood*. Slipping away, month after month, as his expenses outpaced his revenue.

I wasn't sure what I wished for more: that he was aware of how deeply he was in debt or that he wasn't. If he *was* aware, I marveled at his resilience. I'd looked through past documents over the last decade, and the amount of readings and lectures declined sharply in the mid-90s. After that, they were few and far between.

They'd been my grandfather's bread and butter: between ticket sales, the revenue from renting those cabins, and the book sales that naturally occurred after each reading, he'd been making quite a bit of profit for a while.

Why had he stopped? I couldn't imagine there being a lack of interest, except that the mid-90s was the start of the tech boom. A rational push back against the "free love" and hippie mindset of the 60s and 70s. The beginning of internet popularity.

"Huh," I said out loud, looking through his records. I was still slowly making my way chronologically through his journals. Maybe he'd mention it.

The other option was that my grandfather had been blissfully unaware, up until the end. Or maybe not totally unaware —he did pay his bills every month, had to notice the decline in profit. Maybe he was just *unconcerned*.

Which was more like him.

I dug further into the boxes and unearthed a stack of index cards he hadn't pinned to the ceiling. They looked a little older but not much, maybe from five or ten years ago. He must have stuck them in a random box and totally forgotten. I fanned them out, curious.

It's a rare sunny day here in May. My friend and I have been driving up the coast for days. We stopped on in because both of our parents told us about this place. I'm so happy we came here. Before we knew it, we'd spent a few hours talking to Robert, the owner. Browsing the shelves, reading in front of the fireplace. He made us coffee in these old, funky mugs, and we drank it on the front porch, just staring at the redwoods for what felt like days. I couldn't get enough. I bought ten books! Thank you, Robert, for your kindness and this peaceful sanctuary for book lovers.

I smiled, liking this one. So many of the index cards were about authors or poets they had just seen, the power of that experience. But this one was just a simple afternoon in May—and it reminded me so much of the summers I spent with him here that my heart clenched, painfully, in my chest. I knew what it was like to watch the sunrise on that front porch and the sunset on that patio. I knew what it was like to drink coffee from those old chipped mugs and have my grandfather quiz me on my feelings about a particular poem.

My grandfather always encouraged my natural inclination towards nerdiness—the first science fiction novel I'd ever read came from this store. I'd spent the first week of a summer here chatting animatedly about *Star Wars* and my obsession with *Star Trek: Next Generation*. He'd listened with great interest and never made fun of me. And by the end of that summer I'd left with a backpacked filled to the brim with the classics: Asimov, Vonnegut, Ursula Le Guin, Ray Bradbury.

Middle school and high school weren't easy for me—I was too much of a shy wallflower. I struggled to make friends, connections. But my grandfather gave me different worlds: aliens, dystopic futures, and galactic empires. Worlds I could lose myself in for hours at a time.

I rubbed my hand across my chest, a feeble attempt to soothe the ache there. The grief was like this sometimes, a sudden wave you couldn't fight against. I breathed deeply, trying to find my way. Tears pricked the backs of my eyes, and I was just wiping them away when Lucia strode past, popping a handful of blueberries into her mouth.

She was wearing a wide-brimmed floppy hat, torn jeans, and a faded *Abbey Road* tank top. Effortlessly cool, as usual. She happened to make eye contact with me just as I was wiping tears away. She stopped in her tracks, concern and empathy moving cross her gorgeous face. I looked away, my cheeks burning with embarrassment.

"Lu," I heard Josie call out. "I need to fix that eyeliner, *mija*."

I waited a beat, and when I finally looked up, she had moved on, seated in a chair in front of Josie's steady hands.

Sighing, I turned back to the task at hand. I read through more documents, made neat piles, stacked up the index cards for me to pin up later.

Although, really, why bother? I'd need to pack all this shit up a month from now anyway.

I grimaced and then pulled out one of my grandfather's journals. It was slim and black, like the rest of them, but hadn't been in the boxes where he kept the others. Curious, I flipped through.

A random entry from the sixties:

I don't know why I brought Maggie here—she's used to living in big cities, surrounded by her family and friends. And now I've dragged my new wife off to this small town that lacks basic electricity. It's like living in the 1800s out here, totally isolating and different from the coastal communities she grew up in. We don't have any friends, and even though I thought living in a book store was romantic, I think she just thinks it's really, really odd.

There was nothing after that. It was strange, even though my grandfather had his fair share of bad days, or boring days, he very rarely was negative in his journals. And I knew, from his stories and even from my own grandmother, when she was alive, how deeply she loved this place. In a few years, they created such a strong community they couldn't go anywhere in town without people recognizing them. Loving them. It was strange to see this anxious, worrying side of him—that he'd made the wrong decision. That his new wife would hate Big Sur.

I flipped again, the passages suddenly leaping twenty years ahead.

It's hard to visit our kids sometimes. They're grown up now. In fact, they have adult lives of their own. And I know they love

Maggie and I deeply—just as we love them deeply. But our lives are so different. Visiting their condos and apartments in San Jose makes me wonder if I'd chosen the wrong path—why did I choose a path that took me away from my family? From Maggie's? Why did I choose to raise my children in Big Sur? I think this place is magical and wondrous, but to a teenager it's completely dull. Nothing to do. Living alongside the ocean doesn't inspire anything in them. No wonder they left as soon as they graduated high school. What teenager would have stayed?

And I know they think I'm weird. A lot of people do. And I wonder if I'm a bad person since I find myself judging the way they're living their lives too. Which is not bad at all. Any 'normal' parent would be proud and relieved: they're both successful. Make a lot of money. They have nice houses and nice cars and so many things.

But I wonder sometimes where my children went: my children, who used to spend every evening running through the woods until twilight. Racing down the beach until they'd collapse, out of breath and exhilarated, on the sand. They didn't need things then; they just had happiness.

My grandfather could be a judgmental bastard sometimes. That was true. He'd spent his entire life purposefully pushing back *against* what society told us we "should" do or what we "should" be. To him, my parents' lives were boring and uninspired, and he let them know that. But, then again, my parents spent a lot of time telling me my grandfather was an "aging hippie who refused to live in the real world." That he was silly, had no direction. That he lacked ambition.

I had no idea he'd regretted, even for a moment, raising his family in Big Sur. It had always been something he'd taken great pride in—raising his family "off the grid." But my mother and uncle had entered their teen years deeply unhappy, no longer content to run through the woods. Instead they wanted TV and malls and to go to the movies. I always thought my grandfather didn't care.

Except that it was clear now that he had.

I shoved this journal in my back pocket to keep reading for later, intensely curious about this secret journal he'd kept, one of his deepest fears, worries, insecurities. It was different from the jolly, joyful anecdotes of his other journals.

I didn't doubt that both experiences could be true.

CHAPTER 14

Lucia

"Coffee break?" Josie asked, and when I turned to look at her, I arched an eyebrow at the wild look in her eye. She'd had an... *interesting* morning, to say the least. And evening. We both had.

"Please," I said, standing and immediately following her to the back, grabbing a blanket from one of the chairs. It was freezing outside, the wind whipping through the trees. Ray was all about it, on long calls with Shay about how we could incorporate "storm imagery" into his avant-garde style.

Calvin had been hunched over stacks of paper all day and barely glanced my way once. He'd certainly not mentioned the poem I'd drunkenly left outside his door last night. Which was for the best. As soon as I'd woken up—a little hungover, squinting against the harsh daylight—I knew it was a mistake. Embarrassing, even. Supermodels didn't leave secret love poems for guys they had crushes on.

It just didn't happen.

Although, for the briefest of moments, I *thought* I'd caught Cal crying. He'd looked stricken, flipping through some notebook, and when I'd walked past, he was wiping tears from his eyes. I wanted to jump over the desk and give him a big hug.

I wrapped us in the blanket, huddled over the cup of coffee like it was the Holy Grail. Josie had bitten her lip so much I was worried she'd break the skin.

"So..." I started. "The bouquets." Last night Josie had gone home with Gabe, the sexy, bearded bartender—and Cal's closest friend. This morning she'd crawled home only to have a bouquet of irises delivered to her cabin an hour later.

"They kept coming," she said, gulping down caffeine. "Six total, one every half an hour. Each with a card."

I fought to keep quiet, but I couldn't stop the beaming smile. "*Josie*," I squealed, shoving her with my shoulder. "He's a total sweetheart! And he's got the hots for you, for sure."

She shook her head. "We're seeing each other tonight. For a *date*." She grimaced at the word. Josie hadn't gone on a date since Clarke, two years ago.

"That's a good thing."

"It's against the rules."

"Rules-schmules. Just have some fun. We're leaving tomorrow anyway," I said, and a corresponding feeling of dread unleashed in my stomach.

With her best friend sixth sense, Josie turned a sharp look on me. "What happened with *you* last night?"

I shrugged nonchalantly. "Oh you know...got a little drunk and left Cal a poem by Mary Oliver at his bedroom door."

Josie spit her coffee out.

"What is this, *The Three Stooges*?" I asked, sighing.

"You have a crush on Cal."

"I sure don't," I said. Lies, lies, it was all lies.

She let it go, even though it was so obvious I was lying. I hadn't had a real relationship in years—hadn't had real feelings for a person in years. Everything in my life as a model was orchestrated and for the cameras. I dated *opportunistically*. I swallowed against a panicky feeling in my throat—like a cluster of moths was trapped there.

It was fine. I had the rest of my life to fall madly, passionately, wildly in love. But not now.

And certainly not with Cal.

"We've known these guys for three days," Josie said in a calm voice. "I'm really not sure what we're freaking out about."

"I'm not freaking out," I lied again, and she half-shoved me. "So, um, I got a message from Sabine. I'm supposed to call her tonight, to set up travel plans, go over some mock-ups. I should be in Paris by the end of next week."

The words sounded dull to my ears—how was it possible that our time in this... this *place*, this bookstore... was giving me such stark feelings of dismay about leaving for my dream job?

Josie was quiet for a moment, and then feebly said, "*Yay.*"

I laughed. "This is a *good* thing," I reminded her.

"*No estoy segura de que estas feliz,*" she muttered, looking away for a moment. I couldn't parse the sentence.

"What? I can't conjugate Spanish verbs when I'm hungover."

She sighed, biting her lip again.

"You can tell me. I'm not going to be angry."

"No, it's just... Lucia, you've seemed more excited to talk with Calvin, to read poems again, to be in this bookstore, than you are about this photo shoot *or* Paris. I just think that's... interesting."

"It's a big move. I have to leave you. I don't speak the language... it's probably just nerves. But *good* nerves. Happy nerves." The moths were back, cluttering up my windpipe. I was moments away from wheezing on this rain-drenched patio.

Josie looked at me—like *really* looked at me. "You're sure about that?"

"Fuck yeah!" I said, charging my voice with an enthusiasm I didn't feel. I was distracted—worried about how Josie felt about Gabe, wondering if Cal was okay, and noticing that there was a definite poem in the way the puddles slid down the dark wood of the patio—the reflection of the trees, our toes at the edge, like twin sisters about to jump into the ocean. Holding hands, their hair whipping against the foam. The image coalesced in my mind, hardening into the rough outline of a stanza.

It took my breath away. I squeezed my fingers around the mug, attempting to soothe the itch.

"I love you, Lu," Josie said suddenly, wrapping me in a hug. I hugged back, surprised.

"I love you too. And are you okay?" I asked against her hair. "Those flowers really upset you, huh?"

I liked to think of myself as a peaceful person, but if I ever came upon Clarke in a dark alley he was a fucking dead man. He'd made my fiercely independent, free-spirited best friend doubt her feelings, her intuition, her sense of self—smashed her internal compass into pieces. It was hard now, when men like Gabe showed her kindness and not just sex.

"I don't know," she said in a small voice. She pulled back, wiping a stray tear. There was a poem here too.

"I think he's a really nice guy. And I think he has a crush on you, even after one night, because you are brilliant and beautiful. I think it's okay to let yourself have fun with him tonight. Because, well, what are your chances of ever seeing him again?"

"Minimal," she said, resolute. She lifted her chin. "And he's sexy as fuck."

"Thatta girl," I said, punching her arm. "You deserve to get laid."

She nodded, her walkie going off. Ray, wondering where in the hell we were. "And you deserve a guy like Cal."

* * *

Zippers were my fucking arch nemesis. As a model, I'd had zippers on every single part of my body—not just in the normal areas. Under my armpits, along my thighs. Once, in a full bodysuit, along the arches of my feet. I'd spent the entire runway show trying not to laugh (I have terribly ticklish feet).

And now I was stuck in the bathroom attempting to zipper this gauzy, bohemian dress and failing miserably. The gauzy layers kept getting stuck in the teeth of the zipper, and it started awkwardly low on my back, just above my ass.

"Go *fuck yourself,* zipper," I said through gritted teeth, pushing the bathroom door open to find Josie. Instead, I walked right into Calvin.

"Oh... um... hello?" he said, stepping back quickly. "I'm sorry, I didn't—"

"We *have* to stop meeting like this, Cal," I said, flashing a grin. "Or you need to stop following me into tiny, enclosed spaces like hallways and bathrooms."

Cal rubbed the back of his neck, shuffling on his feet. "It's always been part of my charm: following women into small spaces. I'm a total *Casanova*. I spent a lot of high school, just... you know, juggling *too many* girlfriends in *too many* enclosed spaces."

I laughed, leaning against the door. "So was that the title you held in your yearbook? Instead of *Most Likely To Succeed* you had *Uncontrollable Amount of Girlfriends*?"

"Oh, no... I'm pretty sure it was *Never Going to Get Laid*."

Without realizing it, I'd backed further in, and he'd followed me. The glasses, the blushing, the nervous speech: he'd joked about being kind of a nerdy outcast in high school, and I could see how it had happened. And how he'd spent those years developing such a dry wit: nerds in high school always ended up with the best senses of humor when they were adults—it was a weapon, a shield against bullying.

But also, I got the impression Calvin had grown into his good looks kind of recently. Because standing six inches from him in this bathroom, I had to admit to myself that if we'd met in high school (and he looked the way he did now), I would have had a serious crush on him. Like, "can you hold my books; I'll wear your letterman jacket" type of crush.

He was tall, taller than me, which was saying something since I hovered over six feet wearing heels. He didn't seem overly muscular, but he did seem fit—broad shoulders and a trim waist. That crooked grin, his strong nose. Bright green eyes behind his thick glasses. He alternated between clean-shaven and scruffy five o'clock shadow (today it was clean shaven), and I fought the strongest urge to press my hand against his jaw and feel the skin there.

"Lucia?" Cal said, quietly, and I snapped back from my reverie.

"Sorry," I said. "I was just, um... hey, can you help me with this zipper?" I asked, turning around. I'd never been shy about my body—you can't be a model and have any kind of shyness, really. So I usually wouldn't have thought twice about asking someone like Calvin to zip up a dress that *barely* covered my back. It was just skin.

But as soon as I turned—my hands gripping the sink, our faces reflected in the mirror—I realized I'd made a critical error. Because I had a front-row seat to the total shift that went through Cal at the sight of my bare skin. He placed his hands on my body: his left hand, firmly, on my hip. His right hand grasped the zipper, his thumb pressing against my lower spine.

He looked up into the mirror, gaze meeting mine, and

there it was: the shift. That *look*. Like he was a man dying of thirst in the desert.

And I was the oasis.

"Who made this dress, NASA scientists?" he asked, his eyes still on mine.

Two days ago, I would have told him *looking at it* would help, except that would mean he'd break eye contact with me. And I was suddenly desperate to keep his gaze.

He squeezed my hip gently, and a riot of sensations spread forth from the touch—slide his hand forward, and he could slip his fingers between my legs. Backwards, and he could palm my ass.

"Something like that," I finally said, a distinct shake in my voice. "I mean honestly, about eight of these gauze layers are completely superfluous."

"I love that word," he said, yanking on the zipper and smiling at me.

I arched an eyebrow.

"Superfluous," he said, finally breaking eye contact to squat below me. "Sorry, it's just... yeah, all these *superfluous* layers are fucking jammed in this zipper," he said.

And I could have just called for Josie or had someone from wardrobe cut the damn dress from me, but I was glued to this spot. An earthquake could have cracked Big Sur wide open, and Cal and I would still be standing here, suspended in time.

"Me too," I said, aware of his body crouched behind mine. His hand tightened on my hip, his breath ghosting over the small of my back. My eyes fluttered close for the briefest of seconds. The material tugged and pulled around me— evidence of his attempts at freeing me.

"It's not a word I see in poetry a lot," I finally said, wishing he would lean forward and press his lips against my spine. "Or even literature. But I love saying it. Rolls off the tongue perfectly."

A hard yank, and then Cal said, "Victory is mine."

"And yeah, it's the tongue work that makes that word so magnificent." He was suddenly standing back up behind me, and was it my imagination, or was it closer than before? And did he have to say the phrase *tongue work?*

He pulled the zipper up slowly, cautious of getting snagged again. As he did, his thumb caressed up my spine, setting off a round of shivers.

"Should I stop?" he asked softly, and there was a new scrape to his voice.

"No," I said, and there was no hiding the slight moan. I'd just spent the entire *day* being pet and touched and felt up by Taylor, a supermodel, and felt not a single thing.

Two minutes with Cal, and I was aching with lust. I felt it now, full-blown and cataclysmic.

"I won't, then," he said, thumb continuing to stroke up and up and up. The zipper reached its destination, but Cal's fingers stayed on my back, feather-light. I shifted back—barely a centimeter—and met the hard resistance of his erection *right* where I needed it. I swallowed a gasp.

"Were you okay earlier?" I asked. His fingers danced up to the nape of my neck, stroking.

"Yes. I mean, I am now," he said, fingers moving in small circles. I was tempted to move my hips like that, circling on his cock but held off. Not yet. "Thank you for asking. The grief comes in waves."

"I'm so sorry," I said.

His fingers found my hair. He scratched lightly at the base of my scalp. This time I closed my eyes, not caring if he saw. *Wanting* him to see the effect he was having on my body. I couldn't remember ever being so aroused. So *aware.*

"If Mary Oliver wrote a poem about this moment, what would she say?" he asked. His breath stroked the back of my neck. I smiled, happy we were both finally acknowledging the poems we'd been leaving each other.

"Oh, let's see. Something about nature. Springtime, maybe?"

"Why springtime?" We still hadn't broken eye contact, conducting the conversation as if his hands weren't on my body, his cock not pressing deliciously against my ass.

"Bodies. Warm air. Exploration," I said, a poem writing itself in my mind already. My fingers twitched against the bathroom sink.

"Verdant. Flourish. Lush," he said. He half-grinned, fingers still scratching the strands of my hair. They migrated downward, his thumb pressing massaging circles into my neck. I let out a small, breathy sigh, and he gripped my hip so hard I knew it'd be bruised tomorrow.

I loved it. Grew hot at the idea of bruising beneath Cal's hand.

"Wantonness," I said, my mind searching for my favorite words. Words that described *lust*. Because this was a poem about two bodies seeking primal release. Nature at its most lascivious.

"Salacious," I said, his green eyes darkening. I wanted darker. *Deeper*.

"Hunger," I sighed and rolled my hips *ever so slightly*, and Calvin let out a low growl.

"*Fuck*, Lucia—" he started to say, and then we heard the loud clomp of Ray's boots and his voice, calling out.

"And where the *hell* is Lucia? She was supposed to be back ten minutes—*oh*," he said, stumbling into the bathroom. We'd sprung apart at the sound of his boots. Cal was red-faced, and I knew I was breathing heavily. Ray looked between the two of us, arching an eyebrow at me. I shook my head quickly. "My zipper was broken, and Cal here was helping me with it," I said, fluttering my hand his way.

126

Cal nodded in agreement. "Yeah, I, um... have always had a penchant for zippers. Good with my hands," he said, laughing nervously. "So, I'm going to get back to my paperwork. Lucia, happy to be of service," he said, moving quickly around Ray and leaving the room.

I let out a long breath.

"You needed me?" I asked, ignoring the questioning look on Ray's face.

"I mean, we *are* in the middle of a workday, so—"

"*Bossy*," I said, swatting Ray playfully. "Can't a girl take a five-minute bathroom break? We have a union, you know," I said, laughing to cover up the fact I was still trembling.

I walked back out to the Big Room and plopped myself into the makeup chair. Josie gave me one look. "*Tengo preguntas...*" she said beneath her breath.

"*Luego*," I said, glancing at Cal. His head bent over dozens of documents like he'd been all morning. Me in the makeup chair like I'd been all morning.

Both of us as if those minutes in the bathroom had never even happened.

CHAPTER 15

Calvin

I knew the poem I'd leave her. It'd been swirling around my lust-addled brain since Lucia obliterated my entire world in the space of five fraught minutes: an e.e. cummings poem called "i like my body when it is with your." A poem that was visceral and *real*.

I left it outside her cabin door but didn't stay. I knew, deep down, that I'd be tempted to knock softly. Wait for her to open the door, sleepy-eyed and warm. And then proceed to do any number of filthy things I'd been thinking about for days.

I felt like I'd taken drugs, some potent mixture of LSD and cocaine. Never, ever, *ever* did I think there was a world that existed where I, Calvin Ellis, would stroke the nape of Lucia Bell's neck. Feel the soft strands of her hair between my fingers.

It was like dreaming. Are these *my hands* on *her* hip? And since when was I that guy? Since when did I make the first move... on a fucking *supermodel*?

Compelled couldn't even begin to describe it. It was something hungrier and more primal than a mere *compulsion*. It was a need as basic as breathing, my need to touch her, to feel the muscles of her back flexing under the tips of my fingers.

And there wasn't a word in the English language to describe the image of Lucia, bent slightly over at the waist, eyes closed in pleasure as she ever-so-subtly rolled her ass against my cock.

Not a damn word.

So I left her a love poem, starry-eyed and grinning and with absolutely no plan in place.

And then went back to the increasingly tedious and dreary task of preparing to sell a bookstore.

CHAPTER 16

Lucia

I 'd fallen asleep without realizing it—exhausted from my
early morning and intense day of shooting—and woke
to dark, angry-looking clouds sweeping over the cliffs,
turning the ocean a dreary color.

I'd wrapped a blanket around myself and stood, watching,
feeling very much like so many women throughout history,
waiting for the ships to come home.

When I opened my eyes that morning, I didn't reach for
my phone, even though for the past few days I still clutched it,
willing the internet to appear. I thought about social media
constantly—a big world at my fingertips. I was desperate to
receive people's judgments of me: the good and the bad. I
craved it.

Now I craved something different.

Calvin.

Against my door he'd left me another book of poetry. e.e.
cummings. *100 Selected Poems*. I'd had this anthology when I
was in high school. Read it to death, the pages so dogeared the
corners eventually crumbled and tore away.

Part of me knew which one he wanted me to read. And when I opened to the Post-it Note, I was right. This was a bold move for Calvin, leaving me an erotic poem. He'd circled his favorite part, about bodies pressed together. I flushed. Next to the lines he'd written *"I love the simplicity in his words. The quiet yearning."* - Cal

P.S. Not as good as the poem we wrote today.

No one had ever left me a love poem before. Suddenly, I felt the deep chasm of what I'd been missing my entire life as I stood on this cliff, overlooking a stormy sky. My hair whipped by the wind. My skin still trembling from Calvin's fingers.

And a poem, left on my doorstep.

For the first time in my life, I was left without a sarcastic reply or a pithy remark. Because I was genuinely in this moment, genuinely in this experience.

I wanted Cal to kiss me.

Now I was sitting in Big Sur's quirky little internet café, which was also a video store, a quasi-coffee shop, and one-half of the post office. Sabine would be calling in a matter of moments, and I was staring at the computer screen. Staring at my phone.

Surprised at how suddenly I did *not* want to be here.

I opened up the browser on the computer, logging into my email. Just then, my phone connected, and a symphony of alerts sounded: three days worth of texts, Instagram tags, Snapchat stories and Facebook notifications. My neglected Pinterest boards and Tumblr accounts. I looked at it, looked back at my emails. That familiar flurry of excitement started up in my stomach.

Another symphony, my phone vibrating so much it almost fell off the table. I bit my fingernail, watched as emails tumbled into my inbox. One from Sabine with the subject *First ideas*. I clicked before I could stop myself.

Just wanted to send you a mockup of what we were thinking, the email said. *And nothing's set in stone. These are just ideas.* We'd taken them when I'd visited a couple of weeks ago, trying out different looks, seeing if I worked for what they had in mind.

I clicked, pulling up a selection of images: a full magazine spread, billboards in Europe and the US. A commercial, something light and airy, where I was wearing all white and laughing with other women. My face, literally everywhere, for two years.

The mock-ups were pretty and sweet. The shots I'd seen from this week were darker: more sexual, tons of skin, slick with rain. It would be my most diverse set of work yet, and I felt a spark of excitement, imagined being at premieres and answering questions: *"Why thank you. They are very different, but you know, I'm just really very versatile."*

I watched as the notifications lit up the screen of my phone. *So many people* talking about me. Talking to me. This was what it was all about—the adrenaline rush. That fame wave.

I opened Instagram. That morning of chasing down my lost followers felt like a decade ago.

1,682 *new* followers. I swallowed. The last thing I'd posted had been liked more than a million times. Thousands of comments. Questions—where had I been? People had missed me, thought about me, worried about me. Wanted to see what was going on with my life.

My heart rate picked up, a side effect of the rush. I opened my camera and took a selfie—so practiced I could do it in ten seconds. Posted it everywhere, a silly caption about being stuck in Big Sur without internet. That I had missed everyone and appreciated their support and concern.

The reaction was instant, my phone lighting up with notifications within moments. I smiled, delighted, and watched the affirmation roll in. More comments, more messages.

I looked up suddenly and realized half an hour had gone by. My phone lit up again: Sabine was calling.

"*Bonjour*, Sabine," I said, and she squealed.

"I thought you were *dead*," she said. "But finally, I got in touch with your agent who told me that Big Sur had limited connection."

"It's pretty primitive up here," I said, dryly. "How are you?"

I took the phone away from my ear, putting her on speaker. Opened Instagram and watched the wave of comments keep coming in. There were so many.

One negative. *Why do your eyes look fucking weird?*

I glanced into the reflective surface of the computer screen. Were they weird? I mean, I wasn't wearing makeup—hadn't been most of this trip. They just looked like my eyes, except usually they were caked with eyeliner and fake eyelashes.

Did I have weird eyes? Oh god, here it went.

"Lucia, are you there? You saw the mock-ups? Tell me you saw them. And tell me you love them." She was so intensely excited. My stomach began tying itself in complicated knots, but I wasn't sure why.

"I did," I said, glancing back at them. The billboard was *so* extravagant-looking. That, paired with the billboards Shay wanted up from the *Boho* shoot, and you wouldn't be able to drive down any highway and *not* see my face.

"And those are just the beginning, Lu," she said. "I am telling you, the world is going to freak."

"Yeah?" I asked. "Are people really that excited?"

"Your agent and I have been in touch, talking about the release. It's going to be huge. And you know you don't have to live here, in Paris. But I figured, unless you had something keeping you in the States, you'd want to."

"Mhmmm," I said, noncommittal. A thought floated up, unbidden: Cal was in the States.

Wait, what?

"But your schedule would be intense. We are going to need you shooting most of the week, so not sure how many trans-Atlantic flights you're going to want to take, week after week."

"Right," I said, finding my way back to solid ground. "That makes sense. I should probably stay in Paris. Sabine can I, uh, ask you a question?" Josie's words had stuck with me, lodged in some part of my brain I'd rather forget about.

"Shoot," she said.

"This is a good career move for me, right? I know that's kind of an odd question, but we've been up in Big Sur without any contact with the real world, and I guess I'm getting a little... anxious," I finally said, as if "anxious" could encompass the myriad of thoughts, feelings and regrets I'd experienced since arriving.

As if "nervous" could explain Calvin.

"Anxious? *You?*" Sabine asked, breathing into the phone. "I would not have thought it."

"Yeah, well... this place is pretty isolating. Gets in your head, you know?"

"No."

"Oh... okay, so I'm guessing you think this *is* good for my career?" I asked. Maybe Sabine had never had secret desires to be anything *but* a ball-busting, powerful CEO. Maybe that's what Sabine dreamed of as a little girl.

Maybe.

"This is the best fucking thing in the world, Lu," Sabine laughed, as if I was being foolish.

A burst of chimes, and I gained another thirty followers. Ray must have snuck up to the internet café and tagged a few photos of Taylor and I during shooting—there we were, miniature on my phone's screen, but we looked amazing. I looked like a bohemian, flower-child goddess, alight in daisies and body paint.

I smiled. I couldn't help it.

"Your schedule will be punishing at times, but tons of models in your position would kill for this opportunity. Guaranteed work for two years, more money than you'll know what to do with. And afterward, you'll have your pick of jobs."

"Even though I'll be close to thirty?"

A pause, longer than I expected. "Thirty isn't ideal. You know that. But, who knows, you take the right jobs, and you'll be modeling until you're—"

"Thirty-two?" I joked grimly. For years, I'd told myself I needed a plan for when modeling was no longer an option. And yet I put it off and put it off, and now I had no idea what the hell I was going to do.

But Sabine was right—for two years I wouldn't have to worry. To stress. I could take the easy way out and be set, at least for the time being.

"Lucia, you're gorgeous and have a great reputation. Keep it that way, and you'll work for as long as you want." I heard the concealed doubt in her voice. I bet she said that to all her aging models.

"Is there a reason you're asking me all these questions?" she asked, and there it was: the opening I was looking for. To take Josie's advice and just... do something different. Be brave.

"No," I said firmly. Safe. Comfortable. Where I belonged. "I'm looking forward to the opportunity. Immensely. Just... making sure I have all the details."

"Good," Sabine said, laughing at something someone was saying in the background. "You were making me nervous there for a moment."

I laughed weakly. "Nothing to worry about. You'll want me there soon, right? I think my tickets are already booked."

"We'll see you in a week," she said before clicking off abruptly.

A week. I let out a long sigh. Big Sur was a distraction, nothing more. My phone chimed again—more comments. More followers.

I grinned and started to scroll.

CHAPTER 17

Calvin

"We've been interested in your grandfather's property for a long time, Calvin," Shannon said, placing her hand on my arm. She and her business partner, Peter, were hosting me in their offices at Carmel-by-the-Sea. Wall-to-wall windows displayed a view of the ocean.

"Good to know," I said, shuffling the papers I brought with me. "Were you... patrons of the bookstore?"

"No," Shannon said although Peter looked away. "Wasn't really my scene," she said, smiling. They were both older than me, in their mid-60s, which meant if they'd lived in this area growing up, they were aware of The Mad Ones and its literary reputation.

"Oh, okay. Well, you're at least aware of the significance of the property, historically?" I asked.

I was uncomfortable in their swanky offices. I remembered my grandfather telling me he felt like an alien whenever he left Big Sur, and I was starting to feel the same way. I hadn't even thought to dress up, throwing on a plaid shirt and an old pair of jeans, stubble on my face. I had at least run a comb through my hair and cleaned my glasses.

Meanwhile, Shannon and Peter were slick in their suits, hands strapped to iPhones. Peter's fingers flew over the keyboard of a small laptop.

"We are, and rest assured we will do our best to maintain the... essence of your grandfather's legacy," Peter chimed in. "I know building a day spa might seem totally different from a book store—"

"—well, it is," I interjected, aware of the tension in my voice and wondering where it was coming from. *You want this,* I reminded myself.

"Of course, of course it is," he replied, ever the salesman. "But we're building an organic, sustainable, and eco-friendly day spa. It'll be a place for people to unplug from their lives, get off social media, and really relax into the moment. We'll have meditation classes and yoga. In many ways, I feel like it'll maintain the spirit of what your grandfather did: encouraging people to live fully in their lives."

I smiled apologetically. "I'm happy to hear that. It *is* a beautiful property, and I know your clients will feel rejuvenated there."

"Exactly," Shannon said. "And you know we fully intend to keep those cabins—with some major refurbishment, of course."

"Of course. They have beautiful views. And the store itself?" I asked, trying to keep the hope out of my voice.

They exchanged a glance.

"Not sure yet," Peter finally said. "It's a large piece of property, and we'll be building quite a number of buildings on it. I'm sure we could find some use for the original cabin," he said, but Shannon's look was pained.

"I know it's not the fanciest of buildings," I said. "But it holds a lot of respect in the literary community. You might want to consider keeping it open. There are all these fun hide-aways—index cards where famous poets have written these beautiful lines. Books hidden in secret cabinets—" I paused, noticing a distinct lack of interest in their faces. That, and I was babbling—*so* unlike me.

"Yeah," I finally said, sheepishly. "It's... um, it's really cool."

"I'm sure you're sentimental about it," Peter said, smiling at me like I was a child.

I opened my mouth to say something but stopped. Sighed. "I am. And, really, I mean, it'll be yours, so you can do what you want with it."

"Exactly," Shannon said quickly, so quickly I was pretty sure that a year from now, the bookstore would be torn down, a spa built on top of it. I rubbed the back of my neck, unsure why I suddenly felt so conflicted. I'd wanted this for *months*. Couldn't wait to get back to my life.

And it was a *good* deal. Enough money to pay off the debts on the property *and* buy myself a San Jose penthouse with a view.

Fuck, it was enough money that I could retire at forty-five if I wanted to.

They slid the contract across the table at me. "Per this, the property would be ours, and you'd be out—"

"*Everything* would be out," Peter clarified.

"—by the end of November. Which is about six weeks from now."

I exhaled. "All right, then. Sounds good."

I stood to shake their hands. "When do you need my answer?"

"One week from now, or it's off the table," Peter said. "But I'd seriously consider it. You're not going to get an offer better than this one, Calvin."

I nodded since he was right. I'd met with countless other

investors, and their plan sounded the *least* terrible. Everything else was a complete assault on my grandfather's values: Hotels. Clothing stores. At least a spa was kind of bohemian, like him.

I walked through the first floor, awash in the sounds of an office for the first time in months. Theirs had a similar vibe to the tech company I'd worked for: an open-plan cubicle farm, people plugged into headphones and zoned out on laptops. It was quiet except for the tapping of fingers on keyboards.

This used to be my version of paradise. Except now my concept of paradise had shifted to include talking to a customer about a book they loved, a starry sky overhead, the sound of the ocean, and the smell of the forest.

Six weeks. Six weeks to pack away the framed poems, the index cards of memories. The guest book and slim, black journals and miles and miles and miles of books.

And me. Back to my old life, the one I missed so much. Except the memory of that had grown distant without me even realizing it. The shift had been so subtle—like staring at an old picture where you no longer recognize yourself.

The long drive back to Big Sur helped to quiet my thoughts, even though I was more upset than I anticipated. I thought the drive back would be victorious—finally, an ending to this strange period in my life. But still, even with the sadness, even with the confusion, deep down I knew selling was the right choice. The *only* choice, really, since per the stipulations of my grandfather's will, it needed to be sold if I wasn't going to become the owner.

And that...well. That just wasn't possible.

What *was* possible, when I finally pulled up the long driveway to The Mad Ones, was that we were being robbed.

* * *

The storm had officially landed. After days of on-and-off raining, it was striking with a vengeance. The wind was like a battering ram. Trees thrashed against the windows as I let myself in, the sound of rain on the roof drowning out the sounds of the ocean. Everything was dark except for a light on in the small poetry room—even though I distinctly remembered turning all the lights off before leaving for the meeting. I reached behind me, picking up the heaviest book I could find, and held it like a weapon.

What are you going to do—throw it in the burglar's face? I thought stupidly, creeping around the corner. The fireplace was lit, and books lay in disorganized piles on the floor. And there, curled up in a giant sweatshirt and yoga pants, no makeup and her hair in a messy bun, was Lucia.

I'd never seen anything more beautiful in my life.

I let out a quiet exhale, but she didn't look up, completely engrossed in what she was reading. She was chewing on her thumb, eyebrows furrowed in concentration. Every so often she'd bite her lip, flip the page, eyes crinkling at the sides when she liked what she read.

"I know you're watching me, Calvin," she said, eyes still on the page. I blushed immediately and fought every urge in my body to flee.

"Oh... um, hey," I said, smooth as ever. "I'm sorry, I—"

She looked up at me, tilting her head. "Don't apologize. This is *your* bookstore after all," she said, grinning.

"True," I said, coming fully into the room. It was warm from the fire, and the sound of the rain made it feel like we were the only two people left on the planet.

"Sit," she said, patting the floor next to her. I sat, leaning my back against one of the chairs and stretching my legs out in front of me. "I thought you were a burglar," I said, holding up the book I'd picked up. "I was going to throw this at your face."

She pointed at her face, scrunching it up. "Thus ending my illustrious career. Although you're currently seeing me without makeup or my hair done, which makes you part of a very small set of people."

"Like the Illuminati?" I asked.

"Oh, basically. I'm usually, you know, lipstick-ed and hair-sprayed to within an inch of my life."

"You look like yourself," I said honestly. "You're beautiful."

What the fuck are you doing? Every time I was around Lucia, words slipped out before I could spend my usual five to ten minutes obsessively analyzing if it was the right thing to say.

She held my gaze for a moment. "Thank you," she said. "Really." She shifted a few books out of the way. "Where were you tonight?"

"Meeting with the investors who are probably going to buy this property at the end of the month," I said.

"Oh," she said, eyebrow lifting. "I didn't realize that. You mean... you're selling this place?" I was happy to hear not an ounce of judgment in her voice, only curiosity.

"It's been a tough decision, but yeah, I am. I inherited the years of debt he had incurred on this property. The financial future is pretty bleak." I shrugged. "It makes me really sad, to be honest. I spent a lot of summers here growing up, and I *know* how important it is from an historical perspective—"

Lucia reached out, placing her hand on my arm. I stilled, took a breath. "You don't have to explain your choice to me, Cal. Although I'm guessing you're getting your fair share of opinions from other Big Sur residents?"

I sighed, leaning back further. "You got it. Big Sur is the most close-knit community I've ever lived in. It's so small and so..."

"Different," she said. "Everyone who lives here is like a weird blend of frontier-pioneer and commune-hippie."

"Exactly. And they consider this place *theirs*. It *is* a rich part of their history, which I totally get. It's just hard. My grandfather didn't expect to die suddenly, and I didn't expect to inherit such a mess."

We were both quiet for a second, watching the flames in the fireplace. "There is another option," she said, narrowing her eyes at me. Assessing. "*You* could run the bookstore."

I grinned, scratching my head. "Thank you, but no."

"Why the hell not?" she asked, laughing.

"Lucia..." I said. She arched her eyebrows, as if saying *And?*

"I'm a software engineer, first of all."

"You're good with numbers. Check," she said.

I laughed. "I have horrific social anxiety. My grandfather was this charming extrovert. He *loved* talking with people and... and having parties and readings and hosting workshops. I can barely string two sentences together without criticizing myself."

"So you're a little shy?" she asked. "Listen, we're not in high school anymore. I know you have this view of yourself as a bumbling nerd—"

"—Because I *am*."

"—but I've watched you with customers, and you seem pretty comfortable around them."

She wasn't wrong. I'd struggled the first couple months, for sure, but I was feeling more confident every day.

"Yeah, well... I appreciate your confidence in me, but there's still the massive issue of the debt. His sales had been dropping for years before I took over. And there hasn't been a reading here for a decade. I just think... it hurts to say this, but I just think we all need to accept that The Mad Ones isn't what it used to be. Cherish the memories and then let it go."

Lucia pulled her knees into her chest and rested her chin on top. "So you'll just go back to your old job?"

"I will," I said. "I miss it."

"What do you miss specifically?"

"The routine. The order. I knew what to expect every day —worked on the same projects, sat in the same traffic, ate the same food. Both of my parents have a rigid sense of routine, and I'm the same way. Big Sur... running this bookstore, well, it's the exact opposite of that."

Lucia made a face.

"What?" I asked, laughing.

"*Same food. Same traffic.* Cal, your life sounds fucking boring."

I laughed again, trying to cover up the part of me that agreed with her. A part of me that wasn't really there a few months ago. "We're not all globe-trotting models, I know."

She shook her head. "It's not that. It's just, wouldn't it be interesting to live a life where you *didn't* know what each day held? It'd be like a surprise party but every day."

I shuddered. "I think I'd hate that."

"I think you'd like it more than you can admit," she said with a knowing smile.

Before she could dig deeper, I changed the subject. "So now that you know there isn't enough money in this joint for you to rob me, what have you been doing in here?"

"Reading," she said in a small voice, looking almost embarrassed. There was a journal next to her feet, and I could make out the beginnings of a few scratchy sentences, some words circled over and over. "Your grandfather has a great collection of Adrienne Rich. She's one of my favorite poets. I used to have parts of her *21 Love Poems* memorized when I was in high school. It made me *real* popular with the other models."

I grinned. "I think that's beautiful. And I can't imagine

you sneaking in any time for reading with your schedule the way it is."

She shrugged, suddenly looking sad. "Yeah, I uh... well, by the time I was sixteen, I wasn't doing much reading anymore. Even though it was my first love."

"What's this?" I asked, pointing. "Are you writing?"

She looked at me, considering. "I am, actually. That's my second love."

"What are you writing about?"

She smiled slowly, tilting her head. "About you."

CHAPTER 18

Lucia

"I couldn't sleep," I said, which was the truth. Driving back from my phone call, I'd felt buoyant and hopeful, like I'd recaptured that feeling Josie felt I'd lost. But as soon as my head touched the pillow, sleep evaded me, my mind crowded with thoughts. Modeling. Writing.

Calvin.

"So I came here. Before I was a model, the only thing that calmed me down was reading and writing," I said, nodding at my journal.

"Prose?" he asked.

"Poetry," I replied, loving the *tree*-sound at the end of that word. I always had. Calvin looked impressed.

I'd finally found the journal (I never left home without it), but even though I'd had that *feeling* since we'd gotten here, nothing came. I tried to write for more than an hour and ended up tossing it back on the floor in frustration.

But still. At least I tried—for the first time in years.

"Is something bothering you? Keeping you awake?" he asked.

You, I wanted to say. That and... I was horny. Like *really* turned on, in a way I hadn't been in months. Maybe years. And Calvin was not helping, sitting a foot away from me looking scruffy and adorable. He pushed his glasses up his nose, and I almost sighed.

"Well... I mean, I tried to write a poem, and it sucked, and I suck, and everything sucks," I said, laughing.

He smiled. "Writer's block?"

"Of epic proportions," I said. "I haven't written a poem in more than seven years. But I carry my journal with me, always. This is the first time, the first place, that's inspired me in a long time."

We looked at each other. Fuck, he was sexy.

"What were you... why were you, um, writing about me?" he asked.

"Remember when we were in the woods? At your grandfather's campsite?"

His green eyes darkened. "I do, yeah."

"There was this moment... I don't know, I feel silly saying it now..." I trailed off. With the exception of Josie, I really never talked about writing. With anyone. And now here I was freely sharing with Calvin.

Again.

"You were sitting on this log and telling this story about your grandfather. It was just... I don't know, the trees behind you, and the way you were describing things. The color of your eyes. The fresh, clean air." I paused, feeling embarrassed again. "I don't know. It *felt* like a poem. Do you know what I mean?"

"Yes," he said, flashing me that crooked grin again. "I know exactly what you mean. I feel it when I read. When I used to spend my summers up here, I'd spend the whole day watching customers or listening to what they said to my grandfather. Watching their interactions. Or we'd go to some weird, Big Sur event, and something totally unusual would happen. And I'd think: this is a *story*. And I've never been a writer, but there are moments I wish I could be like you." He nodded at my journal. "Pick up and write about it."

I nodded. "That's exactly it, that *feeling*. I love it so much. And it used to be easier for me. But I got out of the habit," I said softly. "And I haven't even really thought about it in years. Not until we came here. In Big Sur."

"Big Sur tends to have that effect on people," he said. "I think that's why writers used to come up here. There are literally no distractions, nothing to take you out of that moment you're describing." He looked around the floor. Books were scattered everywhere. "Have you been here all night?"

"Pretty much," I said. "I haven't been able to just sit in a quiet bookstore in a long time. They used to be my favorite places in the whole world. Like my church." I ran my hands along a small stack of poetry anthologies. "Now there are too many paparazzi, too many fans."

"I thought you loved that though," he teased.

"I do," I said quickly. "Or... I did? I don't know," I paused, looking at him. "This might seem strange, but just three days up here, and every other part of my life feels miles away."

"You haven't tried to phantom-check your social media once this entire conversation."

"I *know*," I said, laughing and squeezing his arm. "Is it strange though? Do you think my reaction to being up here is weird?"

"Not at all. Before the start of every summer, I would dread coming. I'd miss going to the movies or seeing my friends or going to the mall. MTV, my computer, my Nintendo. I was young and desperate to be connected to the world in that way. And even though I loved my grandfather, my parents always told me the way he lived was different. Bizarre. So on the long drive up, every summer, I'd beg my parents to turn around," he said, shifting another inch closer

148

to me. "And I swear to you... within the first thirty-six hours, it was as if my other life never even existed. And I'd *hate* leaving in the middle of August. Hated it. There's an isolation up here, but it's not bad necessarily. It's one of the most beautiful places in the world, and living here changes you. Irrevocably."

I smiled, placing my hand on his arm and leaving it there.

He was quiet for a moment, studying me. I felt my cheeks heat.

"I hope you can keep this feeling with you when you leave," he said. "When you go back to Los Angeles. Tomorrow."

"Me too," I said, trying not to think about it. Trying not to think beyond this perfect moment. "And actually—" I cleared my throat, suddenly nervous. "I just signed a big contract with a makeup company. In Paris."

His eyebrows shot up his head. "Really? Lucia, that's amazing."

"Yeah. It is," I said. "For two years, I'll be the face of Dazzle Cosmetics." I did a jazz-hands thing over my face, and Cal laughed.

"What does being 'the face' of a cosmetics company entail?"

"Oh, millions of ads. Commercials, billboards, being in magazines. I'll be moving to Paris actually. To fulfill the contract."

His face lost a little of its brightness, and I reached over to touch his knee. "It's okay. I'll be back," I said, although I wasn't sure who I was soothing: Calvin or myself.

"Oh yeah," he said, looking embarrassed. "I wasn't... I mean, what do I care? Are you excited?"

"I am," I said, ignoring that strange sensation that kept popping up. "This is the kind of thing that takes a modeling career to the next level. You know, make me even more famous." I liked to brag about these things online, tease Josie about it. But suddenly, facing Calvin, I felt vain and shallow. "Opportunity of a lifetime," I finished, glancing at my nails.

Cal cleared his throat, picking up a book and flipping through it. "I'll, um... I was joking before. I'll kind of miss you. I mean, everyone, really. Having a bunch of Hollywood celebrities up here has been the most excitement we've had in decades."

Calvin was *so fucking cute*, and there was a fire and a storm outside and absolutely no one around. "I'll miss you too," I said because the why the fuck not? After tomorrow I'd never see him again anyway. "I'm just happy you finally started paying attention to me."

"Are you serious?" he asked, incredulous. "You think I've been ignoring you?" He was laughing, and I joined in.

"Either you've been ignoring me, or you're the most respectful man I've ever met," I said. "I basically walked around naked for *days*, and you barely looked up from your book." I slid closer, pressing my leg against his. He pressed back.

He blushed deeply, looking away. "I looked a couple of times," he said softly.

I watched that lust come into his gaze again. God, I was hungry for that.

"I remember," I said. "But other than those *very few times,* what's your excuse?"

"I didn't... I didn't want to be like every other guy. You know, slobbering over you. Staring at you like some kind of object."

"Oh Calvin," I laughed bitterly. "I'm a model. By definition I'm an object," I said, something I used to feel a lot more comfortable with. Now the words were like sand in my mouth.

"You're not, though," he said. "Not to me." He was staring at my lips.

The rain was coming down in sheets now, the fireplace making me feel warm and wanton. And this was not part of the plan. The plan was: Land a huge makeup contract. Finish out a provocative photo shoot for Shay Miller's new clothing line. Fly to Paris. Begin initial stages of world domination.

But really, what fucking plan? What future? There was just me and Cal, alone in a beautiful bookstore, surrounded by miles and miles and miles of forest. I lifted my sweatshirt over my head, tossing it. Underneath I was wearing a plain white tank top, and I could *feel* my nipples hardening under Cal's hungry look. I watched his throat as he swallowed.

"Can I read you a poem?" I asked.

CHAPTER 19

Calvin

"Please," I said, my mouth suddenly dry. This past week I'd seen Lucia in dozens of "sexy" outfits—had even almost seen her naked multiple times.

But right now, she was *captivating*. Her blonde hair was falling out of its messy bun. Without makeup caked on, her eyes were brighter, clearer. It was obvious, seeing her work on set, that she was famous for a reason. I watched her hold still for so long she looked like a wax statue, bend her body into strange shapes while arranging her face to look flawless. But she never seemed *happy*.

Tonight, holed up in this bookstore with me, she radiated a quiet joy.

Lucia curled up at my side, grabbing a copy of *Pablo Neruda: The Sonnets*. She was flirting with me. For real this time. And the sight of her nipples against her white shirt had my cock hard instantly.

"This used to be a favorite of mine," she said, clearing her throat. "Neruda was one of the first romantic poets I'd ever read. His words are so *sensual*. So tangible. I used to dream of having a boyfriend who'd say things like this to me."

"Did you ever have one?"

"No, of course not," she said, grinning.

"And what about now? Have you ever dated someone who said romantic things to you?" I asked, caring about the answer more than I wanted to admit.

She thought for a moment, tugging on a wayward strand of hair. "I don't think so. I mean, I think *they* thought they were being romantic. But Neruda..." She paused, fingers dancing down the page. "There's such a depth to what he feels for the woman he loves. The words he uses are so... carnal? But he's also cherishing her."

"He'd do anything for her," I said, suddenly understanding that Neruda must have had a woman in his life like Lucia Bell.

"Yes," she said simply, gazing at me. Then she flushed lightly, looking away.

"What's wrong?"

"Nothing... I just got nervous. You, watching me read this."

I smiled, covering my eyes with my hand. "Do you want me to close my eyes?"

She laughed, pulling my hand away. "No, no... it's okay. I've walked on a runway in front of ten thousand people. Pretty sure I can read this poem to you."

Lucia cleared her throat, reading me lines about hunger and harvests. A pause as she let the words sink in. Her voice was low and heated, the look on her face euphoric as she read. The fireplace pulsed a golden light around her. I thought she was quite possibly the loveliest thing I'd ever seen.

"I like the phrase *savage harvest*," I said, mesmerized as she placed her hand on my chest.

"It's the hard consonants," she said softly. "Very erotic." She slowly dragged the palm of her hand down my chest.

"He's starving for her," I said.

"The best kind of hunger," she whispered. She caressed my stomach, fingers inching towards my cock.

"Lucia—" I warned, but her fingers kept drifting. Lower and lower.

"Have you ever been that hungry? For a woman?" she asked, running one long finger up the length of my cock.

"Yes," I said through gritted teeth as she gripped me fully. A breathy moan escaped her lips, her eyes widening.

I grabbed her wrist, stilling her. With my other hand, I cupped the back of her neck roughly.

"What are you doing?" My eyes locked on that full lower lip of hers. I'd wanted to bite it from the first moment I met her.

"Touching you," she whispered. "Feeling you."

She lowered her mouth closer to mine, tempting. I held her wrist harder, stroking my thumb across her lips. She sighed.

"Kiss me," she said. She licked the tip of my thumb.

"No," I said, my hands slipping back to thread into her hair. Her eyes searched mine.

"Why not?" she said. The wind roared outside, thunder in the distance. Danger.

"I'm not—" I started to say, but then she crushed her full lips against mine, and it was fucking perfect.

I didn't know what was happening, couldn't believe that Lucia Bell was kissing me, couldn't imagine *why* a supermodel was sitting across my lap, but within seconds every bit of self-doubt in my brain was demolished by the pure carnal need of that kiss.

I tried to take it slow, to linger on her lips. I backed off a little, teasing. Softer, sweeter kisses that did nothing to satisfy the ache inside but followed the awkward narrative of my entire sexual life: Be soft. Be sweet. Don't dominate.

But then Lucia straddled me, pressing herself against my cock, and there was no stopping my darker desires.

I took her mouth. It wasn't sweet. It wasn't gentle.

I *owned* it, loving when she matched me, kiss for kiss, hungry and heated and raw and *real*. I swept my tongue between her lips forcefully, and, *god help me,* she sucked on it. I growled against her, tightening my fingers in her hair and pulling back. She was breathing heavily, face flushed, lips already swelling.

"I'm not going to be able to control myself around you," I said.

My fingers dug into the silky strands of her hair and pulled. Hard, harder than I intended, but I needed her to know. Needed her to *understand*. She gasped, but then her gaze turned ravenous. She lifted her palm from my cock and slowly placed it behind her back, my hand still gripping her wrist like a vise. Her other hand went too, and suddenly I was holding Lucia's hands behind her back like a prisoner.

And she gave me a look so perfectly submissive yet defiant, I knew that Lucia Bell was going to be my goddamn downfall.

"Maybe I don't want you to," she said.

CHAPTER 20

Lucia

The world was falling apart around us.

Literally. The rain fell in sheets against the window like millions of pebbles smacking against the glass. Wind whipped through tree branches, scraping the side of the store in long, ominous scratches. A huge roar, like a freight train, which must have been thunder or lightning or an earthquake, but who in the *hell* cared because Calvin and I were wrapped around each other on the floor, and I'd never felt so alive.

"This is why I fucking ignored you," Cal said, holding my wrists tight in one hand. His other slipped beneath my shirt to press against my stomach. I sighed. "I just knew..." he said, stroking up towards my bare breasts, fingers caressing and stopping *just* below my aching nipples.

"Cal," I moaned, trying to arch myself closer. He leaned forward, breathing in my scent. Pressing soft, gentle kisses up the side of my throat. And then I felt his teeth. He bit my neck. *Hard*.

"I knew you'd bring out something in me," he said against

my ear, fingers still teasing below my nipples. "Something dangerous."

"Yes, *yes*," I sighed, loving his mouth on my ear. I wanted him to bite me again, keep marking every inch of my skin with his teeth. The roar was louder this time, and the floor of the bookstore rattled beneath us. Cal trailed his lips down my jaw. "That day in the woods, do you remember when I left?" Cal gave me a heart-stopping kiss, rough and quick.

"I missed you," I said, loving the way his pupils darkened. "I wanted you to keep watching me. I was... I was getting off on it." His fingers tightened on my wrists, the pain edging the pleasure. A look of hesitancy passed over his face—he was doubting himself for a moment. So I rocked against his cock, both of us groaning out loud, and then he yanked me back against him.

"Dirty girl," he whispered, and I smiled. How did he *know?*

"What did you do?" Those fingers continued to tease, and I was this-close to begging.

"Jerked off. In the *fucking woods*. Because of you," he growled against my ear. His fingers stroked downward, toward the top of my yoga pants, and I shivered.

"Oh *god*," I moaned, rocking steadily against him now. I couldn't control it, could only think about Cal stroking himself to thoughts of me, the sounds he'd make when he'd come...

A shrill ring pierced the air, causing us both to jump. It rang again. And again, unrelenting.

Cal stopped, slowly lifting me from his lap, and I swallowed a sob. "Cal, wait—" and the look he gave me was so sweet it made me ache. He pressed his lips against my forehead, my cheek, my lips.

"I'm so... please," I begged but wasn't sure how to finish

the question. So *close* for sure, already moments away from orgasm. But also so *happy*.

That ring again, and Cal winced.

"Stay here," he said, standing. "That's the emergency phone." He huffed out a big breath, running his hand through his dark hair. "Lucia, I'm... that was..."

My heart was pounding, like a herd of elephants were stampeding across my chest, so loud I was sure Cal could hear it.

"Go," I said. "We'll talk later." He turned, sliding through the door, and I tried to make myself turn back into a normal human being.

CHAPTER 21

Calvin

The ringing wouldn't stop, and as I walked towards it, I could see how bad the storm had gotten. A few trees lay where they'd fallen, water ran in rivulets towards the edge of the forest, the sky a milky gray. I'd felt the earth quake beneath us but thought it was the heat of the moment.

"Yeah? I said, picking up the phone.

I'd only heard this ring once, and that was the summer before my junior year of high school. Two large earthquakes in Sonoma County were causing freakishly large waves on the beaches of Big Sur. "A possible tsunami warning," my grandfather had said, twinkle in his eye. I was freaked out, imagining a wall of water sweeping the bookstore away, my grandfather and I trying to stay afloat on giant volumes of Keats's poetry.

We'd stayed up most of the night, every so often sneaking out to the cliffs to watch the waves crash against the beach—a stupid idea if a tsunami wave had come. It would have swept us away in an instant. But I never forgot that night, seeing the reverse-side of Big Sur's magnificence—the supreme danger of nature when she's angry. The way the waves rocked the shore I could picture, thousands of years ago, the way the water had carved away this beach, eroded the rocks into the very cliffs we were standing on. I spent the next two days reading Moby Dick and shivering, dreaming of monsters beneath the surface.

"It's Gabe. Are you guys okay?"

"We're fine, why?" I asked slowly. *I was this close to having the most intense sexual encounter of my life, but other than that...*

"There were two massive rockslides along Highway 1, one at the entrance to Big Sur and one on the way to San Luis Obispo."

"Is anyone hurt?" I asked, staring outside and into the darkness. A rockslide. That must have been the roaring we'd heard.

"No, thank God. It missed Lisa Davenport's home by a few hundred feet. The mayor's home too."

"Jesus." Natural disasters were deeply felt here—there weren't that many people, and emergency services had a hell of a time getting out to such a remote location.

"Listen, you and I should be fine. Your grandfather had a huge stash of emergency food and water in that pantry, and the bar does too. But you've got to let the Hollywood folks know they're going to be stuck here for a bit. A few days, at least."

I glanced back at the poetry room where Lucia stood, a goddess wrapped in blankets, concern on her face. I tried to ignore my willful heart, uplifted by the possibility she would be staying longer.

"They're not going to be happy about that. For how long?"

"Not sure. Road crews have to get out there. But it's enormous, Cal. I'd say at least five days."

"Holy shit," I said, which caused Lucia to look up at me in

alarm. I pushed my glasses up my nose, shifting on my feet. She tilted her head, and I shrugged. "And I'm guessing whatever cell or internet service we did have has been knocked out, right?"

"For a few days, yeah. You'll deliver the information to everyone tonight?"

"Of course. The first cabin has an emergency phone—it's Ray's, I think. I'll ring him, gather everyone together if it's safe to walk over."

There was a sharp knocking at the back door, and then a crowd of people barged in, including Ray. Lucia clutched her chest, eyes wide, and then she scurried back into the Poetry Room to put on more clothing.

"Or maybe not," I said, laughing. "They all just showed up."

"One thing you should, uh, know," Gabe said, clearing his throat. "Josie's here. With me. The crew was drinking at the Bar tonight, and she stayed. The night."

My eyebrows shot up. "Well... okay, then. I'll tell Lucia."

"Please do. She knows Lucia will worry about her."

"Are... congratulations in order?" I asked, and Gabe roared with laughter.

"Want to come up and drink with me? Soon? I'll fill you in as much as I can."

I laughed too, a sharp ache in my chest. *You'll miss this.* Because as terrifying as a rockslide is, San Jose had none of this community, this sense of connection.

"I do," I said. "Definitely soon." I glanced back at Lucia. "We've got a lot to catch up on."

People were spilling into the Big Room, and Lucia sidled over, grabbing my arm.

"What is it?" she whispered.

"Huge rockslide, on either side of Highway 1. I'm afraid you're, um, well, you can't leave. Not for a few days at least." I couldn't read the expression on her face. "Also, Josie's not here. She's with Gabe. In a... sexual way, I believe," I stuttered.

Lucia did a tiny victory dance.

I laughed despite the seriousness of the moment. And then Lucia high-fived me.

CHAPTER 22

Lucia

"It was a massive rockslide. Two of them, actually," Calvin said, standing in the middle of the Big Room. He was so damn cute. I wanted everyone to leave. I wanted to keep grinding myself to orgasm on his lap.

Focus, Lucia.

"So far no injuries have been reported—the storm was so bad there weren't a lot of people on the roads. But, and this is still just preliminary information, it looks like the rockslides occurred at two different locations, unfortunately. At the entrance and exit to Big Sur, on Highway 1. Until clean-up crews can get out there, we are all, well..." He ran his hand over the back of his neck. "We're trapped here for the time being. There's no way out."

"Oh my god," Joanna said, hand flying to her mouth.

I wished Josie was here, except my girl was spending the night with a bearded hunk. But I was potentially sex-addled and couldn't entirely grasp what was going on.

"I still don't understand what you're saying," I said. *But I understood the way you pinned my wrists behind my back.*

Cal shifted on his feet, looking nervous again. "I'm not

163

entirely sure either. Gabe was only able to pass on the basic information."

"Has this happened before?" Ray asked, thumb already scrolling through his phone's camera. I knew what he was thinking. Shay Miller was a notorious hard-ass. He wasn't the kind of person to take "*I'm so sorry we ran behind schedule. A massive rockslide almost killed all of us*" as an excuse.

"Big Sur has had some strange weather phenomena, yes. Wildfires, mudslides... and because it's so remote, severe weather can be even more damaging. Luckily, most people have planned for this kind of event, so Gabe's bar has plenty of canned food stocked up and water. I do too, and the small grocery store up the road should have enough." He turned to face Ray. "You were going to leave tomorrow, right?"

Which is why I'd given in to my crush on Cal. One more night. No consequences. No feelings. Also, I was technically supposed to be in Paris in a week.

Shit. I wanted to go back to sex-addled.

Ray sighed, shaking his head. "Right. I mean, technically, we were a day behind schedule anyway, but I was hoping Shay would like the shots as is. But if we're here for another few days—"

"—maybe a week," Cal interjected, to the groans of everyone. *Fuck*, Paris. But also... would Cal want to see me again?

"—*Maybe*," Ray said, looking flustered now. "Does your grandfather have any cool stories of getting trapped here with a bunch of poets and, like, taking LSD and running through the rain?"

"I'm sure of it," Cal replied with a smirk. "I'll look through some more of his journals, try to give you a narrative you could work with. I would suggest Big Sur's most famous restaurant, Fenix. Next to this store, nothing more bohemian back in the day than that place. It's on a huge cliff with this gorgeous view of the California coast. Maybe they'd let you do some shots there?"

Ray was writing everything down, making notes in his phone. "Brilliant, Cal. Jesus, what *can't* you do, man?"

Cal and I made eye contact from across the room, and he blushed so furiously I thought he would faint.

"I wish we had fucking internet," Taylor muttered, nudging my shoulder. "People would love this. We could be posting updates on the storm, our efforts to get out of here. Start our own hashtag."

I could see it, I could, suddenly and swiftly aching for the affirmation of fans and strangers. For their comments of love and affection and downright obsession. Like earlier tonight— the constant chiming of my phone as people affirmed my hard-won celebrity.

A wave of anxiety broke open on my skin, and I hated it... hated that half an hour ago I was happy and safe, thinking about poetry and Calvin's hungry mouth, and now I was back to craving the fame. I was kidding myself when I'd told Calvin I was letting go of some of that... that Big Sur was changing me.

You can never let it go. *I* could never let it go. And now I was stuck up here for another week with nowhere to go and nothing to do except obsess over which younger, prettier supermodel was already replacing me.

"Walk you back?" Taylor said, and I nodded, shoving my writing journal under my jacket. Trying not to focus too much on the books lying haphazardly on the floor—a secret sign of our earlier passion.

"Lucia?"

I stopped, turning around, but I knew it was Calvin. He was already blushing, shoving his glasses up his nose.

"Hey," I said, suddenly breathless.

"Here's the book I was telling you about earlier. The one...

um, the one you said you wanted to borrow?" Cal pressed it into my hand, his gaze intense and heated. For the briefest of moments his finger stroked along mine, and then he pulled back. "I think you'll like it."

I nodded. "I'm sure I will," I said, feeling Taylor tug on my arm. "I'll see you tomorrow, I guess," I said, then followed Taylor in a daze back to the cabins.

CHAPTER 23

Calvin

"We had a moment," I said, hefting up a giant box of bottled waters from the basement of Gabe's bar. "That's all. No big deal."

It was the next morning, and I'd barely slept. Between the adrenaline of Lucia's kiss and everything with the rockslides, I'd tossed and turned. Finally, I gave up and called Gabe, who had suggested morning beers.

Ahead of me, I heard his laughter. "You shared a *moment* with one of the most famous supermodels in the world?"

I kept hefting until we reached the bar. I hoisted the box up, breathing heavily.

"I know," I said. "I too did not believe this was in the realm of possibility. Not in this world. Not in any world."

"You're a computer programmer from Silicon Valley," Gabe said, reaching below the bar to grab me a beer. He tossed it and I dropped it, fumbling clumsily. When I stood up, I knocked my head against the bar.

"*Ouch,*" I said, rubbing the bump already forming.

"And you're also... you know, *you,*" he said, grinning a mile wide.

"Thank you for your show of confidence," I said, taking a sip. "And your friendship."

He laughed, digging up a box of candles from the floor. "You think the power's going to go out?"

"Probably," I said. "Swarm of locusts next. Followed by some kind of plague. We haven't had a big storm yet this year. This feels like it might be the one."

"Ah. How romantic. Getting stuck in the dark, no power, raining outside? Might give you an opportunity to close the deal. With the supermodel."

"Lucia," I said quickly. "And she's not just a supermodel, although that by itself is impressive."

Gabe's head titled. "Oh?"

"She's... she's really funny. And smart. And a total bookworm, like me. She's got... layers."

Gabe leaned against the bar, suddenly serious. "And she's been on the cover of *Maxim* magazine, Cal. She's next-level out of your league. Out of *anyone's* league. You sure she's not just bored and messing with you?"

I felt a flurry of butterflies in my stomach because of *course* I worried she was just messing with me. Until last night, I had been sure of it, sure it was a harmless flirtation caused by the fact she wasn't getting her usual affirmations from social media and gossip magazines.

Except I'd had her writhing on my lap with her hands pinned behind her back, my name on her lips. Totally vulnerable.

It had to be real.

Right?

I laughed, gulping down half the beer. "Fuck if I know," I said, trying to keep it light. "So... Josie."

Gabe's grin was enormous.

"You like her, I guess?" I asked, liking this early morning beer-and-feelings meeting we were having.

He looked around, a comedic moment, since no one was in the bar.

"She's incredible. Last night was incredible. I'd be lying if I told you I wasn't just the tiniest bit happy they're stuck here. Does that make me a terrible person?"

"Nope. Because I had the exact same thought," I said grimly because saying it out loud made it too real. Both of us were silent for a moment, weighing what that meant.

"What about when they leave?" I finally asked, wondering if pursuing Lucia would only make it hurt more.

"It'll fucking suck," Gabe said, swallowing half of his beer in one gulp. "And that's why we're not going to think about it. We're just going to live in the moment, content with the fact that two absurdly beautiful women want to be around us... for reasons no rational person can comprehend."

We knocked our beer bottles together at that, and I nodded, agreeing. "Live in the moment. It's what my grandfather would have said."

"Did it ever get this exciting in your old life?" Gabe asked. "I mean, technically, you're leaving soon too, right?"

I'd completely forgotten the meeting I'd had yesterday, forever altering the destiny of The Mad Ones and my grandfather's legacy. It felt so far away now, during a more innocent time when I *hadn't* shared the best kiss of my entire life with Lucia Bell.

I sifted through a dozen answers, trying to defend the quiet life I'd led before this. But instead, rain pouring outside and my lips still swollen, I went with the truth.

"No, it never got this exciting. Not even a little," I replied.

Gabe just looked at me, and I was grateful he didn't try to convince me to stay one more time.

The rockslide was a brief reprieve, but in a few days from now Lucia would be gone, back to her glamorous, famous life. And in a month from now I'd be back in a cubicle.

CHAPTER 24

Lucia

"We had a moment," I said triumphantly as Josie walked through my cabin door.

It was morning, and she knew I'd have one *billion* questions for her about Gabe. Last night it had poured rain on me and Taylor, and after soaking in a scalding hot shower, I'd fallen deeply asleep.

"What? With who? And what's that?" she asked, pointing at my writing journal. "Were you writing again?"

"With Calvin. And you have sex hair," I pointed out, pulling myself up into a seated position.

"Well, that's because I had sex. Really, really, great fucking sex," she said, satisfied smirk on her face. I kicked her.

"Horn dog. What was the dick situation?"

"Huge. Perfect. Just right."

"Any more details than that?" I asked, casually, knowing how secretive she was sometimes but desperate for the dirt.

"Maybe," she said slowly. "But I think I need to think this one through. Let it marinate."

"That good, huh?" I asked since she hadn't said that in a *while*.

She bit her lip, smiling. "Back to the original question," she said, picking up my journal. "Were you writing?"

"Not even. I mean I tried, but as usual, I got nothin'," I said, shrugging.

"So you 'had a moment' with Cal *and* were motivated to at least *try* and write?"

Josie knew what writing meant to me, knew that no romantic partner (real or otherwise) had *ever* known I wanted to spend my days writing poetry. "And you told Cal about it?"

"It came up while we were talking about books."

"*Talking about books*," Josie cried, tossing a pillow at my face.

I laughed. "What is going on with you?"

Her mouth gaped open. "Nothing. Just that you *had a moment* with a cute nerd who you also told about your writing *and* talked about books with." She crossed her arms primly. "Calvin Ellis is your dream man."

I rolled my eyes, ignoring the skip of my heart. "Hardly. I barely know him."

"Doesn't mean he can't be your dream man," she said, all-knowing in the way only best friends can be. "*Yo se que es verdad, chica.*"

"*No puede ser,*" I said. "My dream man is going to be a wealthy oil tycoon I marry in my mid-thirties."

"You've got it bad," Josie said with a laugh, standing up and heading towards the bathroom.

I bit back a grin since she really wasn't wrong, and that's when I saw the book Cal had given me. I'd forgotten all about it. I picked it up (it was *Neruda's Sonnets*), and there was another Post-it Note inside.

My fingers trembled. *I'm sorry we were interrupted,"* he had written, *"because what I really wanted to do was fuck you with my tongue. I can picture it: Your back arching off the floor, your wrists bound above your head. My hands, holding your*

KATHRYN NOLAN

thighs down as I licked you. Deeply. Thoroughly. The taste of you on my tongue for hours afterward. I wanted you to come. And you would have, as many times as I demanded.

And maybe Josie was right because not once in my twenty-six years on this earth had a man written me something so erotic and thrilling. On instinct, my hand pressed between my legs, seeking the aching release Cal had made me desperate for. I pressed my palm against my clit and whimpered.

P.S. Don't make yourself come. I'll know if you do. -C

CHAPTER 25

Calvin

I loved the kitchen in The Mad Ones. It was a long, narrow galley kitchen, and while it was technically my grandfather's, it quickly became another space for people to meet. When I was younger, I'd stumble upon customers having intense conversations about their favorite books in here, drinking cup after cup of coffee, hands shaking.

My grandfather would tell stories about impromptu readings that would happen over a pot of water, boiling for tea. Or writers, struck suddenly with inspiration, scribbling down notes on an old napkin.

The refrigerator was covered in scraps of poetry, articles about the bookstore, old photos of my grandparents. From time to time, I'd pull out a coffee mug and find a note from my grandfather on it—sometimes something ordinary ("Don't forget Chance's food at the store"), sometimes a line from a poem he loved and had to document.

But this morning, there was no scrap of wisdom from my grandfather, only the endless torrential rain. My morning beer with Gabe, while therapeutic, had brought on a bout of melancholy. I held a mug that said "*Keep Independent Book-*

173

stores Open" and dug through a box of his journals, settling into the overstuffed chair by the roaring fireplace. Chance curled up at my feet, and I tried to soak in a moment's peace— before the crew came storming in, before Lucia's presence demanded my attention.

I flipped through a couple, stumbling upon the weeks when my grandparents were just beginning to date.

I do not believe in love at first sight, my grandfather had written about his reaction to meeting my grandmother on a beach in Monterey. *Although I've read about it in books, it is not my personal belief. There's too much about a person to love them instantly—and really, isn't that the best part? To learn, intimately, about every single beautiful thing about them. The way they laugh. What makes them sad. The way they peel an orange. Do they like whiskey?*

I smiled, rubbing Chance's head, sipping my coffee.

When I met Maggie, it wasn't love at first sight, although I thought she was gorgeous. Striking, really, and effervescent. And maybe this is shadowed by time, since we're married now and I think of her as my soulmate—but although I do not believe in love at first sight, I do believe something inside of me recognized her... I don't know, her soul. Or spirit... I'm not sure. Recognized it in a unique way. Like everyone on the beach that day was a dull, pale blue but Maggie was electric turquoise.

She made me so at ease with myself. Things I had buried or things I didn't like—they didn't matter around her. As I fell in love with her, she helped me love myself.

Thunder clapped outside. I thought I heard voices in the distance, which meant my moment of peace would soon be shattered. The voices got louder, and in an instant, my grandfather's small bookstore transformed into a film set. Ray was talking loudly into a walkie-talkie, and the craft services people were struggling to dry off the bagels, which had gotten soaked in the rain.

And then Lucia. Lucia strode in wearing tight black yoga pants and a giant men's sweater, and everything narrowed down to her. Her smile as she brought Josie coffee. The way she'd sneak glances at the bookshelves when she thought no one else was looking. She shimmied her shoulders, tossing a crass joke at the camera crew, and they roared with laughter.

The number of times in my life I'd had the courage and the confidence to leave an erotic note for a woman—a note *with instructions*—was zero. But secretly, I'd always wanted to. Meeting a cute girl at a bar and failing horribly to impress her —I'd fantasize about doing something like that, something that would help her see beyond the socially awkward first impression.

Fear would always get the best of me. That and a nagging feeling left over from high school that I had a very specific role to play with women, and Sexually Dominant Alpha it was not.

With Lucia, the fear and the low self-esteem faded away, like turning the volume all the way down on the TV. For the first time in my life I felt comfortable in my body. Comfortable in my desires. Comfortable to express what I wanted.

And what I wanted was for Lucia to come over here so I could kiss her senseless.

"Where the hell is Taylor?" Ray asked, clapping his hands together.

"Sick," Lucia piped up. "I think it's food poisoning. Ray, I'm sorry—I thought he might be up for it this morning, but he's still completely out of it."

Ray made a face like he wanted to freak out but kept it together. "Yeah, so..." he said, rubbing the back of his neck. "It's just that with the storm and this weather, everything is getting really behind schedule. I mean, Lu, I could photograph *you* all day."

"*Obviously*," she agreed with a grin.

175

"But Shay was clear. And *Rag* was clear. They wanted sexy couples photos. Two people together."

"What about a stand-in?" she suggested. "Also, where are we even shooting today? The roads are closed, and we've done a ton in this location already."

Ray grinned, devious. "I have an idea. It might be dangerous."

"Well, then, I'm in," Lucia said immediately. This entire Hollywood drama had been playing out in front of me, but not a single person had addressed me. Or probably noticed me, as usual. I had shit to do, so I tried to sidle across the back of the room, tip-toeing quietly. If I could just get to my desk...

Except I was so busy quietly sidling that I failed to notice the snarl of power cords, which my foot caught, sending me flying across the room. I dimly heard my coffee mug shattering as I fell, face first, into the floor.

"Mother*fucker*," I groaned, rolling over to stare at the ceiling, willing the earth to open and take me away. Immediately, a trio of concerned faces appeared in my view.

"Calvin," Lucia said, with a wry smile. "Good morning."

"Oh... hello, everyone," I said, sitting up. I rubbed the side of my face that had smashed against the carpet. "How's it, uh, going?"

"Dude, you okay?" Ray said, looking not the least bit concerned. He was on a time-crunch after all. Except, suddenly, his face changed as he was looking at me. "Cal, can you come here a second?" He grabbed my hand and dragged me towards the heavy studio lighting being set up.

"Josie, Joanna, come here," he said, and they trotted over. Lucia came too, sensing something was up.

"We need a stand-in, right?" Ray said, staring at me like I was the Mona Lisa.

Josie's face lit up. "We sure do, boss."

"Good bone structure," Ray said, still staring at me. "This scruff... I like it, Cal. It's very *bohemian*."

Oh no.

"Can you turn around?" Ray asked.

I did, slowly, recognizing that they were picking me apart, examining every square inch.

And Lucia did this every damn *day*.

"I'd like to add that this is the most bizarre thing that's ever happened to me," I said. I made eye contact with Lucia and her smile blazed across my skin.

"It would mostly be body shots," Ray was saying. "I don't think Shay would mind if we replaced Taylor for a day. Especially since mostly I could shoot Lu's reactions to Calvin."

Behind me, I heard Lucia choke on a cough.

"What do you think, Lu?" Ray asked, turning me back around. He gave me a wide smile that I thought was meant to be reassuring but only made me more anxious. "You think you can, you know, get into it with Cal for a day?"

Our eyes briefly met, but then she turned towards the cameras. "I mean... I am a stalwart professional."

Joanna grinned. "You're cute. You've got good hair," she said, winking at me. Lucia saw, her gaze turning murderous for the quickest of seconds.

"Um, thanks?" I said.

Josie looked up from chatting with the wardrobe folks. "How tall are you, Cal?"

"Six foot two, I think," I said. I was a little shorter than Taylor, although we were both pretty slim. She nodded, pulling off a few pieces and holding them against my chest.

"Ooooh, nice. I really think this could work, Ray. Cal, have you ever modeled before?"

I let out a sarcastic laugh. "Oh yeah, in between *Star Trek* conventions, I always squeeze in a little modeling."

Lucia snorted, and I smiled at her.

"Lucia will show you the ropes. You're not going to have to do much; Lu will carry it. You're just going to basically work off her energy. What her body is doing, what facial expressions she's making," Ray said.

"What if I can only make one facial expression?"

Lucia stepped forward, taking my face in her hands. Her blue eyes were practically dancing. "Look at me," she said as if there was anyplace else in the world I wanted to look. "Smile, kind of naturally. Like we're friends and you just told me a funny joke."

I thought about it for a second, thought about last night and the conversation we'd been having. I smiled naturally, and she returned it. I heard a *click* and looked over. Ray was holding his camera, staring at the screen.

He made an impressed face. "You two... well, you do look kind of natural together." Lucia glanced at it, and some feeling crossed her face I couldn't begin to decipher.

"Is it good?" I asked.

"I mean, *I'm* good," she joked, hand on her chest, and I laughed.

Ray *clicked* again. Looked. Made that same face. "You know, when you're not tripping over power cords, you're a handsome guy, Cal."

Lu tilted her head at me, thinking. "That's how I make certain expressions. I play a little movie in my mind, and my face will naturally start to recreate it."

"Okay," I said. "I'm still not sure I can..."

"You'll basically have your face in Lu's boobs for six hours. You'll be fine," Josie said, pushing me into a makeup chair. She smiled at me, arching an eyebrow. "Just try not to get a giant erection."

CHAPTER 26

Lucia

I never thought Calvin and I would be sitting in conjoined makeup chairs, about to be photographed sensually touching each other's bodies for an entire day.

I also didn't expect Cal to have such a nice body. His shirt was off now, and they'd put him in terry shorts—easier to wipe makeup off. I was in a short towel, wishing desperately that we were alone. This close to his mostly naked body, and I wanted to climb all over him.

"You're kind of a hottie-with-a-body," I teased, looking up so Josie could layer on eye-liner.

"Yeah, Cal. Agree. Are you like the heartthrob of Big Sur?" she asked.

"Your sarcasm has not gone unnoticed," he said, eyes closed as Joanna fussed with his hair.

"We're not joking," Josie said. "You, uh... you work out?"

I swallowed a laugh since I knew she was only asking for me because *I* wanted to know how he'd gotten so lean and fit but couldn't ask without raising some eyebrows.

He opened his eyes, giving us a look as in *seriously?* Josie nodded.

He glanced down at himself. "I just have a normal body. I'm a normal person."

"With abs," I said before I could stop myself.

Josie widened her eyes at me, and if we weren't surrounded by people, she would have squealed.

"Um... okay," he said as Joanna rubbed foundation on his forehead. "I don't know, I run every day. I have a pull-up bar I use."

I liked the idea of Cal doing pull-ups. His heavy breathing. Sweat dripping down his lean stomach, the muscles of his broad shoulders bunching. He wasn't bulky-muscular, but he looked strong and hard in all the right places. He had dark chest hair, a smattering on his stomach. I wanted to press my lips against every inch of him.

"What's happening on my face right now?" he asked.

"Foundation. Globs of it," I said.

"You do this, like, every day?" he asked.

I nodded. "I don't always have huge shoots like this. Sometimes it's runway, sometimes it's for a magazine. They're all different. But they all start by sitting in hair and makeup for hours. It's a really unique blend of boredom and relaxation."

"What do you do to pass the time?"

"Well it helps when your best friend is your makeup artist," I said, reaching out to squeeze Josie's hand.

"True," she said. "Lucia and I usually spend a lot of time talking—"

"—Instagramming—"

"—Snapchatting—

"—Talking about our feelings," I said. "Gossiping." I shrugged. "It makes the time pass quickly because, once the shoot or the runway show begins, it's really physically exhausting. Sometimes this is the only time I'll sit all day."

"Really?"

"Well, you do so much *standing* for hours on end. It's why

I have super strong legs," I said, pointing at the limbs in question.

"How many fans do you have?" Cal asked. "I'm curious."

"On which platform?"

Josie snorted. "Lucia's Followers," she said, sweeping blush across my cheeks.

"You say that like she's a cult leader," he said, smiling.

"Because she is. I mean, you have to be in this industry." My hands were twitching at the mere mention of "followers" and "fans." I picked up my phone on instinct, glaring at the *No Service.*

"On Instagram, I have over five million followers," I said. "It's all part of the whole... you know, the whole *persona* you have to have. Friendly but not *too* friendly. Aloof but also approachable. People want to get a glimpse into this glamorous other world but also want to see me eating Cheetos and binge-watching Netflix." I paused. "I am losing followers, so... and not having internet this whole time, I'm sure, is *not* helping."

"*Mija. Basta, ya,*" Josie warned.

"So some people dropped off... what's the big deal?" Calvin asked.

My stomach clenched. *Why was I bringing this up?* It was such a dark, shallow side of myself, and I didn't want Cal privy to it.

"Oh, just..." I started, ignoring the look on Josie's face. She thought I was too obsessed. "As a celebrity, you need to stay relevant. Always doing something new, something different. Standing out. It's how you stay famous. How you keep getting paid." I swallowed. "Models don't have a particularly long shelf-life."

"What are you, like twenty-four?"

"Twenty-six, which is about as old as we get," I said, the words tumbling out of my mouth before I could stop them.

Cal glanced at me, sympathy playing across his face, which clued me in that I was sharing more than I should.

I opened my mouth to make a joke—change the subject—but Ray came over with his notepad. "How do you two feel about heights?" He paused. "And rain?" Another pause. "And high winds? Also cliffs."

"Specific cliffs? Or cliffs in general?" I asked.

"Specific. Specifically, the cliffs in front of the cabins."

"The ones that jut out hundreds of feet over the roaring ocean?"

"Yes," he said.

"I feel fucking *great* about that," I said and watched Cal almost faint out of his makeup chair.

CHAPTER 27

Calvin

"I would like it to be known that I object to this," I said, standing in front of one of the cabins under a pop-up tent that was threatening to blow away any instant. The storm was dying down, and the rain had settled into a gentle drizzle. Really, taking pictures in the rain wasn't the issue. Or the fact that the wind made it freezing.

It was those fucking cliffs.

"Duly noted, Cal," Ray said, examining his notepad. "We'll have you sign a waiver. It's fine."

It was not fine.

"It'll be wild. And dangerous. And totally arthouse," he said, showing us his drawings. "Kind of... I don't know, animalistic. Two people who can't keep their hands off each other, even outside in a fucking storm. And the ocean adds this element of danger." He looked at us, laying a hand on each of our shoulders. "Because really, you could fall in at any moment."

"*Totally*," Lucia said, a gleam in her eye.

"This is fucking ridiculous," I said, but neither one of them heard me. In fact, they were shuffling us closer to where we'd be shooting, keeping an umbrella over our heads. I was wearing a patterned vest, no shirt, and ripped jeans. My hair had weird gel in it, and my face felt sticky with the foundation they'd layered on.

Lucia was a rain goddess. She was in a black, two-piece bathing suit covered in turquoise and white stones with layers and layers of necklaces. Leather sandals laced up her calves to her knees. Joanna had created a large crown of leaves and branches that sat on top of her head, her blonde hair crimped and curled and wild-looking. She had only a little makeup on since the rain could downpour at any second.

"You, um, you look really pretty," I said, as if *really pretty* could describe Lucia Bell.

"Thanks," she said, nudging me with her shoulder. "You're not too shabby yourself."

"Let's go," Ray said, looking at the sky. "The clouds are perfect, and the rain isn't too bad. You ready?"

"*Nope*," I said as Lucia yelled, "Fuck yeah!"

Ray marched us over to the collection of rocks, pointing out the one we'd be leaning against for most of the day. I looked over and down, at the sheer drop. Huge rocks jutted out of the ocean, white water swirling around their jagged edges.

"We're going to die," I said, pointing.

Lucia looked, gave a casual shrug. "Probably. But at least we'll be having fun, right?"

I was already captivated by the sight of water on Lucia's eyelashes. I shook myself.

"All right, Cal, remember: follow Lu's lead. I'm going to be shooting mostly her face anyway. Just be natural. I'll tell you if you look weird or constipated or anything."

"*Jesus*," I said, but then Lucia was backing up against the rock and crooking her finger at me, and my mouth totally dry.

"I think you're in front of me in the beginning," she said.

"Okay," I said, moving slowly towards her.

There was an entire crew of people behind us, shivering under tents and umbrellas, the ever-present Ray, already rattling off a string of instructions to Lucia, who was nodding in understanding.

But really. Really, there was just Lucia, water rolling down her skin, gazing at me like I was the sexiest thing she'd ever laid eyes on.

I placed my hands on either side of her head, firm against the rock. It was freezing, but Lucia was a total professional: no complaints.

"Closer," Ray said, so I did, pressing the lower half of my body against hers. I was hard, and she felt it, her eyes widening.

"Right leg up, Lu," Ray said, and she complied. My hand automatically left the rock to wrap around her lower thigh, holding it against my hip. Beneath my fingers, her muscles flexed gently.

"Beautiful," Ray said. "Keep looking at each other just like that and hold it."

"Um... for how long?" I asked out of the side of my mouth.

"Hours and hours," she said.

"Can we at least talk—"

"Cal, stop talking," Ray called out, and I clamped my mouth shut.

Lu didn't change the expression on her face, but her eyes were bright and dancing. She was *enjoying* this. She moved her hands, slid them up my bare chest, up the side of my neck, and into my hair. She gripped the strands, slowly pulling my face down into the crook of her neck.

"Old model trick," she whispered in my ear. "They won't catch us if we whisper like... once every hour."

I stifled a laugh, accidentally scraping my teeth against her neck. Every muscle in her body stilled.

"Sorry," I whispered.

"Don't be," she whispered back. My eyes closed for a second, and I rocked, as subtly as I could, against her. There was just a thin sliver of fabric preventing me from being inside her—something we were now both very much aware of.

"Get your head out of her boobs, Cal," Ray said, and we both laughed. *Click click* went the camera. "And stop being cute. I need raw. Lu?"

"Got it," she said, eyes on me. "Calvin," she said, hands drifting up my back. I felt her fingernails bite into my shoulders. "You need to, um, *pretend* that you want to fuck my brains out."

"Yeah, Cal, just what Lucia said," Ray called out.

I turned, looking at him helplessly. Did he know? Did they all know?

Ray tapped his watch. "The sooner you rip each other's clothes off, the sooner we can get out of this god-forsaken rain."

I turned back to Lucia. "You have a really weird job," I said.

She pressed the entirety of her body against the rock, arching her back. Water danced between her breasts and down her lean stomach. I almost broke the rock in half with my palm. Like a dream, she reached forward, looping her fingers in my vest, pulling me slowly, slowly, *slowly* until our lips were almost touching. My hand slipped under her other thigh, lifting until she was pinned against the rock, legs wrapped around my waist.

"That's the spirit," she said against my lips. "And you should know your cock is driving me wild." I tightened my fingers on her thighs, giving another subtle rock. The smallest whimper escaped her lips.

"I need to kiss you," I said. We were staring into each other's eyes—so intimate. So vulnerable. In the three years I'd dated Claire, I doubt we'd ever had eye contact this intense.

In fact, not a single part of our relationship—not even the beginning—had been as intense as these moments with Lucia, being pelted with rain against a rock with a bunch of strangers standing around us, taking our picture.

She sighed softly, tilting her head all the way back and exposing her throat. She flashed a look at the camera.

"Beautiful, Lu," Ray said. I already missed her eyes on me. "Keep looking at her like that, Cal. That's great. You look so *hungry*, man."

How was this happening to me right now?

"Good hungry? Or um, like, *hangry?*" I asked, and Ray immediately said, "*Stop. Talking. Calvin,*" and Lucia hid her face behind her hair for a moment, lovely shoulders shaking with laughter. I rolled my eyes, then shifted my body so my lips were against her ear again, hovering.

"Is this payback for last night? For the note?" Her hands traced down my stomach, playing with the button on my ridiculous ripped jeans.

She didn't answer; instead, she pressed herself against my cock again. And again. I was almost fucking Lucia in front of everyone, on this rock, steps from hurtling into the ocean. I slid my fingers up higher, to the very edges of her bathing suit, and left them there. Stroked my fingers along it as subtly as I could. She gave me a look of such deep yearning I knew she'd followed my instructions.

"You didn't touch yourself, did you?" I murmured against her ear.

"All right, new positions. Lu, switch it up," Ray said, moving in closer. He was suddenly a foot from us, dripping with rain. I was too, although I'd been completely unaware. My world was the size of Lucia and Lucia only. "I'm going to get some close-up body shots, Lu. Cal, you just stand there, bro."

"Um..." I started to say, but Lucia was on the move. She slid down my body, grabbed my shoulders, and shoved me. My back was now against the rock (*fuck, it was freezing*), and Lucia was standing in front of me, back against my chest. Her ass lined up perfectly with my cock, her head thrown back against my shoulder.

Which meant I could whisper in her ear, and she couldn't respond with the cameras trained on her face.

I gathered the courage inside me, a growing storm. Had it always been there? Had I always possessed this deep well of confidence or was this new?

I placed my hand on her collarbone, slipping my fingers beneath the straps of her bathing suit. Slid it slowly to the side. My fingers were barely an inch from her nipple. My other hand gripped her hip, squeezing hard. Her hair was blowing all around me in the wind as I lowered my lips to her ear.

"I didn't realize you were such a good girl, Lucia Bell," I said. "I expected you to tear up that note and then finger-fuck yourself over and over."

A hum in the back of her throat. Ray was three feet from us, calling out instructions to Lucia. I could see her nipples hardening through the thin fabric of the bathing suit.

"Good girls get rewards," I said, letting my tongue touch her ear for the briefest of moments. She shivered. "How should I reward you?"

I thought for a moment but not too long. Too long, and I'd realize I was saying the kinds of filthy things I'd always wanted to, but never could. Because of fear, because I didn't think it was right. But nothing had ever felt so right in my life: Lucia's pliant body trapped against mine while I muttered a string of dirty words into her ear.

I'd lived my life before in total darkness. This crucial

moment, like millions of light bulbs flaring to brightness, painted my life in vivid color.

"Let's see..." I said, moving against her just slightly. "I could eat your sweet pussy for hours." Another hum in the back of her throat. "I could tongue-fuck you the way I wanted to the other night. Make you come in my mouth, maybe with a blindfold on? Definitely with these pretty little wrists tied behind your back. Or to my bed."

She stumbled a bit.

"Lu, you okay?" Ray called out.

"Oh, yeah," she said, breathless. "Can we switch?"

CHAPTER 28

Lucia

R ay glanced at his sketchpad for a moment. "Uh...
yeah, why don't you turn around, back towards
Calvin. We can get some good shots of you, like,
fisting his chest hair or something."

Perfect. I was already seconds from coming, my entire
body strung tight as a hair-trigger. If Cal rocked against me
one more time with his cock—firm and *long* and so fucking
right—I was going to orgasm. Here, in front of everyone.

Except I'd never been more unaware of the cameras, the
crew, the endless collection of assistants and techs and makeup
artists and production designers. Because for the past hour I
had his full lips against the sensitive curve of my ear, saying
things to me no lover had *ever* said. Even though I'd thought
about it, pined for it, touched myself to it.

I wanted... I wanted *this. Him.* This gentle, respectful,
intellectual demeanor covering up a man who couldn't control
his baser instincts.

Because of me. Because I pushed Calvin to a dark ledge he
didn't want to acknowledge. But we were both racing towards
it now.

I turned, taking in his wry expression. "Where do you want Cal's hands?" I called to Ray, threading my fingers into the thick trail of hair covering his chest.

I pulled. He winced. I pulled again, barely aware of the *click click* of the shutter lens. "Hot, Lu. Do that again."

I heard a barely perceptible groan from Cal. So I did it again, his cock stirring against my leg. Calvin liked *pain*.

Interesting.

"Okay, okay, before you rip his hair out," Ray said, laughing. "Cal, buddy, hands on her ass."

I cocked my head, letting my hair whip around. Cal hesitated.

"It's not... Cal, it's not real. It's not sexual. She's not going to slap you," Ray said, coming in close. His lens was less than two feet away now.

I re-arranged my face to Ray's verbal cues: *Give me vulnerable. Give me smoldering. Cal's the hot guy at the bar you're about to take home and devour.*

Devour was right.

His hands smoothed down my back and grabbed my ass like he'd been put solely on this Earth to complete that task. I gasped, and he caught it, long fingers sliding between my ass cheeks, hauling me against his lean body.

I licked up his neck, tasting sweat and raindrops. "Are you going to fuck me tonight, Calvin Ellis?" I whispered against his ear.

Every muscle in his body tensed. I grinned, loving this shared feeling of power and control.

Although really, he could have shoved me to my knees and demanded I suck him off in front of all these people, and I would have done it.

God help me, I would have done it.

"I feel like it's the least you can do for keeping a girl on edge for days now. Don't you think?" I bit his ear, dragging the skin between my teeth.

His fingers slipped lower between my ass. My cunt clenched, anticipating. I splayed my hand cross his chest, then caressed down to his stomach. He wasn't a gym rat, wasn't sculpted and hairless like Taylor. But he had the body of someone who was fit because he wanted to be, not because of some abstract desire to look perfect.

His abs flexed beneath the tips of my fingers, and we couldn't stop looking at each other. Staring at each other. *Fuck,* after this everyone would have to know, right?

Ray kept calling out cues, and I followed them, mindlessly, tapping into some muscle memory I'd developed over the past decade that allowed me to be both innocent and sexy-as-sin all at the same time.

The rain whipped against my skin, freezing, but I barely registered it because Cal was molten hot everywhere we touched. Lightning cracked against the beach in front of us, but neither of us jumped.

Click click click went the camera, then Ray's voice, a bit tense. "Listen, I think we need to go back. Like soon."

"Okay," Cal and I both said at the same time, dreamily staring at each other. His eyes were so *green*. I wanted Ray to give us the cue to kiss. I'd done it a million times with other models, and if Taylor was here, he wouldn't have hesitated.

"As in... as in *now*," Ray said. In the distance, I heard sirens, shaking me out of the moment. I stepped back from Calvin, dazed and trembling. He gripped my elbow, a look of concern on his face.

"Right," I said, laughing softly. The rain was pelting harder, almost like hail. Thunderclouds loomed in the distance, and the sirens were growing louder. "Sorry I didn't... I hadn't realized how bad it was getting."

Calvin stepped back from the rock, shaking water out of

his hair. Joanna stepped forward with a towel, and Josie wrapped me in a giant blanket, giving me a squeeze.

"You and Calvin are incredible together." She squeezed again. "Truly."

I nodded, barely making eye contact. My lips were shaking, and Calvin wouldn't look at me. The crew and the camera guys were muttering softly, glancing my way as they spoke. Had it been that obvious? Lightning cracked again, and this time I swallowed a scream.

"And that's a wrap, people. We need to get inside," Ray said, physically pushing me away from the rock and the cliff that would have sent me to my certain death.

I walked, shivering, towards my cabin, only thinking of the words *hot* and *shower*. I watched Calvin walk away, back through those gorgeous, towering trees, not even bothering to cover his head.

Stay, I wanted to say because a hot shower with Cal was suddenly something I wanted more than anything—more than hot tea. More than a good book. Even more than the look of black ink on a crisp white page.

My heart squeezed painfully, a feeling I didn't recognize.

But I'd read about it.

CHAPTER 29

Lucia

H e was expecting me but not in the way I imagined. He'd left no note, had given no indication that he wanted to see me as he'd walked away after the photo shoot, soaking wet and head bowed. *I* had to be the one to come—because I sensed his hesitation as he whispered dirty things in my ear.

He thought we were playing a game.

We weren't.

And as I picked my way along the dark trail that night, I didn't think about a damn thing. Not Paris or my Instagram followers or my waning fame or why I hadn't been able to write a single poetic word in seven years.

I didn't think about how, regardless of what happened tonight, I'd still be leaving in a matter of days—to become the face of a cosmetic line while Calvin went back to programming in a cubicle.

Instead, I thought about how I *felt*, which was wanton. Hot and aching and seeking the shy, sexy nerd who'd gotten under my skin. Who'd worked me into such a frenzy it took every ounce of willpower not to get myself off in the long, steaming shower I'd taken.

But I hadn't—and now, wandering beneath a Big Sur sky, the scent of rain and chaos in the wind, I only wanted to *feel*. Only wanted to do what my body had been made to do—give pleasure. Receive pleasure. After years of denying myself any authentic moments—romantic or otherwise—I felt greedy. Hunger, simple and powerful, pulsing in my veins. Over and over, a rhythm that matched my heartbeat.

I wanted Calvin.

The light from the bookstore guided me the last hundred feet. And how fucking *magical* was that place, lit up, a golden beacon beneath the leaves. So much had happened between those walls: Earth-shattering revelations, words so beautiful you couldn't help but cry. Experiences so perfect they carved themselves into your bones. I felt it even more strongly now as I approached, opening the back door I knew would be unlocked. Walking past the bedroom, the kitchen and into the Big Room. A fire roared in the fireplace, casting Cal in a warm glow.

He was sitting, staring into the flames. Whiskey in his right hand, journal in his left. Hair a little mussed, scruffy jaw, those glasses. He looked up, and a riot of emotions crossed his face.

"What are you writing about?" I asked, leaning against the doorway.

"I want to write about you," he said simply. "But I'm stopping myself."

I paused while we stared at each other. "Why would you do that?"

He looked pained. "Because it's not right. Because you live in a world with a million admirers. You don't need one more."

I took two steps closer, feeling the fire lick along my calves, the arches of my feet. "Who says?"

"I do," he replied. "I let myself... I let myself get out of control. Earlier. In the rain. I'm sorry about that."

"I'm not," I said, reaching up to undo the pin holding my hair in place. It tumbled down to my shoulders. "I'm not the least bit sorry about that."

"You should be," he said, eyes trailing up my legs, stopping at the junction between my thighs. I was already wet. Soaking. I slowly unbuttoned the long shirt I was wearing. I was naked underneath.

His fingers tightened on the glass. "This is reckless. You realize that?"

I shook my head. "I don't think so."

"You're a goddamn *supermodel*."

"And you need to stop thinking so hard," I said, letting the shirt fall away from my shoulders. I knew the effect I had. I knew what my body looked like. I loved it, was proud of it. But nothing prepared me for the look of total reverence that descended on his face, like he would have crawled a thousand miles for the privilege to pray at my feet.

I sank to my knees. The glass broke.

Amber liquid ran through his fingers, but he didn't notice.

"What the hell are you doing?" he asked, voice dangerously quiet.

"You make me feel—" I said before I could stop myself. Because I was naked and on my knees and a sexy man was looking at me like he wanted to eat me for every single meal for the rest of his life. "I know it's reckless. We met four days ago. But you make me... *want* again."

His throat worked, liquid dripping onto the floor. I moved forward, onto my hands and knees.

"Lucia," he rasped. A warning. I didn't heed it. I crawled forward an inch, eyes on him.

"You need to stop," he said, but he was leaning forward,

watching me. I loved it. Had never crawled on my hands and knees to a man before, but I fucking *loved it*.

"No," I said. "You want this."

"Doesn't matter if I want it."

"You *deserve* this," I said, crawling until I reached him. I looked up, suddenly unsure. Nervous. But then I bent down, my ass in the air, and I kissed his fucking feet.

I heard a low growl, like an animal about to attack. I lifted my head, sat back on my knees primly. Raised my gaze to meet his.

"You promised me a reward," I finally said.

"Good girls get rewards. This—" he said, voice uneven. "—is not good. You know better."

I cocked my head with a wry grin. "Maybe I don't."

In an instant, I was hauled up on his lap, my wrists pinned behind my back. I tried to settle onto his cock, but he stopped me, holding me up. Keeping his gaze on me, he slowly removed his glasses. His eyes were emerald and fire.

"I want to give you everything," he said, suddenly serious. He kissed up my neck, heading towards my lips. I needed to reassure him, needed him to know I could handle whatever he wanted to give.

"Give it to me, Cal," I said. "I *need* this." I didn't have time to think about how I'd stumbled over the word *this* wanting desperately to say *you* because Cal was kissing me, and my world exploded. His lips moved over mine, learning me, tasting me, licking into my mouth.

Calvin kissed like a fucking dream. The fire crackled. His hand trapped my wrists. I tried to thrust my hips, to find friction somewhere, but he wouldn't let me, keeping me from the pleasure I craved.

He settled back for a moment, just looking. I moaned, twisting in his grasp. He stared at me so long I could *feel* it, feel his eyes like a caress. Up my legs, around my hips, along my collarbone. I was panting, watching him watch me. The transformation was incredible—gone was the nervousness, the shy demeanor. A week ago, Cal couldn't even maintain eye contact with me; now he *owned* me.

His fingers traced up to my nipple, his lips circling the other one. "Have you ever come this way?"

I closed my eyes, leaning back. What he was doing was so... so...

"What way?" His tongue flicked over my nipple, and I swear I felt it on my clit.

"Nipple stimulation," he said, pinching with his fingers, lapping with his tongue.

"I don't..." I was struggling to focus, struggling to breathe.

Dimly, I heard the storm outside start up again, a loud crack of thunder that shook the foundation of the store. Or maybe that was Cal, playing my body like his favorite instrument. The sensations shimmered through me, unfurled like leaves greeting the sun.

"No," I finally said, and he chuckled against my skin. He kept sucking, scraping his teeth, and I cried out. The pain was something else... only it wasn't pain but merely the knife's edge of pleasure, and he kept me dancing on it for what felt like hours. Nothing but my panting, moaning cries and his sounds of total enchantment. Nothing but his lips, his tongue, his teeth, his skilled fingers moving over my nipples—now so sensitive I could barely form coherent thought.

"So close," I kept moaning, over and over. "So *fucking close Cal please*," I heard myself beg, but he wouldn't stop, just kept methodically bringing me to the edge.

My legs were trembling, and he wrenched me closer, using his body to support mine. I couldn't touch him, couldn't stop him—could only receive this merciless teasing that seemed to have no end. He flicked his tongue quickly, and I knew he'd lick my clit like that. My pussy clenched over and over in time to his tongue, forcing me closer to release, imagining his head between my legs. I could feel the orgasm tightening in my stomach, feel it gathering, ready, so ready, couldn't believe I was going to *come* from this, couldn't believe Cal was going to—

He stopped.

"You mother*fucking bastard*," I groaned between clenched teeth.

He stood in one fluid movement as I wrapped my legs around his waist. Kicked the table away, knocked over the journal, the pen clattering across the floor. His shoes crunched over the dull shards of the whiskey glass.

Outside a low roar had started up—rain and wind again.

I tried to rub myself against him, but he stopped me again, slamming me against a shelf of books so hard every bit of breath left my body.

He pushed, and books fell to the floor, pages open like wings on the ground. I grabbed something, smashing a sign that said Fiction, Women's and a large volume of Margaret Atwood.

Eyes locked with mine, he asked, "Is spanking something that you enjoy?"

"Yes, please," I panted.

He slid me down his hard body, spun me around, and yanked my hips back before I could begin to regain precious air.

"Good girls get rewards," he said calmly before cracking his palm against my ass. I cried out, knocking over a pile of slender paperbacks. "Bad girls—" *crack crack* "—get punished."

He tangled his fingers in my hair, grabbing until I had tears in my eyes. He yanked the upper part of my body up until it was briefly flush against his chest.

"But I know your dirty secret, Lucia," he whispered fiercely.

"What?" I panted. He tweaked my nipples again, and I almost passed out.

"You like the punishment," he growled, throwing me back against the shelf and spanking me so hard I saw double.

Who in the *fuck* was Cal, and how did he know? How did he know how to reach down into the deepest, most intimate parts of myself? I could feel him coming alive, could feel *myself* coming alive under his touch, his mouth, his fervent whispers.

Crack went his palm, one hand still twisting my nipple.

The vibrations from his palm echoed on my clit, deep in my cunt, and within moments I was close again, balanced precariously on the edge, one toe over, ready to fall.

"Calvin, please, I need, I *need*, I *need you*," I begged, out of my mind with lust. I heard a zipper, a condom wrapper, and then the thick head of his cock at my soaking wet entrance.

He slammed every inch inside of me, and I climaxed. I fucking *climaxed*, screaming as he dragged his cock over every nerve ending, dragging out what was probably the best orgasm of my life. He thrust again, and I gripped the bookshelf, novels tumbling to the ground, only able to stand because Cal was holding my hips in a death grip.

One hand went back into my hair as he thrust into me, each thrust rocking the bookshelf, rocking me back to the precipice even as the aftershocks of my orgasm were still sparking up my spine.

He pulled me back against his chest, slapping a hand over my mouth. My eyes rolled back into my head as he continued to fuck me, biting down between my neck and my shoulder.

"You come like a goddamn force of nature," he groaned, breath growing heavy.

He was still in control, but just barely. I moaned against his palm as he circled my clit with his thumb. "You're going to come for me again, Lucia." His thumb circled with the perfect amount of pressure, my back stretched against his chest.

He moved his cock inside me slowly, thoroughly, and it was easy, almost too easy, for another orgasm to ripple through me, gentler this time but no less intense.

I screamed against his palm, body shaking, as he coaxed me through it. "That's it," he rumbled. "I've got you, beautiful. I've got you."

He smoothed the hair back from my forehead, kissing my cheek, my jaw, the corner of my mouth. I sighed happily, languorous with two orgasms, but with Cal's cock still hard and full inside of me. A steady rhythm, and this time the sensations built slowly, deep inside a place I didn't know existed. He was still hard and fully clothed; I was naked and totally blissed out.

He pulled out, turning me around, and kissed me— leisurely, his fingers drifting and slipping inside of me. I hooked my leg around his waist as he stroked my g-spot until I was whimpering again.

Cal pulled back to stare into my eyes—two fingers stroking, working magic on that bundle of nerves.

"Cal," I gasped, feeling my hips start to jerk. "What are you *doing* to me?"

I ripped his shirt open, buttons scattering to the ground, and thread my fingers through his chest hair. I yanked with all my might.

He hissed, a low growl tumbling from his lips. I leaned forward and closed my lips around his jaw, nipping at the skin there. He tasted salty. He tasted like sex. I yanked his hair again, bit his neck. The growl got louder.

He'd broken me in half, exposed my darkest secrets, and I needed to see him broken too. I scratched my nails down his back, drawing blood.

"*Christ*," he groaned, fingers stroking more quickly. I was full-on fucking his fingers now.

"You like pain too?" I moaned against his ear, digging my nails in again.

I reached down to grip his cock, and *Jesus Christ* his cock was amazing. It pulsed against my hand as he tilted his head back, eyes closed in pleasure. I was going to come like this, stroking Cal to orgasm.

I stroked, then pinched his nipple. Stroked and bit his throat. Stroked and pulled his hair. He lost his damn mind, shoving his tongue between my lips, forcing my head back painfully against a row of books until they collapsed to the floor.

He practically *snarled*, hoisting me back up against his waist and crashing me against the shelf again. This time I felt my back bruise and loved it, the pain mixing with the shock of pleasure as he thrust back inside of me.

"Rough, Lucia," he moaned, turning and throwing me against the nearest wall. Picture frames knocked to the ground, his one hand gripping the door frame, the other pinning me in place. "I need you *rough*. I need my handprints on your perfect ass. I need to bruise these pretty hips," he grunted, thrusting faster, his motions suddenly out of control. Desperate.

The sound of our bodies together, the endless *thump thump thump* as he fucked me against a wall. I was on the edge *again*—his words and his cock, hitting my g-spot over and over.

"You're the most beautiful goddamn thing I've ever seen, and I need to fuck you until you can't see straight. Walk straight. Until you've lost count of how many times you've come," he said against my lips, moving his thumb down to circle against my clit.

I screamed then, my third orgasm in an hour threatening to obliterate my senses.

"Oh *god*," I cried out, everything in me snapping. "Calvin, *Calvin, yes*—" and then I watched as his climax took him by surprise, the look of total ecstasy washing over his face.

I followed a second later, kissing him until our breathing slowed, until I felt his arms tremble with exertion. Slowly, he pulled out, lowering me down, holding me tightly—like I was the only thing in the world.

Like I was the only thing that mattered.

He pressed his forehead against mine, cupped my face, thumbs stroking against my cheekbones.

Books, photos, signs, picture frames lay around us, fallen in a bizarre pattern. One of the bookshelves was tipped over. Cal's shirt was ripped, and I'd left huge bite marks on his neck. I knew I'd have bruises everywhere, could already feel a twinge of soreness in my cunt.

There was a poem in this, maybe dozens of poems— because what could be more beautiful than bodies coming together like ours just had? What was more raw, more *real* than this?

Cal looked at me—*really* looked at me, and before his self-doubt could march in, before he could hesitate, I pressed a kiss against his lips.

And said, "Well, *fuck*."

CHAPTER 30

Calvin

I made us a makeshift bed by the fireplace. It was past two in the morning, and I had never been more sexually sated. More in touch with my body and its needs and desires.

I had never been happier.

But even though I'd just fucked Lucia Bell like the world was about to end, I wasn't tired. And I wanted to keep making her feel good.

The entire time I made our bed she sat, curled up in one of the armchairs, wearing my shirt. Her hair was everywhere as she watched me quietly, her blue eyes clear and bright. We didn't say a word to each other, and for the first time in my life, I didn't feel guilty that I'd let my most secret sexual fantasies become a reality.

I re-lit the fire, held my hand out to Lucia. She took it, stepping over the books still littering the floor, and settling onto the blankets I'd laid out.

She lay down on her stomach, head on a pillow, and smiled at me. I massaged her scalp, watched her eyes flutter closed. Massaged her neck, lightly stroked her back—sore and red. I'd bruised her hips, just like I said I would, and now I kissed them, over and over. Rubbed the palm-prints out of her ass, nuzzled her thighs.

"If you keep doing that, I'm going to want to fuck again," she said sleepily, and I laughed.

"You're insatiable," I said, kissing her cheek. I continued to rub her back in large, lazy circles.

"Will you read to me?" she asked, turning onto her side. Illuminated against the fire, she was so fucking beautiful it hurt. No makeup on, hair undone, just natural. Authentic. This wasn't the Lucia Bell of *Maxim* magazine.

She was so much more than that.

"Of course," I said, voice raspy with emotion.

I stood, then stepped over more books, index cards, photos of famous authors with my grandfather, signs. I thought about what she needed in this moment, whose words she wanted to hear. My fingers danced along the spines, the names as familiar to me now as any relative. I picked up *21 Love Poems*, which she said she loved so much.

I didn't think about how she'd be leaving. I didn't think about the severely small odds that I would ever see her again. I was just fully in the moment, about to share words with a beautiful girl after having the best damn sex of my life.

A few minutes later, I settled next to her in the blankets, leaning back against a chair so she could rest her head in my lap. I stroked the golden strands of her hair, flipped through the pages. She hummed gently against my skin every time I scratched along her scalp.

"You make me feel so good," she whispered, nuzzling closer.

I picked up her hand, kissed her palm. "It's an honor," I whispered back. Began reading to her about planets and meadows.

"I'm in love with her words," she said sleepily.

I stroked her hair and kept reading, her eyes growing heavier, the embers of the fire dying.

A substantial silence settled over the bookstore, a completeness. Eventually I shifted her from my lap, pulling the blankets up to her chin. Watched her for a moment, trying to remember every detail: The sweep of her lashes. The freckles on her nose, the way she clutched her hands towards her mouth in slumber.

I wasn't sure what I'd done in this life—or another—to deserve this night, this week, this woman. But I was grateful.

* * *

There's a special kind of feeling in this world when you wake up on the floor and realize you *hadn't* dreamed you'd fucked a gorgeous, funny, poetry-reading supermodel against a bookshelf.

Especially when that same woman wakes you by wrapping her lovely legs around your waist and peppering your face with kisses.

"We've only been asleep for three hours," I said against her lips, amused.

We were lying side-by-side. She was naked—gloriously naked—and as I trailed my palm up her thigh to grab her ass, I wondered, yet again, how this was happening.

"You look hot when you sleep," she said, lips tracing the shell of my ear.

"Really?" I asked, shuddering beneath her touch.

"Mm-hmm," she sighed. "Like a sexy male librarian or something." I laughed, and she giggled.

"If only I'd known this was the secret to getting all the girls." I squeezed her ass, rocking against her pussy.

She laughed again, head thrown back, and I took the opportunity to run my tongue up the column of her throat. I rocked harder, loving the feeling of our bodies moving together in early-morning light, sloppy and messy, just delicious friction.

"How do you do it?" she asked, stopping to meet my gaze.

I stopped too, unsure of what she meant. "Do what?"

Lucia turned away, suddenly shy. "Be..." she bit her lip. "Be one thing last night. Another thing this morning."

I rolled her onto her back, thrust against her again. "You are many things, beautiful. Coy isn't one of them." Thrust again. "Explain."

Her fingernails lanced down my back, re-opening scratches from last night. I hovered my lips over hers as she searched for the right words. "Last night, you were... so *primal,*" she finally said with a sly grin.

Primal didn't begin to describe last night for me. Last night, I was basically a goddamn animal finally let out of its cage.

"This morning you're so... sweet." She kissed me. "Gentle."

I held her hands down, lacing my fingers with her, keeping up a steady rhythm of rubbing my cock right against her clit.

"Maybe I'm both," I finally said since I didn't really have an answer. She was exhaling these breathy moans, smile still on her face.

"Mmmm," she said, turning towards me. "I like that about you." I rocked harder, and she grabbed my ass, pulling me in closer. "And I like *this.*"

"I feel like I'm in high school again," I murmured against her neck. "Dry humping in your parents' basement or something."

She laughed deep in her throat. We couldn't seem to stop kissing each other, touching each other, fitting perfectly together. Lucia's wet heat sliding up and down my cock like some kind of paradise.

And she was still such a mystery to me, the tiny nuggets of information she'd let me see so far painted her as complex. Intriguing. I wanted to know more, wanted to spend more nights reading to her before we fell asleep.

I wanted more nights like last night—to explore this woman who demanded my authentic self when we fucked. Who didn't want me to shy away, to hide it, but to unleash it.

And yet she'd be gone in a few days.

I pushed back those thoughts, focusing on the way her nipples hardened under my fingers. Memories of last night flooded back, of almost bringing her to orgasm this way. The way she thrashed about, trembling, gasping.

"*God*, Cal, this feels good," she sighed, head tilting back, fingers tightening in mine. "Everything you do... everywhere you touch me..."

I shifted her leg up higher, hooking it over my shoulder. Her back arched off the ground, hair fanned around her face. I ground harder, already feeling the beginnings of orgasm tightening at the base of my spine.

"Maybe later I'll fuck you like this," I groaned into her ear, trying to keep our sweet morning-sex sweet but unable to stop the filthy things she inspired in me.

"I'd like that," she moaned, fingernails digging into my skin.

"Dirty girl," I rasped. "You want me to bend you in half." I didn't wait for her answer, hooking her other leg over my shoulder, circling my hips. The new position brought us even closer together. Part of me wanted to fuck her; part of me liked the intense teasing, the fact that we were both close to climax without penetration. That we'd woken after only three hours, too desperate for each other.

"I have so many ideas for you," I said, running my tongue up and down the curve of her ear. Gentle, curious. She panted faster, a flush working its way up her chest. "So many things I want to do to this perfect body."

My index finger slid down the curve of her ass, down to the tight ring of muscle between her cheeks. I circled my finger there, testing. Teasing. Stroking lightly. "You make me want to do illegal things," I said, and she gave me a seductive grin.

"You are full of surprises this morning," she sighed, and she kissed me, sucking my tongue into her mouth. We were balanced on the edge between filthy and sweet, our soft sighs the only sound in the room. Except my finger was pushing gently on her anus, and she was begging me for more. I hesitated for a moment, since this was brand new territory to me, but then my finger slipped inside with a slight pop.

"Jesus *Christ*," she panted. "That's... *fuck* that's... how did you *know?*" And just as quickly, our movements spiraled out of control, our hands clawing at each other, lips bruising, a string of nonsense words spilling from my mouth. I didn't think I could come this way, except as Lucia's climax wracked through her body, mine roared up my spine and stole every bit of breath I had.

I thought she might roll away, but she clung to me instead, shaking, hands in my hair and legs around my back. And when our eyes met, something happened.

A bolt of lightning, an electric current; everything in the bookstore turned a pale blue.

But Lucia glowed, brightly turquoise.

CHAPTER 31

Lucia

The first time I ever saw myself on the cover of a magazine, I was hooked. The first few years of modeling, I did catalog shoots, some smaller stuff. But when I was seventeen, I walked my first runway in Milan —wearing seven-inch heels and a giant headpiece made of heavy metal, no less—and my fame grew from a slow burn to a full-on bonfire.

Sports Illustrated had called my agent, who'd booked it right away. I remember screaming over the phone, my parents giving each other meaningful glances over dinner that night. They knew what it meant.

Now, more than ten years later, I wondered what kind of parents would allow their minor-aged daughter to appear semi-nude on the cover of a national magazine. But that wasn't the kind of thing my parents cared about. They were familiar with the murky gray areas of Hollywood. They lived in them, celebrated them, made money off them. If unions hadn't stepped in, my mother would have gleefully worked a child actor for twelve straight hours and not given it a moment's thought.

At seventeen, I'd just started having the bumbling, awkward sex of teenagers—it *wasn't* sexy. Or erotic. Or hot in any way. But I still knew how to *be* hot and sexy and fuckable for a camera. On the cover (toned down for *Sports Illustrated* —I was still a minor after all), I'm in a classic bikini, big eyes, big hair, bright red lips quirked up. My hands are digging into the sand, knees in the water, a wave splashing up behind me.

The title: *Lucia Bell: The World's Next Supermodel?*

I loved that fucking thing. The article was total nonsense, but if the Milan show had planted me firmly in the world of high fashion, this first cover officially made me a Sex Symbol.

This was before the days of Instagram and Facebook, but I read the online comments on that article obsessively, would refresh the page over and over to make sure I didn't miss a single one. It's a lot to feed a teenager—the instant gratification, the attention. No wonder I became addicted so quickly; it was better than any drug. The most blissful high. Comment after comment of *she's fucking gorgeous. Her body is perfect.* And then I started to get recognized on the street, and that was even better.

And the entire time, I wrote less and less. Read less and less. Stopped worshipping in used bookstores and instead perused the internet for comments about my appearance. I used to see poetry in the world around me, but even at seventeen, I knew there was something almost gruesome about the world I existed in now: the blinking eye of the camera lens, bright lights, slimy directors and agents, stick-thin models doing coke in bathrooms.

A shallow world, vacuous and vapid.

Every so often I'd see it for what it was. I'd look around and wonder how on earth I'd gotten there. How, at seventeen, I was suddenly living the life of a fully-grown adult, flying to Europe by myself and partying with socialites. How had this happened? Who had allowed this?

I still carried my journal with me everywhere, the pages worn thin, but I stopped filling it with stanzas. Because every time I longed for my life to return to normalcy—to get my writing degree or, shit, just go to college—I'd read something else. Be on another magazine cover, walk another runway to widespread acclaim, see my face on a billboard in Times Square and feel my delicate ego grow, like a balloon being filled with air.

Anyone who claims you can't become addicted to fame is a goddamn liar. And I thought I'd never feel a rush like that with anything else. Thought I had ruined myself for all other ways of life.

Until last night. Until Calvin brought me to earth-shattering orgasm three times and then read to me until I fell asleep, stroking my hair.

And then brought me to *another* earth-shattering orgasm.

It wasn't just a physical response I felt. It was words. They'd been hidden somewhere, tucked inside the ventricles of my heart, sleeping in my blood cells. Calvin had shaken them loose.

I had shaken them loose, because last night as I'd crawled towards Calvin, bared myself completely, was as vulnerable and real as I'd ever been, I'd felt a small spark of something else.

I felt *brave*.

CHAPTER 32

Calvin

The first time I ever tried to have sex I was nineteen, a sophomore in college, and feeling the kind of peer pressure all sexually inexperienced people feel when they're suddenly surrounded by people they very much want to have sex with.

I was only friends with nerds, but even still, about half of them were already shacked up with similarly nerdy girls, going to town on each other between board games and marathons of *Battlestar Galactica*. We didn't have parties, so I was left with shyly trying to impress girls in my Engineering 101 classes. My natural social awkwardness didn't dissipate in college—it got stronger, and I spent that sophomore year desperately trying to impress a pretty girl named Kayla. She was a little nerdy, and I think she thought my interests were "cute." At nineteen, mostly my interests were how to get her to take her top off, so I was fine with that—she just needed to be okay with the fact that I had limited sexual experience

But a *lot* of enthusiasm.

I'd started to feel the first stirrings of dominance then, had fantasies that involved ball gags and bound ankles, but I attributed it to being generally sexless for so long. Too much pent-up sexual aggression. I figured it would intensify your fantasies.

I didn't do great with Kayla—at thirty, I was better, but at nineteen, I was so stuck in my head conversation was supremely difficult. Everything I said came out wrong or weird, and I'd spend hours chastising myself. Playing the conversation over in my head, continually analyzing.

Either Kayla had a thing for extreme social anxiety, or she finally took pity on me because one night she came back to my room, and I practically threw my roommate through the window. Pure instinct took over, and half an hour in we were both panting, fumbling for a condom. Which I found, finally, rolling to my side to put it on.

And then rolling right off the top bunk bed.

I landed hard, hard enough to shatter my collarbone and dislocate my left shoulder.

The only things I remember were the school emergency services picking me up off the floor, Kayla wrapped in a blanket with a sympathetic look on her face, and a wild and desperate urge to call out *Wait! Just let me fuck this girl!* The pain was nothing compared to how deeply I felt I needed to be inside her.

And then one of the nurses grabbed my arm the wrong way, and I practically passed out, erection eradicated.

Another sexless, romantically hopeless year passed, and the fantasies came back, stronger this time. I found BDSM websites, submission porn. Thought about girls on their knees, pleading. Thought about the weight of a flogger in my hand, the power. Not all the time, but when it happened, it'd wash over me stronger than a tidal wave, sudden and fierce.

The first time I actually had sex—Rebecca with pink hair and combat boots, punk-nerdy—I lasted for two minutes and thirty seconds, and she never returned my calls. The second, third, and fourth times were similar, but the fantasies continued.

When I landed my first semi-girlfriend senior year of college, we fucked enough that my stamina improved. But when I broached the idea of some light bondage, it wasn't her thing. Same with the next woman. My orgasms were good, but not great, and I was left with an unending feeling of *missing*.

Claire, who I seriously dated for three years and technically *loved*, could not have been bothered. Claire had liked a certain kind of sex—lights off, minimal sounds. When I tried to show her images of what I thought we could do together, she blanched. When I tried to dominate her, encourage her to submit a bit, she seemed to do it just to placate me. Not because it was who she *was*.

It was different. It was... not good.

I was back in the Big Room after an hour of cleaning up the mess Lucia and I had made last night. And this morning. Shelving books soothed me, rain still lightly falling, Chance asleep in the corner of the room. We'd had no customers today because of the rockslide and the unending bad weather, which left me ample time to ruminate on what had happened between Lucia and me.

I needed to go through my grandfather's journals and find some story for Ray to work with, but I couldn't stop writing in my own journal once night had settled.

I always thought what I wanted from a woman wasn't "good" or "right." That it wasn't respectful. Rationally, I knew that wasn't true. Plenty of women enjoyed being dominated sexually, but between my lack of confidence and inability to find a woman to explore it with, I tried my hardest to ignore it. To bury it, put it to rest.

Until Lucia. I can't put into words yet what last night meant to me except to say I felt fully myself. Alive. I wasn't nervous or over-thinking; I was driven by pleasure, carnal need.

And it felt so deliciously good and so wonderfully right I want to do it again and again and again.

Her stay here had been extended a few more days, maybe even a week—through a combination of fate and natural disaster. Did I know what was going to happen at the end of that week? Not at all. Probably what would have happened if the rockslide hadn't obliterated part of the highway. She would have left, back to her world as a glamorous supermodel. I would have stayed here another few weeks, sold the store, and moved on, back to San Jose. Back to *my* world.

I'd have a story, although just thinking about telling anyone about it left me feeling cold. I didn't want anyone to know about a night that was distinctly ours, especially not people who didn't understand the person I was beginning to see beneath the Lucia Bell armor. They'd think I'd banged a hot, model.

But nothing could be further from the truth.

The landline rung, startling the moment, and the last person I expected to hear on the phone was Shannon, one of the investors.

"*Oh*, um, hi there," I mumbled, taken aback. "I didn't expect to hear from you. I still have another week to get back to you, right?"

"That's not why I'm calling," she said smoothly. "Although it's related. We just saw the news about the huge storm and the rockslide, and Peter and I wanted to check on the status of the property."

"Oh," I said. "Like..."

"Like is it damaged?" she said as if speaking to a small child.

"Got it," I said, eyes glancing back at the wall I'd fucked Lucia against. Try as I might, I couldn't get the things to hang straight, like we'd permanently fucked the wall crooked. "Not that I can see," I said. "But I plan to do a full walkthrough after it stops raining. My grandfather built this thing to last," I said, swallowing hard on the last word.

"Good to hear," she said. "And to be clear, if there is significant damage, it could seriously affect our offer. So please let us know as soon as you can. We'll be expecting your call," she said before hanging up the phone.

I sighed, leaning back against the wall, still cradling the phone in my hand. I hadn't really thought about selling this place since Lucia had kissed me. I was sucked into her orbit now, and everything else felt secondary. But I needed to think about it, needed to put shit in order so I could leave Big Sur and get on with my life.

Maybe if there's damage... the thought popped up, unbidden, and I grimaced at the feeling of relief that coursed through my body as I briefly—*briefly*—entertained that thought. I mean, it'd make things easier, wouldn't it?

I'm sorry, but the storm damaged the property, and I'll need to live here at least another year to make sure everything is fixed before I can begin to think about selling.

I called Chance to the bedroom, grabbing a handful of my grandfather's slender black journals and Flannery O'Connor's *A Good Man is Hard to Find*. I needed some gothic literature and for my grandfather's words to convince me to leave this place.

For good.

* * *

I slept fitfully, and in the morning, when I opened my bedroom door, there was an index card propped against it. I bent down to pick it up, the now-familiar sounds of the ocean roaring in the distance, my feet automatically taking me to the kitchen to search for my favorite Walt Whitman coffee mug.

It was Lucia's handwriting, scrawled in blue ink:

Craving, it said at the top, and then a short stanza:
More than what the body needs
It's what the body wants
Fundamentally changing
Cell structures/blood flow
Neat arteries growing flawed/messy
Raw with damaging desire
And a new pulse: thready, like a heart
That's crashing.

The words I wrote last night were feeble compared to this: our night together, compressed into eight short lines. The sound of her hips hitting the wall, the sucking, wet sound of my fingers in her pussy, the grunting, the moaning.

The damaging desire.

And Lucia had *written me a poem*.

CHAPTER 33

Lucia

I 'd written a poem last night.

It hadn't been easy. After soaking my aching body in a hot bath for hours, I found my journal. Re-read some of my favorites, laughed at some of the poems from middle school, high school. So earnest, so much drama. But still more real than some of the things I'd said and done as an adult.

I had a word on my lips. *Craving*. A favorite of mine. Loved the hard 'v', the way it made you bite your lip when you said it. The long 'a' sound, so sensual.

I wrote half a stanza, and it was the worst thing that had ever been written. In all of human history. Ever.

I rolled it up, tossed it in the trashcan.

Wrote another one. Still the absolute worst.

And again. Still bad. But not as bad as the first.

After two hours, I was still drafting, half in journal form, half poetry. Just... putting words on the page.

My favorite writing instructor at the creative writing camp always encouraged us just to put words on a page. That even that simple act was better than nothing—better than giving up. So I did that.

Another hour passed. The night with Calvin played on an endless loop in my mind, and I focused on the crucial, delicate details: his hair falling over his forehead, the flexing of his ass beneath my fingers, the way he somehow managed to be two people at once, rough and gentle. Shy and loud. Sweet and filthy. It was the dichotomy that had me hot and aching after four hours of writing.

I only had one stanza—eight lines—to show for it, but it was enough. It was the first poem I'd written in seven years, and when it was done and finished and I'd left it for Calvin, I walked back through the woods with tears streaming down my face.

The release. Like a hundred-pound albatross flying off my shoulders. Like wildflowers had suddenly burst into bloom, all over my skin. The writer's block was broken, and more than that, I'd felt something split open inside of me, something I'd kept locked up and hidden for years. I couldn't put it back now—hoped, prayed, would do anything to keep it alive, even when we left Big Sur.

Because between my night with Calvin and the hours of writing sensation had flooded back in, sharp and poignant.

The only side effect was a sudden burst of nerves that Cal wouldn't like what I'd written.

Unfortunately, those nerves became a hailstorm that wouldn't cease, keeping me awake until the pink light of dawn. *What if he thought it was bad? What if he didn't like it? What if he told me I sucked at writing poetry?*

I tried deep breathing, meditation, counting sheep. I remembered now the scariest part of writing: other people's opinions. In school, when I could make it to a creative writing class, reading my work out loud—for criticism, for feedback —was the worst part. The praise always helped: something small and precious to think about later, letting it play on repeat in my mind. But the criticism stayed with me in a different way, crystallizing into something hard and immovable.

That happened later with modeling. It was that damn *Sports Illustrated* cover. Buried at the bottom of the marriage proposals and lewd sexual comments was one. Just one. Now, with hindsight, it was so innocuous it was almost funny.

What's with her ears? The person had written. *I mean, she's hot and all, but is it just me or do her ears kind of stick out? Especially the left one.*

I'd never spent more time looking at the human ear than I did that weekend. Looked at my ears from a million different angles. Looked at *other* people's ears, examined baby pictures (Did they stick out when I was born? What about later?), paged through magazines and newspapers.

"Can you get plastic surgery done on your ears?" I'd asked my mother, as casually as possible, on the way to a family function.

"You can pay someone to do plastic surgery on any part of your body," she responded, while in the middle of a phone call with some studio executive. She was barking into a bluetooth every few minutes, and our usual conversational style involved me receiving an answer from her every three minutes.

"Hmmm," I'd said, looking out the window, trying to catch a vague glimpse of my ears in the reflection of the glass. I compared my mother's ears, which looked normal. Maybe... *too* normal.

"Did you get plastic surgery done on your ears?" I'd asked her, and three minutes later she responded with, "Of course not. Although I *have* had thousands of dollars of plastic surgery done in other places. You know that. Why, are you interested in something?"

Her lips. Her forehead (BOTOX). A bit of lipo in the thighs. Also, in retrospect, offering to get a seventeen-year-old plastic surgery should qualify as child abuse.

But she was nothing if not supportive.

"You know, you're not always going to look like that," she'd said, and I'd sunk lower in my seat, dismayed. Three minutes later, she continued. "Women are constantly engaged in a battle with time. The oldest war there is." I rolled my eyes but was secretly listening. "You're going to need plastic surgery at some point, or you won't book jobs anymore. Just the way the world works."

The anxiety eventually died away, only to be replaced with a fascination of the *next* criticism of my body. Or my hair. Or my shoes. Or my teeth. Or the way I spoke to a reporter.

I'd once paid an absurd amount of money to have my (mostly) naturally blonde hair dyed to a rich, mahogany brown. I'd loved it, but the comments from my fans were so swiftly bitter (and upset, like they were taking it *personally*) that I'd dyed it back.

I tossed and turned in bed, hating the highs and lows of my confidence, remembering changing my hair color with a sick feeling in the pit of my stomach. My stylist had *tsk-ed tsk-ed*—she'd have to bleach it out—but I didn't feel good about myself until after it was changed back and the encouraging comments came back.

When had my skin become so thin? Afraid to share my writing. Terrified that some stranger I'd never meet thought my *ears* were weird? When did I let strangers start to control the color of my fucking hair?

I must have dozed off for a bit because I woke to Josie letting herself into the cabin about an hour later, mugs of coffee in hand.

"Where have *you* been?" I asked blearily, suddenly so happy for the presence of my best friend.

"Getting us coffee," she said, tossing her tangled hair over her shoulder and pressing a hot mug into my hands. I gripped it, grateful for the warmth and the caffeine, and narrowed my eyes at her.

"You have sex hair again," I accused as she slid onto the bed next to me. Her eyeliner was smeared, and she looked as bleary-eyed as me.

"Me?" she asked, pointing at herself. "I slept here last night."

"Funny because I had horrific insomnia all night and didn't see you come in once. You left while I took my bath."

"I—" she started and then sighed. Took an extraordinarily long sip of coffee. Then said: "I'll only spill if you do."

"Calvin and I had sex," I said, and Josie basically shoved me off the bed.

"Details, *mija*," she demanded, but I shook my head.

"You go first," she whined.

I shook my head again. "Girl, you just lied to me about sleeping here. *You* go first."

She bit her lip, carefully placing her coffee on the nightstand. And then dropped her head in her hands.

"I messed up," she said. "With Gabe."

"I highly doubt that," I said, stroking her hair.

I could see the appeal. He was huge, like a gentle giant, beard and bun and plaid shirts. Different from her, for sure, but Calvin and I were about as opposite as they came.

"It's true, and everything in the world is ruined," she said, voice tiny against her hand.

"Did you have sex again? Is that what this is about?"

"*Yes*," she said. She looked up, eyes wide again.

"Let me guess. Great sex."

"Life-changing."

"Aw, *shit*," I said, clinking my coffee mug against hers. "Cheers to you. Why are you so sad, then?"

"Because I fucking *hate* men. And I never go back twice. But I did, with him... a lot actually." A fierce blush—so unlike her. Josie's attitude towards men now was slash-and-burn. "And I think... I like Gabe."

"You like his dick, you mean."

Her eyes met mine. "Yeah," she lied. "That's probably it." I didn't push her, knew she'd want to talk more about it later. But I did wrap her in a big hug. She smelled like Josie but also woodsy, like bourbon. I was guessing that was Gabe.

"Whatever it is, I'm sure you can undo it," I said. "You always can." After a few minutes she pulled away, re-arranging her features until she looked as devious as she usually did.

"I'm guessing you like Calvin's dick," she said, eyebrow arched.

I did. I *really* did. Could a dick be beautiful? Because if so, Cal's was. Who knew hiding under those layers of awkward, bumbling nerd was a perfectly straight eight-inch cock?

Josie snapped in front of my face. "Earth to Lucia."

"Hello," I said dreamily. "What were we talking about?"

She tossed a pillow at my face. "Tell me about how you made all of Cal's nerd dreams come true."

I shifted on the bed, tucking my legs beneath me. "It wasn't like that," I said. "It wasn't... it wasn't what you'd think. Calvin is... Calvin was *extraordinary*," I breathed, and a look came over Josie's face that told me she knew exactly what I was talking about.

"Yeah?" she asked.

I gave her the down-and-dirty details, and by the end, she was gripping her mug so tightly I thought she'd break it.

"Jesus."

"Yeah."

"Jesus."

"I *know*, right?" I said.

"What are you going to do?" she asked.

"Spend our extra days here bringing each other to earth-shattering orgasm over and over again," I said. "And I, well... I wrote him a poem last night."

"You did what?" she asked, head tilted.

"I wrote. For a long time actually. And it was *terrible*," I said, smiling. "But then... it wasn't so terrible. And I composed something. For Cal. About... about our night. And left it for him." An uprising in my stomach, the anxiety back in full force. "But then all I could think about was that he probably hated it. And thus—" I said, pointing at the wrecked bed. "The horrific insomnia."

"It's like the ears thing all over again," she said, sighing.

I nodded solemnly. "Yep. I can't handle the heat, Jo. I've never been able to do that."

"Stop," she said, shaking her head. "Not many people could do your job. It's not just... it's not just once in a while. You are criticized *constantly* for every little thing that you do. I couldn't do it. I'd never leave the house. I'd be terrified."

I swallowed, thinking. Was that it?

"But also," she said gently. "Lu, what are you going to do? About Calvin?"

"What do you mean?" I asked, sipping my now-cold coffee

"In a week, you're going home. We all are. If not sooner. The road crews could finish tomorrow, and Ray would have us out of here in a minute, back to LA."

"I know. So?"

"So, you wrote a poem for a man you *like* who just rocked your world sexually. And you're just going to... leave him? And not just back to Los Angeles but all the way to Paris?"

I chewed on my lip, attempting a nonchalant shrug. "I just want to enjoy this week. *You* should too. With Gabe. We'll take it one day at a time."

"Sure," she said, heading towards the shower. "I guess you're right."

"You know I am," I teased, trying to lighten the mood. "Come on, it'll be fun. A *bonus* week of sex and adventure in Big Sur. What could possibly go wrong?"

CHAPTER 34

Calvin

L ate at night I'd finally found the passage I was looking for—the narrative Ray needed:

Spent the night at Fenix too drunk and too stoned to drive home. Readings for a full week at the bookstore, culminating in Pete, the owner, letting us have a giant party. He closed the restaurant off from other patrons, and I sat around with a bunch of writers and idealists, talking the night away around the giant pit fire in the middle of the room. Someone kept jumping up and reciting their favorite poems from memory —Keats, Walt Whitman—and others would do the same, pulling out creased and dog-eared copies of their favorite books from their pockets, their bags, their cars.

I loved being in the same room with people who all had to have a copy of their favorite book on them at all time, for a moment like this. A perfect moment. Saw grown men cry, stanza after stanza, because they thought it was beautiful.

Isn't this what we're alive for? Why else were we put on Earth if not to enjoy the written word? And in the morning, blinking against the harsh sunlight, Pete fried up bacon sandwiches and served strong coffee on the deck, the fog misting over the cliff-side. Nothing could have been better than grease and coffee, fog and ocean, a night well-spent on the floor of an abandoned restaurant as night turned into day. And the day turned into magic.

I'd never been inside Fenix when it was empty. Usually it was so crowded with tourists that you waited hours for a table. But the rockslides had effectively stopped business for a few days, and Pete Jr. (the son of the former owner) was more than happy to let Ray and the crew use their location.

"There was a lot of crossover between these two places," I told Ray, who was scratching his notes into a notebook, nodding along. One half of the restaurant was now hair/make-up/wardrobe, and every cell in my body was aware that Lucia was in the room. Barely dressed. "Parties at the bookstore would end up back here and vice versa. Fenix was more about the music, though, and between the late 1950s and early 1970s, the number of cultural icons—in music *and* literature—that passed between the two was pretty extraordinary."

"Kind of a bell-bottoms and acid type of thing?" Ray asked, and I nodded.

"Spontaneous poetry readings and musical performances happened all the time. A lot of once-in-a-lifetime memories."

"Jimi Hendrix whipping out his guitar after dinner and playing a set," Ray said, grinning. "I fucking love it." He glanced back at Joanna. "*Janis Joplin hair,*" he called out, and she nodded, as if that was a thing a person would just instinctively know how to do.

"I can see it," he said excitedly and then left me, walking over to Lucia and Taylor. "Okay I got it. You two have just fucked in the bathroom, and now you're enjoying drinks right before The Beatles show up."

I swallowed a grin, shaking my head and settling on a bar stool. I'd come along to provide "inspirational narrative" (Ray's words) but also because there was nothing to do at the store—no customers. The internet café was closed (no internet), so I couldn't guiltily check my emails and ignore the ones from Justin inquiring about my exact start date back at the company.

And I couldn't stop thinking about Lucia. Barely twenty-four hours and my thoughts were bordering on obsessive. Or maybe compulsive.

Okay both. I'd re-read her poem so many times I had it memorized. Analyzed what it could possibly mean, what her feelings for me were. If you could have feelings for someone you'd barely known a week.

Could you?

It was still a little stormy outside, and it turned the restaurant into a cozy, bohemian hole-in-the-wall. I grabbed a cup of coffee, settled on a bar stool, and took out my books: the Flannery O'Connor collection and a slim volume of Mary Oliver. Lucia's love for her had re-ignited my interest—plus, since she'd left me something last night, I'd been searching for something to leave her. But I couldn't find the right fit. The right tone to express my gratitude. I wasn't a writer, but I imagined you would have to make yourself pretty vulnerable to do what she had done last night.

And maybe that was why she'd spent this morning avoiding eye contact with me.

Lucia was still in a short, clingy robe, and Joanna was transforming her hair (*Janis Joplin hair*) into a snarled mess. Big as a house and kind of dirty looking. She was grunting with the effort while Lucia sat there, cool as a cucumber, flipping through a magazine. I wandered over as non-awkwardly as I could, and as soon as Josie saw me, she grinned.

Lucia must have told her.

"Mornin'," I said, lifting my mug of coffee in greeting.

Josie gave me a slow look, up and down, appraising. Nodding to herself.

"Good morning to you too, Calvin," she said, testing blush on her skin. She tossed me a wink, and I coughed a little on my coffee, sliding my glasses up my nose. Lucia didn't look at me, still staring at her magazine. Josie noticed and tossed me a sympathetic look.

"Hey Cal, thanks for standing in for me, man," Taylor said, walking up to clap a hand on my shoulder. "That was maybe the worst food poisoning I ever had."

"Sorry to hear that," I mumbled. "But also...you know, it was no big deal. Any time." *Yes, any time. Any time, please let me run my hands all over Lucia's near-naked body.*

"I saw the shots, though. Ray showed them to me," Taylor said, allowing himself to be pushed into a fur jacket, no shirt, ripped jeans and combat boots. He looked retro and way too handsome for his own good.

I looked down at my Chuck Taylors, my old *X-Files* shirt. I hadn't shaved, and I felt scruffy and un-glamorous, like your best friend's little brother that you take to the prom because you feel bad for him.

"Oh yeah?" I asked, not wanting to hear his assessment of my modeling debut.

"Wait, I haven't seen them yet," Lucia said, finally looking up.

"Really? They're great. Phenomenal actually. You two have real chemistry," Taylor said, pointing between us and smiling. All three of us—me, Lucia, and Josie—went still as statues.

"Huh," I finally said after what felt like a million years. "That's so funny. Guess I should give up my exciting career to go into modeling."

Taylor laughed, shrugging. "I don't know, man. There was something about the two of you. Ray was going wild about it."

Lucia and I finally made eye contact—just for a second,

but an electric shock went through me when her blue eyes landed on mine.

Like clockwork, Ray appeared, dailies in hand. "You talking about the shoot the other day? I have some of them. Untouched, obviously, but..." Ray laughed in disbelief, handing them to Lucia.

"But what?" she asked before glancing down.

"Shay might want to use these. They're incredible," Ray said simply.

I looked at the photos in Lucia's hand, sure he was pulling my leg. But he wasn't.

The one on top was me, hands on either side of Lucia's head, leaning us back into the rock. Storm clouds in the background and rain on our skin. Our lips, almost touching.

We looked *fiercely* in love.

Fuck.

"Who knew?" she said, tilting her head. Her fingers were trembling just a little. "Calvin the supermodel."

"Er... *right*," I said, laughing nervously. This was too much —too awkward. I needed to get Lucia alone, to tell her how much her poem meant to me. I hadn't responded in kind, like I usually do, so maybe that's why she seemed skittish this morning.

"So, I'm going to find the bathroom and, um, well, use it," I said, backing away slowly, bumping into about six techs and spilling coffee down the front of my shirt. "So..." I quickly glanced at Lucia. "So, yeah," I said, turning away, praying that she got the message. That she would follow me down the winding, dark hallways.

But she didn't.

In the bathroom, I took off my shirt, scrubbed the coffee stains out of it. Put it back on. Examined my appearance in the mirror. Wondered, briefly, how someone like Lucia could *ever* find someone like me attractive. I put my glasses back on, ran my hand through my hair.

I mean, really. Dramatic shots in the rain were one thing. Reality was different.

I looked back down the hallway. Nothing. Jesus, didn't people always do this in the movies? Now I'd just been awkwardly in the bathroom for a really long time.

So I washed my hands resignedly, shrugging at my reflection. Opened the door and came face-to-face with Lucia. Her Janis Joplin hair like a lion's mane, eyes dramatic with black eye shadow. That short fucking robe clinging to her lithe body.

"Sorry," she said, biting her full bottom lip. "I thought you were kind of, you know, wanting me to come back here, but I wasn't sure, and then Ray was asking me all of these questions, and you were still in the bathroom, so I thought maybe you were just, you know, *in* the bathroom, so I wasn't sure, but now here I am, and we're only allowed breaks for five minutes," she finished, breathless and adorable.

I smiled. She smiled. And then I placed my palm against her chest and pushed her into the open pantry closet across the hall. Kicked the door behind us and, in total darkness, pulled her in for a soul-searing kiss.

CHAPTER 35

Lucia

How a man as timid as Calvin could kiss like he'd
spent the entirety of his life *studying* the art of
kissing I'd never understand. Because this was an
all-out assault on my lips—my head bumping against the wall,
his hands crushing my face, his lips and tongue setting every
nerve ending in my body on fucking fire. I held his wrists,
giving it right back to him, our bodies already starting to move
together in a heavy, grinding rhythm.

"We have four minutes now," I said dutifully, tilting my
neck to allow his lips access. His right hand slid up my thigh,
parting my silk robe and cupping my pussy. I opened my
mouth on a moan, but he covered my mouth with his other
hand.

"You're going to have to stay quiet, Lu," he groaned
against my ear, his fingers beginning to rub soft circles right
over my clit. Pleasure began radiating from his fingers,
through my cunt, down to the tips of my toes and the top of
my head.

"Why did you want to see me?" I sighed, loving his mouth

233

against my neck, his fingers working magic between my legs. "And we only have three minutes now."

"I wanted... I *needed* to tell you how much I loved the poem you left me."

Relief coursed through me, washed together with the mounting pleasure, leaving me breathless, practically weightless with total happiness.

"I read it over and over. Committed it to memory," he said. "It was beautiful."

"Oh," I sighed. "I was...I was nervous."

He pulled back, although his fingers kept moving slowly. "Nervous for me to read it?"

"Nervous you wouldn't like it. It's the first thing I've written in seven years. I figured it was terrible," I said, tracing his cheekbones with my fingers.

"You did that for me?" he whispered, and the moment was so perfect, another poem—the consuming darkness, the shape of his lips, our urgent meeting.

I already knew I'd write about it later.

"Yes," I said simply, and then his fingers started moving more quickly. I was going to come, and soon, if he kept it up. "Yes, *yes*, Cal, just like that—" I moaned, my hips pumping against his. I felt him smiling against my lips, the total darkness adding another layer of eroticism. The tiny space, our quickly disappearing time. "Two minutes..."

"I bet a dirty girl like you can come in two minutes," he said, thrusting two of his long fingers inside of me and hooking up, hitting a bundle of nerves that made me briefly black out. His palm ground against my clit, and I bit his shoulder to keep from crying out.

"*Please*," I said, nodding in affirmation, hands fisting in his shirt. I dragged his mouth against mine, practically inhaled his tongue. I was close. Not at the precipice, but I could see it rapidly approaching.

"Good to know," he said, slowing down his movements, lessening the pressure, gently removing his fingers from my pussy. His kisses grew softer, the ending of something.

"Wait, what?" I panted. "You're not really going to stop?"

"I get to do whatever I want to you, Lucia. You know that." He bit my earlobe.

I shivered. "You're going to torture me all day?" I asked, furious and frustrated and so turned on I could barely stand.

"I don't know," he said, straightening my hair, closing my robe, making me look like I hadn't just been ravaged in a broom closet. "That depends on how many times you're able to sneak down here to meet me."

"For five minutes at a time," I whimpered, wanting to stomp my foot like a teenager being grounded.

His corresponding grin was downright *smug*.

"Sounds about right," he said and then kissed me so sweetly my head spun.

When he pulled back, my eyes narrowed. "You think you can kiss me like that and get me to forget you're a sadistic son of a bitch?"

Cal arched his eyebrow. "Do you have a counter-strike planned?"

I brushed my hair from my shoulders, cocked my hip. "Please. I might not even meet you down here," I said, leaning forward to run the tip of my finger up the length of his cock. He shuddered. "I might leave you down here all day, knowing that I'm walking around upstairs, naked and glistening, and you're hard as a fucking rock with no relief in sight."

Cal's lips quirked up as he stared me down, intrigued.

I maintained my haughty demeanor, even though my legs were shaking and I would have given *all* the royalties from the entirety of this photo shoot to shove Cal's head between my legs and make him finish me off.

Twice.

I felt the familiar buzz of my phone alarm, letting me know it was two minutes past Ray's allotted five-minute break. I took it out, turned it off, kept eye contact with Calvin. He opened the door of the broom closet.

"After you," he said, like the gentleman that he wasn't. I fake-saluted him and then enjoyed the fact that he had to watch my ass the entire way down the hallway. I could practically *hear* his erection, and when I turned back to toss him one last sassy wink, he was staring at me with such voraciousness I tripped.

The entire crew saw it too.

"Where the hell have you been, Lu?" Ray asked, tapping the face of his watch. "Time's wasting away." I rolled my eyes.

"It's *fine*, Ray. Can't a girl have five minutes to herself in the *bathroom*?"

"Seven minutes. And no," Ray said, and I glanced back at Cal. Gave him a look, as in *see what I mean*?

But then again, if Calvin Ellis thought he could get me off in five-minute increments over the course of a five-hour photo shoot, I was willing to let him try.

CHAPTER 36

Calvin

We were an hour into the photo shoot, approaching the first call for a five-minute break from Ray, and I was only 40% sure Lucia would meet me for our five minutes in heaven in the broom closet.

What she *was* doing, however, was giving as good as she was getting.

It started when she began changing right in front of me. In front of everyone, really, but no one seemed to care, used to models stripping off clothes throughout the day. But she'd always used a privacy screen—until now.

Now I had to pretend to read my books with the willpower of a goddamn saint. Because every twenty minutes or so, Ray would yell "*change*," and she'd pop out of whatever strange pose she was holding and immediately strip down to the pale white thong she was wearing. And nothing fucking else.

"You know, Ray," she called out at one point, "I kind of like that this shirt shows my nipples. What do you think? Very boho, very vintage, huh?" she said, pulling the fabric tight against the nipples in question.

"Provocative," Ray said, snapping his fingers. "Shay'll love it."

Lu bent over constantly and took every opportunity to look at me while she was on camera. Sucking her fingers between her lips. Arching her back.

"Fucking *inspired*, Lu," Ray called out. "This is gonna get us banned in all the magazines," he said to laughter from the set.

A few minutes before the break, I gave Lu a pointed, pained look. *You won*, I tried to convey so hard I could barely see straight.

I paced in the tiny broom closet—well, not really, but I could walk a step, turn, and walk another step. My hand pressed against my cock, sensation coursing through me.

I glanced at my watch. She wasn't coming, and she was right after all—here I was, no relief in sight, my only comfort the endless images in my mind of her beautiful, tanned body. Her breasts, small and perfectly rounded. Those *legs* went on for days, toned like a dancer's. Jesus, I was going to have to jerk off, or I wouldn't be able to go back out there.

She'd really won, and the dominant side of me was aroused yet furious. I saw punishments in my mind—days of orgasm denial, keeping her tied to my bed and on the edge from sun up to sun down. I liked that fantasy. Liked it a lot, and my cock was out and in my hand when Lucia slid through the door. Dropped to her knees. Took the entire length of me in her wet, warm mouth.

"Sorry I'm late," she said, running her tongue to the top, closing her eyes in pleasure. "And you taste delicious."

I fisted both of my hands in her hair, watched in total amazement and wonder as my blonde goddess sucked my cock with total devotion. I was panting, unable to stop, even though I knew I needed to be quiet. Even though I didn't want to come, didn't want to give her the satisfaction, *needed* her to come first, over and over.

"How many..." I started to say, head falling back on a groan as she hollowed her cheeks with suction. "Holy *fuck,* Lucia," I rasped, and she looked up at me, not playfully. Not bratty or defiant. But shining with arousal.

"One more minute," she sighed, tongue working quickly over the head, so I hauled her up, and she squealed, laughing, as I pushed her against the wall. Yanked down the flimsy shirt she wore and sucked her nipple into my mouth, slid my fingers inside her hot cunt, the pad of my index finger gliding against her g-spot.

"If I was a poet, Lucia, I'd write a goddamned sonnet about this pussy," I growled, biting her nipple and then licking it tenderly.

"Forty-five... forty-five seconds," she breathed, back arched against the wall. "And don't stop, *please don't stop.*"

"Lucia, I'd love nothing more than to feel you climax on my fingers right now," I said, flattening my tongue and moving it over both of her nipples. "The way you'd drench me, I'd carry your scent on me for the rest of the day. Fucking getting *off* on it."

"Twenty seconds. *Calvin please fuck me,*" she begged, and *that's* what I wanted, what I *needed* from Lucia right now. Not on her knees and owning my cock but up against a wall and mindlessly seeking the release only I could give her.

And then her phone buzzed: the alarm, signaling the end of our time together.

Lucia slapped her hand against the wall and let out a string of curses that would have made prison inmates blush.

"I can't go out there," she said. "I'm going to accidentally brush against a table leg or something and come in front of everyone."

"I'd pay good money to see that," I said, stroking her hair, kissing her cheek. Trying to soothe her, but who was I kidding —even as we tried to break apart, one of us would keep grabbing the other, and even now she was stroking my cock through my pants, grinding her palm against it.

Her phone started to ring, and her head fell against my shoulder.

"Calvin," she whined.

"Lucia," I replied, rubbing her back, nuzzling her ear. "When we get more than five minutes together today, I'm going to fuck you so deeply you'll feel me there for weeks." She gave me a look of such longing I had to kiss her, kept kissing her until she answered her phone.

"Yes, Ray," she said, mouth still against mine. I heard a fiery volley of words that had her rolling her eyes in the near-darkness. "Don't make me Norma Rae all over this fucking photo shoot," she replied calmly, pulling herself together, pressing a kiss against my cheek and exiting the broom closet.

She was laughing into the phone now, and I heard that sunshine-sound echo as I watched her walk down the hallway and away from me, the intensity of our moment together not gone but burrowed beneath my skin.

CHAPTER 37

Lucia

"I'm going to demand a lunch break," I moaned, my fingers in Calvin's hair. "Thirty fucking minutes lo— oh *fuck*, yes."

He responded by growling against my skin, and I felt the vibrations in my stomach. Another hour of sweet torture had gone by, and as soon as I'd skipped down here (run, really, although I'd never tell Calvin that), he'd shoved my floaty, ephemeral skirt up above my hips, fell to his knees, and plunged his tongue inside of me. One knee hooked over his shoulder, his thumb kept teasing around my clit, never quite hitting it as he devoured me.

He licked so deep I saw stars, and I was so used to being kept on the cliffs-edge of orgasm at this point I welcomed it, tried to sneakily get there without Cal realizing it.

But the man could read my body like a book, backing off just as my hips would buck against his lips.

"Christ, you're good at that," I groaned, knowing we had less than two minutes left. "What do I have to do to get you to let me... to let me..." I stilled, body poised for flight because his tongue was now tracing my clit in slow, lazy circles, and my orgasm was rushing up like high tide. I made the mistake of tightening my hold on his hair, grinding on his face, and he stopped, standing up to lick his tongue into my mouth.

I bit down on it, giving his chest hair a good yank.

"You're such an asshole," I said, biting his tongue again.

"And you're driving me *out of my mind*," he said against my mouth, hoisting me up against the wall and spreading my legs as wide as they would go.

He dragged his hard cock against my clit, and only his palm against my mouth stopped the entire restaurant from hearing my scream of pleasure.

"When will that lunch break be?" Another thrust. His biceps were bunched against my thighs, the veins of his neck standing out. A drop of sweat slid down his throat, and I caught it with my tongue.

"Soon," I said. "Soon soon *soon*," and then my fucking phone alarm went off, and we both groaned in frustration so loudly there was no way we weren't going to get caught.

"Okay, okay," I said, trying to calm us down. "Let me talk to Ray. I'll tell him my... I don't know, my blood sugar is low or something, and I need to eat." I sighed because Cal was still rocking against me while licking my neck at the same time. I was literally just a bundle of nerves, primed to go off.

"Do it," he commanded, dropping me quickly and backing away. "You're um... you're—" he said, pointing and I looked down. He'd practically shredded the outfit I was wearing.

"I'll have to tell everyone this happened in the bathroom," I said with a wry smile. "Quick. Give me a reason."

"Swordfight with a dragon," he suggested. "Or an encounter with a werewolf. It *is* a full moon."

"Maybe a coyote? Are there coyotes in Big Sur?" I tried to put the dozen floaty skirt layers back in place, pushing my Janis Joplin hair out of my eyes.

"Toilet fought back?" Cal said, chuckling a little.

I shoved him playfully. "So I *shouldn't* say it's because I've been sneaking down here to let you dry-fuck me to the edge of orgasm."

Cal pressed his hand against my cheek, and I leaned against it, a moment that was sweet until his thumb brushed my lips, and I sucked it into my mouth.

"Lunch break," he rasped.

I nodded, then bit his thumb hard enough to draw blood.

CHAPTER 38

Calvin

I t was still another forty-five minutes before Lucia could talk Ray into a break. Even Taylor was against it.

"Lu, come on. Just chug a handful of almonds so we can push through the final hours. We'll get done faster, and then we can grab dinner in town or something," he said, stretching his neck out and sipping lemon water.

I was dutifully turning the pages of my book, pretending not to care, cultivating a kind of nonchalance I was faking the hell out of.

"Ray," Lu said, ignoring Taylor. "I need a break. We've been going hard this whole time and... well, my blood sugar is low."

Ray arched an eyebrow. "Your *blood sugar* is low? You've never complained of that before."

"Well, it's a thing I have now," she said, hand on her hip. She nodded at the crew. "Come on, don't you guys want an actual lunch break?"

"It's true," Josie said, stepping in to save the day. I shot her the kind of look a drowning person gives their rescuer. "Her blood sugar has been way low this entire time, really. She needs to sit down and eat something."

"For at least thirty minutes," she said. Her cheeks flushed a little. "Maybe even forty-five minutes."

What I would do to Lucia Bell in forty-five minutes.

"How do you know her blood sugar is low?" Ray asked, narrowing his eyes at Josie.

She shrugged. "Best friend thing." She paused. "You wouldn't know about it."

There was a long silence in which I saw my life end (cause of death: blue balls), but then Ray reluctantly nodded. "You get twenty-five minutes. And then you're back here until we're done shooting. No more breaks."

He'd barely finished speaking, and I was already sidling towards the door. Lucia caught my eye, and I mouthed the word *car* to her. She gave me the briefest of nods before saying loudly, "Well, I'm off to go take my lunch outside."

"Hey, I'll come with you," Taylor said genuinely, standing up. She shook her head forcefully, and he stepped back, a little hurt.

"No, oh, shit, I mean, sorry, Tay. I just, the low blood sugar," she said, fluttering her hand up to her forehead. I thought Josie was going to burst, her shoulders shaking in silent laughter. "I need to be alone for a bit. Is that okay?"

But before he could even answer, she'd grabbed a banana and a bottle of water and walked towards the other door.

I left—exhaling the longest, horniest breath of my life— before walking around the back end of the restaurant and digging for my keys. The air was almost balmy with the threat of rain, the waves angry-sounding against the shore, mirroring the pull of my body towards Lucia, who was walking towards me looking like a fantasy.

We reached the car at the same time, her hands all over me

as I tried to pull my keys from my pocket and slip them into the lock.

"Twenty-four minutes," she whispered, shoving her hands beneath my shirt and sliding them up my chest. The key finally *clicked*, and I threw the door open, shoving her into the back seat.

"Take your fucking clothes off," I said, tossing off my shirt and yanking my pants off.

"Do we have time?" she breathed, fingers at her lips, staring at my body.

"I need to feel you," I said, finding the condom I'd stuck in my jeans pocket this morning. "Off," I said, but she was already halfway naked, kicking off her dress and sliding over until she straddled me, her hair like a curtain, sheltering us from the real world.

Her bare breasts brushing against my chest, my arms wrapping around her naked back. With trembling fingers, she took the condom, slid it on. And slammed herself down my cock, taking every single inch of me.

The sound we made together wasn't human.

"Oh my *fucking god*," Lucia screamed as I snarled against her neck, marking her with my teeth. Nothing had ever felt as good, as right, as *tight*. I squeezed her ass, spreading her cheeks as she rode me. Fast, sloppy, the only goal to get us both off.

For the first time, I had no words, couldn't think to form a single, coherent thought—just licked her nipples. Pulled her hair. Slapped her ass every time she thrust down. The windows steamed, the car shook. She was clenching around me a minute later, her first orgasm tearing through her, tearing through *us* because I could feel her milking me, her gorgeous face contorted in pleasure, her name falling from my lips.

A tear worked its way down her cheek, and I caught it with my tongue.

"I'm sorry, I'm sorry," she panted, still rocking against me, shuddering. "It just felt... Calvin, I never... it was like..." and I soothed her with a kiss, grabbing her hips and thrusting up into her. Hitting the spot I knew she loved. She screamed again, and in an instant, I had her flat on her back, both legs over my shoulders.

"Never apologize for that," I said. "And now I need you to come again, beautiful," I bit out, the new position intense. I tried to go slow, aware of the angle, but she bucked against me.

"Fuck me *harder*," she groaned, and I spanked her so hard her eyes widened, throat tilted back.

"I'll fuck you—" I grunted, one knee on the car seat, other foot planted. "As hard—" I grabbed onto the ledge of the car window, drilling faster, grinding my pelvis into her clit. I reached down, picked up my shirt and shoved it into her mouth. "—as I fucking *want*."

And then something in me snapped, the need to fuck an orgasm out of her overwhelming, my own orgasm already threatening to spill over. I was a blur of motions, my hips moving faster and deeper than I thought possible, and she climaxed again, clawing at my back, screaming into the cloth, tears streaming down her face, and I came with such ferocity my world went black.

CHAPTER 39

Lucia

"Nine minutes left," I murmured, Cal's body still on mine, my legs around his waist, arms wrapped around his back. I was stroking his shoulder blades, his lips in my hair.

Everything was bliss.

"Do you think anyone noticed?" he asked.

I laughed. "Noticed a car in the parking lot rocking like two people were fucking the shit out of each other in it? Yes. I do think a few people probably noticed."

He moved his head to look at me, grinning. "Good," he said, kissing the tip of my nose, wiping away a wayward tear.

"I feel so embarrassed that I cried," I whispered. I'd never cried during sex before. And *definitely* not after only the second time with someone.

"Please don't," Cal said kindly. "Was it because... I mean, do you know why you cried?"

"I just felt so connected to you all day," I said honestly. "And both of my orgasms were kind of world-shattering. I don't..." I stopped for a moment, collecting my thoughts. "Modeling doesn't leave a lot of time for relationships.

And the brief ones I had were more—" I bit my lip. "—opportunistic I guess. More about image or money. We never talked about anything *real*. And we certainly didn't have sex like this." I shifted beneath him, moving my weight so I could press more tightly against him. "I used to fantasize about it being like this," I said, and Cal's gaze darkened.

"Me too," he said. "Only I used to think it was wrong."

"Why?"

"I'm the nice guy, Lu," Cal said, smiling down at me. "I guess I thought nice guys didn't fuck like this. Treat women like this, like... like an object to be used."

I placed my palm against his face. "I don't feel used. I feel *alive*." He kissed my fingers, threading them together with his. "I think that's why I cried," I said, feeling myself break open in front of Calvin. Feeling this moment lodge itself in the chambers of my heart.

"I feel alive too," he whispered, eyes searching mine. "Thank you. For letting me..."

And that's when we heard Josie's voice, loud across the parking lot. "OH HI RAY," she yelled, and Cal and I jumped up like a couple teenagers caught smoking behind the bleachers. "WAIT DON'T GO OVER THERE. I THINK I SEE WHALES."

"Josie can't act for shit," Cal said, and I started laughing uncontrollably, yanking my underwear from under Cal's leg. He joined in, pulling on his jeans and almost kicking me in the face.

"Watch it, lover boy," I said, kissing his cheek as I handed him his shirt. The shirt he'd shoved into my mouth to quiet my screams. "Sorry I got spit all over this."

"Ah, my favorite shirt from high school."

"*That's* from high school?"

He looked down, pointing at *The X-Files* logo. "Oh yeah.

This shirt got me all the girls. High school chicks dig guys who are into sci-fi."

"I'm sure," I said, rolling my eyes. "You know, I would have had a crush on you if we were in high school."

Cal laughed so hard I thought he'd fall out of the car.

"*You*? No way in hell," he said, pulling up his zipper and finding his left sock.

"Why not? I think you're totally cute," I said, blushing a little, even though not ten minutes earlier I was begging him to fuck me.

His lips quirked up. "Really?" he asked, and I nodded. "I would have thought you were cute in high school too. I had a thing for nerds, especially bookworms."

Cal looked at me in amazement, drinking me in. "We would have caused quite the stir, Lucia Bell."

"Hey, we *would* have been Prom King and Queen." I paused. "If I had gone to prom."

"That's right, I forgot you missed it," he said. "Don't worry, you didn't miss much."

"I wish I'd gone though," I said softly. "I remember I had an event that night, runway, in New York City. I spent the entire time wishing I was putting a corsage on my date's lapel. And then feeling equally as embarrassed that I cared about that kind of thing. Everyone around me was so much older, so much more mature. If I'd told them I was missing my prom that night, they would have laughed at me."

We were out of the car now, and Calvin shyly took my hand. I smiled at him.

"Okay, then," he said, "if we'd gone to prom together, what kind of dress would you have worn?"

I sighed. "Princess-style. Full skirt, corset top. Curls and taffeta just *everywhere*," I said, laughing. "And you would have worn a powder-blue suit."

He grinned. "Yeah?"

"Yeah," I said firmly, seeing it in my mind. "You would have tried to, you know, *dirty dance* on me, but I wouldn't have let you."

He cocked an eyebrow.

"*What?*" I said, fluttering a hand to my chest, "I'm trying to keep my virtue here, Cal." We were nearing the restaurant, and I reluctantly let go of Calvin's hand. I leaned over to whisper in his ear: "But I would have let you deflower me under the bleachers."

And then I planted a kiss on his lips and traipsed back inside.

I was barely able to stand. There was a twinge of soreness between my legs I would remain aware of for the rest of the day. And every time I'd think of the car and what had happened there, I'd grow so flushed even Ray would notice.

"*Focus*, Lu. Where's your head at?" he had to say to me multiple times, but I didn't care.

Cal left after that, back to the store, but his collection of Mary Oliver poems stayed on the bar. Hours went by, and at the end of the shoot, drained and exhausted, I grabbed the slender paperback. Flipped through it to find a note to me, from Calvin, bookmarked in the middle.

Come watch the sunrise from my patio tomorrow. - Cal

My heart tripped over itself, and I smiled so brightly my cheeks hurt.

CHAPTER 40

Lucia

"You know I've only been here seven days, but I've woken with the sunrise on every single one," I said, leaning against the entrance to the bookstore patio. Cal was stretched out with a book on a large deck chair in front of the fire pit, which he'd lit. For the first time in a while, the sun was out. The storm clouds had been cleared away, leaving a clean blue sky. Through the redwoods, you could just make out sly fingers of sunshine beginning to lift from the horizon.

"Good morning," Cal said, voice still husky from sleep. He patted the spot next to him, and I gladly joined, wrapping a blanket around both of us. A steaming mug of coffee was pressed into my hand—the same Virginia Woolf mug from our first day together. Chance slept at our feet. Cal was cute and ruffled in the morning, his thick hair messy and scruff closer to a beard.

"I used to only go to *bed* at sunrise, if you can believe it," I said.

"Wild nights in LA?" he asked.

I shrugged. "Wild nights of being a model. An agent is

always pushing you to 'be seen' at different places, with certain people. Calling the paparazzi and pretending you didn't know they were going to follow you, looking fabulous in a short, slinky dress that the readers of *People Magazine* could then vote on."

Cal's forehead crinkled. "Vote on what?"

"Who wore it better, of course." I said, taking a long, grateful sip of hot coffee.

"Let me guess," Cal said sardonically. "You did."

"Every damn time," I replied. "But we've only been here seven days, and already..." I paused, searching for the right words. "It's like what I told you the other night. Is it wrong to have this kind of reaction to a place? I haven't checked my phone or mindlessly texted friends I no longer like or counted the number of comments I get on Instagram or compared myself to some new, younger model or analyze the way I look in a certain picture." I stopped. I was babbling.

"Do you miss it though?" Cal asked quietly.

"Yes," I said, quickly. "I do. It's been my life since I was fifteen. There's an *adrenaline* to fame. It's different than just sitting here, enjoying the sunrise. Everything is about getting on top, and, when you lose your footing, getting *back* on top. An endless cycle," I said.

"But you still feel different? Like you're changing?"

I turned to look at him, unsure of how to answer. "Do you feel that way? Has Big Sur changed you?"

He sighed, staring out at the forest. I could hear the waves and something else: the absence of cars. Back here, you couldn't hear the constant drone of engines and exhaust pipes, the lullaby I fell asleep to every night in LA.

"You know, my mom and my uncle hated it here," he started. "My grandfather and grandmother, well, they *were* Big Sur. Every single person who lived here attended both of their funerals. They were like... unofficial mayors of this town. And

KATHRYN NOLAN

this bookstore meant *everything* to them. Created entirely in my grandfather's image, but you know my grandmother did more than people realize. I think there's this sense that she was always in the background, but she wasn't. Half the authors who came here were because she'd read them, contacted them, pushed my grandfather to support them. She was a voracious reader. And at night, after my grandfather went to bed, she was the one who'd stay up until dawn, right on this patio, talking with the writers." He paused. "This was a dream they shared equally."

"I would have loved to grow up here," I said. "When I was a little kid, I used to have this fantasy where my parents would discover I had a long-lost uncle or something who owned a bookstore, and they'd send me to live with him. In the bookstore." I smiled at the memory. "I wrote a story about it when I was in fourth grade. It was called *The Girl Who Lived in the Bookshelves*."

"Creepy," Cal said, grinning.

"Oh, totally. And completely unintentional too. I just loved the idea of being a little kid and spending your day between bookshelves, falling asleep on stacks of paperbacks." I shifted on the chair. "The beginning went something like, 'Hey there, readers. *I'm* Lucia, and guess what? I live in a bookstore! But that's not all. Books are my best friends!'"

Cal snorted into his coffee, wrapping his arm around me and squeezing.

"But the title did sound like a horror story. And *anyway,* that was a tangent. Why didn't your mom like it here?"

"My grandparents happened to have children who were the exact opposite of them. They were numbers kids, like I am. Or was. Or—" Cal paused, brow furrowed. "I guess I'm both, to be honest. But my mom ended up going to school for computer engineering, and my uncle is a physicist. They're very rational. They don't go to poetry readings or

254

stay up all night with a good book. They thought all of this —" He indicated the store behind him. "—was kind of pointless."

"But your mom sent you here every summer. She must have thought it had some value."

"True," he said, thinking. "After my grandmother died, I think she saw how lonely my grandfather was. He and I were always very close."

"You're like him," I teased.

He shook his head. "Except for the fact that we share a distinctive nose, we're nothing alike."

"Hmm," I said, finishing my coffee. "I don't know about that." But I let it drop since it was clear to me he was sensitive about it.

And so clear to me that he and his grandfather shared more than just the same nose.

"What are you reading?" I asked, nudging his book with my toe.

"I just finished a Flannery O'Connor anthology."

I made a sound of affirmation. "The first time I read *A Good Man is Hard to Find* I had nightmares for a week."

"I would have loved to peek inside her mind, just for a minute. Or watch her writing process. How did she get so dark?"

"She's a genius," I agreed. "Now what?"

Cal smiled. "More Kerouac. Back to the Beats for a bit. I picked up some Bukowski last night."

"Talk about intense," I said. "Kerouac make you want to fling away the remnants of your former life and embrace something wild?"

"I have to give the investors an answer tomorrow," Cal said. "So no more adventures for me, sadly."

My stomach clenched. "To sell this place," I said. We hadn't spoken about it since that first night in the poetry room. "For some reason, I keep thinking you're *not* going to sell."

"Nope," he said, resolutely. "It's what's best, really. They were concerned about damage from the storm, but luckily there wasn't any. I'll be back in San Jose by the end of the month."

"If you know you're going to sell to them, why haven't you given them an official answer yet?" I asked, curious. I could *feel* his hesitation. Try as he might, Calvin couldn't hide his feelings—they were written all over his face. "Can't you just call them and say yes?"

Awareness washed over his body, and he leaned against me. "Probably, yes," he hedged. "I should, right?"

"It's not my decision," I said softly. "Maybe you just like extending the fantasy a bit longer?"

Cal pressed a quick kiss to the tips of my fingers. "I guess that's what this feels like, running this bookstore in the middle of paradise. A fantasy. Not real life."

"But it *could* be, Calvin," I pressed. "You could make it your life."

"I'm not Kerouac, Lu. I'm just a regular person." Cal looked at me. "Hey, do you remember that night we had the party out here?"

"Of course."

"You surprised me with your literary knowledge. And I remember thinking, well—" He stopped, coughing a little.

"Surprised I wasn't shallow?" I asked with a teasing grin. He reddened, and I reached forward to kiss his cheek. "I'm just giving you a hard time. You wouldn't be the first."

"I feel bad about it now, to be honest," he confessed. "I made such a snap judgment about you. And it was totally wrong."

"It couldn't have been *all* wrong. I am sometimes..." My tongue tripped on the words. "I can be shallow. It's part of the world I live in. But also you're the first person, except for Josie, that I really let myself talk about the things I love with. I usually hide it. People like it when I'm silent and beautiful."

Cal tilted his head. "You're not silent, though. I feel like you've got this huge personality on set. You're so funny. And you're kind of weird sometimes. You're, well, you're very *Lucia*."

I laughed. "Ah, my agent would call that '*getting a reputation*.' When I was twenty, I'd just smile and nod. Now..." I shrugged. "I see more of the bullshit. Eleven years of modeling is a long time. Plus, it gets harder and harder just to sit around and smile prettily. Like you're a piece of finely crafted furniture."

The sun was lifting higher, unyielding, and I had the oddest feeling that Calvin and I were the only ones left on Earth. He ran his fingers through my hair, pulling on a strand to the very end.

"Do you think you'll feel that way in Paris?" he asked, which rocked me back to reality, like having a bucket of ice-cold water thrown in my face. It was so easy to forget, wrapped up in this sweet, sexy man.

"Oh..." I started. "Shit, I don't know. Maybe." I paused. "Probably."

"*Opportunity of a lifetime*," he said, quoting me from the other night. "Even if you do feel that way, it's just two years. Two years, and then *boom*. Your face is everywhere." He paused. "Well, *more* everywhere. I do feel like before you came up here, I saw you on magazine covers all the time."

"Sure, but with modeling... there's always someone younger, prettier, and more exotic coming up from behind you, trying to take your spot. For a twenty-six-year-old to get a makeup contract is a big deal actually."

"I mean, you're *basically* The Crypt Keeper," Cal said dryly.

I rolled my eyes. "I *know* it's ridiculous. But not in modeling. In modeling, I'm a grandmother, someone the younger girls look up to." I paused. "And I say 'girls' because they are literally seventeen years old."

"And yet none of them can hold a candle to you," he said.

"You're sweet."

"I'm being serious. I've watched you every day. The way you transform your face, move your body, the poses you hold... you just *shine*. I don't know what it is, but you've got this light, and everything else seems dim beside you."

I laid my palm against his cheek. "Thank you, Cal. That was... thank you," was all I could say.

We spent about a minute staring into each other's eyes, goofy as lovelorn teenagers.

"Did you write last night?" he finally asked.

"I did," I said, butterflies in my stomach. "And it was all terrible. But also so, so wonderful. Just the sight of pen ink on the cream-white pages of my notebook was enough to keep me going." I paused. "Big Sur is helping me discover there's no better feeling than reclaiming something you thought you'd lost forever."

A moment stretched between us. Nearby, a sudden burst of birdsong. Chance shifted at our feet, paws moving in his dreams.

"Did you write something for me?" Cal finally asked.

"Maybe," I said. "Yesterday was very inspiring," I said, leaning into his hand in my hair. He scratched my scalp lightly and I purred. "Darkness. Our breathing, the condensation on the car window." Cal's gaze darkened, nostrils flaring. "The feeling I got when I'd race down the hallway to meet you." I splayed my hand on my stomach. "Like getting to the top of the roller-coaster. I was so present in the moment, so present in my *life*. The anticipation." I stopped, biting my lip. A few minutes around Cal, and I automatically started to spill like I never did around any other people.

Cal gazed at me, his green eyes standing out against the green of the trees behind him. Leaned forward, thumb tilting my chin up. Kissed me slowly, his lips on mine a sense of two halves coming together. His tongue explored my mouth, fingers moving to grip my hair. I tried to move closer to him, but he kept me in place, content to keep kissing me, his only goal sensation. Touch. Longing. After what felt like hours he finally pulled back, barely an inch, breath hovering. Our eyes met, something searing and honest passing between us.

"What are you doing to me, Lucia Bell?" Cal asked.

"Same thing you're doing to me," I whispered.

In the distance, I heard Cal's landline ring. His eyes closed, face pained.

"Do you have to get that?" I whispered.

"Yes," he said. "It's the emergency phone again."

We stayed an inch apart, breathing in each other.

"How come every time we kiss each other, there's an emergency?" I asked, running my tongue along the seam of his lips.

He groaned, but then the phone seemed to get louder, more persistent, and he pressed a kiss to my forehead, standing.

"Hold that thought," he said, taking his coffee and Chance with him.

I settled back against the chair, tilting my face up to catch the first rays of sun. A hummingbird flew past, hovering for a moment in front of me, wings a blur of motion, its head the sultry red of a pomegranate. I wanted to write a poem about this bird, seeking sweet nectar.

If the original calculations were correct, we had at least another five days here. I stretched my legs out, surprised that I was looking forward to five more days being off social media, five more days when my agent and Paris and fans couldn't reach me.

Five more days with Calvin, exploring every inch of his leanly muscled body, memorizing the way pleasure moved through him, moved through me. Maybe we could go for a hike. Maybe he'd take me to the ocean, ravaging me on the sand. Maybe I'd stay up all night reading to him. Maybe—

"Lucia?" Cal said, stepping out. For a second, the sun's rays sparkled behind him.

"Hey," I answered. "What's up?"

"That was Gabe. The road crews worked faster than they originally expected. By midnight tonight, they expect both slides to be officially cleared." He swallowed hard. "It means you'll be leaving tomorrow morning."

CHAPTER 41

Calvin

"You're more than welcome to stay another night," I said, shifting nervously on my feet. "Especially since the expected time for people to be able to access the roads again isn't until after midnight. But, yeah... that's about it. You are officially no longer trapped in Big Sur."

There was a cheer from the camera crew, and Ray was already in motion, a whirling dervish. If we had cell service here, he'd be on a Bluetooth earpiece, coordinating logistics like an air traffic controller. But he didn't have that, so he just barked instructions at people and pulled Taylor and Lucia into the corner. I couldn't hear what he was saying, and Lucia's face was unreadable: professional, nodding in agreement.

I sighed heavily, glancing at the calendar, looking around at the store. I'd meet with the investors tomorrow night—for my "final decision"—and then I needed to call Justin, confirm my start date back at work.

I was suddenly filled with dread. With the sunlight streaming through the wall-to-wall windows, details I hadn't seen for a week were springing to life. The way the index-cards in the children's section weren't white but yellow and shaped like tiny stars. The hand-written love note my grandmother had written—who knows when—that my grandfather had framed next to an article in the *San Francisco Chronicle* calling The Mad Ones a "cultural touchstone for poets, street kids, bohemians. A magnificent display of literature, a Mecca for book-lovers," and stuck to the side of the frame, a Post-it Note with a message scrawled in blue ink: *And I fell in love here. Married fourteen years this spring.*

No indication of who wrote it, just a memory my grandfather saw fit to leave there, as he saw fit to leave all the memories here, woven into the walls, pinned to the ceiling, shoved haphazardly into coffee mugs and tea kettles.

Everyone was whirling around me, so no one noticed that I grabbed my grandfather's journal and settled behind the cash register, sipping my now cold cup of coffee, my delightful morning with Lucia now a distant memory. It was the journal where he recorded his darkest, most anxious thoughts. His regrets, his fears. I needed him to talk me out of the small kernel of an idea that was forcing its way into my consciousness.

From the mid-nineties:

People don't want to spend the day wandering around a bookstore anymore, collecting novels, discussing their favorite authors. Or just sitting in a chair and letting the day slip away. Everything is move-move-move, checking things off a list, our culture pushing people to be too busy, too overbooked, always in a hurry. I don't know if The Mad Ones can stay alive in a culture like that. It is the very antithesis of the American desire to stay in constant motion.

And from just five years ago:

Sometimes feel like I am the only one left who likes to read.

Nothing else—just one line. And it didn't come as a surprise to me either. Just one year out of college, I had almost entirely stopped reading. Too distracted, too tired, too stressed out from work.

As soon as I moved up here, though, it was all I could do. I kept a count by the bed, and in five and a half months, I'd read 128 books. Almost one a day. It was exhilarating, like falling in love again.

And then, from just two years before he died:

Living here is a choice I made, fifty years ago, and I wouldn't change it for the world. Today I visited my children, and we had a lovely dinner where my son, for the first time in years, didn't try to get me to move to the city, into a retirement village. We didn't argue about my lifestyle, and I was able to look around and honestly congratulate them on their new house. I didn't suggest they were corporate drones in a system of greed. And they didn't remind me the Summer of Love had been dead and gone for decades. We'd reached an impasse—both seeing the other's life choices as distinctly theirs to make.

A reminder that Big Sur is only as isolating as you make it. Years when I didn't make it down for holidays or birthday parties: a choice. Or when they didn't come up for poetry readings or concerts I held: a choice. It's a small, wild town, but it's not in Madagascar. Maggie and I certainly didn't expect to have children so different from us, in almost every single way. And it's not been easy, but I think we've taught each other patience. Respect. Each of our lives are our own. What a gift. And what a privilege.

I remembered that dinner. I'd come home for it and remembered how happy I was just to see my grandfather. He'd brought me books, as usual, and we sat together, talking about them excitedly. Usually our family dinners would have at least one tense moment when my mother or uncle would chide him for his "dirty hippie lifestyle," but they didn't this time, somewhat content to let the evening linger happily.

I'd been reading so long that when I looked up most

people were gone, including Lucia. As quickly as she'd appeared in my life, now vanished.

I thought about my grandfather's words: *What a gift. What a privilege.*

I shivered, the meaning not lost on me. Tomorrow night I would sell the store, and after that I had no idea what my future held.

But I had today—Lucia's last day in Big Sur. Our last chance to spend time together before reality rushed back in.

What was I going to do?

CHAPTER 42

Lucia

Josie and I were packing our bags with slow movements and heavy sighs.

"It's not that bad," I said, wondering why on earth I'd packed *so many clothes* since I'd ended up wearing the same yoga pants and giant sweater the entire time. My journal was sitting on the nightstand, safe with the now four (four!) poems I'd written.

"It is," she said, completely miserable. "It's bad, Lu."

"What are you going to do, quit your job and live with Gabe in a bar in the middle of Big Sur?" I asked, feeling desperate.

"I am. Just like you're going to quit modeling to live in this bookstore with Calvin."

My heart shouldn't have been able to slam against my chest so loudly. So excitedly at the prospect of waking up each morning next to Calvin Ellis.

"We need a reality check," I said quickly, coming around to the bed and grasping her hands. "Look at me," I said, and she did, eyes already filled with tears. I swallowed hard since we couldn't both be crying.

"You just met Gabe. One week ago."

"Right."

"How well do you *really* know him?"

She sighed. "I guess... I guess I know him as well as you can know someone in a week. But—"

"No buts," I said firmly since I knew what she was going to say. The same thing I would say: *But it's different than that. Different than anything I'd ever felt before.*

"What conceivable future do you have?"

"None. Which is why this is so terrible. I mean, my career is in LA. My contacts are in LA. There isn't a big need for makeup artists *here*. And Gabe? This place is his life. He's who everyone comes to for wisdom over a drink. For a kind word. He'll probably be the mayor in twenty years."

I was nodding. "Which means leaving here to move to Los Angeles with a woman he barely knows is just not in the cards, now is it?"

Josie's face hardened. "Lucia, who are you trying to convince here?"

I closed my eyes. *Busted.* I leaned forward, letting her wrap her tattooed arms around me. "I'm sorry. I thought... with your history... I don't know. Do you want to be talked into something? Or talked out of something?"

"I think I just want to be sad," she whispered.

"Okay," I said, "I can do that." I leaned back, and she looked so miserable my heart physically hurt.

"I'm guessing Calvin isn't interested in continuing to see you after this?" she asked.

I scoffed. "I haven't... we haven't even... I mean, whenever we're together we have mind-blowing sex and amazing conversations. But we haven't once said anything..." I couldn't even continue since it was so far beyond any realm of possibility. "I think we both knew... it couldn't last past this time. And he

266

knows about Paris, so." I shrugged, attempting to appear nonchalant and failing terribly.

"Here's a radical idea," Josie said, tilting her head.

"Oh no."

"*Don't* go to Paris."

My jaw dropped open dramatically. "Turn down an opportunity of a lifetime for a guy I hardly know?"

"You always say 'opportunity of a lifetime' as if modeling is the only life you're ever going to have." Her tone softened. "You've been unhappy for the past year. I know you've ignored me the past three fucking times—"

"I didn't ignore you," I said defensively, "I heard you. I really did. And I appreciate your concern. But I'm just tired. Burned out. Paris will be different. It's a launching pad."

"Or it's more of the same. The same bullshit. The same fake people. *You* having to smile and nod and eliminate all the interesting parts of your personality."

I sighed. "Josie, don't make this harder on me. You know I need to do this. To stay relevant, to stay on top."

What if instead I let this Shay Miller shoot be my last one, go out with a loud, provocative bang, and then took some time to re-evaluate what I wanted to do next?

Yeah, right. You're a little fame addict.

"You're thinking about it," Josie said, smiling. She shoved me lightly. "Plus, if you go to Paris, I won't be there. You'll have some boring, stodgy makeup artist who won't be your best friend in the entire world." The thought of being separated from her for two years felt like too much burden to bear.

"I mean, who will listen to me obsess over Calvin and whether or not he's dating another supermodel?" I sighed dramatically, although I was secretly serious.

She lay back next to me, our hair a blend of dark and light. "How could he ever date someone again after he's dated The Lucia Bell?"

We laughed, a moment of levity in the middle of a shitty day. Which was a shame since the morning had started so beautifully, so peacefully, watching the sunrise with Calvin.

What if every day started that way?

"You know Paris won't change a thing with us," Josie finally said, softly. "But in all seriousness, I want you to go for *you*. Or not go, for *you*. It's your life; you need to decide what's best for it."

A knock on the door, startling us both. "It's probably Ray, trying to figure out if we can helicopter out of here earlier," I said. Which was funny since a week ago I would have tried to do the same thing. My cell had run out of batteries on Monday, and I hadn't even charged it, content to let it stay at the bottom of my purse.

And when I opened the door to see Calvin standing there, I couldn't fight the way a smile broke across my face.

"Hi," I said.

"Hi," he said.

"*Calvin*," Josie said, tossing him a saucy wink.

I shooed her away, closing the door behind me. "I didn't tell her anything, I promise," I said. "Except that you're a sex god. I did tell her that," I finished, avoiding his gaze. His laughter caught me off-guard.

"Do you want to go on a date with me?" he asked, cheeks so red I thought for sure he'd pass out.

"Um," I said, completely and totally surprised, and he immediately backed up.

"No worries," he said, waving his hand. "You probably have things to do—"

"I'd love to," I said, taking a step closer. "Sorry, you just surprised me is all. I don't have anything to do tonight—"

"—and it's your last night here, I thought, you know, why not make it special?" His smile was timid.

"Yes," I breathed. "I'd absolutely love that."

His smile widened. "Also, I don't know if this is weird or anything, but today is my birthday. My 30th birthday, to be exact."

"*What*?"

"It's not a big deal. I'm not even sure why I'm telling you. I've never been a birthday person, and to be honest, I almost forgot—"

"You almost forgot your own 30th birthday?"

"Yes," he said, looking sheepish. "But, to be fair, my birthday wish was to drink coffee while watching the sunrise with a beautiful, brilliant poet." He reached forward, brushing my hair back from my shoulder. "It came true, so the day has already been absolutely perfect."

My toes curled.

"Let me plan tonight," I said impulsively. "For your birthday. I didn't get you a gift, so let me do this."

He arched an eyebrow. "You sure? Also, there's not much to 'do' here, so if you need recommendations or something, I can help."

I shook my head. "Nope. Just pick me up in your car at eight. I'll handle it from there."

"Okay," he said. "If that's what you want."

"I've already got some ideas," I said, tapping my finger against my temple. Which was bullshit (I had none). "And I'm going to give you a 30th birthday you'll never forget. Promise."

I gave him a salute and a wink, and he responded by backing me against the door and kissing me passionately, both hands squeezing my ass. I looped my arms around his neck, kissing him back happily. When I was breathless and starting to grind against him, he stopped.

"I can't wait," he said against my lips.

* * *

I pooled together all the random brochures that had been left in the tiny cabins, used Ray's landline, and after a couple hours had put together not a half-bad night for Big Sur on a Tuesday after an incredibly damaging storm.

Cal was definitely going to love it.

We were definitely going to fuck.

And we were probably going to be arrested.

Not necessarily in that order.

Josie and I did an entire clothing montage straight from a 90s movie, but in the end, I went with something simple: tight black jeans, ripped at the knees. A black tank top. Hair up in a high bun. And my only nod to my glamorous life: blood-red lipstick.

"Cal's about to have the best 30th birthday any straight man has ever had in the history of the world," Josie said, spinning me around to see my appearance. "And I will bail you out, of course. Unless you want me to let you guys stay in there, and it can turn into a *sexy* jail stay?" She waggled her eyebrows.

I tapped my cheek, thought about it. "You know, I bet Big Sur doesn't even have a jail cell. You just have to sit quietly for a little bit and then say you're sorry."

"Aw, *sweet.*"

"But yes, please do bail us out," I said, laughing. "And thanks for the clothing montage. And the support. And for not telling me that seeing Cal one last time tonight is only going to make tomorrow even harder."

"You're welcome. And thank you for not doing the same thing when I tell you I'm also going to see Gabe tonight."

I gave a little cheer, tossing the red lipstick her way. "Lucky lady! You're just now telling me?"

She looked bashful—so not Josie. "It's after he helps you with your date."

"Small role," I said, pinching my fingers together. "I'll only need him for, like, an hour tops."

"No, it's good. He's a good friend to Cal. I like seeing that. Clarke didn't have friends the way Gabe does, didn't have relationships the way Gabe does. Gabe is..." She splayed her palms out. "Just really fucking kind."

Oh Josie. The last time I'd seen her like this, Clarke had just proposed.

"I think that's beautiful, Jo. Tell him what you're feeling. Just be honest."

She snorted. "I will if you will." We stared each other down for about thirty seconds before I said, "Fine. I'll do it."

"Same." She reached her hand out. "Pinky swear, *chica*." I did it, my heart slamming against my ribcage.

"Let's go be brave," I said, and like clockwork, I heard Calvin knock on the door.

CHAPTER 43

Calvin

When Lucia opened the door, I realized two things: I was about to go on a date with the most beautiful woman in the world.

And I was totally overdressed.

"Jaw closed, Cal," she teased, closing the door behind her. She was in tight black jeans that hugged every gorgeous curve. Her delicate neck exposed. Cheekbones that could cut glass. Full lips glossed in crimson.

I swallowed, couldn't find any words to adequately express how perfect she looked. So instead I brought my left hand from behind my back, producing a sprig of jacaranda I'd cut from the garden.

"I love this flower," I said. "And every time I see it, since you've come here, I think of you. It's so vibrant. All these other flowers bloom near it, but it stands out from the rest." I paused. "Just like you." I was looking down at my feet but glanced up, bravely, to catch a swirl of emotions on Lucia's face.

She took it from me, fingers brushing mine. "Thank you. So much. It's beautiful. I have these growing in my yard back home. Hummingbirds love them," she said, tracing the frail petals. She reached up, weaving it into the mass of hair on top of her head. "How does it look?" she asked, striking a quick pose.

"Perfect," I said. "And, uh, sorry I'm so overdressed." She looked trendy and cool, like we were going to a coffee shop. I was wearing a dark gray suit. Like I was going to a funeral. "I haven't been on a date in a little while. Kind of forgot the rules."

She shook her head, pressing her fingers against my lips and stepping closer. "You look incredibly handsome." And then she did a quick walk around me, hand in her chin. "Actually, Cal... I think the word *People* Magazine would use is *hot*."

I laughed, hands in my pockets. "Right," I said sarcastically, but I appreciated it. I'd taken my glasses off for the evening, shaved away the stubble. Tried my hardest to look like the kind of man who might be attractive enough to take a woman like Lucia Bell on a date.

"Shall we?" I asked, holding out my arm. She linked hers through it. "Also, where are we going?"

She laughed. "It's a surprise, Cal. Just sit back and enjoy the ride." She fished her hands in my pocket, fingers just grazing my cock. And then pulled out my keys.

"And I'm driving," she said as we started our way through the trail back through the woods, linking her hand through mine. It was an amazing night—stars silvery in the black sky. Oddly warm, everything feeling clean after the torrential downpour of the last week. Lucia nimbly stepped over logs and rocks.

"Look at you. You've got this trail memorized now," I said, impressed.

She looked back at me, smiling. "I've walked it enough. I love it. It's like walking through a secret tunnel to two

273

wonderful things. On the one end, a beautiful ocean. On the other, all the books you could ever want."

I squeezed her fingers, agreeing.

"So when was the last time you went on a date?" she asked.

I thought back. "Honestly, probably almost four years ago. Claire and I only broke up about six months before my grandfather died, and we were together for three years."

"Serious, then?"

"Ye-es," I hedged. "We did live together but only because it seemed like the right thing to do. The next step. Claire and I weren't a good match. I think I checked off all the boxes for her: nice, a good job, a car, no criminal background. And I'd never had a long-term relationship before, so all the classic warning signs that it was time to break up flew right past me."

"She dumped you? Or—"

"She broke up with me, yeah. Which isn't to say it wasn't pretty much amicable, but Claire was like that. See a problem, solve it. And I was a problem. We weren't compatible really, except that we lived in the same city, both worked in the tech industry." I shrugged. "She didn't like the things I liked and wasn't willing to give them a try."

"I'm guessing no *Star Wars* conventions?" she asked but seriously. Not teasing.

"No, uh, nope. She was always begging me to not bring those things up when we had dinner with friends or at parties. But in all my years as a total nerd, there's one thing I know—most people are nerds. Your nerd interests might not be the same, but I just like meeting other people who are as passionate about, I don't know, *forks* as I am about science fiction. Or gaming. Or *Star Wars* conventions, yeah. Claire was the opposite of passion. She liked things appropriate, always in forward motion." We both stepped under a low-hanging branch. "I started to be like that too a little bit, and my grandfather totally called me on it." The time we'd visited, our long walk in the woods.

"He was disappointed?"

I laughed at the memory. "My grandfather was always really honest. Never blunt or hurtful. But he'd tell you what he was thinking. And yeah—Claire and I came up here about a year before he died. He pushed me, on how I was living. We walked right through here," I said, smiling. "And he asked me if I was living the life I wanted."

"What'd you say?"

"Yes and meant it. I did at the time. It's not always obvious it's time to make a change, and my life was in no way terrible." Then, I corrected myself, since I'd be going back to that soon: "I mean, my life *is* great. Good job, good apartment, good friends." I trailed off, lost in thought.

Lucia nudged me with her shoulder. "Why do you sound so unsure right now?"

"Do I?"

"You do," she said, turning those blue eyes towards me and temporarily leaving me speechless. "You sound really unsure."

"Let's not—let's not talk about the future, okay?" I pulled her toward me, pressing my lips against her temple.

She nodded, and I felt a weight lift from her shoulders. "I'd like that. Now get back to telling me about your dates. Also, you should know I was always more of a Luke Skywalker girl myself. Han Solo had too much ego," she said, wrinkling her nose.

I laughed. "Well, that's good, since I never had his charm anyway. The last dates I went on before I met Claire were all blind dates. And they all stood me up."

Lucia looked shocked, but I just arched an eyebrow. "I'm the kind of 'nice guy' older women are always trying to set their daughters up with. They almost always stand me up."

"I'll murder those bitches for you," Lucia said, and I laughed again. Couldn't stop laughing.

"It's not necessary, although thank you for the offer. It's much appreciated. Other dates... I don't know. I didn't have a ton. I'm too shy to talk to women in a bar, too nervous at parties. I get in my head about all the ways I might mess up, say the wrong thing. And then some handsome doctor with tons of swagger comes along, and I'm toast. I actually always wanted to meet a nice girl in a bookstore."

"Yeah?" Lucia said, smiling. We were near my car, and she was twirling my keys around her index finger. She planted a kiss right on my lips. "Well, I can't say I'm a nice girl, but you *did* give me the three best orgasms of my life in a bookstore."

"That's right," I said, growing hard at the memory. The image of Lucia coming around my cock would stay with me for the rest of my life. "A lot of my dreams seem to be coming true this birthday."

I slid into the passenger seat, eyes gliding over Lucia's lithe body as she slid behind the wheel. Turned on the car, revved the engine like a racecar driver.

"Oh, Calvin. And the night hasn't even started yet," she purred, turning towards me. Leaning across the seat to trace her lips along my ear. Her hand drifted down my front to grip my cock. I hissed in a breath. "Did I ever tell you I fucking *love* a man in a suit?"

"N-no," I stuttered. She stroked the length of me with a hum of appreciation.

"Well, I do. I was ready to fuck you from the moment I opened the door."

She kissed down my neck, lazily stroking. I knew she wasn't going to let me come, but I was enjoying the swell of sensations, the confidence boost her whispered admission was giving me. "And you should be making a list of things you'll be doing to me later."

Another stroke.

"*Sir.*"

* * *

"You're taking me to Gabe's bar, right?" I guessed.

"*Shhh,*" she squealed. "You'll ruin the surprise."

I laughed. "Lu, there's like one road in this entire town."

"Maybe we're going off-roading," she said.

"Right."

"Maybe I'm driving us all the way to Mexico. It *is* your 30th birthday, after all. Aren't you excited?" she asked, eyes on the road.

"I am now," I said, settling back in the seat. "I'm not sure how I let this sneak up on me, but I've been kind of wrapped up in other things. Decisions." *Falling for you.* "Running the store, that kind of thing. But if there was any person I'd want to celebrate thirty years on this earth with," I said, nervously clearing my throat. "It'd be you, Lucia."

She smiled at me, biting her lip. "Thank you for letting me plan it. Quick question: you *do* appreciate clowns?"

"Oh, always."

"Great. And are you 'pro' or 'con' circuses?"

"Pro, of course."

"Fabulous. And you *have* always wanted to skydive, correct?" she asked.

"Actually, I've always wanted to skydive *with* a bunch of clowns *into* a circus tent," I replied.

"Well, *hot damn,* Calvin Ellis! Looks like I planned your perfect birthday."

I'd never seen her in such a good mood. And I felt like jumping out of the car and doing cartwheels down the highway because *I* was the source of that goodness.

"If Pablo Neruda wrote a poem about this night, what

would he say?" I asked, remembering the moment everything changed between us.

"It would *definitely* be about sex, but this is nice timing since a lot of his poetry is about sex but also food. And we're about to go have your birthday dinner, so..." she said, pulling into a space at Gabe's bar. There was no one else there. She undid her seat belt, turning to look at me. "He would use words like *languorous*," she said, fingers at her lips. "And he would describe the night as..." *Tap tap* went her fingers. "Heavy with scent... the moon a smooth fruit."

"Stars like a dash of salt on a dark cloth," I said, and her eyes widened.

"I love that, Cal. *See*? You inherited a bit of your grandfather's romanticism. Don't you think?" She was digging around for something—a notebook.

"Pen?" she asked, already flipping through pages.

I produced one from my pocket, handing it to her. She sat, scribbling, and I was content to watch, fully in the moment. The silence stretched out, but not awkwardly, and after a minute she pressed the journal into my hand.

"It's a first draft, and I just wrote it, now, in like, forty-five seconds, but what do you think?"

Our night was heavy with scent;
weighted, like gold scooped from the earth
The moon, a smooth fruit
Untouched, stars scattered like salt against
Your favorite black tablecloth
And isn't it sweet?
This golden night
This starry sky
Our hearts, tender as peonies
Languid with sunlight.

I swallowed against a rising tide of emotions. "Lucia... it's beautiful."

"You're co-author on this one," she said, teasing, but I shook my head.

"You're an amazing writer. Please never stop," I said, kissing the inside of her wrist. I could feel her pulse against my lips, beating rapidly.

"Okay," she said softly. "I'll make a copy of it for you. It can be your birthday present."

I nodded. "I'd like that." Another long, heavy silence.

And then Lucia grinned and said, "Let's fucking *eat*."

* * *

"Man of the hour," Gabe said, opening the door and bringing us inside. The bar was dim and quiet. "And I'm pissed you didn't tell me it was your birthday."

I shrugged. "It's no big deal."

Lucia cocked her thumb my way. "He's been saying that all night."

"Your *30th* birthday," Gabe said, shaking his head like he was ashamed of me. "Good thing Lucia had the sense to call me."

Lucia was watching Gabe move around the bar, grabbing keys, picking up a few glasses. She had a secret smile on her face. "Thank you for this, Gabe." She coughed, nudging me. "*Josie* said you'd be the perfect person to help." She winked, waggled her eyebrows.

"What?" I asked, looking around. "Do I have something on my face?"

"No," Gabe said, laughing his big, booming laugh. "Lucia is trying to tell you, not-so-subtly, that Josie and I had sex again. Like a lot," he said, indicating we should follow him.

"*What?*" I asked, throwing my hands in the air. "I thought it was just going to be one night."

"Nope," Lucia said, sighing with happiness. "It's been *every* night."

"Why am I the last person to find out about this?"

"Because, dear Calvin, you have been otherwise *distracted*," Gabe said with a huge grin, opening the door to his kitchen. He'd strung up a few lights, put out a tiny table with a white tablecloth. Tilted his head at the row of cooking equipment and handed Lucia two beers.

"It's all yours," he said, and she squeezed his arm.

"Thank you. I promise we won't have sex here," she said, and he laughed, giving me a slap on the back that almost knocked me over.

"Good luck with this one," Gabe whispered, with a look that said *you're a goner*. Which I was, through and through.

Lucia shuffled me forward into a seat and poured me a beer.

"What is this? What's happening?"

"I, Lucia Bell, am cooking you dinner. A birthday dinner." She glanced at the wall clock hanging over the oven. "But a fast one because we have someplace to be."

"Where's that?"

"*Secret*, Cal. And would you like to know the number of dates I've cooked for in my life?" She had tied a jaunty little apron around her waist, pulling things from the refrigerator.

"Fifteen."

"It's *zero*. Question," she said, turning around with a spatula in her hand. "And this will actually determine a lot for me. Do you like grilled cheese?"

"I do, actually."

She grinned. "Good, because that's the only thing I know how to make. And the only thing we're eating tonight."

From the front of the bar, we heard Gabe yell, "Check in the drawer next to the fridge!"

Lucia looked slightly startled, but complied, pulling open

a drawer and throwing her head back in laughter. "I'm going to guess Josie called him," she semi-whispered, and not a moment later Gabe yelled, "Josie called me. Said she didn't want Calvin to starve to death."

I laughed too, reaching forward to grab chips, pretzels, and a plate of chocolate chip cookies.

"Okay, I just want to say I don't think you would have *starved* to death," she said, reaching forward and cheekily popping a pretzel into her mouth. "But it's appreciated."

I leaned back, sipping beer, and watched Lucia start cooking.

"You don't like cooking?" I asked.

She snorted. "I *loathe* it. Never been my thing. When I'm at home, which is rarely, I either make myself grilled cheese. Or cereal."

"Is it because of work that you're never home?"

"Yes," she said, tearing off a piece of cheese and munching on it. "When I was younger and modeling was so *new*, I loved that part. Wake up in a different city every week, the adrenaline rush of paparazzi waiting for you in airports. Learning you have fans in other countries. Feeling so damn *lucky* I got paid to see the world. I've tried so hard to never take that for granted. But..." she trailed off.

"You can still feel lucky and no longer love what you do," I said. "It's complicated but possible."

She dunked the bread into a small bowl of butter, looking sideways at me. "Yeah... yeah, I get that now. Sometimes I'll be standing in the middle of... I don't know... *Rome* and wish I was back in my LA apartment. In my home. And then feel terrible that I wish that. But I do, if I'm being honest. You do get tired of eating on the road all the time, surrounded by strangers, sleeping in hotel beds."

"Watching you all these past two weeks has helped me learn a lot. About what you do, how hard it is."

The first grilled cheese hit the pan with a sizzle. She shrugged, a piece of hair slipping from her bun. "It's my job. I do it *very* well. But I do think people assume it's just glitz and glamor. Not standing in nine-inch heels in a wind tunnel while you balance two lion cubs in your arms for six straight hours..." Lucia winked at me. "Which I've done by the way."

"Of course you have," I cracked, the scent of sizzling butter making me hungry.

"And my parents freaking love it. We're a perfect Hollywood family. We even get to show up to film premieres together."

I sensed a bitterness there I wanted to explore more. But later, maybe later. "Can you tell me what it's like?"

"What?"

"The... Shit, Lucia you're *famous*. You're a celebrity. I knew who you were before you came here."

She wrinkled her nose. "It's weird, right? I forget that sometimes. I've only ever dated or had friends who are in the 'business.'"

"Weird and surreal," I said honestly. "Everything you do, every decision you make, everywhere you go... people see it. Have feelings about it. Have an opinion on it."

"I'm not *that* famous. I'm not a movie star," she said, flipping the grilled cheese. "There are some supermodels with twice the online following that I have."

I laughed. "Yeah, but we're still talking about millions of people here, right?"

"Yeah," she said shyly. "That's the weird thing about fame, Cal. I mean, if you woke up and had millions of followers on Instagram, what would you do?"

"Get their help to keep the bookstore open," I said, utterly surprising myself with my answer. Lucia turned, cheese dripping from the spatula.

"We're going to come back to that," she said, pointing

with the spatula, and some of it splattered me. I laughed, trying to pick cheese off my dark suit.

"Maybe," I said, trying to dodge her narrowed eyes. We'd *said* no talking about the future, yet I'd just let it dangle out there awkwardly. "So, okay," I said, quickly getting back on track. "The point of your question is... what would *you* do if you had millions of followers on Instagram?"

"This is fame. Because I do have millions of followers, which fifteen-year-old-me would have puked in excitement over. Just puked *all* over my Backstreet Boys bedspread. But now, when I see 'millions,' my first thought is 'how do I get another million?'"

She slid the sandwiches onto a plate, cutting them delicately down the middle. Even from where I sat, I could see the cheese oozing out.

"Actually, if I'm being brutally honest here, and it's *only* because it's your birthday, my first thought is *why* don't I have another million?" She paused, swallowing. "I mean, do people... do people not like me?"

"Oh, Lucia..." I said, reaching forward for her, but she dodged me.

"No, that kind of came out wrong," she said, but it didn't seem like it had. "What I mean is, could I be doing something better with my spotlight, to attract more people?"

"Hmmm," I said, pouring Lucia the beer Gabe had left for her. "So is it a sense that nothing is ever enough?"

She nodded. "Always bigger, always changing, always more, more, more. Once you get a taste of that, it's one of the hardest things in the world to give up. It might appear totally irrational from an outside perspective, but—"

"No, I get it. My grandfather experienced something like that once. It doesn't come close to your life, but The Mad Ones was 'famous' for a while, especially in certain circles. There were articles about it; these authors were desperate to do readings. People would drive across the country just to meet my grandfather."

"Then what happened?" Lucia asked.

"I don't know. From what I can gather from his journals, a few things happened. A lot of those authors unfortunately passed away, many of them young, leaving this big hole during that time in literature. The eighties showed up, and suddenly no one cared anymore about the revolution. People wanted computers. The landscape of books and bookstores changed, and about fifteen years ago, tons of independent bookstores had to close."

"Walmart, Target, Barnes & Noble."

"And I don't know..." I started, sighing. "I also don't think he wanted to keep up with the times. His business was in horrible debt for more than a decade, and instead of changing his ways, doing online marketing or reaching out to new authors or thinking of new programs he could offer, he stood his ground."

"He refused to change," she said, taking a big bite of her grilled cheese.

I did the same. "Fuck, that's good, Lu," I said, mouth full of cheese.

"I know, right? It's my one thing. And that's interesting about your grandfather," she said, blue eyes boring into mine. "When the bookstore was at its peak, those must have been heady days. I mean, can you imagine waking up, in that paradise, and being like, 'Well, got to plan for Kurt Vonnegut stopping by today.'"

"And then, for the last twenty years, you just see kids coming, faces glued to their phones, no interest whatsoever. In books or literature or any kind of counter-culture lifestyle. No more articles being written about you or your store. No more late-night parties or camping in the woods. No more young artists showing up in the middle of the night because they

"Passion," she said. "Drive. The ability to take the store back to its glory days. It was obvious to me the first moment I met you."

"Most people just think I'm awkward when they meet me."

"Well... they're stupid," she said, stealing another chip. We both took a long sip of beer, watching each other over the rims of our glasses.

"Thank you," I finally said. "I... well, that's much appreciated."

And completely irrelevant. Since tomorrow I was walking into that office and signing the contract to sell.

Right?

She stood up suddenly, brushing off her hands and putting things away.

"Time's a-wasting, Calvin," she said, loading dishes into Gabe's industrial dishwasher.

"Can I help?"

"Nope, you just sit back and enjoy the view," she said, bending over, flat back, ass pointing at my face. I wanted to fuck her like that, both of our pants barely off, her panties shoved to the side. Hot and hurried. Desperate.

"This morning, we had coffee. And you wrote me *another* poem. And cooked me dinner." I reached forward, I couldn't help it, and glided my palm up the back of her thigh and over the swell of her ass. "This *is* the best birthday I've ever had."

"And it hasn't even really gotten started," she said, pushing back into my hand.

I squeezed, and she let out a breathy little sigh.

"Oh yeah?"

"Yeah. You know the Crescent Moon Institute?"

"Oh... I mean, yeah. Everyone around here knows it." The Institute had been built in the seventies and had a long career as a 'spirituality retreat,' but because of the cloak of mystery wrapped around it, it still wasn't clear exactly what it was. There were cottages on site, large buildings, classes...you had to drive up a long driveway just to get to the entrance, and when you could see through the thick plants covering the fence, you could see tents and yurts set up sometimes. String lights and bonfires.

They were also famous for their natural hot springs. They had two, carved into the side of a hill, overlooking the Pacific Ocean. But you had to be staying there to use them.

"You ever been?"

"No way... I'm not even entirely sure what it is, to be honest."

Lucia nodded, clearing our final plates and pausing to check her lipstick (flawless) in the reflection of the microwave. She reached underneath the table behind me and brought out two white, fluffy towels."

"Um...what—"

"I had Gabe store these for me. We'll need them later tonight."

"Why?"

"Because we're going to the hot springs at the Institute."

"Lucia... you can't use those hot springs unless you're staying there. Plus, it's—" I looked at the clock. "Past ten at night. Everyone will be asleep."

"Exactly." Her hands perched on her hips, chin tilted up. "Which will make it even easier for us to break in."

CHAPTER 44

Lucia

"So... what's your plan?" Cal asked nervously. We were staring up at the giant wooden fence, blocking our entry.

"I told you. I'll boost you over this fence, the alarm will sound, you'll get arrested, spend the night in jail. I'll bail you out in the morning... *classic* 30th birthday shenanigans," I said sarcastically, eyebrow arched.

"*Lucia.*"

"Okay, okay... I don't necessarily have a *plan*, in the traditional sense of the word *plan*."

"... What the fuck."

"Cal," I said, turning to him, "before you came up here, what was the wildest thing you'd done? Like in your previous life?"

"One time I got turned down by ten women in a row at a bar," he said, hand rubbing down his jaw. "Pretty wild night. I think I ended up going home and binge-watching *Game of Thrones.*"

"You're a real adrenaline junkie, aren't you?"

He sighed, thinking. "I don't know, Lu... nothing comes to mind, to be honest."

"No wild nights? Drunken mistakes? Slept with five women at once?"

Cal laughed, leaning one arm against the fence. He looked hot as hell in his suit, and even though I was actually a huge fan of his glasses, without them his gaze was even more intense. I'd had to actively work not to strip that suit right off his body the entire night. I wasn't sure how *any* woman could have turned him down.

"Okay, wild girl... What's the most reckless thing you've done?"

"Past week? Past month?"

He looked surprised. "Um... okay, *month*."

"A month ago, I was on camera on a very famous and well-known cable morning show." Cal opened his mouth, but I immediately said, "I'll never tell which one. And I was being interviewed by a famous news anchor—it was me, I think Taylor was there, a few other models. Some segment called... gah, I don't even remember. *But* the point of the story is that ten minutes before I was supposed to go on, Josie and I sweet-talked some of the security, and we snuck into this famous news anchor's dressing room. And took pictures with all of his wigs."

Cal's smile brightened his face. "I gotta say, I'm impressed."

"And the week before that, I was in Milan and had been flirting with some tech all day. I fucked him in the elevator of our hotel *during* the busiest time of the day. So everyone was just waiting around, listening to two people going at it." I paused, tapping my chin. "I'm actually pretty proud of that one."

Cal took a step closer, then another one. My back was flat

against the fence as he boxed me in, one fluid motion. So smooth.

"Did you tell me that story to make me jealous?" he asked, lowering his face toward mine. His leg slid between mine, applying pressure right against my clit. "Of how you fucked some other guy in an elevator?"

"No," I said, hating the tremble in my voice. "I told you that story because I think you need to take more risks in your life. Like breaking into a potentially secret cult headquarters to swim in their private hot springs." His gaze narrowed; his knee pressed harder. "Also... I think I felt comfortable telling you that story because the sex I had with him barely registered. I mean, I did it for the adventure, not for the orgasm."

"He didn't make you come?" Cal closed his teeth on my bottom lip and pulled before releasing me.

I shook my head.

"Speak," he said, and my pulse pounded at the command in his tone.

How had I gone my entire life only fantasizing about this —fully submitting to a dominant lover? There was no going back now, no turning away. Because the orgasms my sexual partners had given me were few and far between, yet Cal could snap his fingers and I would climax.

"He didn't make me come," I breathed, rubbing myself against his leg. Totally shameless, and yet Cal loved it, arched over my body, watching me.

"Why not?"

His palms slid up my rib cage, stopping just below my breasts.

"He didn't... he wasn't like you," I said.

"And what am I like?" His thumbs slid up, stroking my nipples. But only once.

"In control," I said on a moan. "Of my pleasure."

"I own your pleasure," he said simply, like it was the oldest known fact in the world, stroking again, and I was about to say *fuck it* and just let Calvin ravish me against this fence when his face changed.

"Lucia, look," he whispered, pointing. He moved his leg, and I fell forward in a horny heap against his chest.

"I have a better idea," I started to say, but then I did look.

"Oh, shit!" I said, shoving Cal on the chest. "It's a fucking *hole!*"

CHAPTER 45

Calvin

I t was a hole all right, right in the middle of the high wooden fence. Lucia crouched down, and I realized now why she'd worn all black.

"You dressed like a cat burglar—" I pointed out. "—so you wouldn't be seen tonight."

"Maybe," she said, voice muffled as she attempted to wedge the fence further apart. "And you wore a dark suit, which means neither one of us will get caught." She looked up, winking. "My plan is working."

"You said you had no plan."

"Did I?" she said breathlessly, sitting back on her heels. "Also, I think I fixed this hole. Fixed it so we could slide through, I mean."

"Do you think I'll do well in prison? Emotionally, I mean. I could always go back to school, get that master's degree I always wanted..."

"*Chill*, nerd," Lucia groaned and then shimmied her way through the hole. I blinked—there one second, gone the next.

"*Lucia*," I hissed. No answer. I crouched down to peek through a hole that would allow me in *just fucking barely*. Her gorgeous face appeared, laughing silently. "Come and get me," she whispered.

"If I slide through here, I'm going to get stuck, and firemen are going to have to cut me out."

"Classic 30th birthday shenanigans, Cal," she said, reaching through the hole to grab my arms. "And that won't happen because I'm going to pull you."

"This is ridiculous."

"This is *fun*. Now come on," she said, giving me a look that told me her naked body and wild, primal sex awaited me on the other side. So I got down, in the dirt, and gave my hands to Lucia.

"If we wrote a poem about this moment, what would it be?" I said through gritted teeth, working my body through the fence as Lucia yanked on me.

"This isn't a poem," she said, slightly out of breath. "This is a moment in your life you'll remember forever, when you're back at your boring-ass office job, doing whatever-the-hell it is you do with numbers—"

"Software engineer, and I—" My hip was caught on something, but if I jiggled it, I could just—

"And you'll remember this time a snarky supermodel pulled you through a fence hole at a mysterious spirituality retreat."

With a hard yank, I slid all the way through—with my face in a pile of dirt, my tie smearing mud everywhere, my shoes getting caught on ragged edge of the fence. I looked up, to see Lucia surrounded by moonlight, and burst into nervous laughter.

"*Shhh*," she said, laughing too. "*Shhh* or we'll both go to jail."

"I'm sorry it's just—" I said, trying to catch my breath. "It's so *quiet*, and I have this feeling that any second now, a giant security officer is just going to wallop me on the head with a flashlight."

A pause. Hands back on her hips, corner of her lips twitching. "Excellent use of the word *wallop*."

"Thank you," I said, still flat on my back, dirt on my face.

"Are you ever going to stand up?"

"No, I, uh... I like it here. Feels safe—" But I barely finished the sentence before she hauled me up, dusting the dirt off and straightening my tie.

"Christ, you're strong."

"Have you ever held lion cubs? They're heavy. And squirmy. And *you* need to bring the volume of your voice way down," she said in a dramatic whisper. I bit my lip to keep from laughing—it was the whispering. And the drama. And the fact that we were now standing in the middle of a large field, dozens of cottages, and not a single soul was out except us. She took my hand, leading the way in the darkness.

"Do you know where we're going?"

"Not a clue."

"Okay, good." Her hand was warm, the night was slightly cool, and I knew, without looking, that the stars would be phenomenal. We walked in silence for a minute, the threat of being caught hanging over us. We could hear the sound of the ocean, and Lucia instinctively headed that way, passing a white gazebo, a yoga center, trees decked with Buddhist prayer flags like splashes of bright paint. Meditation pillows, gongs, the slight scent of sage still on the wind.

A large, low wall with a huge mural appeared out of nowhere. I couldn't tell what the background image was, but the letters stood out stark and white against the night sky. We both read the quote silently, Lucia's hand squeezing mine in recognition.

"Now *this*," she whispered. "—is an actual poem. And, dear Calvin, a sign."

In large white letters was a quote from Mary Oliver, a quote both of us knew, a famous quote, urging us to consider the preciousness of our own lives.

I looked over to catch Lucia wiping tears from her cheeks. I pulled her closer.

"It just happens when I read a poem I love," she said. "Always has. And I *love* her. Not just the message, what she's trying to say, but the juxtaposition of the words she chose to use. It makes my heart ache." She turned to me. "What about you?"

"I don't know how a person can sum up the full magnitude of life's beauty and life's wretchedness in so few words," I said.

A pause. "I love the word, 'wretched,'" she said.

I pressed a kiss at her temple. "I like using words that you love."

We kept walking, but the gravity of that moment—those words, at that time—had settled over us like a heavy cloak. Not in a bad way, necessarily, but Lucia and I were two people meeting at a crossroads in our lives. This night might be like pressing the pause button, but once the sun came up, we would both split, back on our separate roads.

We passed a large, nondescript building, a statue of Buddha. The fields here had been cleared, and almost immediately we could see the ocean: a black, swirling mass ahead of us, white caps of waves illuminated in the moonlight. We reached the cliff's edge. I could smell, faintly, the scent of sulfur, which meant the hot springs were close, but Lucia seemed glued to this spot, staring.

"*This* is a poem," she said. "This is why I fell in love with poetry when I was a little kid."

"What specifically?" I urged.

"Just... the power behind each word. It's not the same as prose; there's no natural wordiness or the ability to prattle on.

You're reading the words a writer has chosen out of *every* word in the universe. Sometimes using words to describe things you could never imagine doing—or a moment in time, like this. A moment in our lives we'll forget if we don't write it down. Before modeling, all I wanted to do was to write like that. I had a very Emily-Dickinson-style sense of my life."

"Being discovered after you die?"

"No," she said smiling. "But a quiet life, writing poems in my little cottage in the country. No distractions, just creativity, dry wit, and a pencil to keep me company."

"I can't quite imagine you in such a... *matronly* life."

She shook her head. "I'm no matron. But even a few years into modeling, when I was still writing on the side, I thought I would go back to it. Just make a shit-ton of money, enroll in the country's finest creative writing program, and then... well, to be honest, I don't know what after that."

"That's okay. I don't think dreams have to be completely fleshed out—there's always a level of uncertainty." I paused. "It's what makes them so terrifying." We were both silent, watching the waves. "Why didn't you do that? Go back to school?"

"Oh, well, I got famous, I guess. As a teenager, which *really* screws with your head. You already have this grand, egotistical sense of yourself, and then when you see your face on a magazine cover, it's like your brain just explodes." She laughed quietly. "I remember tossing that little poetry journal into a suitcase and forgetting about it for years. But then, every so often, this... *feeling* would roar up inside of me. I'd get antsy and anxious, and my fingers would actually itch." She looked at them, bathed in moonlight. She had beautiful fingers. "And this feeling would always coincide with long periods of unhappiness."

I moved closer to her, my hand making big, soothing circles on her back.

"You know what's funny?"

"What?"

"I've been feeling off this past year," she said. "Different, about things. Even Josie's noticed. I didn't write, but I think that's where some of the feeling was coming from. And when I stepped out of the car that first morning and saw the bookstore and the trees and... and you, the feeling came back. And it hasn't let up since."

"Big Sur is the ultimate writing inspiration."

She held my gaze for a long time, and I felt trapped by it, drawn into her web. *Never leave me,* I suddenly wanted to shout, and when she stood on her tiptoes and pressed a passionate kiss against my lips, I almost did.

"So are you, Calvin. So are you."

CHAPTER 46

Lucia

"I think they're this way," he said as we stepped gingerly along the cliff.

I'd seen pictures on the brochure, of calm, blissed-out looking people soaking in water against the dramatic backdrop of the sun setting over the Pacific Ocean. If the pictures were accurate, we were close by.

"Do you think your grandfather ever did this?" I whispered.

I watched Cal smile in the darkness. "Oh... probably. I think when he and my grandmother were younger, they were very romantic. Very adventurous. They used to close the bookstore for a month in the summer and go someplace new. Sometimes expensive and far away, when they were doing well. Sometimes just to go live in the woods. Shake things up."

"See things from a new perspective," I said softly since the last two weeks here had just about split my life in two. I understood the urge now.

"Do you have a favorite memory of your grandfather?"

"Yes," he said. "The one I shared at his funeral. It's more a collection of memories, but one thing we used to do, all the time when I stayed here in the summer, was we'd read poetry or books out loud and discuss them. It was like a book club, but it only had two members. I thought it was so magical as a kid. To be introduced to words that way. We'd always drink hot chocolate or roast marshmallows around that fire pit. Sometimes his friends would come over, and we'd all talk about the section we were reading. It's funny now to think of people like Gabe's father coming over to discuss *The Giving Tree* with me as a little kid."

I grabbed his arm. "The first poet I ever loved. Shel Silverstein."

He looked at me, gaze searching. "That's what I told everyone at the memorial service. We'd read Silverstein, and he'd ask me these questions, get me to really think about what was going on in the poem. Then, later, when I'd come out and talk to him about... I don't know, *Star Trek: Next Generation* or —"

"Magic: the Gathering?"

Cal gave me the kind of look a husband gives his wife on their wedding night.

I actually squirmed. "What? You're not the only nerd here."

"Y-yes," he said, stumbling. "Things like that. He could tell I was going to be into science fiction, so then we'd start to read the classics."

"*1984?*" I guessed, and he nodded.

"*Fahrenheit 451. Brave New World. The Left Hand of Darkness. Kindred.*"

My skin broke out in goosebumps. "I can only imagine reading such brilliant books on that deck, surrounded by the entire universe. The stars and the moon and that *kid* feeling."

"Yes," he whispered, reverent. "It was like Christmas every morning."

"Because every Christmas you'd get tons of books and then spend the entire day reading?" I guessed.

He laughed, turning against me and putting his head against my neck, muffling the sound. I broke out in goose-bumps again, shivering as his breath coasted along my skin.

"I'd do the same thing," I said, and he kissed my cheek.

The hot springs were upon us now, two small pools, no bigger than hot tubs, in the side of a mountain. Directly in front of them was a view of the ocean that made my chest ache it was so damn beautiful. Beautiful and a little lonely—that moment when you realize how small you are against the expansiveness of the natural world.

"Wow," Cal breathed.

"Indeed," I said, stepping forward. The hot springs threw off elegant, pale steam that caressed my face as I lowered it towards the water. I dipped my fingers in.

"Oh, Cal," I said, turning towards him. "It's perfect." As I turned towards him, already lifting my shirt, I thought about the sheer number of people I'd undressed for in my career—not lovers but makeup artists and hairstylists and wardrobe assistants. Men like Ray and Taylor who viewed my body as a piece of art to move and manipulate, not sexual. Just legs and arms and a stomach draped in expensive clothing that some teenager in Middle America would beg her parents to buy her. *That* was the purpose of my body, of this body.

But as I tossed my shirt to the ground, shivering in the cool air, my body existed to submit. To yield. To receive the pleasure Cal needed to give, needed to lose himself in. I unhooked my pants, sliding them down my thighs with the balance of a ballerina.

I watched Cal's transformation—it would never get old. He slid off his jacket, one hand already unbuttoning his shirt.

I unhooked my bra, the night air like a lover's touch.

His shirt slid down his arms. There was no last gasp of

awkwardness, no shy blushing. Only Calvin with his messy hair, his broad shoulders, his lean stomach. I blinked, and his pants were sliding from his hips.

I swallowed as I saw the outline of his cock. I slid my underwear off, tossing it at him coquettishly. I winked, trying to lighten the mood, but Calvin took his cock out, stroking the length with my panties in his hand.

"Get in the fucking water," he said firmly, and I did, turning around and slipping my toes, then my ankles, then my calves in. The air was cool, almost cold, but the water was so perfectly hot I couldn't help but let out a low, keening moan. I undid my bun, dipping my head back and letting my hair soak in the steamy warmth. I slipped lower, until the water came up to my chin, and then I turned around.

Calvin was right there, pulling me towards him and wrapping my legs around his waist. Kissing me roughly, hands in my hair, his cock already pushing at my entrance. I wanted him already, wanted him to fuck me into oblivion, but he had other ideas. He moved us towards a large rock, lips against my neck. I sighed happily.

And then he lifted me up onto the rock, spreading my legs wide, baring me to the night air. My first instinct was to cover myself, close my legs, but he held them open with a punishing grip.

"Do you want to know what my favorite word is, Lucia?" He asked, eyes pinned on my pussy.

"What?" I asked, mesmerized by the look on his face.

"Cunt," he said, sliding a long finger inside of me.

"Oh *god,*" I said, as he stroked my g-spot. Slowly, no hurry. Exploring. He added a second finger, then a third, fucking me. We both watched his fingers moving in and out, slick in the moonlight.

"I've always loved it," he said calmly. "It's filthy and raw and *real*. And your cunt–" he said, bending down to take a long, slow lick. "—is perfection." He removed his fingers, replacing them with his tongue, which licked inside my body so deeply I thought I would pass out.

"Calvin—" I gasped, holding his head there.

A low growl escaped his lips, and he grabbed my hands, holding them at my sides. His tongue moved, fluttering against my nerve endings. He pulled out, his tongue tracing up to my clit, circling. I swallowed a cry.

"Your cunt tastes like the ocean. Your cunt tastes like chocolate." Another lick, and he sucked my clit into his mouth, humming. "Your cunt is the best fucking thing I've ever tasted."

He pushed me back gently, my back against the rocks, warm from the hot springs, the steam everywhere. The sky was a riot of white stars, the ocean waves drowning out the sound of my heart, slamming against my rib cage. I felt almost over-whelmingly alive, my body like a work of art, Calvin's head between my legs, his tongue dancing over my clit.

I knew we had to be quiet, but even still I couldn't stop moaning, my hand over my mouth, as Cal worked his tongue over me. He was groaning too, and as he slid two of those fingers back inside of me, my hips thrust up, desperately seeking the orgasm already building.

"This pretty cunt is going to come for me," he said, flat-tening his tongue and lapping at me greedily. I could only nod, my head thrashing on the rocks, the entire universe flooding my nervous system as I came, explosively, against his mouth. I let out a long wail, not giving a *shit* if anyone heard me, because nothing in my life had ever felt so magnificent.

"Cal—" I started to say, hips jerking as he kept licking, stroking back inside of me, drinking me in. My muscles clenched around his tongue, and he gripped my ass so hard I knew I'd have fingerprint bruises tomorrow. His thumb wandered down to the ring of muscle below where his mouth was working, thumb tracing the sensitive nerve endings.

Cal was a filthy little *freak*, and my back arched as his thumb slipped inside my ass, tongue working my g-spot, his other hand finding my nipples. Tweaking them roughly. And all of a sudden, Cal was going to tongue-fuck me into another orgasm, or maybe I was still riding the *same* orgasm, but either way my body was suspended in pleasure, tiny climaxes exploding like light against my skin. I was being devoured, and I fucking loved it, nothing to do except lay back and enjoy the all-out assault.

Another orgasm beckoned, but before it reached me, Cal pulled me back into the hot springs.

CHAPTER 47

Calvin

"I can't believe this is happening," Lucia sighed against my lips as I wrapped my arms around her body, pulling her close. I couldn't tell where my body began and hers ended, and I liked it that way. Liked that the musky scent of Lucia's pussy was on my fingers, my hands, my lips, my tongue. Liked that for the rest of my life I'd have the memory of her coming in my mouth, the delightful way Lucia Bell climaxed, her endless capacity for pleasure.

I was on my knees, her legs wrapped around me, and as I thrust inside of her, part of me wanted her like this. Slow and lazy, riding me like we had all the time in the world. Her rhythm was sensual, perfect tits in my face, my lips against her throat.

But then I looped my fingers in her hair and pulled, instinctively, and the plaintive sound that came from her flipped a switch deep inside of me.

I flipped her around, forgetting to be gentle. Hauled the entirety of her body out of the hot springs, arms outstretched and ass in my face. I bit her inner thighs, and she whimpered.

Wondered about the sounds of my hand spanking her, how many people it might wake up, our odds of being caught.

But then she shook her ass, and I cracked my palm against it so fast she cried out in surprise. I liked the look of her pussy like this—wet with arousal, inches from my mouth. I ran my tongue over her ass, spreading her cheeks. I rimmed her asshole, sucked her pussy lips into my mouth, spanked her again.

I couldn't get enough of her—something inside of me worried this would be our last time together, and I wanted to taste, to feel, to *know* every goddamn inch of her.

I slid her back down, back against my chest. Wrapped a hand around her throat and thrust inside of her. She started to work herself against my cock, but I spanked her under the water.

"Don't you *fucking* dare," I said, hand still on her throat, other arm wrapped around her hips, holding her in place.

"Feel me, Lu," I groaned. "Feel *this.*" I lifted my hips, rocking in small circles, cock moving inside of her. She whined, fingers gripping the rock in front of her as I made subtle, slow movements deep in her pussy. Like stoking a fire from banked coals, making her wait, so that when I finally started fucking her in short, fast strokes, we both let out primal sounds of rapture.

Lucia fell forward onto her elbows, and I gripped her hips, lifting her in the water. The ocean waves roaring, the hot water steaming, and my cock deeper than I thought possible.

If there was ever a moment in my life to bare my soul, this was it. "You are the most intriguing woman I've ever met," I groaned against her ear, and she leaned back, sighing happily, lying her head on my shoulder. "Funny and smart and passionate, and I was head over heels the first moment I saw you."

"*Calvin,*" she moaned, and I circled her clit, giving her what she needed.

"I will never meet another woman like you in my entire life, Lucia," I said fiercely. "*Never*. And this?" I fucked her faster, and she cried out. "*This* is a fucking privilege."

I turned her head so I could give her the kind of kiss I'd always wanted to give a woman, taking her mouth like I owned it.

Because I did. Because Lucia was unraveling beneath my touch, my cock, *my* thrusts, and that knowledge alone was enough to make me come so hard I bit her shoulder to keep from yelling.

Lucia fell with me, shuddering for minutes, mouth still glued to mine. My heart lurched as slowly disentangled herself me, but she only turned to wrap herself more closely, kissing my cheek, my jaw, my neck. Squeezing me so tight I knew she was thinking about the same thing I was.

Tomorrow.

"Lucia," I said, heart still pounding, but she shook her head.

"Just let me... Cal, just let me have this moment."

So I did, holding her tightly, rubbing her back, whispering the same things I'd said to her roughly only moments ago but now softly.

I will never meet another woman like you.

I was head over heels from the moment I met you.

But I didn't ask her to stay.

Say something, my inner monologue kept yelling. *This is your life. You don't get another one.* And, really, wouldn't life with Lucia Bell be so much sweeter? What was the worst that could happen?

Lucia, I'm falling in love with you. And then... well, I didn't have an *and then*. I guess it would be something like: *give up the opportunity of a lifetime for a man you barely know. Move into a financially failing bookstore and run it with me.*

A thousand scenarios ran through my head, and all of

KATHRYN NOLAN

them ended with Lucia laughing hysterically before traipsing off to Paris.

But then she pulled back to look at me, pressing her palm against my cheek. Her blue eyes were filled with tears, threatening to spill over. Her thumb stroked—it looked like she was trying to *memorize* me.

Say something.

"I want... I want to talk to you about—" I said, and I swear the look on her face was so beautiful, so filled with yearning, I wanted to freeze us permanently in this moment.

And that's when the security guard showed up.

CHAPTER 48

Lucia

"Is shining that flashlight directly in our faces *absolutely necessary*?" I asked, bringing my hand up to my face.

I was pissed, wishing I was back in the most perfect post-coital moment of my entire existence. And *this close* to a possible breakthrough with Calvin. Of what, I wasn't entirely sure, but I wanted him to finish that sentence *so fucking badly*, and now a security guard was standing there, light in my eyes, and I wasn't about to have any of it.

"I'll repeat the question," he said. "Are you actual guests of the Institute?"

Calvin was frozen in terror, a deer in headlights. He'd jumped in front of me to cover my nudity, but I just rolled my eyes, pushing him gently aside. About half the population of the world had seen my tits (or close to it).

"Yes," I said firmly at the exact same time as Calvin said, "No." We looked at each other. Busted. I bit my lip to keep from laughing.

So much for playing it cool.

"Is that a *yes* or a *no*?"

"Do we not look like guests of the Institute?" I asked haughtily, tossing my wet hair over my shoulder.

"You don't. Because I actually know what every current guest looks like. And you two—" He shined the light back and forth between our naked bodies. "—look like a couple of hippies up to no good."

Couple of hippies?

I turned to Cal and said, dryly, "Your grandfather would have been proud."

"What?" he whispered at me, eyes as round as silver dollars.

"Well," I said loudly, waving my hands as if I was about to say something hugely important.

Both men waited on me to speak, but instead all I did was toss the towel in the guard's face and yell "*Run!*" at Calvin, leaping out of the hot springs and scooping up my clothes.

He didn't need telling twice, doing the same, the guard calling out, wearily, "Please don't run. I'm not even going to call the cops—"

But it didn't matter because I was racing through the cottages, the twinkle lights, Mary Oliver quotes and meditation pillows, Cal behind me, laughing uproariously now.

I joined him, and for a second I was laughing so hard I had to double over, Cal pushing me to keep going. We reached the fence, and I threw my clothes over the wooden slats, military-crawling through the hole.

I slid through easily, turning around to grab Cal's hands. He'd thrown his pants on, and mud was smearing all over his chest and arms. I was a literal hot mess, twigs in my hair and cuts up and down my legs and laughing so hard I could barely hold onto Cal's hands.

"He's not even going to call the cops, Lu," Cal wheezed, shimmying through the hole.

"I *know*, and that's what makes it funnier."

"He called us *hippies*... like we were in an eighties after school special," Cal said, and I snorted, dragging him up when he made it through.

"In this after school special, did I corrupt you? Or did you corrupt me? And which of us smokes weed?"

"Oh, it's clear that *you* are the corrupting force here, Ms. Bell," he said.

I slid into the car seat, taking Cal's keys and revving the engine. "We gotta make a quick getaway."

I glanced at the clock as we left the Crescent Moon Institute, winding our way back down Highway 1, nothing but hills on one side and the ocean on the other. No people out, just us.

"I'm sorry to tell you this, but it's after midnight. No longer your birthday, and you're officially thirty years old," I said, reaching over to squeeze his hand.

As the adrenaline of our madcap chase slowly left my body, I remembered what we'd been doing before the guard had gotten there.

What was *about* to happen, maybe, possibly?

"No more birthday," Cal said softly.

"How do you feel?" We were close to the bookstore, but I felt myself slowing down, dragging out this night. I didn't want it to end.

"Fucking fantastic," he said, and I laughed with him. "Hands down, best birthday I've ever had."

"Mission accomplished," I said, pulling up the long drive to The Mad Ones, going about five miles an hour now. Woodland creatures were scampering along more quickly than we were traveling. We'd been talking nonstop the entire night and now, as the old sign came into view, we both stopped.

I parked the car, turned off the engine.

I'll just never open the door, I thought.

But then Cal opened his, and I silently cursed. We both

311

climbed out, staring at the bookstore, quietly slumbering. The lights along the trees glowed like beacons.

I'd be leaving in six hours.

"Will you send me the poem? The one you wrote tonight?" he asked, breaking our silence. I turned, startled.

"Oh... oh, of course." I rummaged in my bag, pulling out the journal. Tore the page out and handed it to him. "An original. You'll have the only copy."

His eyes widened. "You don't want it?"

I shook my head. "It's your birthday present."

It'd hurt too much to read it. And now reality was really settling in. My feet felt like heavy, red bricks.

Say something. But instead, a thick, tangible silence stretched out between us. I needed to go, he needed to go, but we remained still.

"Thank you, again, for tonight. I think it was the most perfect five hours of my life," he said sincerely. I didn't laugh because I was suddenly about to burst into tears.

"Some hot springs, huh?" I finally croaked out.

His laughter was similarly restrained.

But then his face turned serious. "I'll never forget that, Lucia," he said, the words he'd whispered fervently as I climaxed roaring back.

I was head over heels the first moment I saw you.

It had been the most romantic moment of my life. And I'd said nothing, even though the urge to tell him my true feelings had swept up like a tornado inside me. Even though I'd promised Josie I'd be brave, baring my soul with no thought to the consequences.

But what was I going to say? *I think I'm falling in love with you. Will you sell this amazing bookstore and move to Paris with me?*

How fucking selfish. Even though, deep down, there was another option, and I knew it. But reneging on this contract would end my career. To do that... for Calvin, for a week in Big Sur, for a moment in a hot spring...

It was foolish, right?

"I'll never forget it either," I said. "I'll never forget the things you said. Thank you."

Cal looked away from me, suddenly as shy and nervous as the first day we met.

"Thank you for seeing me." I gulped since *that* was pretty brave. And true. Cal had seen past the gauzy, shallow layers and seen *me*.

"Don't worry about it," he said, looking up at the trees. "Just kind of... swept up in the moment, you know?"

"Oh... of course," I said, recovering. "Me too."

This is what you wanted. A few days of hot and heavy fun with a guy I'd never see again, swept up in the moment. Live a little—that's what I'd said to Josie.

"You know, this is the last time you'll see this place," Cal said.

I swallowed thickly. *Oh, and that too.*

"Yeah," was all I could manage.

"The investor's plan is to bulldoze the store, build an organic spa. Use the cottages for private massage suites."

"Yeah... okay. Sounds like you made your choice—" But I wanted to say *please don't.*

I wanted to say *this is the most beautiful place I've ever seen.*

"Selling it is the right choice. I know it," Calvin said.

He stumbled at the end. Hesitant. But I pretended to ignore it. I wiped my face, catching a tear before he could see it.

"Do you, um... do you want to stay the night?" he asked, catching me totally off-guard.

More than anything. "I think... don't you think that'll just make it harder? I'm leaving... tomorrow morning," I said, and my voice definitely cracked. I cleared it.

God, this was terrible.

"Right, of course," he said quickly, backing away from me. I went to move closer but then stopped myself.

"You're probably right." He smiled weakly.

"Calvin," I started to say, but he interrupted me.

"So, Paris, huh? You'll be there soon. Exciting." It was like awkward party small talk. My emotions were a fucking mess. I didn't know, entirely, what I wanted Calvin to ask me, but I wanted him to *ask me*.

"Opportunity of a lifetime," I said again, shrugging, the words like ash in my mouth. I shouldn't have agreed to tonight —too much salt in the wound. "You'll have to let me know the first time you see my face on a billboard here in the States."

As if that mattered anymore.

"I will. You can, um... well send me a postcard? And I'll see you, you know, on Instagram."

Another follower, mindlessly liking my posts, feeding my ego.

"I'll try and post some topless ones for you," I said, and he gave me the sweetest smile. The entire week came rushing back, every moment we'd spent together. I was going to need Josie to physically restrain me in the car tomorrow or I'd stay here, curled up next to Cal, reading books. Writing. Being truly happy. Forever.

"And, you know, I know it's not... um, *likely*, but if you're ever in Big Sur again—" A pause, while he corrected himself. "I mean, if you're ever in San Jose, give me a call. We could grab coffee or something."

Coffee. This was starting to sound like the end of an awkward one-night stand. How had our walls gone up so quickly?

"Yeah, okay," I said, and I was definitely crying now— buckets of tears. Cal reached out, concerned, touching my wrist, and just that was too much.

"Lucia? Are you—I'm sorry, did I—?"

But I was walking backwards, shrugging my shoulders and attempting to laugh through my tears.

"So anyway," I said, speaking over Cal's concerned words. "Happy birthday. We'll always have the hot springs. And, uh... see you around some time. We'll have coffee. In San Jose."

He called out to me, a few times, but I ignored it, just pushing my way through the trail, branches snagging on my clothing, tripping over rocks.

Going back was only going to tear my heart to pieces.

* * *

I crawled into bed with Josie who, from the looks of it, had had the same kind of night.

I reached out, held her hand.

"Were you brave?" I asked.

She bit her lip, tear sliding down her cheek. "It's a long story. Yes, but also... no. It's not going to work out."

Silence for a moment. I stroked her hair.

"How about you?" she asked, sniffling.

The whole horrible scene replayed itself in my mind—Calvin and I both obviously leaving words unsaid, neither one of us willing to put themselves on the line. And also, maybe, like he'd said... we were just swept up in a moment. A week in Big Sur, no consequences, just great sex with an undercurrent of intense, possibly life-changing, emotional connection.

Yet neither one of us could do it. Be brave.

"A little bit," I said. "But mostly no. Not at all. And it was awful."

* * *

315

I held Josie's hand and cried all the way back to Los Angeles. Except when she needed to cry, and we'd switch spots, saying the same things over and over. *This is for the best. It wasn't meant to be. It was just great sex, nothing more.* A continuous stream of complete and utter bullshit but the kind of bullshit you say to your best friend when she's sure she'll never love again. I said it to Josie, and she said it right back to me.

Because of course I was fucking going to Paris. The farther we got from Big Sur and the closer to civilization, I felt Big Sur's hold on me loosen. Shake loose from my bones. As Josie read through the latest celebrity news, got me caught up on gossip, my world shrank back to size.

I wondered if I'd be inspired to write in Paris or if it'd be more of the same... listlessness. Disinterest. But my apartment was too small, and I missed the constant sound of the waves, the giant redwoods, that lingering scent of forest and moss.

Calvin wasn't in my bed, and in the morning when I woke to make my flight to Paris, there was no book of poetry left at my door with a post-it note inside scrawled with his favorite lines.

I was head over heels the moment I met you.

I cried on the way to the airport and during the flight— received my fair share of odd looks, and it wouldn't surprise me if I didn't end up in some gossip column later. *Lucia Bell in tears at LAX—what happened?*

I arrived in Paris in a daze, greeted Sabine's people numbly, barely glanced around my cute Parisian flat. Just laid down on the bed and fell into a restless, unhappy sleep.

And in the morning, I strolled onto the set, plopped into a chair, snapped for a latte and took out my phone.

CHAPTER 49

Calvin

I had to meet with the investors.

I'd spent the night staring into the fire, drinking the last of my grandfather's really good whiskey. It felt overly dramatic and melancholy, but I didn't care.

I realized I'd never truly been heartbroken before, my relationships with other women seeming very shallow and surface-level now even though they'd lasted longer. This, this gut-wrenching, nauseating sense of loss felt *exactly* like heartbreak.

If my grandfather were alive, he'd say "the kind the poets write about." And I'd have to agree because I just wanted to lie down in the middle of the Big Room, weeping, until the investors came and kicked me out. I wanted to go back to my old, boring job, my old life, and forget any of this ever happened. Heal my heart and try to forget a bunch of rich people were getting massages in a building that had once been America's most important literary touchstone.

When I finally fell asleep, my dreams were filled with Lucia, and when I woke, I thought I'd imagined the whole thing. Woke up in some world where the gut-punch of harsh reality didn't exist. In the morning, making coffee, I avoided the Virginia Woolf mug. At the register, I couldn't look at the photo of Mary Oliver or the collection by Pablo Neruda that Lucia had left there, opened to a favorite line.

I could imagine us here, every morning, opening the store. Drinking cup after cup of coffee, reading out loud from whatever book we were currently reading. Laughing about a strange customer. Kissing on the armchair, in front of a fire.

I was a goddamn mess. How had I fucked this up? Why had I bared my soul to Lucia and not asked her to at least *consider* staying with me. She must have thought I hadn't meant it, the way she'd cried against the Christmas lights strung up on the trees. The way she'd run from me.

We were probably just swept up in the moment.

I was a fool. I'd only said it because fear had suddenly raced up my spine, freezing my thoughts. Halting my decisions.

And making Lucia cry would now go down as the shittiest thing I'd done in my entire life.

I was mindlessly shelving books, looking for a distraction before the meeting, when an envelope flew through my legs, landing about a foot in front of me. *Calvin*, it said on the front.

My grandfather's letter—the one his lawyer said he'd left for me with his will. I scooped it up, amazed. After his lawyer had given me the inheritance news, I'd completely forgotten about this. Must have shoved it this bookshelf in a total daze.

I sat back down, opening it up. The letter was worn yellow, the creases soft, the handwriting faded and barely legible. I thought he'd written it recently, which was silly. It wasn't like he'd written it the day before he died, but in my mind, I thought of it that way. He must have written it when he made his will, which might have been ages ago.

Dear Calvin, it started.

I think it is very likely that you're reading this letter and hating me right about now. I mean, first I decided to die (very *inconsiderate), and then I left you with a sinking ship in your hands. I don't know when you're reading this, but unless I won some kind of lottery, it's likely you're inheriting The Mad Ones <u>and</u> its debt, which I am deeply sorry for. There is no excuse, and please do not think I didn't try to stop this; I did. But I think, at a certain point, The Mad Ones would have benefited from a different leader, someone different from me, who had a bit more business sense. Less of a poet's heart—because really, at the end of the day, all I wanted was a space to be surrounded by words and the incredible people that create them. Making money, turning a profit, was never the goal, and maybe it should have been. I wish, for your sake, I was filled with more regret about that, but I'm really not, Cal. I have lived my life exactly the way I wanted, in as pure a way as possible. Not driven by the choices or demands of others. Not hemmed in by the pressures of society.*

This is not to say my life has been easy, even though it might have appeared to be: I suffered and struggled, fought and lost hope. Felt lost and sad, listless and bored. I think it's easy, when you live in paradise, doing your dream job, to paint my life in broad strokes: aging bohemian. Weirdo. Old hippie. I <u>am</u> all of those things, and proudly. But I'm a human being like everyone else—life up here was sometimes very hard. When your grandmother died, the first few years after her accident were only darkness, my only pinprick of light your summer visits.

I say all of this not to make you scared of inheriting The Mad Ones; quite the opposite. I just want you to know the full reality of a wilder life. I would say I went to bed happier, more content than many—that happens when your life choices align with your values.

But life <u>still happens.</u> The anxiety will chase you, depression can find you, and one night, while she's picking up milk at the store, your soulmate might drive off the road and die, years before she was supposed to.

Your life is different now, Calvin, and it's quite possible you no longer have the love and hunger for books that I saw in you during our summers together. You may want to burn this shambling old shack to the ground—and I wouldn't blame you.

First of all, I'm dead, so who gives a shit? Not me. But secondly, your life might be brimming over with happiness and moving up here, taking this over, could be the absolute last thing you want to do. So don't do it. I left it to you not as a punishment or a burden, not to pressure you into the shape of the life I had lived. I left it to you because, years ago, it was beyond obvious to me that you had that same tender poet's soul, the heart of a booklover, the desire for solitude and tranquility. And you're different from me—you could do the things The Mad Ones needs to stay afloat.

Also, I just believe in you, Calvin. So whatever choice you make, make it your choice. If not, you'll only spend the rest of your life regretting it.

If I didn't say it enough: I love you, very much. Think of me when you read Shel Silverstein to your children. Ask them questions. Help them open up their world.

Go a little mad.

I couldn't turn around, so convinced was I that my grandfather would be walking out into the Big Room, mid-laugh, whiskey in one hand and a book in the other.

My grandfather hadn't wanted me to live a life of regret, yet the five years before he died I visited him twice, saw him at a few holiday gatherings. "Too busy," I'd always said. "Too stressed with work," as if either of those things were actual excuses. And meanwhile, he stayed up here, continuing to think the world of me, even as I stayed away.

Whatever choice you make, make it your choice.

And just like that, I knew what I had to do.

It was going to be so much fucking work. And I had no

plan, no idea, no clue how to run a bookstore, let alone one that had completely fallen to pieces.

Nothing would be easy about this. Nothing in my life would be the same. The thought of the countless knots of my life I'd have to undo made me dizzy. And yet.

And yet. My grandfather believed in me. Lucia had believed in me.

I looked around, at this place I loved so much, and saw something: a future.

Maybe it was time to go a little mad.

CHAPTER 50

Calvin

"Right, no, I understand you've never heard of us before," I said into the phone, waving to some customers as they strolled in. "We are... well, *were*, famous for a long time, and I'm working to... right. No, I understand, and I sure will," I said, sighing as I hung up the phone.

I took out my red pen and crossed another name off the list.

"No luck?" Gabe asked, staring at my computer screen. He'd been coming by to help me set up some financial systems for the bookstore. Turned out, Big Sur had a lot of experts, and when your best friend had been running a business for his entire life—you should start there.

"Nope," I said, shrugging. "But the list is long, and I'm only 10% through it. They'll come," I said with a confidence I didn't really feel.

Gabe and I had taken a second look at my grandfather's finances, and as I suspected, the bread-and-butter of his business—when it was good—had been readings and lectures.

Getting them started up again was another question entirely.

"Your sales are up 3%," Gabe said, clicking through a report and printing it for me. "Not too shabby."

I looked, impressed as the small line on the bar chart moved up. Slow but steady.

"That's good news," I exclaimed so loudly a few of the customers glanced my way. I smiled at them nervously. I still lacked a lot of my grandfather's gregariousness, but I was getting better.

"It is," Gabe said slowly, slapping a hand on my back. "But your expenses are still outpacing your revenue significantly. Almost *shockingly* so."

"Fuck."

"I'm still letting you drink for free," he said with a wry grin.

I winced a little—for every ounce of good financial news, it didn't seem to be able to chip away at the massive amount of debt.

"Much appreciated," I said grimly, turning back to my list.

After I'd let down the investors—who had a few choice words for me—I called my parents. They thought it was a terrible idea and told me so. A few friends agreed. My boss didn't seem to care—they hired the intern, like they promised —but he did express a fair amount of disbelief over my decision.

The first month was exhausting. Between getting rid of my apartment, moving my things, running the store, and starting marketing classes at the community college, I barely had a moment to myself. And when I did, I spent it drinking with Gabe.

Hard, just like my grandfather had said. Some days it felt like I was pushing a mountain from one end of the earth to the other.

Others were sublime—a run along the beach, whales in the distance. A great book catching me by surprise. Seeing a bear, with two cubs, walking along the path leading to the cabins. A quiet contentment had settled in my bones.

And I knew what I was doing: distracting myself. Pushing myself so hard I didn't have time to think of Lucia, yearn for Lucia, ache for Lucia. Every so often—watching the sunrise over the cliffs or reading a line of poetry I knew she'd love—it would hit. Swift and sure, breaking my heart anew. Shattering that quiet contentment. I hadn't heard from her, but I also hadn't reached out. One night, during a fit of insomnia, I'd looked at her Instagram account.

She looked happy in Paris.

For the next two days, I felt like I was drowning, unable to fully catch my breath. It was the photos of her laughing, the curve of her lips. The interesting way she captioned things—I noticed, now, the poetic style of her writing.

The two poems she'd written for me were shoved into my grandfather's copy of *On the Road*.

I couldn't bring myself to read them.

I dialed the number of the next author, looking over Gabe's shoulder as he did something I couldn't begin to parse.

"You're an accounting genius," I whispered, sound of the phone ringing in my ear.

"That or I'm stealing from you," he said, waving up a customer.

I watched as he listened to them gush about the books here, handing them an index card. I'd decided to re-start the tradition. According to our new Yelp page (all five-star reviews... we just weren't making enough *money*), customers raved about it. Loved its quirky charm.

A woman picked up on the other line—Noel Hartford, a local poet that the Big Sur Channel was raving about. Surely, she'd be interested?

"At The Mad Ones?" She semi-squealed, and I grinned, appreciating the response. "I thought it closed down."

"Nope," I said. "It is alive and well, and we'd very much like to start up the writers' programming my grandfather used to run."

"I used to go to those," she gushed. "I was little and didn't always understand what was going on, but I begged my parents to take me."

My heart beat painfully, thinking of Lucia, begging her parents to take her to a bookstore. The way she'd denied those things to herself now in pursuit of a career it was so obvious she was ready to leave. I hoped, wherever she was in Paris, she was reading. Or writing.

"Well, would you like to be the inaugural author?" I asked, crossing my fingers under the desk.

My grandparents stared out at me from their wedding photo, hanging above the register. *You can do it*, they seemed to say. Because really, I could.

"I'd love to."

And just like that: hope.

CHAPTER 51

Lucia

Y ou'd think it'd be easy to fake putting on mascara in
a mirror for six straight hours, all while saying, "*I
hate it when my mascara clumps. Don't you?*"

It's not.

By the second hour, your wrist is so cramped that you can
barely hold the wand. And the phrase *I hate it when my
mascara clumps* starts to echo in your mind like a scene from a
horror film.

Over and over and over again.

It was nearing midnight when I finally left, waving
goodbye weakly to the crew. My makeup artist was a stern
woman who spoke only French and who routinely looked like
she was going to stab me in the eye with an eyeliner pencil.

It sucked. I missed Josie, terribly. Every time she called, I'd
burst into tears.

Plus, there was no sexy nerd in glasses standing in the
background and intensely undressing me with his eyes.

Every day on set, I felt... empty.

I slept poorly that night, like I had every night since
leaving Big Sur. Insomnia plagued me in Paris—a feeling I

finally recognized as regret taunting me as soon as my head hit the pillow.

My only thoughts were about Calvin. The bookstore, our conversations, the hot springs. The night we fucked against a bookshelf, wild and free. Our naked run. Cal's kind eyes and generous spirit. The words, flowing from my pen.

In the morning, I dragged myself from bed, made an espresso, and sat on my little deck, wrapped in a heavy wool blanket. My poetry journal lay in front of me: the blank pages like an accusation. I wasn't inspired to write—at all. But every day I'd try, waking up at dawn just like in Big Sur. Waiting for the words to come.

Nothing did, even though Paris was filled to the brim with inspiration. The cafés, with their thimble-sized cups. The red geraniums that had grown in my planter boxes, even through Christmas—even when it snowed, continuing to lift their heads to the weak winter sun. The adorable schoolchildren that waved to me as I walked to the studio every morning.

There was so much *life* here.

Nothing.

I couldn't even write an awful, angsty, teenaged poem about Calvin and how he was probably already dating six other women.

I was fucking miserable.

But my Instagram followers were skyrocketing, just like I'd hoped, and I did interviews in *Vanity Fair*, pretending to dodge the paparazzi while I shopped for baguettes, looking fabulous. And the obsessive affirmation flowed in, as steady as a river.

The *Rag* photo shoot came out, and people loved it—the images were gritty and raw, and I looked like a seductive wood nymph in all of them. Taylor told me some magazines were carrying the ones of Calvin and I, but I couldn't look at them.

Miserable.

Every month I told myself it'd get better, listened as Josie did the same, reminding me, in soothing tones, that it was only two years. It'd lead to bigger and better things. And I'd prattle on about some interview with *E!* or a segment *People* wanted me to do and feel absolutely fucking nothing.

As I walked to the set that morning, I tried to stay present in the moment, take in the world around me so I could break this loathsome writer's block and feel alive again. Even pining over Calvin—*that* was something I needed to write about. To process what had happened, what he'd meant to me.

How I couldn't stop thinking about him, even three months later. Night and day, he was ever present in my thoughts.

I walked past the café I frequented, stopping in for another espresso. As I waited, I watched an older gentleman with shockingly white hair read to his grandson. A sweet moment—the sun shining around them, the hazy air of the café. They were reading in French, and I couldn't catch it, but the look on his grandson's face made my heart hurt. I knew that look. I knew that feeling.

I felt tears suddenly, which seemed to happen all the time now. But I wiped them away, grabbing my espresso from the harried waitress.

There was a poem back there—-in the way the grandfather watched his grandson. The curling French vowels. The melancholy fact that the grandfather might always remember this moment but the grandson will probably forget it.

The tears came again, but I wiped them quickly. Josie told me Calvin had kept the bookstore, hadn't ended up selling it at all. Which had made my heart soar—it was the right thing to do. And he was living his life, truly unafraid and hopeful. I'd wanted to send him a little note, maybe a poem in the mail, but I'd stopped myself.

Too painful. And what good would it do?

As I walked onto the set, Sabine grabbed me before I could plop myself into a makeup chair.

"Can I speak with you for a moment?" she asked, surprising me.

"Of course," I said. "Is everything okay?"

She led me up the stairs to her office. "How are you liking things here? Settling in? Enjoying the Parisian lifestyle?"

I laughed weakly, remembering the last time I'd been here, before Big Sur, when I thought this job was going to change my life.

"Um... sure," I said. "A little homesick, but that'll pass." I hoped.

"Right, right," she said, distracted in that way that made you know the person didn't really want to ask you a question and especially didn't care about the answer.

She closed the door, offered me a seat.

"Let me start, Lucia, by saying you're doing a great job."

I raised my eyebrows. "Oh, well... thank you."

"You're probably the most beautiful woman on the planet—"

"Doubt it—" I interjected before I could stop myself.

"—and the camera loves you."

"Great," I said, surprised at how little I gave a shit. I glanced at the wall clock. What time was it in Big Sur? With the time difference, I figured it was nighttime. Cal, closing up the store. Grabbing a good book and settling down with Chance.

An ache pierced me like an arrow.

"But I'm going to give you a bit of feedback, and I hope you take it well. Because it's all about learning, you know? How to be better at your job."

I shrugged. "Of course. What is it?" I could really care less about doing better.

"You just seem to be... going through the motions. Not

giving 100% or even 80%. Your expressions, the look in your eyes... dead," she said, doing a kind of spirit-fingers gesture over her own face. "There's nothing there. No passion or feeling. Here at Dazzle, we want our models to be... to be engaging! Fun, free-spirited. We want women to see you in a magazine and think 'she looks like she could be my friend.'"

"Okay," I said slowly, not entirely disagreeing with her. And she was off by a long shot—I'd say, on average, I was giving 15% to this job. On a good day.

"Right now, you're coming off as that morose friend everyone secretly hates."

I snorted. I couldn't help it. But Sabine didn't crack a smile.

"Sorry, I just thought that was funny," I said. "See? I'm not even *that* morose."

Still nothing. I missed Calvin. I remembered the night at hot springs, crying at the Mary Oliver mural, talking about how valuable our lives were.

"The reason I bring this up is because we want you to be happy here. This is a long-term investment we're making in your future. We have another twenty-one months on this contract, and we want you to embody, well... to embody the Dazzle way. Do you understand?"

I nodded slowly, something shifting inside of me. *We want you to be happy here*. I thought back to the last time I'd been truly happy.

Could I do another twenty-one months of this? The first month here I chalked up the constant, unyielding longing I had for Calvin as minor heartbreak—a crush. A heavy flirtation. A week of pleasure and joy I'd always remember but could never have again.

But instead of fading, as all crushes do, my feelings only intensified: of regret. Of sadness. Of love.

Because I was in love with Calvin Ellis.

I didn't know what my chances were—if I went back to California, to Big Sur, he might not have waited for me. He could be engaged to some cute, nerdy writer living my dream life, and I would have missed out. On my chance—on the opportunity to create the life that *I* wanted.

But if he hadn't...

"You bring up a critical point, Sabine," I said, my voice shaky. My heart was beating like a pack of wild horses, tearing through the plains.

Be brave. "Because I'm actually not happy with this job. I'm actually not happy with my life."

Sabine waved her hands around, *tsking*. "Darling, no one's happy with their life. Get used to it."

I sighed. Oh, Sabine. Cal had done it. *I* could do it.

And maybe what I was thinking about doing was risky and stupid. And maybe I'd regret it, and my whole life would stumble off-course—my career, everything I had worked hard for.

Or maybe... or maybe I'd spend the rest of my life running a quaint bookstore with a person I was quickly determining was my soul mate.

Here goes nothing.

"I quit," I said, as a beehive of nerves unleashed inside of me.

Sabine almost fell out of her chair. Since what model, in my position, would do such a thing? The rumors alone...

"You're serious." She looked murderous.

"As a heart attack," I said, the beehive nerves causing my fingers to tremble. But just a little. "I appreciate what you've done for me and this feedback. I've learned a lot during these three months." My agent was going to fucking kill me. *Kill me.* "And if I can help in any way at all, just let me know."

"Is this really happening? Just because I criticized you?"

I shook my head. "No, I get that all the time actually. Did

you know my ears stick out a little?" I said, tilting my head to show off the body part in question. "It's really happening because I want to live differently. And I'm sorry I wasted your time—I truly am. I hope you can salvage what you can before finding my replacement."

Sabine narrowed her eyes at me. "This is going to end your career," she snapped, the mask lifting.

"I know," I said, grinning like a loon. "And it's going to be great."

"They'll tear you apart in the papers," she said, standing up. Hand propped on her hip.

"Let 'em," I said. "I won't have internet where I'm going anyway."

I left her office in a daze, saluting my stern makeup artist and grabbing a bagel on the way out. I traveled home in a stupor, floated up my stairway completely unaware of my surroundings.

The beehive nerves had taken over my entire body; they were dancing the polka on my lungs, my chest, my heart.

What the *hell* did I just do? And did I really just do it?

I slid out my suitcase, pulled out my phone. A slew of social media notifications popped up, but I ignored them.

Josie picked up on the first ring. "Oh my god, I have *so much* to tell you about Gabe."

I grinned, hearing the good news in her voice. "Perfect. How do you feel about doing it in person?"

I was ready to take a giant, scary leap towards my future. Good or bad, no matter what happened. I'd regret it forever if I didn't.

Josie squealed, and then I did too, and buried deep down beneath the bees, beneath the fear and the nervousness and the worry, was something warm and beating, like a tiny heart.

Joy.

CHAPTER 52

Calvin

"Diane di Prima once tried to levitate my grandfather," I said, facing the tiny audience of ten people who had shown up Noel Hartford's reading tonight.

The ten people chuckled softly.

"She wasn't successful, in case you hadn't guessed," I said, and they laughed again.

I still hated public speaking but was trying to get better. At least my voice was only shaking a little bit.

"But Diane was just one of the hundreds of authors, writers, poets, and artists who called The Mad Ones home from the late fifties through the 1980s. Sadly, those readings slowly stopped happening, and the last ten years this bookstore has merely been a quirky local artifact, far from its original glory."

Movement at the back, a latecomer. My heart leapt. Every person counted.

"My grandfather died nine months ago," I said, and the audience made a combined noise of sympathy. "It was peaceful," I said, smiling. "And he left the bookstore to me, to take up the mantle. Return it to what it used to be. Which has been hard, for sure. But my goal is to bring the literary community in this area back to life with readings and writing workshops and authors-in-residence," I said, smiling when I saw folks nodding their heads in agreement.

Gabe was there, big shit-eating grin on his face, and I wondered if something had changed with Josie.

"This is the first reading at The Mad Ones since 1997, and we're happy to have local poet Noel Hartford, who's here to read from her chapbook, released last week."

Polite applause, Noel beaming like this was the best moment of her life, which it might have been. I slipped away, towards the back, taking the second to last seat near the small Poetry room.

Noel started, and I was immediately entranced, rocketed back to a memory of sitting here, on my grandfather's lap as a small child, watching someone read. My heart lifted optimistically. This was the beginning. If I could just pay off the debts...

I was so involved I didn't hear the latecomer slide next to me, but the scent of coconut shampoo turned my head, and I was suddenly face to face with Lucia Bell.

I almost fell out of the chair, but Lucia caught me, laughing silently.

"What are you doing here?" I whispered in absolute amazement. She was dressed simply in a long skirt and a t-shirt, hair up in a ponytail. No makeup. She looked jet-lagged and gorgeous.

"I missed you so fucking much, Cal," she whispered, and if we weren't surrounded by people, I would have kissed her.

"Am I dreaming this?"

She shook her head with a secret smile. "Let's talk after her reading. I want to hear her poetry."

"Um... okay," I said. "Can you give me a summary of what you want to talk about, just so I can prepare? Like, what's the topic sentence?"

She rolled her eyes, giving me a goofy grin. Why were all these people here? Why weren't we naked? She took out her poetry journal and a pen, scribbling something quickly.

Roses are red
Violets are blue
I came back to say
I'm falling for you.

I dropped the piece of paper, grabbed her hand, and dragged her into the Poetry room. Pushed her up against the back of the far wall, away from prying eyes and listening ears. We could hear the poet, the quiet applause.

"Cal, I'm sorry. I'm so fucking sorry. I'm the sorriest person who's ever walked the face of the Earth," Lucia whispered frantically as I hooked her leg around my waist, sliding my hand up her firm thighs.

I reached her panties, gripping and tearing them immediately. Her eyes widened. "Wait, what's happening?"

"I missed *you* so fucking much," I said against her lips, my thumb finding her clit and circling it firmly.

She jolted in surprise, lips open to moan, but I kissed her, covering the sound. "And we have a lot to talk about, and we will, but first, you are going to come for me. Right here, right now." I circled quickly, worried it was too much pressure on her clit—too fast, too soon—but she'd already been wet, and as I stroked, her head fell forward onto my neck, breath coming hot and fast. She whimpered, the smallest of sounds, and I was instantly rock hard and aching.

"I thought about what you looked like coming every night you were gone," I whispered as her legs shook. "Dreamed of your taste, the way you smell, the look on your face when you climax. So fucking beautiful, you are *so fucking beautiful*," I growled as she panted one word, *'yes'* over and over, my fingers moving as quickly as possible as she writhed and trembled and came, explosively, my lips on hers, minutes later.

335

"What the *fuck*," she sighed, head back, as my fingers gently disengaged. I placed her leg down, put her skirt back in place, tucked a wayward strand of hair behind her adorable ears. "I should leave for three months more often."

I gave her a hard, rough kiss. "Please don't ever leave me again."

CHAPTER 53

Lucia

Calvin's hand was warm in mine as we sat and watched Noel read. She was a beautiful writer, and as she spoke, my eyes filled, and spilled over, with tears. I was sitting here, back in this perfect place, Cal next to me.

I didn't expect him to give me an earth-shattering orgasm moments after I arrived, but that was Cal for you.

Everything felt right, like slipping on an old, worn coat, and listening to Noel, surrounded by readers, my fingers itched.

Inspiration.

There it was, brimming just beneath the surface.

I missed you.

When the poet was done, Calvin gave an adorable speech about the re-launch of The Mad Ones, looking at me the entire time.

I smiled broadly, nodding. I'd made a list of ideas that I had and couldn't wait to talk to him about it. And I couldn't wait to hear his. As people stood and saw me, a few folks recognized me, and I waved, friendly, but they didn't give me a

337

hard time. I got the sense Big Sur would be cool with a former supermodel making her residence here.

As people trickled out, Cal kept his eyes on me constantly, and after the last person left, I heard him throw the deadbolt.

I looked up, and he was right in front of me: crooked grin, glasses and scruff, hair a mess. Completely fucking adorable.

He pulled me towards the couch. I had tons to say. And a gift to give. I reached into my pocket, closing my hand around the thin piece of paper.

"Josie told me you'd kept the bookstore open. I'm so proud of you, Cal," I said. He squeezed my hand.

"Thank you. It's... well, it's been a lot since you left."

"Tell me," I said. "Tell me everything."

Silence for a moment. He looked so comfortable in the store. He looked like himself.

"The day after you left, I had the meeting with the investors. Or, was supposed to. I was ready to sell, totally over it. I wanted—" He looked at me. "Well, I wasn't entirely sure what I wanted, but my time was up. Then, right before I left for the meeting, I found this letter my grandfather had written me. The lawyer gave it to me the day she read the will."

"What did it say?"

His smile was huge. "All the right things to wake me up. I'll let you read it someday."

"I'd love to," I breathed. "And I'm really happy you found that letter. I mean, you would have made a good life for yourself wherever you ended up. But I think, if you had sold it, moved back—"

"—I would have regretted it. Deeply." His eyes glittered emerald against the crackling fire.

"So... you're living your dream now," I said, nudging his shoulder "What does it feel like?"

He rubbed his hand down his jaw. "Exhausting. Exhilarating. I don't know, Lu. Every day it feels like I'm fulfilling my wildest dreams. But then this place is in so much debt..." He trailed off, a look of frustration on his face. "It was way easier to be like 'Look at me! I'm achieving my dreams!' before I had to fully confront how much shit this place is in."

"What's your plan?"

"Things like tonight, hosting readings with authors and poets. Gabe is helping me with the finances and the accounting. I'm taking some marketing classes, trying to figure out the best way to lure customers back."

I nodded. "I love that you're bringing authors back. I think that idea is beyond perfect."

A timid smile. "Thanks, it felt right. Felt like my grandfather was here tonight actually."

"I felt that too," I said softly. My hand grabbed the paper. *Be brave.*

"You know, my grandmother cried every time she heard a good poem," Cal said.

"A woman after my own heart," I said with a wry smile. "It just happens. I've never been able to control it."

"And I hope you never do," he said firmly, leaning forward to kiss me until my head spun. "Did you really leave Paris for good?" he finally asked, a slight look of disbelief.

"You look like my agent," I joked. "Well, except my agent is no longer my agent. Because I fired her."

"Lucia... wow. Why?"

I shrugged, biting my lip. "Because I was miserable in Paris. I used to love being a model, I really did. And that contract with Dazzle is going to be the right opportunity for someone else, someone who wants to be in the spotlight for as long as they can. But it doesn't feel good anymore. I feel like I had to wear a second skin." I shook my head. "I don't want to live a life where I'm not myself anymore, even for a job. *Especially* for a job."

I looked at him. "You taught me that." I kept going before I lost my courage.

"I was also miserable because I was pining for you," I said, and realization dawned over his face. "Every day. I couldn't sleep. I couldn't write. Everything around me was brilliant, but I just felt... dull. And the moment I got to Big Sur, as soon as I stepped into The Mad Ones..."

I searched for the right word. "*Magic*. And as soon as I saw you—" Cal reached forward, brushing a tear that was sliding down my cheek. "—as soon as I saw you, my heart was just so happy."

He placed his hand on my chest, right over the organ that was beating rapidly—in excitement. In anticipation.

"I brought you something," I said, hands shaking as I took out the piece of paper.

"A poem?" he asked, and I laughed.

"It's *not* a poem," I said. "It's a check."

He took it from me, brows furrowing, and when he saw the amount, he almost dropped it.

"That should cover all of the debt, right?" I asked. "Josie asked Gabe, who gave me a ballpark number."

"Lucia, this is an *extraordinary* amount of money. Where did you—"

"That's all the money from the photo shoot for Shay Miller. A chunk of my savings. And the first three months of work for Dazzle. They probably won't end up using any of my images, but they still had to pay me. A lot."

"Lucia, I'm not sure if I can accept this," he said, face filled with concern.

"It's a good-faith gesture," I said softly, placing my palm against his cheek.

"Of what?" he asked, voice choked with emotion.

It was time to jump. The doors were flung wide open, the

whole world outside. It was scary and hard, and I didn't know what the future held but I had to do it.

I *had* to.

"I'm in love with you," I said. "Passionately. Hopelessly. And all the other words a poet would use. And if you'll have me, I'd like to stay here. With you, in Big Sur." I let out a long breath. "There, I said it. And if you won't have me, I will kindly show myself out and will then drive all the way to Mexico where no one knows me and I can live out my days as a recluse."

Calvin cupped my face in his hands, smiling broadly. Laughing. "These past three months, all I've done is regret not asking you to stay with me. Because I love you so much, Lucia Bell, I don't know what to do with myself. And please don't live as a recluse in Mexico."

"Well, I don't have to now," I said, feeling the need to dance ecstatically across the floor.

If fireworks had exploded out of the cash register, directly in front of us, we wouldn't have noticed.

"Do you feel a bit like we're jumping out of the airplane but *without* the parachute?" Cal asked, pulling me hard against his body. His lips hovered near mine.

"Yes. But what's the worst that could happen?"

"We both go bankrupt," Cal said, ticking on his fingers. "You realize I'm not the man of your dreams. Two weeks in you realize how much you miss being famous and you miss Netflix and Snapchat."

"Well..." I said, pretending to consider, "I mean, all of that is *technically* true. But also, our other options are: go back to our old lives. Be miserable for decades. Retire. Be filled with regret that we hadn't been young and uninhibited and decided to run a bookstore together." I shrugged. "Have terrible sex with people we don't really like. Never read or write or be truly happy." I paused. "But, in all seriousness, what are we waiting for? This is our *life*."

"This is our life," he said softly.

"Ours. Together," I said. "Now can we please make out now?"

And Cal laughed his deep, rich laugh. Joyous and free. He grabbed my hand, and I was up against a wall in an instant.

"I have thought about this," Cal said as he tore away my skirt, my shirt, my bra. "For three *fucking* months."

I gasped as his teeth closed against my neck, biting possessively. I threaded my fingers in his hair, holding him close as he made quick work of my underwear. He stepped back for only a moment, swearing under his breath when he saw me naked.

I never saw a man get undressed so quickly in my life.

"*Calvin*," I squealed as he picked me up, carrying me to the bedroom. He tossed me onto the bed, and my mouth watered, staring at his abs flexing in the moonlight. His hand around his hard cock, stroking. His mouth was everywhere, his tongue on my clit before I could take a full breath.

"I got myself off to fantasies of you at least twice a day," I moaned, squeezing my legs around his head. Keeping him there.

He responded by finger-fucking me to an electric climax, my back arching completely off the bed. Holding my wrists down, he spread my legs, fucking me in long, even strokes for what felt like hours. Sweaty, panting, my orgasms as tangled together as the bed sheets.

And when Cal finally groaned with a shaking release, I felt our lives intertwine in a way that was scary and beautiful and soul-shaking.

We talked all night long, the ideas pouring out, our excitement over the business a tangible thing, our thirst for adventure tethering us together.

Cal's fingers stroked my hair gently; he was half-asleep and so handsome lit up by the moonlight slicing through the curtains.

I could hear forest sounds, the pounding of ocean waves. Big Sur was breathing, the night alive and filled with magic.

Somewhere in the world, a little girl wrote poems in her bedroom, pouring herself onto the page.

Somewhere in the world, a little boy sat and marveled at the strange and wonderful universe he discovered through books.

"Lucia," Cal said sleepily.

"I'm here."

"If this moment were a poem, what would it be about?"

My fingers itched. Tomorrow, I'd write. Tomorrow, everything would be new.

"That's easy. A poem about falling in love."

Epilogue - Calvin

ONE YEAR LATER

I'd never seen Lucia look so nervous. It wasn't her style. But still there she stood in a brand-new red dress, hair in curls, looking like she was going to barf.

"Everyone is going to love you," I whispered, squeezing her hand.

"Says you," she said, biting her lip and looking down at her notes.

"True. I *do* love you."

She looked up, a quick smile. "I love you too. But I'm also about to become the first poet in existence to throw up in the middle of her reading. Do you think that will *encourage* fans or *discourage* them?"

"If you're making snappy quips, you can't be that nervous," I chided, and her lips quirked up as she fought a grin.

People were filing into the bookstore, at least 250, squeezing into the back, leaning against the shelves. It was one of our larger audiences—people in Big Sur were curious about the supermodel turned bookstore owner turned poet who'd been living here for a year.

Which was why Lu was so nervous. It was big news, at least in the world of celebrity gossip, when *The* Lucia Bell left the world of modeling to run a small bookstore with her new boyfriend. People wanted interviews; fans were distraught. Lucia ignored most of it, limiting her social media accounts to one (Instagram) where she posted updates about the store. Books we were reading. Snippets from her writing.

She was right—she *did* lose fans. A lot of them. But the ones who stayed saw Lucia for who she really was and celebrated the courage she had to life an authentic life.

A couple of them were even in the audience tonight.

"Everything I've ever written is terrible, Cal. I can't believe you're letting me do this," she said.

I laughed. "That is not even remotely true."

I leaned forward, pressing soft, lingering kisses up her neck until I reached her ear.

"After this is over, I'll be doing a number of filthy things to you," I promised.

She shivered, blushing slightly. "You do filthy things to me *every* night," she said, reaching down to squeeze my hand.

"You're right," I said, chuckling. "But they'll be even *filthier.*"

She rolled her eyes at me, but she looked a little less nervous.

A few months after she came back from Paris, Lucia did a brave thing, going back to get her bachelor's degree in creative writing. Four times a week, she made the drive to Monterey to take classes, staying up late most nights writing and doing her homework. Running the store in the morning and on weekends. She remained the hardest worker I knew, and even though she was often bleary-eyed in the morning, she'd never been happier.

And sometimes she even let me read her writing. And it

was so poignant, so gorgeous, it made my heart physically hurt.

"Thank you everyone for being here tonight," I said, stepping in front of Lucia to begin.

Public speaking didn't bother me as much anymore. In the past year, we'd averaged a reading a week, and slowly but surely things were turning around. It was going to take a long time, but Lucia and I were committed.

"Many of you in this room knew my grandfather, Robert, and how much poetry meant to him." I indicated the large room. "At least once a day, I'll re-shelve a book or find a stack of new books, and there will be a piece of white lined paper with a few lines scribbled on it. Sometimes his handwriting, sometimes the handwriting of a poet long dead, anonymous but vital. Poetry is alive and well here, and as you know from this past year, we are doing our best to make sure it stays alive."

Most days, Lucia left me a love poem stuck to the register —sometimes long, sometimes just two lines, always perfect. At night, I read to her as we lay curled up by the fireplace. Or she read to me from my business management and marketing textbooks in silly, weird voices, sometimes striking a pose from her modeling days, making me laugh while I learned all the ways to keep The Mad Ones afloat.

My grandfather would have been proud of me. *I* was proud of me.

"So thank you for your dedication to this bookstore, to books, to writing. To the Big Sur community. It means so much to Lucia and to me."

She was effervescent in the light, holding my hand, gazing at me like I was the only person in the world. My love for her was endless.

"Many of you also know that my business partner, and girlfriend, Lucia Bell is a poet. And tonight, she'll be doing her very first reading."

Lucia smiled nervously, clearing her throat. The audience went wild for it—she was a fan favorite in Big Sur, attending town hall meetings, always quick to help a neighbor, dancing with the mayor at Gabe's bar on the weekends. People were usually surprised to learn she wasn't born-and-raised.

"I couldn't be prouder of her," I said, turning towards her, squeezing her hand again. "I mean that, Lucia," I said softly, just for her.

I reluctantly sat, since I would have been content to hold her hand all night long, but this was her moment, her spotlight.

She took the podium, placing her poems down delicately. Gathered her confidence—the same vivacious spirit that had drawn me to her from the beginning.

"Thank you everyone for taking a chance on me," she said, and I grinned at her.

She grinned back, bright and shining. My heart spun on its axis. "Tonight's reading is dedicated to Calvin, whose love brought me back to life. You'll always be my inspiration."

And then she squared her shoulders, standing tall.

Flipped open the pages and began.

Still want more?

Dear readers: I hope you enjoyed Calvin and Lucia's swoony and emotional love story. They truly have a piece of my heart! If you'd like to see their love story two years after Bohemian ends, click here to receive a special bonus epilogue.

Not ready to leave Big Sur yet?

Read Gabe and Josie's story in my book LANDSLIDE and fall in love all over again!

Bonus Epilogue - Lucia
TWO YEARS LATER

I wondered if watching the sun come up through the redwoods would ever get old.

I'd been writing nonstop the past few weeks, charged with a seemingly endless amount of inspiration. In the middle of helping a customer find a book, or ringing someone up, or helping pin note-cards to the ceiling, I'd stop. Grab the pen I always had in my back pocket. And scribble down words onto the first surface I could find.

The other day, Calvin had laughed as I'd grabbed his bare forearm and written the words, *"fullness, intention, how does my body fit"*—a hodgepodge of thoughts that later became the third stanza of a poem I'd been stuck on.

So I'd been missing the sunrise, instead choosing to curl up next to the fireplace and write my little heart out. It was a compulsion—each morning, it felt like stanzas and syllables were *physically* yanking me from slumber, demanding my attention.

But I also hadn't been feeling well the past couple weeks, a fact I'd been ignoring. And this morning, I woke up bone-tired and aching, like my joints no longer fit right. I'd slept for more than ten hours, but was so exhausted I wanted to cry.

Thankfully, the stanzas and syllables were muted today. So I took a mug of tea and a giant blanket and sank into the old couch on the deck of The Mad Ones.

I inhaled the sounds of the forest—Big Sur was waking from its slumber. Bird song echoed through the leaves, and the first tendrils of sunrise unfurled with rosy fingers.

I scanned my body, taking note of the tangible exhaustion, a strange lightness I had in my belly. Maybe the intense period of inspiration was having some kind of physical effect—all of my energy directed toward creating poems, draining the rest.

A whisper of anxiety fluttered through me, but I shook it off.

Nothing was wrong.

Right?

"Good morning, gorgeous," Cal said sleepily, shuffling out onto the deck. I smiled, patted the couch.

"This seat isn't taken, in case you were wondering," I said, sighing as he wrapped his entire body around mine. The whisper of anxiety vanished.

"I thought you'd be writing," he said and pressed a kiss against my neck. I shook my head.

"Wasn't feeling up to it this morning," I said, closing my eyes. "This is nice though. Can we do this all day?"

He stroked his hand down my hair, and when I opened my eyes, I saw a flash of concern on his face. "We can do whatever you want. It's a Wednesday, slow day for us. Do you want to open late? Or I can make up some story about pipes bursting and buy us a whole day off."

I meant to protest, since nothing made me happier than running this bookstore with Calvin. And I'd just spent two years of my life balancing a crazy-ass schedule so I could get my degree. So I was a little tired—who wasn't?

But when I opened my mouth, I surprised myself by saying, "That would be nice."

He kissed me tenderly. "How about you go back to sleep and I cook you breakfast?"

I nodded, then walked back into our house and collapsed onto the bed.

I was asleep a minute later. In fact, I slept through sweet Calvin leaving me French toast and bacon. Slept through Chance curling up next to me, and Cal drawing the curtains.

And when I finally woke up, I felt like I hadn't slept at all.

I shuffled out to the Big Room, where Cal was reading *And Then There Were None* and looking so adorable I almost couldn't stand it.

"Good day for a classic mystery, huh?" I asked, pointing at the Agatha Christie.

He grinned. "Yeah, just felt right. You know how this book ends?"

"I do," I said through a yawn. "Read it when I was eleven years old, and it scared the shit out of me. Do *you* know how it ends?"

"No, and don't tell me," he teased, dragging me onto his lap. I stroked my fingers through his hair, scratched along his scruffy beard. "Also, in case any Big Sur resident *ever* asks you, commit this date to memory and swear up-and-down that our pipes burst, making it impossible for us to have customers."

"I've been cleaning up water for hours," I said with mock innocence. "It's so awful."

"It really is," he conceded, giving me a wink. "And how do you feel?"

"Sleepy," I said. "Maybe I'm just getting sick." I swallowed against that flutter, back with a vengeance.

Cal looked at me for a full minute, searching my gaze. "You've been really tired for a little while actually. I've noticed."

"A lot's going on. All of the authors coming through. Plus the reading I did last month. All the writing I'm doing." Another casual shrug—I was getting really good at ignoring that flutter. "It's all catching up to me."

His thumb stroked along my cheek. "I'm not so sure, gorgeous." I couldn't read his expression, and when he shifted me off of his lap and stood, I automatically reached for him again.

"Where are you going?"

He bit his lip nervously, a slight blush on his cheeks. "I bought something. For you, because of the last few weeks. And you're probably going to laugh me right out of this house. Or break up with me. Which, I'd just like to say, please don't break up with me."

I laughed. "Never. Ever. *Never*," I said again. "And what did you *get* me?"

One more nervous glance, then he left for a moment. I laid my head back down on the couch, closed my eyes. Dozed off for another thirty seconds, and when I opened them, Calvin was standing there.

Holding a pregnancy test.

* * *

"What the *fuck* is that?" I asked as Cal crouched in front of me.

"You take this test. It tells you if you're going to have a baby," he teased.

"Cal," I warned.

"Okay, I'm sorry," he said, palms up. "But just...you've seemed off for weeks now. And I know you're on the pill, and we're always careful, but...maybe you should take this."

I grabbed the stick from his hand, noticed that my fingers were trembling. Pressed my palm to my stomach.

"You think I might be pregnant?" I asked.

"I have no idea," he said, with a hint of a smile. "I'm not even *remotely* an expert. So this might be crazy. And if you're not pregnant, you have permission to tease me mercilessly about it for the rest of our lives."

I could hear my heartbeat rushing through my ears. I hadn't realized it was possible to feel every single feeling you'd ever felt, all at once.

"I don't know what to do if I am," I said in a small voice, and he pulled me in for such a deep, passionate kiss it made my head spin. When he pulled back, his lips were swollen.

"I want to experience every single thing possible with *you*, Lucia Bell. Everything. I know we don't talk about the future much, but you're my person. You know that, right?"

"I do," I said. I'd never once doubted our future together. It was as obvious to me as the blue in the sky and the green in the grass. "You're *my* person."

"Good." He smiled. "So let's take that test, okay?"

I took a deep breath, shocked when a tear rolled down my face. "Okay."

I went to go pee on it, hands still shaking, Calvin standing right outside the door. I placed it on the counter, turned on my phone timer, and sank to the floor.

He joined me.

"Do you remember the first time we were ever in this bathroom together?" he asked, leaning his head against mine.

"Of course." I laughed, grateful for the distraction. "You helped me fix my zipper. In a most erotic fashion." Our fingers laced together.

"That day changed my entire life," he said softly. "Before that, I had what I thought was a harmless crush on you. A crush that would go nowhere." He turned to face me. "But then we had...this *moment*. Here."

"And you left me that e e cummings poem," I said, my heart beating faster at the memory. "And everything changed."

"Everything changed," he repeated, the words hanging in the air as the seconds ticked away. "For what it's worth? I think you'll be a beautiful mother."

"Calvin," I said, and it was on a half-sob. I didn't know why I was so *emotional*, except that this moment had a charged, heavy vibrancy to it. The sense that our life was about to fork into a different direction. Terrifying and thrilling all at once.

"Think about your childhood, Lu. About what your parents made you do. The modeling and the pressure and all that shallowness." He tilted my chin up so we were eye-to-eye. "If we had a child together, what kind of life would you want her to have?"

I wiped my eyes. "Happiness. To...to love her body as *hers*, and not as the property of other people. Not to sell things, but to carry her through life. Strong and...magnificent. No shame in her imperfections. I'd want her to embrace them. Celebrate them."

He was nodding. "And not make her think that her passions were silly or childish."

Another tear. "Let her be herself. Let her be a *child*. Not in front of a camera. But...but in the woods. In this bookstore. Running through a field of flowers." I closed my eyes, saw a little girl with my blond hair and Calvin's green eyes. Saw her jubilant and imaginative, racing through the Big Sur woods, laughing in the sunlight.

I looked at my phone. Thirty seconds. "What kind of life would *you* want our child to have?"

Cal grinned easily. "I'd want her to cherish her life. Live in the moment. Read books, love words, allow her world to breathe and expand through literature."

Ten seconds.

"What if it's really hard?" I asked.

"I think that's okay too," he said. "I think it's okay if it's beautiful and hard and wonderful and frustrating and life-changing and scary. All at the same time."

I squeezed his hand. Kissed him. Picked up the stick to find two lines, clear as day.

Neither of us said anything for a full minute. Just the sounds of our breathing and the forest outside.

"What does that—" he stuttered. I burst out laughing, a joyous sound.

"That, dear Calvin, means we're going to have a baby."

* * *

He had me scooped up from the bathroom floor in moments, a feat that still amazed me since I was almost as tall as he was. He carried me gingerly into the bedroom, laid me down, stared at me like I was the single most important thing in his world.

"Lucia," he whispered, tears in his eyes, "I don't have any words yet for this." One hand was gliding up my bare leg, lifting the long tee shirt I was wearing. Slowly exposing my bare skin to the morning air.

In a second, it was off, and I was completely naked.

"It's okay, it's okay," I said, reaching for him, holding him against my chest. He stayed there for a moment until our heartbeats felt connected. Cal's big palm rested on my stomach, stroking.

And then his mouth found my nipples—a tender, almost hesitant exploration. I sighed, arching off the bed, and he slid his hands along my back and held me there. Suspended.

"I thought I would know," he rasped, kissing my breasts. "I thought I would...Lu, I didn't know it would feel this way."

"What way?" I asked, moaning as his mouth moved down

my rib cage. "Talk to me." A long swipe of his tongue around my belly button. A bite on my hip-bone. Then he settled between my legs, gazing at my cunt like it was a priceless work of art.

"Like every single decision in my life was leading me here. To you. To this moment. To...to *creation*." He buried his face against me, inhaling my scent. I threaded my fingers through his hair, loving his lazy perusal. His fingers glided through my folds, teasing and stroking, but never dipping inside.

Then I felt his tongue flutter against my clit, and I arched clear off the bed again.

"Tell me what *you* feel," he said, eyes on mine as he fluttered his tongue again. My fingers twisted in the bedsheets.

"Amazed," I panted. "Terrified." A harder swipe of his tongue, and I whimpered. "It feels like...Cal it feels like..." I couldn't place the feeling, like a warm light had suffused every inch of my body. A deep intuition I didn't know I had, letting me know we would be okay.

That we were meant to have this baby.

He slid two thick fingers inside me, and a tear slid down my cheek.

"Too much happiness," I finally said on a groan, our eyes still connected as he lapped steadily at my clit, fingers sliding against my G-spot. Slide and lick, and suddenly that warm light transformed into an orgasm that swept through my entire body. I hadn't even stopped climaxing before Cal had crawled up my body and thrust the entirety of his cock inside of me.

"Look at me, Lucia," he said, my face in his hands. I was still crying.

"Too much happiness?" he asked, thrusting gently. Too gently. I trailed my fingers down his strong back, then dug them into his ass.

"Faster," I groaned, and a low growl slipped from his lips. "*Please*."

"Anything you want, gorgeous," he said, sliding my leg up higher, onto his shoulder. Our faces were an inch apart, and I could see his every emotion: fear, exhilaration, worry, completion. Our emotions mirrored each other, and that alone was enough to make this moment, this gorgeous and unexpected morning, the most connected Calvin and I had ever been.

"And *yes*," I moaned, "too much happiness." He smiled, bright as the sun, and I pulled him down for a soulful kiss, lips claiming each other. And we stayed like that as he rocked both of us into a powerful climax.

* * *

We didn't leave that bed, except when Cal carried me out front to watch the sunset. We'd fucked and napped and kissed and talked and cried. He couldn't seem to stop touching my stomach.

But neither could I. That lightness, the flutter, confirmed what I'd known all along.

The love Calvin and I had for each other was magic.

I watched him smile at the setting sun.

"Everything can change in a day," I finally said, resting my head against his shoulder. "For better or for worse."

"And we're very lucky because on this day everything changed for the better." A copy of *Where the Sidewalk Ends* was sitting in his lap. The copy his grandfather had read to him when he was a child.

"I bet she'll like Shel Silverstein," I grinned.

He laughed. "I sure hope so. Because she's going to have to listen to me reading it nonstop." The sun slipped down beneath the trees, stars just beginning to wink in the twilight.

"Do you think she'll be a poet?" I asked, threading my fingers through Calvin's.

"I know she'll be," he said. And then we went back to bed.

Acknowledgments

I started writing *Bohemian* at the Big Sur Bakery, surrounded by all the natural beauty that town has to offer. I finished the first draft in a public library in Portland, Oregon. The second draft was finished in Jasper, Canada. And the final draft was polished in Polson, Montana. I wrote, and published, *Bohemian* while traveling in a van with my husband across the country – and each beautiful location had a profound impact on this book.

Big Sur, California is indeed a real place. And it will change you. If you are lucky enough to go, visit Nepenthe (the inspiration for Fenix) and the Henry Miller Library (the inspiration for The Mad Ones). The Ventana Wilderness is a beautiful stretch of forest, and you can hike through most of it. Unfortunately, as I was writing this book, Big Sur did indeed suffer from several natural disasters—wildfires and floods. Tourism is essential to their livelihood, so if you're ever there, I highly encourage you to support their local businesses.

For Faith, whose constant guidance, feedback, and support means more than I can say. I could write a whole book just on our friendship.

For my amazing family, who took me to Big Sur for the first time where I promptly fell in love.

For Joyce, Jodi, and Julia: my Wonder Women. I'm not quite sure what I did to deserve their support and friendship, but I am immensely grateful for it.

A huge thanks to the amazing Carla Peterson for double-checking my Spanish and fixing all of my errors. Any mistakes are my own.

For the Hippie Chicks, the grooviest ladies around! Thank you for taking a chance on me and on this book. #GirlPower forever! And for the endless support from fans, readers, authors, and bloggers: you are the reason I wake up so early in the morning to write.

Finally, for my husband: your boundless courage inspires me every day. I am so happy we embarked on a six-month road trip together.

About Kathryn

Kathryn Nolan (she/they) is an Amazon Top 25 bestselling author. Her steamy romance novels are known for their slow-burn sexual tension, memorable characters, and big, hopeful feelings.

Kathryn is a bisexual bookworm and femme cutie with big Leo energy. They love to spend their free time hiking, camping and traveling. When not on the road, they live in their hometown of Philly with their cute husband and giant-eared rescue pup, Walter.

Sign up for Kathryn's weekly newsletter to see what she's writing, what she's reading/watching and get all her travel stories (plus an abundance of Walter photos!):

https://www.authorkathrynnolan.com/join-my-newsletter

Books By Kathryn

FREE FALL

Fifteen years as a bodyguard and Elijah Knight has never been tempted to break the rules. His pristine reputation is the reason why he's about to secure the promotion of a lifetime. So the last person he needs anywhere near him is Luke Beaumont, the very definition of temptation. And the man he's just been ordered to protect at any cost.

STRICTLY PROFESSIONAL

Edward Cavendish III and Roxy Quinn couldn't be more different. He's a polite, wealthy hotelier from England. She's a scowling, bad-ass tattoo artist. But when a night of heartbreak brings them together, their chemistry – and connection – is electrifying. Seeing each other romantically is not an option – until they meet again under *strictly professional* circumstances.

NOT THE MARRYING KIND

Fiona plans to be married to her soul mate by the time she turns 30. Unfortunately, she agrees to plan a benefit concert with Max, a cocky bad boy who swears he will never settle down. But when romantic sparks fly between these two friends, will they let their rules get in the way of true love?

BOHEMIAN

Shy, nerdy Calvin inherits his grandfather's bookstore in funky Big Sur, but has no idea whether to sell the bookstore – or take on the challenge of keeping the store's literary legacy alive. When a bohemian-style photo shoot brings famous super model Lucia Bell to Big Sur, sparks fly between these two total opposites.

LANDSLIDE

Gabe Shaw has the perfect life in Big Sur. He's the third-generation-owner (and bartender) at The Bar, the only place in this funky small town where the quirky locals can drink in peace. A hopeless romantic, Gabe's only lacking one thing: his soul mate. And when a sudden storm traps a sexy, funny make-up artist named Josie in Big Sur, one night of searing passion turns into much more. Too bad Josie doesn't believe in falling in love.

RIPTIDE

Avery Dacosta is an ambitious property developer, intent on building a luxury hotel on Playa Vieja's last untouched beach. And she has no time for Finn Travis, the laid-back, hippie surfer who decides to protest this hotel – and her workplace – every day. Unfortunately, Finn's not only the most aggravating man she's ever met – but sexy as hell. Can these two enemies-turned-lovers ever find a middle ground?

SEXY SHORTS (VOLUME 1)

A sweet, dirty collection of fourteen sexy short stories.

BEHIND THE VEIL (CODEX Book #1)

Private detective Delilah Barrett is entirely unprepared for her new assignment: hunt down a stolen rare manuscript that's hidden within Philadelphia's glamorous high society. The only catch? Delilah must go undercover as a fake married couple with her new partner Henry Finch -- a devastatingly handsome librarian. But as the danger intensifies...so does the temptation to let their fake desire become real.

UNDER THE ROSE (CODEX Book #2)

To infiltrate a secret society, private detective Freya Evandale and FBI agent Sam Byrne must go undercover as a pair of thieves in a dangerous world of shifting alliances. But can these lifelong rivals close the case...without falling in love?

IN THE CLEAR (CODEX Book #3)

While chasing a famous book thief in London, two private detectives work together while dodging danger at every turn. But can aloof, serious Abe and charming, mysterious Sloane resist their instant attraction to one another? Or will passionate temptation risk this case – and their careers?

WILD OPEN HEARTS

Luna's cheerful, hippie reputation is ruined when her billion-dollar company is caught in a scandal. And only a burly, dog-rescuing biker can help her. As these opposites give in to their electrifying attraction – will their differences keep them apart? Or will they learn to trust their wild hearts?

ON THE ROPES

Former pro boxer Dean Knox-Morelli is shocked when his new neighbor is Tabitha Tyler – his childhood friend and the woman he's had a secret crush on for years. But when flirty filmmaker Tabitha tries to tempt Dean into a sexy, summer fling, will he finally get the girl? Or will she only pack her bags and leave him heartbroken?

OUT OF THE BLUE

When famous surfer Serena Swift is provided a bodyguard by her new corporate sponsor, she's pissed to find it's her ex-husband, Cope McDaniels, tasked with keeping her safe. But these two ex-lovers soon find themselves in the midst of corporate espionage, and the only thing more dangerous than the secrets they uncover is letting the simmering sparks of their second-chance-attraction burst into flames.

RIVAL RADIO

Popular radio host Daria Stone despises her romance-obsessed adversary, Dr. Theo Chadwick. But when these workplace rivals are forced to share an on-air timeslot to save their radio station, will their sparks burn everything to the ground? Or can they play nice and save the day...without falling in love?

OFF THE MARK

When dirt bike racer Charlie needs a reputation fix before the biggest race of her career, she asks her friend Rowan – cocky ex-baseball player and flirty playboy – to fake date her for the cameras. But what happens when Charlie falls for the one man she knows will break her heart?

KEEP YOU BOTH

In this spicy, MFF novella, a blizzard traps wedding planner Paige Presley in a cabin over New Year's Eve weekend with the couple she's planning a wedding for. The only problem? She's secretly in love with them both.

Printed in Great Britain
by Amazon